THE CAST IRON MAN

THE CAST IRON MAN

Michael Legat

SOUVENIR PRESS

For
Tricia

1

Edward looked pleadingly at his mother. If only she would understand. If only he could convince her that it was not just a whim—his whole future was at stake.

'Now, listen to me,' she said. 'You cannot, at your age, expect to know what is best for you. You must allow yourself to be guided by older and wiser heads.' She smiled at him, hoping that he would respond.

'Mr Vincent says that Cambridge—'

'I'm sure he does. Teachers always encourage such ideas.'

'But I'm top in maths, and—'

'Edward, my darling, I know you think I'm being unreasonable—'

'I don't, Mama. But I just want to make you see how important this is to me.'

'Wilful!' his grandmother broke in, banging her walking stick on the floor. 'The boy's always been wilful. It's not having a father to bring him up. You've spoiled him, Sarah.'

Sarah controlled her temper. Really, the old woman was getting more impossible every day. 'I should be grateful if you would leave us, Mrs Harcourt.' She could never bring herself to address her mother-in-law in any less formal way. 'I cannot talk seriously to Edward with your constant interruptions.'

'Oh!' Mrs Harcourt began to weep. 'Oh, was ever woman treated so? You will only be happy when I am dead and gone.' She wept noisily for a moment or two; then the tears stopped suddenly. 'Very well,' she said, struggling to stand. 'I shall go. I know when I'm not wanted.'

Edward went to his grandmother and helped her to the door.

'You're a good boy,' she said, smiling at him. She turned as she went out of the room. 'Though how you contrived it with such a mother, I'm sure I don't know.'

When the door had closed behind her, Edward laughed.

9

'Grandmama's funny, isn't she? One minute she's saying I'm wilful, and the next she says I'm a good boy.'

'It's not for you to criticise her,' Sarah Harcourt said mildly. He was such a good-looking boy, she thought, with that shock of dark chestnut hair, and the strong-boned face. He was already taller than she was, and beginning to fill out now, and he looked so smart in his Norfolk jacket—his first grown-up clothes. He was at a difficult age, of course, but at least he did not sulk. Indeed, he was still smiling at his grandmother's rapid change of opinion, and she could not blame him for that. 'Now, Edward,' she said, 'let us hope that we can have a reasonable discussion. You must understand; I just cannot continue to run the mill alone, and the sooner you join me and begin to accept your responsibilities here the better. I certainly don't want to wait until—when would it be?—1895. You just have to accept the fact that going to university is out of the question.'

'Oh, please, Mama!'

The smile had faded, and the misery in his face suddenly irritated her. 'I fail to understand this burning desire to go to Cambridge. Oh, no doubt Mr Vincent has filled your head with all sorts of nonsense about a degree being a passport to success. But you don't need that—your future is assured, and a university degree is of little use to a silk maker.'

'Maths would be useful, Mama. Dealing with accounts ...'

'You can add up, can't you? What else do you need to know?'

'In any case, I don't want to be a silk maker.'

'Oh, don't talk nonsense, Edward! Why ever not?' She paused. 'Well, Edward? I am waiting.'

He could not stop himself, although he knew it would infuriate her. 'I'm sick to death of mourning crape,' he said.

'For heaven's sake!' she said angrily. 'You're seventeen! Do try to talk sensibly and not like a child of two!'

Edward gazed at her. It was always like this—a pretence at consultation and discussion, which would turn to anger on his mother's part, and end with her imposing her will on him. 'Anyway,' he said, not caring that he was still being childish, 'mourning crape's on the way out—everyone says so.'

'Who is "everyone", I should like to know?'

'The boys at school say their mothers . . .'

'The boys at school! What do they know about it?' Sarah shook her head irritably. 'I have no time for such nonsense. Crape is still *de rigueur* for mourning, and will continue to be so.'

She was wearing a dress of black silk, heavily trimmed with crape, though she could have gone into half mourning years ago. He wondered suddenly whether she dressed in this style in order to advertise the mill's products, rather than out of respect for his long-dead father. After all, she did not wear a widow's cap, such as his grandmother affected—or was that simply because she did not want to hide her still lustrous dark chestnut hair?

His attention had wandered. 'I beg your pardon, Mama—what did you say?'

She rose, and began to pace up and down, speaking rapidly. Edward recognised the signs. This was what she always did when she had run out of patience and had made up her mind.

'That's typical!' she said. 'How you would expect to get on at a university without any powers of concentration, I don't know. Anyway, you won't be going. And since it is crape that you object to, you shall go to your Uncle Richard in Wensham. Perhaps you will find the brocades that he makes more to your taste.'

'But, Mama, it isn't a matter of crape or brocades—it's the whole silk business. I'm just not cut out for it.'

'That's not for you to decide. I'll not hear another word, Edward. I shall write to your uncle straightway, and if he agrees, you shall spend the rest of the school holidays with him. And I hope he'll prove a better teacher than I have been, and that you'll return here in a more co-operative frame of mind.'

Edward swallowed. 'Mama, please listen to me. I know you think I'm just being difficult, but I've thought about this a lot, and—'

As far as Sarah was concerned, the discussion was over. Now she was ready to resume the part of a doting, if preoccupied, mother. 'Edward, my darling, I just haven't got the time to listen to all this. The latest making of waterproof crape has to be checked, and if I don't do it, no

11

one else will. I shall write to Uncle Richard while I'm at the mill. Come, give me a kiss, my darling.'

Despite his disappointment, the change in her mood struck Edward as being as absurd as his grandmother's had been, and he could not help laughing. 'Oh, Mama!'

'Edward, really!' Sarah said, in some exasperation. 'Well, I don't know what you find so funny, but I'm glad something amuses you. Come, give me that kiss.'

Edward went to her and she put her arms around him and hugged him. He could smell the familiar scent of lavender which she always wore.

The embrace was over almost before it had begun. Sarah walked quickly to the door.

'Mama.'

'What is it now? I really haven't time for a chat, Edward.'

'Please stay—just for a few minutes. You'll be home from the mill late tonight, as usual, and even if you're early, Grandmama is always there and we can't talk, and there are things I want to know. Please, Mama.'

Sarah recognised the note of special pleading, and decided to give in. 'Oh, my poor Edward. I've been neglecting you. That's the penalty of having a business woman for a mother, my dear.' She returned to the sofa, and patted the seat beside her. 'Come, sit down. Now, what's it all about?'

'Well, if I'm going to go to Uncle Richard's, I want to know about Aunt Louisa.'

Sarah looked at him sharply. 'What about her?'

'You don't like her, do you?'

'Whatever makes you say that?'

'I remember the way you looked at her when they were married.'

'Edward, you can't possibly remember that far back—you were only four or five at the time.'

'I can remember as clearly as anything. We were in a church, and I was standing next to you, and I looked up at you and there was a funny expression on your face when you looked at her, Mama. You didn't like her then, and I've never seen you smile at her since—with your lips perhaps, but not with your eyes. Why, Mama?'

She gave a little laugh. 'Oh, what a funny boy you are! Is that all that's bothering you? Very well. I will admit that I do

12

not greatly care for your Aunt Louisa. Some time after Uncle Richard's first wife died—she was your father's sister, Jane—he became engaged to be married, but it was broken off, and he then met and married your Aunt Louisa in what is vulgarly called a whirlwind romance. Do you understand the expression "she caught him on the rebound", Edward?'

'I think so, Mama.'

'Well, I have always believed that this happened in your uncle's case, and that your Aunt Louisa caught him on the rebound. Such marriages are often unsuitable.'

'Is that all?'

Sarah paused. She knew she should say no more, but could not help herself. 'No, it is not all. She has changed your uncle. Crushed him, in fact. He used to be so . . . so strong and independent, and now . . . That is why I dislike her.'

'But he always seems happy.'

'When you grow older, my dear, you will realise that you cannot always judge by surface appearances.'

'You are very fond of Uncle Richard, are you not, Mama?'

'We worked very closely together for many years,' she replied smoothly. 'He learned to make crape at Prideau's in Franton, and when he came back here to Brentfield, he and I together made Harcourt's Mill prosperous.'

'Why did he leave?'

'There was a quarrel with your father. Uncle Richard went off to Wensham, and started his brocade business there. He's been a great help to me since. Of course I'm fond of him.'

Edward smiled. 'You should have married him, Mama, after Papa died.'

The remark shattered Sarah's mood. 'Please do not make remarks of that nature, Edward. It is not a subject for joking.'

'I'm sorry, Mama.' But, in a flash of insight, he realised that the flush on his mother's cheeks was more of embarrassment than of anger. Perhaps, by accident, he had hit upon the truth. Perhaps they had wanted to marry. Then why hadn't they?

'I have no time for any more of this nonsense,' Sarah

said. 'Heaven knows what's happening at the mill.' She rose.

Edward grinned at her. 'You work too hard, Mama. I'm sure the mill can carry on for an hour or two without you.'

Her mouth set into a hard line. 'I will not have criticism of the way I manage the mill, and especially not from you. If I say that I need to be there, then I need to be there.' She walked quickly to the door, and then turned to him. 'But how could you understand? It means nothing to you that you're a Harcourt, does it?' She went out.

Edward thought what a strange woman his mother was—flying from a genuine, if brief, interest in him to a concentration on the family business which seemed to exclude everything else from her mind. Did she really care for him? Did he love her as he knew he should? The other fellows at school sometimes spoke slightingly of their parents, but he knew that the flippant criticisms were no more than a veneer to hide their deep affection. And they never seemed to find their parents funny. He was fond of his mother, in a detached kind of way, which was why it was so often tempting to laugh at her, but he was not sure that he really loved her. And that thought made him feel guilty. He wondered again whether there had been any possibility of a marriage between her and his Uncle Richard. Perhaps Richard had been unwilling to play second fiddle to a silk mill.

*　　　*　　　*

'Say what you think, boy,' Richard Goodwin told him, traces of the flat Essex accent still in his voice. 'It's better to have it out in the open, and you needn't worry about upsetting me; I don't get upset easily.'

Edward smiled. Although with others he often felt diffident and shy, it was easy to talk to Uncle Richard, and always had been. From the earliest days of his childhood, Richard had treated him as an equal, listening seriously to what he had to say and answering with honesty instead of the half-truths that most adults used. Not that everything had been serious—Uncle Richard could play the fool to make a small boy laugh, and join in the merriment himself. Nevertheless, Edward hesitated now. How do you tell someone that you find his life's work boring? 'I just can't understand what you find so fascinating about silk,' he said at last.

Richard laughed. 'Do you really want me to tell you? We shall be here for the rest of the day, and for most of tomorrow, too. For a start, don't you think it's extraordinary that the silkworm spins itself a cocoon consisting of a single thread of silk which may be half a mile long?'

'Not really,' Edward said, smiling to take any impertinence out of his words. 'It's no more extraordinary than an elephant, say, or the stars in the sky, or . . . or almost anything in nature, including human beings.'

'Oh, I'll grant you that,' Richard said, 'but the fact that the whole of nature is filled with marvels doesn't prevent me from admiring each and every one of them. I still believe the silkworm to be an extraordinary creature.'

Edward pretended to consider. 'I tell you what, Uncle, I still don't think that it's extraordinary, but I'll concede that it's remarkable.'

'All right, you young sea-lawyer, let's not split hairs.' Richard always enjoyed being with Edward. The boy had a great sense of humour, which was surprising, since neither Sarah nor Tom Harcourt had been much given to laughter. It was a marvel, really, that he had such a pleasant manner, considering the upbringing he had had, with a mother who veered between spoiling him outrageously and ignoring him for days on end. He looked like her. The hair, which had been golden in his childhood, had gradually darkened—ripened, one could almost say—into a dark chestnut much like Sarah's, and he had her green eyes and the high cheekbones. Not that there was anything effeminate about him—on the contrary, there was already more than a hint of masculine strength in the boy's features.

'The next thing that happens in making silk,' Richard went on, 'is also, at the very least, remarkable. I have always wanted to know who first discovered that, by putting the cocoons in hot water, it is possible to wind off the silk, and then, by twisting several threads together, to make a yarn that can be dyed and woven and turned in a hundred different ways into the most beautiful materials in the world. Isn't that enough to justify my fascination with silk?'

15

'Go on,' said Edward. 'I like hearing you talk about it.'

'Well, look at the process of making crape. It's something I spent half my life doing, which means it's commonplace to me, but in fact the whole process is quite strange—almost bizarre. First, the silk has to be thrown. You know what that means?'

'Twisting the threads together. And I know that the yarn for crape has to have a very high throw—meaning that it is tightly twisted.'

'Very good. We'll turn you into a silk maker yet.' Richard ignored the slightly closed look which came over Edward's face, and went on, 'What happens next?'

'It is woven, into a thin gauze.'

'And then?'

'It is biased.'

'How, Edward?'

'One side of the material is pulled in one direction, and the other in the opposite way, so that the weft threads are no longer at right angles to the warp. I've never understood why.'

'Because the material now goes through the rollers to be embossed with the pattern that is characteristic of crape. Now, remember, silk is made of a continuous thread, unlike wool or cotton, and if you subject it to pressure under heat, as in the embossing process, you will snap the weft threads. In a way, you might say that wool or cotton or linen—anything which has to be spun by hand before it can be woven—is more elastic, or flexible than silk.'

'Why did you give up making crepe, Uncle, when you loved it so? I know you left Brentfield because of some quarrel, but why didn't you start up a rival crape-making mill?'

'For two reasons, Edward—firstly because I couldn't afford to do that, and secondly because I didn't want to compete with Harcourt's. That would have seemed very disloyal. But brocade is fascinating, too, and almost equally complex, in a different way. Whereas the weaving of the material which becomes crape is the simplest thing about it, in brocades it is everything. There is magic in it, boy—pure magic. When I look at those beautiful designs, when I touch the delicate opulence of the silk, that's

16

when I find it all so wonderful and that's why I never tire of it.'

Richard got up and walked over to the window of his office in the Wensham mill. He moved his right arm in Edward's direction. 'My only regret is that this stupid arm prevents me from working the machines myself. Don't ever do what I did, Edward; don't try to work a machine by yourself when you're so tired that you'll fall asleep at the drop of a hat. If I hadn't done that, I might have been sitting at a loom this very moment.' He took out his pocket watch and gave a start. 'Good heavens! It's twenty to one. We'd better hurry, or we shall be late for lunch, and your aunt will never forgive me. And we've still got to spare a moment—a long moment—to show you to Mr Hill, because *he* won't forgive me if I don't. Do you remember Mr Hill? I first met him at Prideau's, and then he joined Harcourt's, and he has looked after the financial side of my own business almost from the beginning.'

Edward laughed. 'He must be almost as old as Methusaleh.'

Richard smiled. 'He's no chicken, but he hasn't exactly got one foot in the grave yet. Come on.'

He led the way out of his office and into the adjoining room. There, behind a desk piled high with papers, sat Mr Hill, a small man with a round, bald head, and pince-nez, behind which his eyes seemed to Edward to be permanently a-twinkle.

'I've brought this young rapscallion to see you, Mr Hill,' Richard said.

'And very welcome, too.' Mr Hill rose and came round his desk to shake Edward's hand. 'How are you, young sir? How you've grown! A trite remark, for which I crave your pardon. And is your estimable female parent in good health, too?'

'Yes, thank you, we both are. And I trust you are well?'

'That is a question which at my age can no longer be asked in full confidence of an affirmative reply. It would be preferable to express a muted surprise at my continued survival, a miracle which, as your uncle will tell you, I ascribe entirely to the selfless ministrations of that long-suffering lady who was foolish enough to unite herself with me, back in the dim beginnings of time, in holy matrimony. I refer, of course, to Mrs Hill. A paragon,

Master Edward. I would strongly recommend you to find yourself a similar companion for the road through life, though I realise that this advice is difficult to follow. Paragons are not met with every day. One cannot simply go into a general store and order one. More's the pity.' He chuckled. 'And you are soon to be finished with schooling, I suppose, and what then? No doubt your mother will be pleased to have your assistance.'

Edward did not answer, avoiding Mr Hill's eyes.

'I think Edward is rather more interested in brocades than in crape,' Richard said. 'Isn't that it, Edward?'

'Yes, sir, but—'

'He's going to spend some time with us, Mr Hill, and make up his mind about his future.'

'I see. In that case I have one thing to say to you, Master Edward. With the immodesty which is the privilege of age, I would suggest that you should listen with your best attention, since I believe it to be most excellent counsel. It is this: make up your own mind, and when you have made it up, do not be swerved from your purpose.' He paused very briefly. 'I speak as one who has never made up his mind about anything in his life, but then, as I have already told you at inordinate length, I am the fortunate possessor of an helpmeet who relieves me of the need to do so.' His eyes twinkled. 'That, of course, is a little joke, and you are permitted to laugh politely.'

Edward smiled.

Mr Hill shook his head sadly. 'Well, a smile is more than I get for some of my best witticisms, so I must be content. I shall hope to see you again, Master Edward, during your stay in Wensham.'

'I hope so, too, sir,' Edward said.

'Make sure you do, make sure you do. And if I can possibly contrive to remain silent for a few moments, you shall tell me all about yourself and your plans for making a mark in the world, as I am certain you will. In short—a preamble which is never to be believed in my case, since I am becoming more and more garrulous, I fear—in short, as I say . . .' He broke off, shaking his head again. 'But, no. I must stop, I must stop really! Go, Richard, go quickly, before I start again.'

Edward was smiling as he walked with Richard the

short distance home from the mill. 'Is he always like that, Uncle?'

'Mr Hill? Yes. I remember him saying that we all have a besetting sin. Mine, he said, was ambition, and his own was verbosity. He was right at the time. I think most of my ambition has been fulfilled, or vanished. But his verbosity has certainly not decreased. On the other hand, he is worth his weight in gold, and I don't know what I should do without him. Spend some time with him, Edward. He can tell you a great deal about the business, and about Harcourt's. I don't expect you to work all the time that you are here in Wensham—you are on holiday from school for the rest of the month, are you not?—but I would like to follow your mother's wishes, and show you as much of the way a brocade mill operates as possible.'

'Yes, Uncle. Thank you.'

* * *

Richard's house lay on the outskirts of the village of Wensham. Not quite so large as Harcourt Place, where Edward had been brought up, it was still a sizeable mansion, in which Richard and his wife and daughter lived in considerable comfort, together with Richard's unmarried sister, Frances, who had a sitting-room of her own, although she often joined the others in the evenings.

Soon, Edward and the family were sitting down to lunch. There was no joint to carve, so Aunt Louisa presided, dishing out the steak and kidney pie with a lavish hand. Edward, remembering what his mother had said, was fascinated by her. She was quite tall, and very upright, and more than a little plump, and her stays creaked as she moved. She certainly seemed to rule the roost, and Uncle Richard acted differently at home from the way he did at the mill—he was quiet, and somehow, Edward thought, smaller. 'Now, Edward,' she said, and proceeded to fill his plate with a quite enormous helping of pie.

'I shan't be able to eat all that, Aunt,' he protested.

'Nonsense! You are a growing boy, and need to keep up your strength.'

His cousin, Mary, stared at him. They had not met when he arrived the evening before, since she was already in bed.

19

He was not sure how old she was—twelve or thirteen—and, although it was really beneath his dignity to notice a girl of that age, Edward had to admit that she was very pretty. She had fair hair, like her father's, and the same bright blue eyes.

'Why does Edward need to keep up his strength?' she asked.

'Never you mind, miss,' her mother said severely. 'Speak when you're spoken to, and not before.'

'Yes, Mama. Sorry, Mama.'

'All young people need to eat well,' Aunt Frances said in a placatory manner. 'Growing bones need plenty of nourishment.'

Edward liked Aunt Frances the best of them all. She was thin, and rather plain, and sometimes there was a sad look in her eyes, but she always had had time to talk to him when he had visited Wensham as a child. Often then his Aunt Louisa had been preoccupied with Mary, and his mother had disregarded him as usual, so that if it had not been for Aunt Frances, he would have been ignored. But she would talk to him, and show him the kaleidoscope and teach him to play solitaire.

He remembered asking his mother once why Aunt Frances was not married. 'Oh, she was crossed in love,' Sarah had replied, and had gone on to say that the man concerned had been quite unsuitable for her, though she had not explained why.

When everyone had been served, Aunt Louisa said to Richard, 'Grace, my dear.'

They all stood while Richard asked a blessing on their food, but when they had resumed their seats no one began to eat until Louisa had taken up her knife and fork and said, 'Very well. You may begin.'

The pie was excellent, and Edward found no difficulty in eating all he had been given. It appeared to be the rule in the Goodwin household that meals were eaten in silence. Edward glanced around the table, and wanted to laugh. Everyone looked so serious, chewing away for dear life. What a funny business eating was, and how extraordinary to think that nearly everyone in England must be doing exactly the same thing at that very moment.

Just as the meal had finished, one of the maids knocked at

the door, and was bidden by Aunt Louisa to enter. 'The post, sir,' she said, handing some letters to Richard. As she turned to leave, she caught Edward's eye, and gave him a pert smile. She was young, and shapely, and had already smiled at him at breakfast that morning.

'One for you, Frances,' Richard said.

Frances glanced at the envelope, and went pale. 'Will you excuse me, Richard, Louisa?' She rose, and hurriedly left the room, the letter held close to her bosom as though it was precious.

'I think it's from Alfred Bunn,' Richard said.

'Who, dear?' Louisa asked.

'The gentleman she was friendly with many years ago.' Richard's voice was heavy with meaning. 'A thoroughly decent sort, old Alfred. But he has not written to her for a very long time, if I am not mistaken, and—'

'I am sure we should not discuss it in front of the children,' Louisa said firmly.

'No, my dear. Of course.'

Edward has been hoping to hear more, but his disappointment lasted only a short while, for after a few minutes Frances burst back into the room. Her eyes were shining, and she looked happier than Edward had ever seen her, as she waved the letter in the air. 'It's from Alfred, Richard. He wants to come and visit me—just for a day, he says. Oh, he may, mayn't he?'

Richard looked at Louisa. 'That will be all right, won't it?'

'Why do you ask me? You are the master of the house.'

Richard tightened his lips, and turned back to Frances. 'Of course he may come. Of course. Does he indicate the purpose of his visit?'

'Well . . . no . . . not really. But I think . . .'

'I beg you not to allow yourself to think too much, Frances,' Richard said seriously. 'Undoubtedly he will merely be paying his respects to us all.'

Frances smiled at him serenely. 'If that were so, my dear, he would have written to you, not to me. But don't worry, Richard. I am not a schoolgirl; I have no remaining capacity for wild, romantic dreams. I am delighted at the prospect of seeing an old friend—that is all.'

'Forgive me, my dear,' Richard said. 'I spoke only because I do not want you to be hurt.'

21

'I assure you that I have developed a shell of remarkable toughness.'

'When is his visit to be?' Louisa asked.

'Next week, he says, if that is convenient.'

'Of course,' Richard said. 'Discuss it with Louisa, my dear, and make whatever arrangements you wish. He can simply join us for a family meal, or you can ask the Hills to come, too—I expect he would be glad to see them again—or perhaps you would like me to book a private dinner for you at the Wensham Arms. You don't have to decide now. Think it over, and let me know.'

'Thank you, Richard. Excuse me again—I must reply by return.' And Frances hurried from the room once more.

'I am afraid she is very vulnerable,' Richard said, when the door had closed behind her, 'despite her brave words.'

'My dear,' said Louisa, warningly, indicating Mary and Edward by movements of her eyes.

* * *

It was really not much of a way, Edward thought, of spending his school holidays. Early each morning his Uncle Richard would take him to the mill, where he would stay until midday, watching every process in the manufacture of brocade while it was explained to him in detail and he would then be given the chance of trying his hand at the work.

He saw the bundles of raw silk, or books as they were called, arriving and being unpacked, and the throwing, when the strands were twisted together into a thick enough thread to be workable. All that, of course, he had seen often enough before in his mother's mill at Brentfield. The dyeing, too, was familiar enough, although here many different colours were used, whereas the crape was invariably black. It was all boring. The weaving, however, did interest him, the patterns depending on the interchange of colours and variations in the regularity with which the weft threads were interwoven into the warp. Many of the patterns were very beautiful.

'Your Aunt Frances designs them you know,' Richard told him. 'She always has—right from the time I first started. She used to help with the designs for the cylinders which emboss the pattern of the crape that I used to make at Harcourt's, but this work gives her more opportunity to use her talents, and she enjoys it far more.'

'Do you use the same patterns over and over again?' Edward asked.

'Bless you, no. We have to change constantly—the public always wants variety, so your aunt is kept busy all the time. Now, you sit down there, and see how you get on at working the loom. That's it. Now bring the red in—that's the style. Oh, no, no, no! You must follow the pattern. See, it means going under the next three warps. You'll have to unthread and do that again.'

Richard would stand watching, doing his best to remain patient and kindly, while Edward struggled to carry out his instructions. The boy really did not try hard enough—he just did not have the right feel for it. And though he seemed to like the colours and patterns of the brocade, Richard had looked in vain for any sign on his face of the sensuous, voluptuous feelings that he himself experienced simply by handling the cloth. Silk had such smooth richness, such delicacy—to touch it was like touching the skin of a beautiful woman.

Richard might have been more encouraged had he stayed to listen on the couple of occasions when he had turned the boy over to Mr Hill. Edward had responded immediately to the little man, with his mannered and self-mocking way of talking, and had wanted to know everything about the financial side of the business, and how it compared with his mother's trade in crape. He and Mr Hill were soon buried in a mass of figures—the cost of the capital equipment, the wages that the workers earned, the prices of the brocades of different qualities and the discounts given to the retailers. And although it was all business, they laughed together a great deal.

Mr Hill was fascinated by Edward's interest, and by the quickness of his mind. 'That young man has a remarkable talent for figures,' he told Richard.

'I'm glad you think so,' Richard said. 'I have found him less then interested in any of the manufacturing processes. I had thought to send him back to his mother with a report saying that he would never become a silk maker. However,

I suppose I can now tell her that he should be found a place in her accounts department.'

'What he really requires,' Mr Hill said, 'is the opportunity of additional education. I don't know whether his ability is entirely instinctive, but I suspect that it has been sharpened by the efforts of some gifted pedagogue. If you ask me, what he needs is to go to university. I have little experience of such places, but have always been given to understand that, with the right material, they can make, as it were, brocade out of raw silk, if you will forgive a metaphor drawn from our daily round.'

Richard heard him out. 'I suppose the young man has put that idea into your head himself.'

'No, he has not. It is entirely my own. I would say "a poor thing, but mine own," except that the quotation is properly, "an ill-favoured thing," which is not so appropriate.'

'You mean he has not talked to you about going to university?'

'No.'

'It is precisely because he has that ambition that his mother sent him here. She hoped that I could talk some sense into him.'

'Just be careful,' Mr Hill said, adjusting his pince-nez, 'that in talking sense in, you don't talk out the sense that is there already.'

'I don't know what that is supposed to mean,' Richard said, 'but I see no reason at all why he should go to university. I didn't. You didn't. The place to learn about silk making is in a mill, or if he is to become his mother's accountant, in the accounts office.'

'I don't often disagree with you, Richard,' Mr Hill said seriously, 'but this time I do. I am not sure that I can justify it by logical argument, but some instinct tells me that the boy would profit enormously if you grant his wish. He might even learn there to love silk as much as you do.'

'How could he possibly do that? It's a ridiculous thing to say.'

'I suppose so. I often say ridiculous things.' He mused for a moment. 'So does Edward, sometimes. He has a keen sense of the absurd. It's one of the reasons I like him so much. A keen sense of humour indicates a balanced mind.'

24

'Provided it is kept in check,' Richard said.

'Ah. Is that so? I shall keep it in mind.' Mr Hill chuckled.

*   *   *

Edward was not expected to work at the mill in the afternoons, which he usually spent with his Aunt Frances and Mary. Of his Aunt Louisa he saw far less; if she were not going out in the afternoon, she usually retired for a rest, and was not seen again until she appeared for dinner.

His cousin Mary was inoffensive, as far as he was concerned. A little in awe of him, she did not make a nuisance of herself, as he would have expected a girl of her age to do. And though his mother always talked of his Aunt Frances disparagingly as a dried-up spinster, Edward knew that she was far from being the bitter and insignificant woman that his mother's words might imply. He found it easy to forget that she was so much older and his aunt, and began to think of her simply as a friend.

The three of them went for walks, or, when it rained, as it seemed to do very frequently that summer, played three-handed whist, or looked at the photographs supplied with the stereoscope which Mary had been given for her recent birthday. Once or twice, Edward accompanied his Aunt Louisa when she went shopping, but he found these expeditions tedious, and when she announced that she and her sister-in-law and Mary would be going that afternoon to Norwich to visit several clothing shops and haberdashers and milliners in search of a new outfit for Mary, he asked her to excuse him.

After his aunts and Mary had left the house, he wondered what to do. He got up from his chair, walked over to the window and looked out idly. There was nothing to see except the shrubs in the garden. He came back and fingered the ornaments on the mantelpiece, sat down again, rose, took a cushion from the settee and kicked it violently towards the door. Fortunately it did no damage. Guiltily he picked it up, replaced it, and then went out into the hall.

The house was quiet. The next door along was open. That was his uncle's study. The room was sparsely furnished; a large desk and a chair stood near the window, and there

25

was a table against one wall, and close by it a large leather-covered horsehair chair. The whole of the other wall was provided with shelves, divided into spacious pigeon-holes, and these were filled with old ledgers, files of correspondence and the like. More papers lay on the table and the desk.

Also on the desk was a copy of *Lippincott's Magazine*. With little interest, Edward picked it up and flicked through the pages. In it was a chapter of a novel, *The Picture of Dorian Grey* by Oscar Wilde. He had heard of that, and how outrageous it was. It was not very long—he could read it easily before his aunts and Mary got back from Norwich. But he had better not do so here in the study. He hid the magazine under his jacket, and ran upstairs to his room. The extract was not nearly as shocking as he had hoped, but to read it was still to taste forbidden fruit. Besides, he was delighted by the fireworks of Wilde's epigrams.

Suddenly there was a knock at his door. Edward started, then hastily thrust the magazine beneath the eiderdown on his bed. 'Yes?'

The door opened, and he saw one of the maids standing there. It was the girl who had smiled at him. 'I was just wond'ring, was you wantin' something, sir?'

'No. No, thank you.' He noticed that she was not wearing her usual apron.

'Are you sure, sir?' She slipped into the room, and closed the door behind her. Then she looked at him, still smiling, and placed her hands at the waistband of her dress and slowly moved them down, smoothing the material over her thighs. 'Me name's Tessie . . . and you're Master Edward. Nice name, Edward.'

He looked at her uncertainly.

The tip of her tongue appeared and slowly she licked her lips.

'Edward,' she whispered. 'You don't mind if I call you Edward, do you? Seeing as we're alone, you and me. Wouldn't you like a little kiss and cuddle, eh? Come on. I won't bite.'

Edward's interest in girls had developed rapidly in the past two or three years, but he had had little opportunity for any contact with the opposite sex. Whenever he had met young ladies of his own age—sometimes when they came

with their parents to visit their brothers at his school—
they had always been strictly chaperoned, and he had merely
exchanged a few shy words. He had been left wondering
what it would be like to take one of these strangely
different creatures in his arms, to allow his hands to travel
caressingly over those swelling curves, to discover, indeed,
just what lay beneath the clothes which exposed so little
and left everything to the fevered imagination.

And now he gazed at Tessie, half eager, half frightened.
She really was quite pretty.

She held out her arms to him. 'Come on,' she said again.
'Give us a kiss.'

He went to her, awkwardly, and put his arms around her
waist. She pulled him closer, and turned her face up to his,
closing her eyes. Gently he kissed her.

She moved her head away. 'Not like that, silly. With your
mouth open!'

He tried again, and tasted the sweetness of her lips, and
was immediately intoxicated. Her tongue flicked against
his, and he responded, and as their embrace continued, he
became more demanding. He broke away to kiss her cheeks
and her neck, and he was aware of the softness of her skin
against his, and could smell the faint odour of the soap she
had used. He could feel himself becoming aroused. Daringly,
he put one of his hands on her breast.

'Oh, oh!' she cried, laughing. 'Naughty, naughty. None
of that, Master Edward. You've gone far enough already.
'Sides, I'd better go.'

'No. Not yet.'

'Maybe I'll come and see you again one day, if you're a
good boy. Would you like that?'

'Yes. Oh, yes.'

'We'll see, then.' She disengaged herself, and went to the
door. 'What was you doing when I come in, shut in your
room like this, eh? I can guess.' She gave her little laugh,
showing her small white teeth.

'I was reading,' Edward said.

'I don't see no book. Oh, it's a dirty book, eh? So you 'id it,
is that it? Well, don't you go reading them dirty books, and
doing what little boys do with themselves, 'cos there's
better things than that, and maybe I'll show you one day.'

And then she was gone, leaving Edward dazed and

27

almost wondering whether he had dreamt the whole episode. Hastily, he went downstairs and returned the magazine to his uncle's study.

From then on, he made every excuse he could think of—a letter to be written to his mother, school holiday reading which had to be done—to stay in the house alone while his aunts and Mary were out. And Tessie came again to his room, and each time allowed him a little more liberty.

On the fourth occasion, as he was caressing her breasts beneath the rough material of her dress, she said, 'I bet you want to see, don't you? I'll lock the door, shall I?' She did so, and then came back to him. 'They're just buttons. They undoes like any other buttons.'

And as he began to unfasten them, his fingers clumsy in his haste, he felt her touching him on the outside of his trousers, and then was aware that she was deftly opening his fly, and slipping her hand in to hold him. His senses reeled. He could not move, and stood there with his fingers frozen on the sixth button of her dress, conscious only of his own sensations.

Suddenly her warm, infinitely exciting grasp was withdrawn, and she was pushing him away, and he looked at her in puzzlement.

'Go on,' she said. 'Take 'em off—your trousers. We'll be 'ere all night if I wait for you.' She turned away from him and hurriedly unfastened and stepped out of her dress, and loosened her bodice so that the pink-tipped breasts were free. When she turned back, Edward had taken off his trousers. 'Go on,' she told him, 'the underpants, too. Gawd, 'ow funny men are.'

And then she fell back on his bed, and pulled him to her, and showed him what to do, and did not mind when his excitement brought him to an almost instant climax, and promised him that it would be better next time.

And it was.

'You won't tell no one, will you?' Tessie asked as she began to dress.

'Of course not.' Edward clambered back into his trousers. 'Tessie? When can we . . . when can we do this again?'

She laughed. 'Oh, you'd like that, would you?' She put her nose in the air. 'Well, I'm not sure that I want to any more.' He looked so woebegone that she relented. 'Oh, all right. You was good, you was. But I don't know when. A girl's got to be careful, you know.'

'In case there's a . . . a baby, you mean?'

She laughed again. 'Lor' bless you, no. I know what to do about that sort of thing. No, I don't want to lose my place 'ere. This is a good 'ouse to work in. And they'd chuck me out, sure as eggs is eggs, if they thought I was 'aving fun and games with you.'

Edward thought for a moment. 'I wouldn't let them. I'd say it was all my fault,' he said.

'Save your breath. They wouldn't believe you, not in a month of Sundays.'

They were both silent for a while. Then another thought struck him. 'Tessie.'

'What now?'

'Do you want some money?'

'Money?'

'Yes. For what we've just done.'

The smile dropped from her lips. 'You bloody little bastard,' she snarled. 'Think I do it for money, do you? Think I'm a bleeding 'ore?'

'No. No, Tessie. I'm sorry. I didn't mean to offend you. I didn't think . . . Please.'

Her anger vanished as swiftly as it had come. 'There, there, love. I know you didn't mean it—not the way it sounded. Tell you what, Eddie boy, you can buy me a little present one day.'

He laughed with relief and pleasure. 'What sort of present?'

'I don't know. Anything that takes your fancy.' She had finished dressing. 'Now you be a good boy, Eddie, and don't say nothing to nobody, and Tessie'll come and see you again whenever she can. Bye bye, love.' She kissed him briefly on the nose, unlocked the door and disappeared.

Edward sat on the bed. 'My God, my God!' he said to himself. Then he went to the dressing-table to gaze at himself in the mirror and see whether he looked any different.

*　　*　　*

Alfred Bunn needed to summon up his courage to ring the

doorbell of Richard Goodwin's house. The letter he had received from Miss Frances had been polite, but had given no indication of whether she would be really pleased to see him.

The door was opened by a maid, a pretty, pert young woman. When he gave his name and said that he had called to see Miss Frances Goodwin and was expected, the girl looked at him saucily. He felt his cheeks redden, which angered him. 'No better than she should be,' he said to himself when she had gone to tell Miss Frances that he was here. 'A baggage, a proper little baggage.'

He looked around the room into which he had been shown. Blinds of cream silk had been drawn down to keep out the afternoon sun, but they were almost translucent, and bathed everything in a cool, pale golden light. There was a great deal of furniture—numerous occasional tables and whatnots, a tall mahogany bookcase and a little writing-desk, and, grouped in a wide semi-circle around the fireplace, a settee and a number of large easy chairs. It all looked comfortable and lived-in. On one of the little tables were several silver-framed photographs, including, to his delight, one of Frances. He picked it up and gazed at it.

Hearing the door-handle turn, he hastily put the photograph back. She was there. His Frances—if she was his Frances still—looking almost exactly the same, just as in the photograph. He stared at her. The flesh around her jaw might be a little heavier, and there were delicate crow's feet at the corners of her eyes, and a deeper line between her eyebrows—the line that came when she was concentrating on her drawing, and which he had seen so often before—but there was no grey in her hair. It was more than fifteen years—no, eighteen—since they had last met; she had been in her mid-twenties then, so now she must be forty-three or thereabouts.

'Hello, Alfred,' she said.

'Miss Frances.' He could barely speak.

She seated herself in an armchair, apparently much more at ease than he was. 'Do please sit down.' Just as he had done, she was drinking in his appearance, registering the changes that time had wrought. The hair was thinner and iron-grey now, and his face more deeply lined, and the stoop he had always had was much more pronounced.

30

Otherwise, he was just the same—thin and gangling and awkward, not knowing what to do with his hands, wrapping his arms around his body, all bony elbows and knees. She laughed, and he looked at her curiously. 'Oh, it's all right. I laughed because I'm so happy to see you again, Alfred. It is such a long time.'

'Yes.'

'You haven't changed at all.'

He opened his mouth as though to speak, and then gave a half-smile and looked away.

'No, you haven't changed at all,' she repeated, thinking how much older he seemed. 'You don't look any different from the last time we met. It's amazing.'

'My hair,' he said. 'Gone grey.'

'Oh, rubbish!' she said petulantly. 'I'm not talking about silly things like that.' And seeing a kind of hurt in his eyes at her brusque tone, she went on, gently, 'You must be tired after your journey. Would you like a little refreshment—a glass of cordial, or tea or coffee? Oh, Alfred, it *is* good to see you.'

'Do you mean that, Miss Frances?'

'Indeed I do. Now, what shall it be—tea, coffee, or a little wine?'

'I wanted to come before,' he said, 'but I wasn't sure that I should be welcome. I want to be sure now, begging your pardon, or else I'll go away and not trouble you again.'

'Oh, Alfred, what a funny thing to say, when you've only just got here.' She was aware that she was twittering, but could not help herself. 'And you still haven't said what you would like. And did you have a good journey? How *are* you, Alfred?'

He did not answer her, but rose, and began to pace about the room. Suddenly he turned to face her. 'My circumstances have changed, Miss Frances. My wife has died.'

Frances gazed at him, her eyes wide, and hope beating in her heart. Was it really possible that he still wanted her to marry him? If so, the years that had passed, while he was still bound by his Catholic faith to a wife who had long ago deserted him, would no longer seem so wasted.

He began to speak again, not looking at her. 'I heard that she was on her deathbed. I went to see her, and I am glad to say that we were no longer . . . estranged . . . when she

31

passed away, and I was able to attend her funeral and pay her the respects that were her due. But I would be false to myself if I pretended to any great sorrow.'

'I understand, Alfred.'

'And so I am free. But I do not know, Miss Frances, if—'

'Could you not call me Frances?' she asked softly. 'Miss Frances sounds so . . .'

'I do not know if the change in my circumstances is of the least interest to you, Miss . . . to you, Frances.'

'Why should it not be?'

'I wondered . . . perhaps if there was someone else . . . or if perhaps you considered it too late. You might feel bitter towards me. Some might say that I have blighted your life.' He glanced at her. 'Oh, please don't cry, Miss Frances, I beg of you. Perhaps I should go.'

'No!'

It was a cry of anguish, and he looked at her with a mixture of astonishment and anxiety.

'Please,' she said then, and began to speak very quickly, in a strange, high-pitched voice. 'Please sit down again, and let us talk as though none of what we have said so far had happened. And I will ask you what sort of journey you had and you will tell me, and then I shall offer you refreshment, and you will say what you would like and I shall ring for Tessie and tell her, and then I shall say . . .'

He interrupted. 'Do you feel unwell, Miss Frances?'

It was her turn to ignore him. 'I shall say, I have waited eighteen years for this day, and there is no one else and it is not too late, and I don't feel bitter or that my life has been blighted. Am I being very foolish, Alfred, or am I right in believing that you have come now as I have prayed you would one day?'

He stretched out his arms towards her, and she got up and went to him. He took her hands in his. 'I am still not sure, my dear. How can I ask you to share my life when it means exchanging a home such as this for the squalid rooms I rent? I have gone back to my bad old ways, you see—I accept only the engraving commissions which please me, so I work irregularly, and live from hand to mouth. I can offer only uncertainty, rather than security. Besides, your family is here in Wensham, your friends are here, but in London you know no one. And I am a Catholic and

32

you an Anglican. Oh, I was a fool to come, and I will go now.'

'Alfred—'

He let go of her hands. 'I hope you will forgive me. I am sorry if I have distressed you, and I promise that I will not disturb you again. Kindly give my regards to your brother. I had hoped to see him, but . . .' He turned away. 'Goodbye, Miss Frances.'

'Alfred! When have I asked for security? What do I care about Wensham? Haven't I told you already that I have waited for this day? I don't think you have listened to me, and from you I have heard only nonsense, which I do not believe you meant. Oh, Alfred, listen to me! Let me cast aside all modesty and say simply that I will marry you, with all my heart. If only you will ask me.'

Slowly he came back towards her. 'Do you mean it? Truly?'

'Ask me, Alfred, ask me!'

He gazed at her for a moment in wonderment, and then whispered, slowly and seriously, 'Will you please be my wife?' And then, without waiting for her answer, he folded those long arms around her and pulled her to him and kissed her with a passion which took her breath away.

In later years it became a joke between them. 'I never actually said "yes",' she would say. 'You married me under false pretences.'

And he would reply, 'I think you did more proposing than I did, Mrs Bunn.' And then he would echo her words as she said, 'And a good job, too!'

*   *   *

That evening at dinner, to which Mr and Mrs Hill had been urgently summoned, a special toast to Alfred and Frances was drunk, and afterwards Richard and Mr Hill reminisced with Alfred Bunn over the old days when they had all worked at Harcourt's Mill.

Meanwhile, Louisa and Mrs Hill were quizzing Frances about what sort of household she would be mistress of, and what her bridal gown would be like—silk, of course—and other matters of feminine interest.

'Of course, there will be no question of your becoming a

Catholic,' Louisa said. 'But it will cause many problems, mark my words.'

'Oh, but I shall,' Frances replied, 'if Alfred wants me to.'

'That would be most unwise. You cannot abandon your own faith so easily.'

'I don't know about that,' Mrs Hill said. 'If Mr Hill wanted me to change, I should not hesitate. The main thing is to keep your man happy, my dear. They worry about such unimportant things. If you ask me, the good Lord doesn't much mind which way He's worshipped, and it would never surprise me, if I ever get to Heaven, to meet—oh, Hindus and Buddhists and goodness knows what else there.'

Louisa's lips tightened. It was quite obvious that she found this a profoundly shocking statement, and Frances looked around for some way of changing the subject. Her eye lit upon Edward. He had been sitting by himself, turning without interest the pages of a magazine. 'Oh, how selfish we have been,' she cried. 'Poor Edward, sitting there with nobody taking any notice of him. Edward! Come and talk to us.'

'Yes, Aunt Frances.' He rose, and went to sit on a small chair between his two aunts. Once there, however, he could find nothing to say. All he could think of was the possibility that his Aunt Frances and this Mr Bunn might one day be doing what he had done with Tessie. It was a strangely exciting thought, and also somehow distasteful.

'I asked you to talk to us,' Frances said, 'and you haven't said a word. Oh, I mustn't tease you. It's just that I'm so happy today that I don't know what I'm saying half the time. And to tell you the truth, your old aunt has drunk just a little more wine than she ought.'

Edward laughed.

'That's better. That's more like you. Now tell me, Edward, have you made your mind up yet about what kind of silk you want to make? Is it to be crape or brocade?'

'No, Aunt Frances.'

'Do you mean no to crape, or no to brocade, or no, you haven't made your mind up? Or is it no to all of them? What, has the cat got your tongue? Come, it's a day for honesty—tell us everything, all the secrets of your heart.'

'It's past ten o'clock,' Louisa said firmly. 'It's high time the boy was in bed. Go along, Edward. You have to be up early in the morning.'

With obvious relief, Edward said goodnight to the company and went. Frances watched him go with a sense of unease. Her teasing had been unkind, and there was something more than shyness in his refusal to answer her questions.

She put it out of her mind, and reverted to a discussion of the date of the wedding, which was to be as soon as possible, bearing in mind the fact that she would first have to take instruction and then be received into the Church of Rome. But later it came back to her again.

The Hills had gone home and Louisa had retired to bed, and after an affectionate farewell, Alfred had departed to spend the night at Wensham's only hostelry, the Wensham Arms. He had of course been invited to stay in one of the guest bedrooms, but, always preferring independence, had politely but firmly refused. Frances was alone with her brother.

'Are you pleased for me, Richard?'

'You know I am.'

'It's not going to be easy, I know that. I think we shall probably be quite poor, and living in London will be very strange, and so will hearing the Mass in Latin. But it's what I want, it's what I've always wanted.'

'I know. And Alfred's a good man. I'm very happy for you, my dear. I shall miss you, too.'

'I shall miss you. And we'd better stop talking like that, or we shall both burst into tears.' It was then that the thought of Edward came back to her. 'I'm worried about Edward,' she said.

'Why?'

'He seems unhappy.'

'That's because he's got this absurd idea that he should go to university to study mathematics. Sarah sent him here hoping he would get it out of his head.'

'You didn't tell me.'

'I didn't see any need. The sooner he forgets about it, the better.'

'But why?'

'What's he want to go to university for? He'd better

35

knuckle down and start earning his living. Good heavens, I was working when I was nine.'

'Is that any reason why he should not have a better education? It will give him confidence, allow him to grow, turn him from a boy into a man. And it will provide him with qualifications.'

'He already has all the qualifications he needs to work in his mother's mill or mine. But I don't think we're good enough for the young gentleman. He doesn't seem to have any interest in silk.'

'And why should he? It's not the only thing in the world. Oh, Richard, I have no patience with you. You're expecting him to behave as though he's grown up. He's only a boy—and a very nice boy, too. He's good-natured and as honest as the day is long, and clever into the bargain. And he's got a great deal of charm. He's awkward at times, and I suppose his mother finds him difficult, but that's because he's just finding his feet in the world. Of course he must go to university, and you shall tell Sarah so. It will be the making of him.'

Richard pondered. Frances was usually so sensible in her advice. 'Do you really think so? You're serious? You're not just . . . well . . .'

'You mean, has becoming engaged to be married addled my wits? No, it hasn't, Richard, and I'm as serious as I can be. What's more, I know Alfred would agree with me.'

'Alfred? Surely you haven't discussed it with him?'

'No, but years ago he said to me that he wished he had been better educated. "Education's the best thing a man can have," he said. "It's not just that you learn things, you learn *how* to learn them. That's what's important." Those were his very words.'

Again Richard considered for a while. That Alfred Bunn should have spoken in those terms for some reason impressed him more than the earlier pleas had done. 'Well, I'll think about it.' He caught the smile on Frances's lips. 'You needn't think you've won,' he told her sharply. 'It seems you're all against me—Mr Hill said much the same thing as you—but I'm only going to think about it. And I shall certainly discuss it with Louisa. Don't you say anything to him on the subject. He'd better behave himself in the next few days.'

'Whatever makes you think he won't?'

'Oh, I don't know. Nor why we're talking about him. We should be talking about you. You'll still design for me, won't you? Even if you are living in London.'

*　　*　　*

When Richard came back to the house earlier than expected one afternoon a few days later, the door was opened by a rather flustered cook-general, unaccustomed to such duty.

'Where is Tessie, Mrs Midgley?'

'I'm sure I don't know, sir.'

'Is the Mistress in?'

'No, sir. She and Miss Goodwin and Miss Mary have gone visiting. Master Edward's in his room, I think.'

Richard decided to take the opportunity to talk to the boy. It was perhaps time that he should make a decision about his future. As he mounted the stairs, Richard could hear voices, and laughter, coming from Edward's bedroom. One of the voices was feminine. Without hesitation, he opened the door.

He was met by the sight of Edward's bare buttocks. Beneath the boy, on the bed, lay Tessie. As far as he could tell she was naked, too. In a frozen moment of time, he was aware that their movements had ceased and that two frightened, guilty faces were turned towards him. Then the girl gave a scream.

'Get dressed, both of you. Edward, you are to stay in this room until I send for you.' He turned to Tessie. 'You will come to my study as soon as you are decent.'

A short while later, dabbing at her eyes, scarlet-faced, the maid stood in front of his desk.

'Here are your wages for this week.' Richard held out three shillings. 'You are dismissed, without references.'

'Oh, no, sir! Please, sir! It weren't my fault. 'E took advantage of me.'

'I do not wish to hear. You will pack your bags and leave.'

'It's not fair!' Tessie wailed. 'I'm only a poor girl. 'E forced me. Please, sir! I won't do it no more.'

'You certainly won't—not in this house. Now go.'

'Oh, no! No! Please, sir!'

Richard put the coins down on the desk and turned away to look out of the window. He was aware of the girl taking the money and leaving the room, sobbing.

He waited until Louisa had returned, and explained to her what had happened. Her anger was immediate, and directed as much, if not more, against Edward than against the girl. Nothing Richard could say in the boy's defence altered her opinion. He sent for Edward.

'How long has this been going on?' he asked.

'It's been . . . several times, sir. You haven't sacked her, have you?'

'Of course. What else did you expect? I am very disappointed in you, Edward. You have abused my hospitality.'

'Yes, sir. I'm very sorry. But it's not her fault. I take all the blame, and I'll accept the punishment, whatever it is. But please don't punish Tessie. I . . . I made her do it.'

'Are you saying that she was unwilling? That you forced her?'

'Yes, sir.'

Richard knew the boy was lying. 'I do not believe you, Edward. I know exactly what sort of girl Tessie is, and where the chief fault lies. It may seem noble to you to try to protect her, but in fact it is foolish.'

For the first time, Edward looked him straight in the face. 'I beg your pardon, Uncle, but I do not agree. I took advantage of her, and I cannot let her take the blame. Please give her another chance.'

'I admire you for saying that, Edward, but it is pointless. In any case, she has already left. As for you, I have discussed the matter with your aunt and she—and I—are of the opinion that you, too, had better leave as soon as possible. I shall not tell your mother why you are being sent home, but shall simply say that it does not seem advantageous for you to spend more time here. I see no future for you in the manufacture of brocade.' He paused. 'You spoke just now of punishment. I suppose it would be punishment of a kind if I were to support your mother, with all the power at my command, in her belief that for you to go to university would be a waste of time. But I have decided against doing so. I therefore intend to advise her

38

strongly to send you to Cambridge, if that is where you wish to go.'

Edward was stunned. He looked at Richard incredulously. 'You mean it, Uncle? Oh, that's . . . that's wonderful!'

'You should not, however, escape scot free. Some punishment is necessary and deserved. Perhaps it is something that you should impose on yourself. I think you are ashamed of yourself, and that shame must stay with you for a long time—even for the rest of your life. That is the punishment that you will live with.'

The joy that had been on Edward's face vanished. 'I shall hope one day to earn your forgiveness, Uncle. And I promise you that I shall forget neither my wrongdoing nor your generosity. You shall never again have cause to reprimand me. And I shall always be grateful to you.'

'Very well. You had better go and prepare for your departure. You may, of course, make your farewells to your aunts and your cousin. Your Aunt Frances and Mary will be surprised at the suddenness of your leaving, but we shall say that you and I have discussed your future this afternoon, and have agreed that you should return home as soon as possible.'

'Yes, sir. Thank you.'

'That is all, Edward.'

Impulsively, Edward stepped forward and offered his uncle his hand. Then he turned and went out.

Richard looked after him with affection.

2

Sarah gazed at her son with pride. In the years he had spent at Cambridge, he had filled out, and his shoulders were broad, and when he stood, she had to look up at him. A handsome young man, she thought, and what a good thing that he did not take after his father. She studied his face—there was strength there in the firm jaw and chin, and an honest, open gaze in his eyes, and when he gave that wide, ready smile, as he so often did, he was even more attractive. How many hearts had he broken already, she wondered. 'Well, Edward,' she said, 'what do you intend to do with your degree, now that you've got it?'

He hesitated. 'I'm not really sure, Mama.'

'Oh, surely. You must have something in mind. Teaching, perhaps.'

He laughed. 'No, that's the last thing I want to do.' Then he said, 'Jack Chetwynd—you remember, Mama, we shared a room at Cambridge—he's thinking of starting up a new publishing house, and he wants me to join him.'

'And you need a degree in mathematics for that?' Her tone was only faintly ironical.

'Not really, but . . .'

'Does it interest you? It will need quite a lot of capital, won't it?'

'Not really. And for a start, neither of us would take any money out of the business. Jack's father is fairly well-to-do—he runs a cast iron foundry in Shropshire—and he's always been generous to Jack. And I can manage perfectly well with the money that Grandmama left me.'

Old Mrs Harcourt had died two years previously, and her will had given Edward an annuity of two hundred and fifty pounds a year.

'I see,' Sarah said. 'Then if that's what you're set on . . .'

'I'm not sure that I am. It sounds attractive, but . . .'

'But?'

'Jack's an awfully good sort, but he's a bit . . . well . . . unreliable, I think.' He pushed back the lock of hair which had fallen over his brow.

'Oh, dear. Then what *are* you going to do?'

Edward got up and went to stand by the fireplace. 'I've been thinking about it very seriously, Mama. I think I ought to join Harcourt's, if you'll have me.'

'What? Why on earth didn't you say so before?'

'I suppose I was afraid to.'

'Afraid to? Oh, Edward, I'm not such an ogre as that, am I? But are you sure about it? You say you *ought* to join Harcourt's. That doesn't sound particularly enthusiastic.'

'Yes, I'm sure. I'd like to learn how the business is run, and gradually take the burdens off your shoulders. You've carried them for far too long, Mama.'

'I'm not thinking of retiring yet,' Sarah said sharply.

He smiled at her. 'Oh, don't be so prickly, Mama. I know you're not. But I'm thinking of the future—of my future, as well as yours. It's the family business, and it's where I belong.'

'You always said that silk was boring—especially crape.'

'That was years ago, Mama. I'm not the same person that I was then. But of course, if you're against the idea, I'll have to think again.'

'I'm not against the idea. Whatever made you say that? I'm delighted, of course. I just wonder why you had to go to university at all.'

'If I hadn't gone, perhaps my feelings wouldn't have changed, Mama.'

'H'm. Well, I must say it is a surprise, but a very welcome one, my dear. When do you want to begin?'

'As soon as possible.'

'You'll start at the bottom, Edward. A mill owner should be able to do any of the work that the employees do.'

Edward laughed. 'I don't think I'll ever be the sort of silk maker that Uncle Richard is. I doubt if you are, either, Mama.'

'You seem to find everything so amusing, Edward. Silk making is a serious business, and you must learn all the processes. After that, you should meet some of our customers, and I will explain the business side to you. And

41

you must go and see Mr Leroy in London, who supplies us with the raw silk. You're going to have a busy time, Edward.'

'The busier the better.'

'Come, give me a kiss, my dear. I've dreamt about this for years—almost since you were born. It seems too good to be true. Sit here beside me.' She patted the sofa. 'Oh, Edward, I never thought I would have to carry the responsibility for Harcourt's for so long. Such a struggle! I have often been tempted to give up.'

'Nonsense, Mama—you've enjoyed every minute of it.'

For a moment Sarah was minded to stand on her dignity, and reprimand him again for his levity. Then she decided to laugh, too. 'Yes, I have. But I would willingly hand over the reins. I am weary of it.'

'I thought you said you weren't going to retire yet.'

'Neither am I. You're not ready. But when you are . . .' She broke off, and then said, almost archly, 'Tell me, Edward, you have not found any young lady to your liking yet?'

'Several, Mama. But what a strange question.'

'It isn't strange at all. You should be thinking of marriage. You are twenty-two, and that is by no means too early. Marriage is very steadying for young men.' She thought with irony how little such effect it had had on her husband, Tom, a womaniser and a drunkard to the end of his days.

Again Edward's sense of the ridiculous came to the fore. 'Oh, Mama, really! I'm only just down from Cambridge! And do you feel that I am in such great need of steadying?'

'I shall make it my business to introduce you to some suitable girls.' She paused for a moment. 'I know—I shall invite Mr Prideau to dinner, and ask him to bring his granddaughter.'

'I thought he was Harcourt's arch-enemy.'

'A competitor, but not an enemy. I have met him on many occasions recently, and we get on very well together.'

There seemed to be a special significance in her words. 'You are not . . . you are not thinking of marrying again, Mama?'

It was Sarah's turn to be amused. 'Good gracious, no!

And if I did, I certainly should not choose an obstinate autocrat like Mr Prideau. Besides, he's old enough to be my father. But he is pleasant company, as you shall see.'

* * *

During the next weeks, Edward worked in the mill. He had wondered how he would be received—perhaps the workers would not take kindly to the owner's son coming in to be in fact, if not in name, an apprentice, when it was obvious to the slowest-thinking among them that one day he might be their employer. He need not have worried. They liked his habit of joking with them and his willingness to learn, and were clearly ready to extend to him the affection in which they held his mother—'our Missus' they called her, and spoke of her with pride.

Much came back to him of what he had seen so often during his childhood and in the weeks he had spent with Richard in Wensham. Nevertheless, there were many differences between the manufacture of brocade and that of crape. The weaving and the looms were much simpler, because there was no need to produce a pattern in the filmy gauze, but after that began the biasing, and the passing of the material through the rollers. The upper roller was of brass, engraved in a complex design of ridges and hollows, while the lower was covered in *papier maché*, carrying a reverse impression of the design. When the gauze passed between them, under pressure and heat, it was imprinted with the pattern of the brass cylinder. Then it had to be unbiased, and dyed, and steeped in liquids which would give it the required matt finish, and those which would make it waterproof.

As he learned, Edward also observed. It seemed to him that many of the practices in the mill were old-fashioned and laborious. There must surely be machines now that could take over some of the functions which were done by hand, and much of the existing machinery was nearing the end of its useful life, too, and might well be replaced. He also watched the workers carefully. Most were efficient enough, and knew their jobs, but nearly all were at some time or other idle; it should be possible to train at least the best of them to perform more than one function in the mill,

43

and thereby cut down on the hours wasted when they had nothing to do.

He said nothing of his thoughts at this stage to his mother. It would be time enough to suggest changes when he had learned some of the other sides of the business. He was longing to have a look at the company's finances—there, he felt, he would really be at home. And he had to choose the right moment to talk to her—he had known since childhood that she had to be approached carefully if he wanted her agreement to anything. A simple request on the wrong day could often lead to a tirade and an adamant refusal even to consider whatever it was that he was asking.

* * *

Edward had to admit that his mother looked at her most regal as she stood in the drawing-room to receive her guests. She was wearing a new gown of pale lilac silk, trimmed around the hem with black. The puffed sleeves were black, too, and emphasised the whiteness of her arms, bare above her gloves. Edward was surprised and privately a little amused to see that there was not, this evening, an inch of crape in her attire.

The dinner party had been arranged with the purpose of persuading Mr James Prideau to bring his granddaughter, Miss Alice Ouvray, to the house. The other guests were a Mr and Mrs Ashton and their daughter Edith, and Mr Derwent, a middle-aged bachelor.

They had heard a carriage draw up a few minutes earlier. 'That will be the Prideaus,' Sarah had said.

'It might be the Ashtons, or Mr Derwent.'

'No, dear. I told *them* seven forty-five. Miss Ashton is quite a pleasant girl, and you could do worse, but it is Miss Ouvray I want you to meet. She is an orphan, you know, and Mr Prideau's only heir. Most of his children died in infancy, and the two daughters who survived to adulthood are now both dead. So sad for him. They tell me that Miss Alice is very intelligent, and she's extremely pretty—ideal for you in every way.'

Edward had already decided that he disliked this paragon, and had seen no reason by the end of the evening to change

44

his mind. Everything had been carefully contrived; his mother insisted that Miss Ashton should look at a collection of pressed flowers, while she herself conversed animatedly with Mr Prideau, Mr and Mrs Ashton and Mr Derwent, leaving Edward free to talk to Miss Ouvray. At dinner he was seated next to her, and afterwards, when she was persuaded to play the piano, Sarah immediately volunteered his services to turn over the pages.

It was true that she was pretty—dark-haired, with brown eyes in a heart-shaped face, and a complexion that needed no artificial aids. She was not really beautiful, he thought—the features were a little too sharp for that. Her nose was long and her lips, sharply defined, might almost be called thin. No, not beautiful, but certainly extremely pretty, and her face was expressive and lively. She was fairly tall, and her gown of white silk revealed a figure of which she was entitled to be proud.

But whatever his mother had been told, he saw little signs of a high intelligence—she had been shy and silent at first, and then, her reserve melting, had gushed at him, and finally responded to his conversational gambits and his little witticisms with a tartness which he thought barely polite. He had enjoyed rather more her accomplishments on the piano, but when he complimented her on her talent, she received his comments with such warmth, thanking him so profusely, that they both became embarrassed. He was relieved when Mr Prideau announced that it was time to go.

Sarah was delighted with the evening. 'Tell me, my darling,' she said when the guests had gone, 'what did you think of Miss Ouvray?'

Edward knew better than to tell her the truth. 'She's very charming, and very pretty.'

'I knew you would like her,' Sarah said. 'And wasn't I clever to leave you alone with her so much? You should be very grateful.'

'Oh, I am, Mama.'

'I hope you arranged to see her again.'

'That would have been somewhat impetuous,' Edward said smoothly. 'I wouldn't want to frighten her off.'

'No, of course. How wise you are, my dear. I am so glad I had the idea of sending you to Cambridge. It has put a polish on you—it has given you . . . quite an air. Oh, no girl will be able to resist you! Poor little Edith Ashton couldn't take her eyes off you—did you notice?'

'Not really. I was more interested in watching you and Mr Prideau. You seemed to be much engrossed.'

'He was on his usual tack—asking me when I would sell Harcourt's to him. I'm used to it—just as he's used to my refusal. How did you get on with him?'

'I barely spoke to him, Mama.'

'Not when you gentlemen were enjoying your port and cigars?'

'He talked to Mr Ashton the whole time. I had a rather sparkling conversation with Mr Derwent.'

Sarah smiled. 'Such a bore. But a single man is useful to make up one's table.'

Suddenly Edward saw the opening he needed. 'He wasn't as bad as all that. He was asking me about what I was doing, and I told him how I'd been working in the mill, and hoped soon to learn the other side of the business—the financial side, and so on . . .' He looked at her surreptitiously to see how she was taking it. At least there were no signs of storm clouds.

'You're not ready to leave the mill yet,' she said, but her voice was soft, indulgent. 'Why, if you were not my son, you would spend years there as an apprentice.'

'But, Mama, I *am* your son,' Edward said, keeping his tone light, 'and you must believe me when I say that I'm never going to be a practical silk maker. I don't need to be, any more than you do. I don't want to boast, but I think I have learnt enough—I know all the processes; I know what the machines do. I can tell whether or not they are operating efficiently, and I know which of our workers are reliable and quick and skilled, and which aren't. If I had to, I could do a stint on any job.'

'You're very clever, Edward, I know.' She patted his arm. 'Is there still some brandy in the decanter?'

'Listen, Mama. I must learn more about the business, and as quickly as I can. While I'm learning I'm not contributing anything, so the sooner I've finished this apprenticeship—and you're right to call it that—the better. I'd like to spend some time on the accounts.'

'No! Not yet, Edward. I agree that it is time for you to

46

enlarge the scope of your training, but I think it would be best, before you get involved in our financial affairs, to visit some of our customers. You can learn a great deal from them. Pour me another glass, dear.'

He did so.

Sarah sipped at the brandy, looking at him over the rim of the glass. 'Yes, you'll learn quite a lot. Including why we can't alter some of the old-fashioned ways which I am sure you are itching to change.' She looked up and smiled as she saw that the shaft had gone home. 'I'm not a fool,' she went on, though amiably rather than with irritation. 'I know there are many things which you must have your eye on—economies, greater efficiency, this and that—but you may find that there's a good reason for working the way we do. So, yes, my dear, go out and visit our customers, by all means. Start with Mr Montgomery in Norwich. He has always been a good friend to us, and he knows the trade backwards. I'll write you a note for him in the morning.'

'I'd rather just go in and introduce myself, Mama.'

*   *   *

The next day, Edward travelled to Norwich. Montgomery's was a large shop, divided into two, one half dealing in haberdashery and materials, the other a ladies' outfitters.

Edward went into the haberdashery. The shop was smart, clean and well-lit, with good displays of a wide range of goods, and it was busy. Edward guessed that its customers came almost exclusively from the well-to-do middle classes—the kind of people who would buy crape in large quantities whenever they were in mourning, not only for themselves but for their servants, too. And since large families were the rule, there was hardly any time when they would not be in mourning, whether it was the year-long expression of bereavement for a husband or wife or the few days of wearing black if a remote cousin should die.

As soon as one of the assistants was free, Edward went up to him and asked to be shown some mourning crape.

'Yes, sir. What quality?'

'I am not sure. Perhaps you could advise me.'

47

For a quarter of an hour the assistant brought out various crapes, while Edward examined them, and asked which manufacturer had made them and what the prices were.

'This is Harcourt's Mourning Crape for Gentlemen,' the assistant said, bringing out yet another roll of material. 'It has been the staple line for Harcourt's ever since they went into crape. You will see that it is a rather more substantial material than that designed for the ladies.'

'And is it popular?' Edward asked.

'Oh, very. At least it has been. The demand is dropping a bit these last years. People don't seem so keen on mourning as they used to be, sir. Signs of the times, I suppose. Now, sir, can I show you anything else, or can I perhaps serve you with something you have seen already?'

'I think not,' Edward said. 'I should like to see Mr Montgomery.'

The man's face immediately showed apprehension. 'I'm very sorry, sir. I hope I have not given you cause for dissatisfaction.'

Edward gave him his warmest smile. 'On the contrary. You have been most patient and helpful, and I shall tell Mr Montgomery so.'

'Yes, sir. Thank you, sir. Who shall I say has called?'

'I do not wish to give my name. Tell Mr Montgomery simply that a gentleman wishes to have a brief word with him, if he will be so good as to spare the time.'

The man soon returned, and led Edward up some stairs at the back of the shop to a landing piled with cardboard boxes and bales wrapped in brown paper, which scarcely left room to walk, and then knocked at a door.

'Come in.'

A tall, thin man with a long, narrow face, came towards Edward. His high-domed head was bald, but he wore a short grey beard. The lower lids of his eyes drooped slightly, giving him a look of spaniel sadness. 'Morning, Mr Harcourt,' he said, extending his hand.

Edward was taken aback. 'I was going to surprise you, Mr Montgomery. How did you know my name?'

'Been watching you.' he indicated a somewhat dusty window which looked down into the shop. A small round hole had been cleaned in the dust. 'My spy-hole. Look out

48

periodically. Saw you. Saw the crape. Very like your mother. Put two and two together. Seat.'

Edward sat down. 'I'm amazed, Mr Montgomery, and grateful to you for seeing me like this. And I must congratulate you on the assistant who served me—he tried very hard, and he helped me a great deal. But then, if you were watching, I suppose you know that.'

'Know it anyway. Know my staff. But curious why you looked at every crape we carry.'

'I will confess everything, sir,' Edward smiled. 'I wanted to talk to you about the market for it, but I thought I had better familiarise myself first with the range that you have, and perhaps find out something about how well it sells.'

Mr Montgomery gave what Edward thought was intended to be a smile. At least for a moment his customary sorrowful expression changed. 'You discovered?'

'Your assistant says that crape is no longer as much in demand as it was.'

'Quite right. Going out of fashion. Had a long run. Can't grumble.'

'How rapidly is the market declining, would you say?'

'Oh, slowly, slowly. Few years yet.'

'But you would advise Harcourt's to avoid any future reliance solely on crape.'

'Competitors already branching out. Sensible. Anything else, Mr Harcourt?'

'No, I don't think so, Mr Mongomery. I'm most grateful for your time and courtesy.'

'Pleased to make your acquaintance. Very busy. Forgive me.' He shook hands with Edward and turned back to his desk.

Edward visited other retailers, each time making enquiries in the shop before speaking to the owner, or the buyer in the larger stores. Everywhere he was given much the same information. Occasionally, he was offered orders for Harcourt's, but these he gently but courteously refused to take—a travelling salesman would call to collect them or they could be sent by post—his intention was simply to visit, make the acquaintance of the customer and enquire as to the state of the market.

Sarah was always eager to know how he had fared, but he fended off her questions, merely saying how interesting

49

the visits were. Nor did he tell her of his intention to call upon Mr James Prideau.

* * *

Prideau received him affably. 'Well, young man, what can I do for you? I suppose it is too much to hope that you are an ambassador come to tell me that your mother is ready to sell Harcourt's.'

'Indeed, it is, sir. And even if my mother were minded to sell, I should try to dissuade her.'

'Ah, you Harcourts—always obstinate.' But he smiled as he shook his head. 'What is it, then?'

'I wondered if you would afford me the privilege of looking over your mill. I should like to learn something of how you achieve your success.'

Prideau chuckled. 'So that you can put it into effect at Harcourt's?'

Edward smiled. 'Yes, sir,' he said chirpily. 'Not that I expect to be able to rival Prideau's. Just a quick look round, and perhaps a few questions . . .'

For a moment Prideau glared at him. Then he chuckled again. 'You have a damned cheek, do you know that? I ought to throw you out on your ear, but . . .' He chuckled again. '. . . but you've got courage, I'll say that for you. Come on, then.'

The tour of the mill was fascinating to Edward. The whole place smelled of efficiency, and was clearly working to full capacity. They began by visiting the crape rooms, passing first through doors which had to be unlocked for them.

'We never normally allow visitors into the crape department,' Prideau said, 'and our hands are sworn to secrecy. However, since you are in the same business . . .'

The processes were similar to those used in Harcourt's Mill, though Edward noticed that the machines were both larger and newer, allowing a faster operation and the production of wider material. He was interested to see that comparatively little mourning crape was made. Most of the dyeing vats were filled with colour, and the fabrics produced were of every hue.

'Ten or fifteen years ago almost the whole mill was given

50

over to mourning crape,' Prideau told him, 'but we have cut back production, and expanded into coloured crepes and chiffons and other light materials. We also make some brocades. I'll show you that section next.' As they walked past the brocade looms, he went on, 'I suppose you have seen this kind of thing at Mr Goodwin's mill?'

'Yes, sir. I worked there for a time before I went to Cambridge.'

'Indeed? No doubt you know that as a young man he was employed here. A pity we ever let him go. It caused us a great deal of bother, because he went off to your family mill and started making crape there. And he lured away the best accounts man I ever had. No doubt you've met Mr Hill.'

'Yes, sir.' Edward had heard the story many times. 'You will not take offence, sir, if I tell you that I have been given to understand that my uncle was unfairly dismissed from your company.'

The old man looked at him sharply. 'Perhaps. Equally, you will not take offence if I say that he did not deserve the treatment that your father meted out to him. Ah, well, there is no need to worry about Richard Goodwin. He has fallen on his feet, as I knew he would—he is that sort of man. I admire him. Just as I admire your mother. Mind you, she can be very—' He broke off. 'I was about to say "obstinate", but perhaps "strong-willed" would be a more acceptable term. But she is a fine woman, and if you take after her, you won't do too badly.'

*   *   *

Christmas and the New Year of 1896 came and went, almost unnoticed. Even when Edward was small, his mother had been reluctant to celebrate the occasion, apart from the obligatory attendance at church on Christmas morning, regarding it as an unwelcome day of idleness at the mill.

Edward had been waiting for a suitable opportunity to raise with Sarah the matters which were uppermost in his mind. As he faced her now, on an evening early in January, he remembered Mr Prideau's words. She had certainly been obstinate in her refusal to let him into the secrets

51

of Harcourt's financial position. He had been able to examine the current accounts, which showed that the company was trading in little better than a break-even situation, and he had gathered confirmation of the decline of the business over the past few years. But he had been given no information about the capital reserves, nor did he know how much money his mother was taking out of the business. He suspected that she might well be drawing nothing at all—perhaps even putting in funds out of the personal profits she had accumulated in earlier, more prosperous years.

They were in the drawing-room after dinner. How familiar this picture of his mother was, Edward thought—sitting upright in her favourite high-backed chair, beautiful, serene. The only changes from the days of his youth were the few streaks of silver which had begun to appear in her rich chestnut hair, and the absence of the elaborate antimacassar which old Mrs Harcourt had crocheted for Sarah, which she had always hated and which she had removed as soon as the old lady died.

At dinner, she had seemed in a fairly relaxed mood, and now she was reading a book, while sipping at the glass of brandy which she liked to enjoy in the evening.

'Mama, please let us talk. There is so much that I want to say.'

She sighed, and put down the book. 'Oh, very well. But I warn you that I think you are being impatient. You expect to come into the business and learn it all in a few short weeks.'

'Even in a few short weeks, Mama, I have seen things which I must talk to you about. Are you not worried about the state of the business?'

'It is not as buoyant as I would like, at present, but I see no cause for concern. I presume you do.'

'I see it at every turn. Many of the machines in the mill are outdated and inefficient. Our methods are old-fashioned, and the workers lack enthusiasm. But what worries me most of all is that we are not working to capacity because our market is declining, and quite rapidly. I went to see Mr Prideau, and—'

'You didn't tell me that,' Sarah interrupted sharply.

'He has reduced his output of mourning crape substantially, and is making coloured crapes and other light silk fabrics, and even some brocade. I think it's essential that we should do the same, Mama.'

Sarah rose, and paced up and down as she spoke. Angry spots of colour appeared on her cheeks, and her hands were clenched into fists. 'You know nothing about it, nothing at all! Yes, our machines are old, but they are serviceable still, and it makes no economic sense, as a graduate in mathemetics should know, to get rid of them while they are still working well. As for our employees, I will listen to no word against them. They are loyal and hard-working, and though you may not see their enthusiasm, believe me, it is there. Anything I ask, they will do, and willingly. They love me—yes, love me—and I love them.'

'Mama, I am not trying to criticise—'

'Not trying to criticise! I like that! Do you think I am a total fool? Do you think I am not aware that demand for crape has slackened recently? But the market is always volatile. You would know that if you had been in the business as long as I have, and I assure you it will pick up again.' She turned, and faced him. 'Tell me, Edward, who do you think leads the fashion in this country?'

'If we are talking of crape, I suppose it must be the Queen.'

'Yes, the Queen.'

'But, Mama, younger people think differently, and—'

'Younger people! I don't care what younger people think! Nor do I care what Mr Prideau chooses to do in his mill. And I most strongly resent the fact that, without so much as a by-your-leave, you should visit him, and take what he says for gospel. I am most disappointed in you, Edward.'

'Mama, please listen to me,' Edward pleaded. 'I may be young, and I may not have your experience, but every single piece of evidence that I have found in the past few weeks says that the future of Harcourt's is in jeopardy. We have a duty to our workers and to ourselves to recognise change when it comes; to plan wisely for the future.'

Sarah did not reply at once. She went over to the side-table and poured herself another glass of brandy, and drank it quickly. Then she looked at Edward, smiled in a strange way, and said calmly, 'Tell me, my dear, if I gave you control of the mill you would make these changes that

53

you speak of? You would replace our old machinery? Where would you find the money?'

'I don't know, Mama. I don't know what reserves we have.'

'No doubt you could raise a bank loan if necessary. And what of the workers? Sack some of them, pension others off? And abandon mourning crape, and follow James Prideau's advice? Is that your plan?'

'I do not have a plan,' Edward said gently. 'I am asking you to consider the situation and act accordingly. I believe that change is inevitable, and that it will be for the good of the mill.'

Again there was a pause. Sarah put down her glass. 'I do not wish to discuss this further. I am very disturbed, Edward. Ever since you announced your sudden change of heart about the mill, I have been aware of a highly critical attitude. Whatever you say, you have no interest in silk making, no real interest in Harcourt's, and the kind of ideas you have in mind would ruin us in weeks.' Again she strode angrily up and down.

'Mama—'

'Be quiet! I am thinking.' After a while, she turned to face him. Her voice was calmer, but cold. 'It pains me to say this, but I believe it would be much better if you were to leave the mill. I am thinking of your future, as much as mine. Go somewhere else. Find your own employment, somewhere where your progressive ideas will be acceptable.'

Edward looked at her in dismay. 'But, Mama, I assure you—'

'I do not want your assurances.' Suddenly her anger flared again. 'I will not support your constant criticisms and importunities. And no doubt you have been spreading these wild ideas among my workers, sowing dissension and—'

'No, Mama! Of course not.' Edward could scarcely believe his ears. His mother seemed beside herself, almost unbalanced. 'Please let us forget all that I said. I will do whatever you want. I did not mean to upset you, and I am certainly not criticising you.'

'Oh, no! You only want to change everything, to undo all that I have achieved in a lifelong toil. My mind is made up. I wash my hands of you. You had better go to bed.

54

You can tell me in the morning what you propose to do.'

'But, Mama . . . Please listen to me.'

But Sarah had returned to her seat and picked up her book, staring at the page unseeingly, and she did not reply.

He tried again. 'Mama . . .'

She did not look up, and when Edward went to her, and bent to kiss her, she averted her head.

*   *   *

As Edward entered the dining-room the next morning, Sarah finished her cup of tea, and stood up. 'I trust you have got over your outburst last night,' she said.

Edward smiled to himself, thinking it was a fine case of the pot calling the kettle black. But he said solemnly, 'Yes, Mama. I am sorry, and I beg your forgiveness.'

'Very well,' Sarah replied. 'For my part, I am prepared to overlook it. You will come to the mill as soon as possible, please. I have had a message that Ellerby, the head weaver, is ill, and, since you believe yourself to be so competent, you are to take over his supervisory duties as best you can, until he returns. You will not be expected to weave yourself. Just make sure that the work is carried out properly, and report to me immediately if anything goes wrong.' She hurried from the room.

For the next three days Edward worked in the mill. It was not difficult, since the workers knew their duties well, and no major problems were encountered, but he was far from happy, especially since, at home, his mother barely spoke to him, busying herself with papers while they ate, and retiring to her study as soon as the meals were finished. Edward was careful to obey her every instruction to the letter, in the hope that she would eventually give him back her confidence.

At breakfast on the fourth day, Sarah said, 'Ellerby is back today, so the question is what you shall do now. I have decided that you shall travel for us. You are so concerned about falling orders—perhaps you will be able to increase our trade. I have here a list of customers in the North of England. You may set out as soon as you please to visit them.'

An alarm bell rang in Edward's head. 'Is that to be my future position in the company, Mama?'

'Perhaps.'

He could not conceal the bitterness. 'It will keep me out of your way, I suppose.'

'Please do not adopt that tone with me. I am in no mind to turn over to you any of my responsibilities, not when you have already made it clear that if I did so you would act in a manner entirely contrary to my wishes.'

Edward tried to control his feelings. Clearly, she intended to humiliate him, and he could look forward only to a succession of junior posts in the firm. Perhaps she still wanted him to leave. Carefully, he said, 'You suggested the other evening that it might be best if I were to leave the mill and find some other employment. Is that still in your mind?'

'No!' Then she looked at him hard, and the anger dropped from her face, to be replaced by a kind of relief. She nodded her head slowly. 'Well, it is your decision, my dear, but perhaps it might be wise. Oh, Edward, I did hope that we might work amicably together, but you can see how difficult it would be. Our views are so diametrically opposed. You will be happier somewhere else.' She smiled at him, affectionately. 'Whatever you choose to do, I know that you will be successful, and you shall come back here and tell me of your triumphs. This will always be your home—you know that.' She held our her hands. 'Come, kiss me, my dear, and tell me that you still love your foolish old mother, just as she loves you, and that you bear her no grudge.'

Dazed, Edward went and kissed her, unable to believe for the moment that, despite the affection she professed, his mother was not merely dismissing him from Harcourt's, but in fact turning him out of the house.

*   *   *

That afternoon Edward called at Richard Goodwin's mill in Wensham. It had taken him little time to make up his mind to leave home at once. He had packed as much luggage as he could carry—the rest could be sent for later—and had composed a brief note to his mother telling her that he was

56

going first to his Uncle Richard, and that he would write again as soon as he knew what his immediate future would be.

He tried to analyse his feelings, and somewhat to his surprise realised that he harboured no feelings of bitterness towards his mother, nor was he downcast. Instead, there was a kind of excitement, and a confidence in himself, and a belief that somehow everything would work out.

Richard was astonished at Edward's report of what had transpired.

'I suppose it was my fault, really,' Edward said. 'I tried to push Mama too hard. Besides, we're so different in so many ways. She gets so serious, and I find myself laughing at her. It's affectionate laughter—at least, I think it is—but it always upsets her.'

'You should control yourself.'

'I try to. There wasn't much laughter last night, or this morning.'

'H'm. Well, what do you want me to do?' Richard asked. 'Talk to her?'

'I don't think there would be much point,' Edward replied. 'Do you?'

'Not really. Sometimes I can influence her, as I did over your going to university, but she's never been easy to deal with when it comes to the running of Harcourt's. So what are you going to do?'

'I hoped I might come and work with you, Uncle.'

'I thought you weren't interested in silk.'

'I've changed my mind. I've grown up—at least a bit. I don't think I shall ever be a silk maker, because I don't have the sort of feel for fabrics that you do, but I'm very interested in the business side of it. Is there anything I could do in that line?'

'As a matter of fact, there may be,' Richard replied. 'I have been wondering what to do about Mr Hill. He's not as young as he used to be, and he suffers with his chest, particularly in the winter. Sooner or later he's going to have to retire, and that's going to leave a big hole in the company. You might take over, in time. We'll have to see what Mr Hill thinks about it, of course, and how you get on when you're working with him.'

Mr Hill was quite willing to accept Edward as an

assistant. 'Young men have more virtue than old men, as Samuel Johnson has it,' he said. 'On the other hand, Francis Bacon tell us that young men are fitter to invent than to judge, fitter for execution than for counsel, and fitter for new projects than for settled business. We shall discover, no doubt, which of those pronouncements applies to you. When are you going to start?'

'As soon as I am permitted,' Edward replied.

'Tomorrow morning,' Richard said. 'Now, Edward, you had better come home with me. You will be welcome to stay with us until you are ready perhaps to take on a domicile of your own.'

'Are you sure, Uncle? I thought perhaps Aunt Louisa might . . . After all, the last time I was here . . .'

'Oh, that is all over and done with, and I'm sure your aunt has forgotten it.'

Edward was not so sure of that when they reached the house. His Aunt Louisa made a pretence of welcoming him, but her attitude was cold. A little behind her stood Mary, eyes modestly cast down. Now seventeen, she had blossomed. At first he was aware only of her blonde hair, piled on top of her head, with a fringe of fluffy curls at the front, and her pale blue dress, curving with the gentle swell of her bosom and hips. Then she stepped forward. 'Come, Edward—we are kissing cousins, are we not?' And she raised her head and smiled at him, and he saw the wide blue eyes, and the full lips. A little shyly, their cheeks brushed, and Edward felt a sudden surge of delight. How right he had been to come to Wensham. Not only had his uncle immediately welcomed him, without any difficult inquisition about his relationship with his mother, but now he would have the companionship of this entrancing girl. And he would be as deferentially charming as he could towards Aunt Louisa, and do his best to win her over.

*   *   *

Edward enjoyed working with Mr Hill, who made no bones about revealing to him all the financial details of his uncle's company. Although he believed that some of Mr Hill's methods were rather old-fashioned, and might one day be changed, the firm was efficiently run and highly profitable.

Richard Goodwin lived well, and rewarded his employees at a rate which was high for the industry, but despite this a good proportion of the profits was ploughed back into the business and used not only to buy new machines and to keep the premises in good order, but also to provide substantial reserves against future expenditure.

One thing only puzzled Edward, and that was why his uncle did not expand his company further. He asked Mr Hill about it.

'A deliberate policy, my boy, and one of which I heartily approve. Your uncle is well aware that he could build on to the mill; become a major producer. But he knows equally how easy it is to grow too big, too fast. "Vaulting ambition, which o'erleaps itself," you know.'

'Surely,' Edward protested, 'some growth would be possible.'

'It seems very difficult in this trade. You are either large, like Prideau's, or comparatively small, like Harcourt's or Goodwin's. There is no half-way point.'

'Then perhaps he should think of major expansion.'

'No, because above all that would mean a loss of the personal touch. As it is Mr Richard knows every one of his employees, and indeed looks upon them as his friends. Double, treble, quadruple the work-force, and managers and under-managers and goodness knows who else would have to be brought in, and the family atmosphere of the firm would be lost.' His eyes twinkled. 'In a long career, my boy, however undistinguished it may have been—though I shall not attempt to argue with you if you wish to challenge that remark—in my not inconsiderable experience, I have learnt that a good personal relationship between a master and his men results in a larger output and better quality. And that, as I am sure I need not tell you, brings bigger profits, and satisfaction all round. *Quod erat demonstrandum*— if you will forgive me for showing off my little Latin. I shall not bother you with my less Greek. And that's twice in two minutes that I've quoted Master Shakespeare, which means that as usual my tongue has run away with me.'

As the weeks went by, Edward enjoyed himself more and more. Work alongside Mr Hill was a pleasure, and his uncle began to speak of a time, perhaps a year ahead, when Edward would take over as his accountant. 'I have already discussed the matter with Mr Hill,' he said, 'and he has accepted the idea without too much dismay. I have promised him that he shall remain as a consultant, and his wisdom and experience would be at your beck and call.'

Edward had written to his mother, and received a cool reply, which consisted mainly of complaints about the burdens which she had to carry. It worried Edward, but there was no hint in her letter that she wanted him to return to Brentfield, and indeed the only reference to him came in the last line—'I am glad to hear that you are settled in Wensham'—and in a postscript—'I trust you will remember your duty, and visit your mother from time to time'.

Edward fully intended to do so, but not for the moment—especially since, when he was not working, all his attention was centred on his cousin Mary. He was completely bewitched by her, and was delighted to find that she appeared to enjoy his company too. They spent most of the evenings together, playing bezique or just talking and laughing; they sat next to each other in church, and went for walks on Sunday afternoons.

Edward discovered that there were many facets to her character. At times she was full of fun—one evening when some friends came to visit, she organised a game of Dumb Crambo, and kept everyone in fits of laughter with her acting. Even Aunt Louisa was persuaded to join in the game—Mary was the one person who seemed able to make her mother unbend. And Mary was interested in books and art and music, and brought an enthusiasm to everything she spoke of. She was deeply religious, too, but wore her faith without embarrassing piety, and the good works to which she was devoted were performed without condescension or any feeling of a duty, but simply because she enjoyed helping others.

On the first Sunday in every month, she was in the habit of taking jams she had made, and pies and cakes she had baked, to some of the poor families in the village. Most of the people of Wensham worked for her father and were well paid, but there were some families who were near to starvation. Mary was always welcome when she visited their squalid cottages, which sometimes consisted of no more than two rooms housing nine or ten human beings, talking to the parents as a friend, holding the babies in her arms or allowing the small children to crawl onto her lap. She did not always visit the same families every week, but never failed to call on the Smiths—'my poorest of the poor', she called them—who lived in a hovel on the outskirts of the village. Luke Smith was a drunkard. Occasionally he found temporary work on a farm, but his wife scraped a living for the family by gathering herbs and selling them at the weekly market, and contrived to keep bodies and souls together with the eggs from the few scrawny hens which pecked the ground around their cottage—hens which many suspected had been stolen.

Edward took to accompanying Mary on these expeditions, carrying her basket for her. He was appalled when he first entered the Smiths' cottage. Luke Smith lay snoring on a filthy pile of rags, sleeping off the previous night's drinking, despite the noise of the five small children, all dressed in rags, their stick-like arms black with dirt. Mrs Smith, gaunt and old beyond her years, was pregnant again. The stench in the room was almost unsupportable.

As they emerged from the hovel there were tears in Mary's eyes. 'Oh, Edward, they are so poor. It makes my heart bleed to see their children so thin and undernourished, and Mrs Smith in . . . in that condition. I doubt she has the strength . . . Those children will surely die if she is no longer there to care for them. Oh, that Luke Smith—I would . . . I would like to shake him!' She laughed wryly. 'Not that it would do any good. Oh, why are some men such brutes? Next time I come here I must bring more food, and I will ask Papa to see that they get milk every day.'

'I think you're wonderful,' Edward said. 'You don't seem to mind the dirt and the smell. I almost retched in there.'

'Do you think I don't want to? I always have a bath and put all my clothes to be washed when I get home.'

'I think you're wonderful,' he repeated, and gently took her hand in his.

She did not draw away, but looked into his eyes and said, 'They are human beings, Edward—God's children—and we must love them.'

'They certainly love *you*.' And then he added quietly, 'And so do I.' He laughed with pure happiness.

She said nothing, but the blood rushed to her cheeks. She

61

squeezed his hand softly, and then withdrew it, and they walked home in silence, both embarrassed.

That evening they sat together reading, since card-games could not of course be played on the Sabbath, and after a while, Edward looked up and whispered, 'It's true, what I said this afternoon.'

Mary did not speak, but smiled at him, and his heart leaped for joy.

As he lay in bed that night, his mind was filled with her. The certainty grew in his heart that they were meant for each other, and he determined to ask her to be his wife. The only question was when. They were never alone in the house for more than a moment or two, so it would have to wait until their next Sunday afternoon walk. But the next Sundays were wet and cold, and he had to possess himself in patience, and be content with ardent looks and the occasional opportunity to press her hand in his.

March came in more like a lamb than a lion. The first Sunday was quite warm, and as he and Mary set off on their mercy errands, it felt as though spring had come. There were snowdrops everywhere, and the primroses and the wild daffodils were in bud, and birds filled the air with song.

After they had left the Smiths' cottage, Edward suggested that they should walk the long way home, through the woods. The afternoon sunlight filtered through the trees, and danced on the water of the little stream. Edward made for a clearing that he knew of, where an old tree trunk lay; a passable seat. He led Mary to it. 'Sit there,' he said.

'It's not as warm as that, Edward.'

'Just for a moment.' As she sat, he knelt on one knee beside her, and took her hand. 'Mary,' he began, and had to clear his throat. Then the words came out in a rush. 'Mary, I love you very much, and I want you to be my wife. Will you marry me?'

For a moment she gazed at him, solemn-faced. Then, blushing, she gave a little smile, and nodded.

'Oh, my love!' He rose and drew her to her feet. 'You mean it?'

She nodded again, still unable to speak.

'May I kiss you?' he asked. 'You said once we were kissing cousins. Now we're more than that.' He drew her towards him, and bent his head to hers. It was the sweetest kiss he had ever known. 'I shall ask your father for your hand tonight,' he promised.

'Oh, Edward, I've prayed for this. I love you, too, very much. But Papa—he'll say that seventeen is much too young, and ask us to wait, I am sure.'

'I'd wait for you for ever.' He laughed. 'Or at least until you're of age!'

'Don't ask him tonight, Edward. Let's keep it as our secret for a little while.'

'But I want everybody to know.'

'Let me get used to the idea first.'

'All right. But soon—let me go to him soon. Oh, my dearest Mary, I shall love you till the end of time.' He took her in his arms again and kissed her long and tenderly, not daring yet to show her the passion that he felt.

And when the kiss ended, he said, 'I love my love with an A, because she's adorable, and a B, because she's beautiful, and a C, because she's . . . because she's clever, and a—'

'And I love my love with an L,' Mary interrupted, 'because he's always laughing, and an I for intelligent, and an H for handsome.'

'You're supposed to go through the alphabet in the right order,' Edward protested.

'All right. An A because he's awful, and a B because he's beastly and—'

Edward stopped her words with another kiss, and then they both laughed for joy, and walked slowly home together, his arm around her waist while they were still in the wood, and hand in hand once they had left it and might have been observed by strangers.

*   *   *

Lying in bed, Richard watched his wife as she plaited her hair. She seemed preoccupied, and he wondered what was on her mind. Well, she would soon tell him.

She put down her hairbrush. 'I'm very worried about Mary and Edward. I think they're falling in love.'

'Oh, nonsense!' Richard said. 'They're just good friends. I'm glad to see them chatting away so happily.'

'Don't tell me it's nonsense, my dear. I see what I see.

And I must remind you that Edward is not to be trusted.'

'That's unfair,' Richard protested mildly. 'He was only a boy when all that happened, and it was the girl's fault anyway.'

'I'm not so sure.'

'Well I am.'

Recognising a tone of finality in his voice, Louisa decided not to argue on that score. 'Anyway,' she said firmly, 'he and Mary are much too young, and we'll have to put a stop to it before it goes too far. It might be a good idea to send her to stay with your sister for a while.'

'Yes, dear,' Richard said resignedly.

Later, as he settled himself for sleep, he found himself thinking of the women in his family: Louisa, whom he loved dearly, somehow not resenting the fact that she imposed her will relentlessly on him as well as on his household; and Frances, now happily married to Alfred Bunn and living in comparative comfort since their income was supplemented by the money Richard paid her for her work as his designer; and, of course, Mary, his darling child, whom he loved above all else. Was Louisa right about her interest in Edward? He would have to watch them together, he thought, and indeed put a stop to it before it went too far. He thought suddenly of his older sister, for whom Mary had been named—his betrayed sister, who had died following a bungled abortion by a so-called wise woman. Old Granny Winspear. He had not remembered that name for years. Pray God that nothing like that ever happened to his daughter. He would watch carefully; carefully and closely.

*   *   *

Richard and Louisa were invited to dine, some ten days later, with nearby friends, the Charlesworths. Louisa was loath at first to accept the invitation, knowing that Mary and Edward would be alone in the house, but finally gave in, since Richard was very eager to go. But she instructed one of the maids to make regular appearances in the drawing-room. 'I want to be sure that the young people are properly looked after,' she said.

When, after a meal, a little soirée musicale began, and

Louisa discovered that she had forgotten her music, she insisted on going home to fetch it.

'I will go,' Richard said.

'You shall not. It was my fault. And it is only two doors away.'

'We will send a servant,' Mrs Charlesworth said.

'No, I insist. It will give me the opportunity of seeing that my daughter and my nephew are being properly looked after.'

Mrs Charlesworth knew Louisa well enough not to argue.

Meanwhile, Mary and Edward had dined, and then had gone to sit in the drawing-room, sharing a sofa in front of the small coal fire which had been lit because the evening was chilly.

Edward put his arm around Mary and drew her to him, so that her head rested on his shoulder, and then, as they whispered their love to each other, he punctuated his words with little kisses. Gradually, their mutual passion grew, and the kisses become long and urgent. There was no question of any greater intimacy—Mary was no Tessie to be treated as a wanton—but kisses were legitimate, and so were the words which Edward used to tell Mary how beautiful she was and how much he adored her. And kisses were not only for the mouth, but could extend to the creamy skin of her neck and shoulders, revealed by her pale cerise evening gown.

Neither of them heard the door open.

'What is the meaning of this?' Louisa's voice was like thunder.

They scrambled to their feet and faced her, both scarlet with embarrassment.

'Go to your room at once, Miss!'

'Mama—'

'Your room!'

There was no possibility of disobeying. With her head bowed, Mary walked to the door, turning to flash Edward a look of love and encouragement before leaving the room.

'Stay here,' Louisa told Edward coldly, and went out, shutting the door. Outside, she called for a maid. 'Go to Mr and Mrs Charlesworth's house,' she told her. 'Give my apologies to Mr and Mrs Charlesworth and say that I am a little unwell, and ask Mr Goodwin to return home immediately. Make certain that you stress that the illness is nothing serious.'

She had made no effort to keep her voice down, and Edward heard every word. The front door closed behind the maid, and a seemingly interminable wait followed. Then he heard his uncle return, and a long conversation between him and his wife. This time the voices were low, and he could not make out what was being said, except for his aunt's final words, 'I insist that he leave this house this very night!'

The door to the drawing-room opened, and Richard entered.

'I can explain everything,' Edward said.

'No doubt. But you will sit down and listen to me.' He paced up and down, apparently in some embarrassment. 'I seem to remember,' he said at last, 'that we have been in this situation before.'

Edward was stung to anger. 'No! You would hardly compare your daughter to a maid, I hope. And the situation is quite different.' He controlled himself, and went on, 'We were merely kissing. What is the harm in that? I love Mary, sir, and I wish to marry her. I have proposed to her, and she has accepted me.'

Richard turned sharply, pale with alarm. 'What? Oh, my God, it has not gone as far as that, has it?'

'I would have sought your consent before this, sir, but Mary wanted it to remain a secret between us for a while.'

Richard sat down heavily. 'You have not . . . you have not . . . *touched* her?'

Edward flushed. 'No, sir. Of course not. I honour and respect her.'

'Thank God for that. Marriage? That's out of the question, quite out of the question.' He seemed almost to be talking to himself, and there was no anger in his voice, but only a kind of despair.

'But why, sir?' Edward asked. 'I know Mary is very young, but we are prepared to wait for as long as you wish.' Receiving no response, he went on, a little desperately, 'It's not because we're cousins, is it? But we're not really related at all, are we?'

Richard had buried his face in his hands, and still did not

66

answer. At length, he went to the side-table and poured himself a whisky. 'Perhaps you had better have some of this, too, Edward.' He poured a second glass, and brought it over. 'I have something to tell you—something which will be very painful for us both.' He seated himself and sipped at the drink. When he spoke it was awkwardly, with long pauses. 'It is very difficult to tell you . . . very difficult. I have been . . . a fool. I should have put an end to this. Long ago. But I had no idea it had gone this far. No idea. Although your aunt . . .'

He seemed to have stopped, and Edward, his glass untouched, said, 'I don't understand, sir.'

'No, how could you? How could you? Oh, my God, I had hoped this would never . . .' He tried to pull himself together then, and after taking another sip of whisky, went on, 'You said just now that you and Mary were not related. But you *are*. You are half-brother and half-sister.'

Edward looked at him as though he was insane. 'I don't understand,' he repeated.

'You are my son, Edward.'

Edward's mind reeled. 'I don't believe it.'

'It is true.'

'But why have I never been told before?'

'I was hoping never to do so. It must never come out, Edward. For your mother's sake, it must never come out.' He was aware of Edward gazing at him in shock. 'I owe you an explanation,' he continued. 'Your mother and I were very fond of each other at one time. I begged her to marry me, but she was unwilling to divorce Mr Harcourt.'

'But after he died . . . couldn't you have married her then?'

'We had changed, Edward—both of us had changed.'

'I see.' Edward drank his whisky in two quick gulps, and when he spoke again his voice was harsh. 'It takes a lot of getting used to—to be told that you are illegitimate. And what about Mary? This could kill her. Oh, God, you should have said! You should have told us long ago. Then this would never have happened.'

'I know. But I couldn't tell you. I couldn't tell anyone. I swore a Bible oath that I would never damage your mother's reputation.'

'So your wife does not know that you have a natural

67

son?' Edward said. 'A nice surprise for her that will be!'

'I don't blame you for your bitterness, Edward. Of course, I shall tell her now, and I shall tell Mary. I pray that God will give them both strength to stand the shock, and—'

Edward gave a short laugh. 'Oh, Aunt Louisa is strong enough to stand anything, I'm sure.'

'That is impertinent, Edward,' Richard said quietly, 'and unworthy of you.'

'I am sorry. I was thinking of Mary, and . . .'

'I am thinking of her, too. I hope she will not blame herself in any way. You must not blame yourself, either. The fault was mine, and I regret it with all my heart.'

'It's easy to say that!' Edward cried. 'Very easy, isn't it?' Suddenly his anger evaporated, and he was near to tears as he cried, 'What am I to do? Oh, God, what am I to do?'

'Your aunt insists,' Richard said, 'that you should not see Mary again, and I believe she is right.'

'Yes, I heard her—I am to leave at once, am I not? But I must see Mary first!'

'No. Think about it, and I am sure you will see that your aunt is right. It would only mean more pain for you both.' At the look on Edward's face, he cried suddenly, 'Do you think it is easy for me? Do you think I want to see my son disappear from my life for ever? I have been so proud of you, Edward. I still am. And if you want me to be punished, then believe me, that punishment is about to begin.'

Edward paused, thinking of what Richard had said. But in his own anger and despair, he had no room for sympathy. 'How can I go?' he cried. 'Where can I go? I can't go home to Brentfield, to my doting mother. Why didn't *she* tell me? Oh, Christ! Mary! Mary!' The tears came then, great racking sobs.

Richard went to him, and put his hand on the boy's shoulder, gripping it tight. But he could find nothing to say.

After a while, Edward's sobs subsided. 'I'm sorry,' he said. 'Not very manly, to cry my eyes out like that. You're right, I suppose. I had better go. But where?'

'To London perhaps,' Richard suggested. 'To your Aunt Frances. She would take you in until you have found your feet again.'

'Does she know?'

'No. I think she may have suspected at the time, but she

did not know for sure. You may tell her, of course.' He paused. 'Edward, I beg you to say nothing of this to anyone else—and especially not to your mother.'

'Why not? She knows.'

'I gave her my promise that you would not be told.'

'So I am to remain silent to save you from her anger.'

'No! It is for her sake, not mine.'

Edward considered for a while. 'Very well. As for anyone else, I am hardly likely to go about advertising my illegitimacy, am I . . . *Papa?*'

Richard did not respond to the taunt, but looked away.

A little unsteadily, Edward got to his feet. 'I will go and pack.' He gave a short, bitter laugh. 'The second time I have left your house suddenly and in disgrace. At least the time before I didn't know that I was a bastard.' He walked to the door, and then turned. 'Tell Mary . . . tell Mary that I love her . . . as a brother should.'

As Edward crossed the hall to the stairs, Louisa rose from the chair where she had been waiting. 'It is all right,' he told her. 'I am going to pack.' Knowing that it was she, rather than his father, who was turning him out of the house, he went on, 'But your husband has some *un*packing to do. He's going to open a cupboard and take out a skeleton which I hope will give you the shock of your life.'

He hurried up the stairs, angry with himself. That had been cruel, and there was going to be enough unhappiness in the house.

3

Edward looked at the newspaper he had bought at the station. The printed words made no sense to him, and he put the paper down and gazed unseeingly out of the train window, reliving over and over again all that had happened that evening. He was no longer thinking of himself, but of Mary. How would she respond when she learned that theirs had been an incestuous love? 'Oh, Mary, Mary!' he whispered to himself, and buried his face in his hands, trying desperately to shut out the guilt which threatened to overwhelm him.

A gentleman sitting opposite him leaned forward. 'Are you unwell, sir?'

'No. No, thank you.' The intervention came just in time for him to regain his self-control. Aware of his fellow passenger's concern, he stared out of the carriage window again. There was nothing to see in the darkness, except the occasional light from one of the scattered houses. But before Edward's eyes was a vision of his mother, lying naked in the arms of his uncle—the man he must now think of as his father. Nausea rose in his throat, and bitterness towards them both filled his mind. How could they have left him in ignorance for so long?

Realising that he was sinking into self-pity, he tried to force himself to think of other things—his future, the reception that he might expect from his Aunt Frances, the possibility of joining Jack Chetwynd in his publishing venture after all. But each time his mind returned to Mary, and . . . 'Edward Goodwin,' he thought. 'That should really be my name, not Edward Harcourt.'

At last it seemed as though his tired brain was refusing to respond, and he sank into a kind of stupor. He was suddenly conscious that the gentleman who had previously spoken to him was gently shaking his shoulder. 'We're here,' the man said. 'London.'

Late though it was, Edward could not face the loneliness

that a night in an hotel would mean. He would go to Aunt Frances, and hope that she would be willing to take him in, even though he was arriving unannounced. As the cab trundled the long journey to the small terraced house in Battersea where the Bunns lived, Edward tried to think more rationally. There was an element of absurdity in his situation—sent packing twice from the house in Wensham —but the humour was bitter. He knew he needed to call upon every reserve of mental strength, so that he could conceal from Aunt Frances at least some part of his distress. Somehow, he had to learn to live with the new knowledge, and the guilt, and the loss of Mary. He would do so, he vowed.

By the time he arrived in Battersea, he felt he had recovered something of his equilibrium. He knocked at the front door.

Bolts were drawn back, and the door opened sufficiently to reveal the thin face of Alfred Bunn. He looked at Edward without recognition. 'Yes?'

'It's Edward. Edward Harcourt.'

'Oh! Oh, my goodness! Come in, come in. But we weren't expecting you.'

'No. I'm sorry I couldn't tell you I was coming.'

'Mrs Bunn!,' Alfred called. 'Mrs Bunn! A visitor. Come and see who it is. Let me take your luggage, Edward.' He was wearing a coat, hastily thrown over his nightshirt.

Frances came in, doing up the belt of her dressing-gown. Marriage evidently suited her, for she had put on a little weight, and the slightly pinched look about her face had gone. She seemed to exude contentment as she smiled a welcome. 'Edward, my dear boy!' She embraced him. 'What a surprise! Why didn't you let us know you were coming?'

'It was all rather sudden, Aunt. I didn't know myself until a few hours ago. I've just come from Wensham.'

'Oh, but you must be starving! There's some cold mutton, and . . .'

'No, thank you. I'm not hungry.'

'But you must have something. Alfred, my dear, put the kettle on, and make some toast by the fire. You'll not say no to that, Edward.'

Edward could scarcely refuse, and followed his aunt into the sitting-room. It was simply furnished, and uncrowded

71

—Frances had never been one for the clutter which was so fashionable. The remains of a fire, which Alfred poked into life, burned in the grate, and the gas lamps, turned down below their full brightness, threw friendly shadows.

'Come and sit down and tell me all your news.'

'It's a long story.'

'Then we shall talk all night.' Frances smiled at him warmly. 'Unless you'd rather go straight to bed. You must be tired.'

'No. No, I'd rather talk. But what about you? I'm keeping you up.'

'That's all right.'

Alfred Bunn returned at that moment, carrying a kettle and a plate of bread, on which a dish of butter was precariously balanced. Under one arm was a toasting-fork. He set the kettle on the hob and put the butter in front of the fire to warm.

'There now,' Frances said. 'Wait until the kettle's nearly boiling before you make the toast, my dear. Settle yourself down, and let us listen to Edward.'

Alfred obediently sat, twisting his long legs around each other, and folding his arms about his chest.

Edward decided to plunge straight in. 'Do you know about my parentage, Aunt Frances?'

'What about it, my dear?'

'Do you know whose son I am?'

Frances glanced at her husband, with what might have been a warning look. 'Why,' she said, 'you are the son of Thomas and Sarah Harcourt.'

'So I thought, until today. Today I have learnt that the man I have always called my Uncle Richard is in fact my father.' He paused for a moment. 'You do not look surprised.'

'No, Edward, I am not surprised. I have always suspected as much, though my brother has never given me any indication that it might be so. Is that why you are in London?'

'Oh, yes, that is why I am in London, sent from Wensham in disgrace.'

Alfred Bunn uncoiled himself. 'Would you . . . would you prefer that I should absent myself while you talk to your aunt?'

72

'No,' Edward said. 'You are part of my family now, my real family. You might as well hear it all.' He took a deep breath, and poured out his story, from the arguments with his mother up to his arrival in London.

Frances listened in total silence, but there was deep sympathy in her expression. When Edward had at last finished, she said, 'Oh, my poor Edward. Oh, you have had the most dreadful shock. I am so sorry. Now, do you want to talk about it, or would you rather go to bed?'

'There's nothing more to say, is there?'

'Then perhaps you had better have something to eat, and then get some rest. You can stay here as long as you like. The spare room has a comfortable bed, and we would love to have you here, wouldn't we, my dear?'

Alfred nodded vigorously.

'I'll go and get everything ready for you,' Frances continued. 'Pour some hot water into a jug, my dear—I'm sure Edward would like a wash—and then start making the toast, and the tea.' She bustled out.

*   *   *

It was late the following morning when Edward awoke. He felt drained and listless.

When Frances gently brought up the subject of her brother's family, he did not respond, and she decided to probe no more until he indicated a desire to talk of it himself. She made him some breakfast, and seeing him toy with it, spoke almost sharply. 'Now do eat up. It will do you no good to starve yourself. Will you go and see that friend you told us about today? What was his name?'

'Jack Chetwynd.' Edward chewed reluctantly at another forkful of ham. Swallowing it at last, he said, 'Not today. I am not ready to face him yet. But I'll write to him, to say that I shall call.'

'Yes, perhaps that would be best. Then today you shall help me.'

For the rest of that day she found him a hundred little jobs to do, insisting that he should accompany her to the shops, begging his assistance in the folding of her washing, even setting him to peel potatoes, and all the while chattering of friends and neighbours, of herself and Alfred,

73

and of the work that they did—his engraving and her designing. Edward had never before known her so talkative. When she could find no further employment for him, she sent him to watch Alfred Bunn as he worked in one of the attic rooms. He was engraving a silver tankard with an elaborate pattern of intertwining hop stems, and Edward was fascinated by the skill with which his deft fingers outlined the serrated leaves, the delicate flowers and the cone-shaped heads.

The next day a note from Jack Chetwynd arrived by the morning post. 'My dear old Chap,' it said. 'Delighted to see you any time. Champers will be waiting. But not before 11. Your old pal, Jack.'

Chetwynd had rooms in the Albany, an address which meant nothing to Edward. He was amazed by the opulence he found, and gazed at it all, open-mouthed.

Jack had evidently just got up, and his short, plump figure was swathed in a long and resplendent dressing-gown of bottle-green velvet. He was amused. 'Pretty good, eh? Pardon me if I complete my toilet, old chap.' He took a comb from his pocket, went over to a mirror on the wall, and carefully parted his hair in the middle, and smoothed it down.

'Your father gave you all this?' Edward gestured at the room—the silk-upholstered furniture, the thick carpet, the Chippendale tables, the paintings, the statues. 'It must have cost a fortune.'

'The old man? Good heavens, no! He'd consider it a shocking waste of money.'

'But he's always been very generous to you.'

'Indeed he has, but not to this extent. No, since you and I last met, I've had a bit of a windfall.' His nondescript fair hair arranged to his satisfaction, he began to open a bottle of champagne which was standing in a cooler on an occasional table. 'An uncle, who was a fearful miser while he was alive, turned up trumps and left me a fair old bit. What you might call a small fortune. So I was able to escape from the family mausoleum, and set up here. I couldn't have lived at home anyway. As you know, the old man and I don't see quite eye to eye, and I don't get on with my stepmother either, nor with her daughter.'

'You've never mentioned a stepsister.'

74

'Haven't I? The gorgeous Beatrice? Oh, I must have! She's a funny old stick. Not all that old, really—about thirty, I suppose. She's a bit odd. As a matter of fact, they had to shut her up for a bit—she went slightly funny in the head. But she's all right now. Very clever. Does the old man's accounts.' He handed Edward a glass of champagne. 'Let's drink to dear old Uncle Philip, who provided me with all this.' He downed his glass, and then said, 'Sit down, old chap, while I go and slip a few togs on, and then we'll go out to luncheon. Simpson's in the Strand suit you? My treat, of course. Help yourself to more champers.'

The roast beef at Simpson's was superb. As they ate, Jack talked of the society he mixed in, the plays he had seen, the galleries he had visited, and then, taking another mouthful of Yorkshire pudding, asked, 'And what brings you to the Metropolis, old chap?'

'Well, I really came to see you.'

'That's uncommonly decent of you. Why?'

'Well, I was wondering . . . You see, I've finally come to the conclusion that the family business is not my cup of tea. I'm just not a silk man. And I remembered that you talked about started a publishing firm, and I wondered . . .'

'Oh, I'm not doing anything like that right now.'

Dismayed, Edward said nothing.

'What's the matter, old chap?'

'I've got to find work somewhere. I've got to do something with my life—other than teaching.'

'So have I,' Jack said seriously. 'The old man wants me to go into the family business, but I've told him it's not for me. Can you imagine me in a cast iron foundry? "I suppose now you've got your uncle's money, you think there's no need to do anything at all," he said. Well, I shall, if only to prove him wrong. I decided I'd take a few months just to enjoy myself, and then I'll make up my mind what to do. And when I do, I'll do it properly, I'll tell you that. What's more, there'll be a job for you, Edward, if you want it. That's a promise. In the meantime, you can enjoy life with me. I'll introduce you to my friends. For a start, we'll go and see the new Gilbert and Sullivan, *The Grand Duke*, tonight. After that, we'll have a little supper at the Café Royal, and then there'll be a party somewhere that we can go on to.'

'It's kind of you to suggest it, but I can't.'

75

'Why not?'

'For one thing, I couldn't afford that sort of thing. I've got a little money, but—'

Jack laughed. 'But my dear good idiot, I'm not suggesting you should put your hand in your pocket. My treat. And don't let's have any high-flown nonsense about not sponging on me. I've got more money than I know what to do with. It'll be my pleasure. Oh, Edward, you can't think how I've longed to have someone like you to share with. And we'll find some girls somewhere, and have a high old time.'

'I can't anyway. My aunt and uncle are expecting me for dinner.'

'That's no excuse.'

'No, really. It's very kind, but I just can't.'

'Tomorrow, then.'

Edward smiled. It had always been impossible to resist Jack. 'All right.' A thought struck him. 'But how will you get tickets for *The Grand Duke*? It's bound to be sold out.'

Jack grinned. 'Money talks, old chap. We'll take a box.'

*   *   *

As he went back to Battersea, Edward was surprised to find that he did not feel as depressed as he might have expected. The disappearance of the publishing job seemed simply a part of the disruption of his life. Without Mary, his future mattered little to him. Sooner or later he would find some kind of occupation, and in the meantime, he might just as well enjoy the entertainment that Jack had to offer.

His thoughts went back to Mary. How had she taken the news of their relationship? A shock of that kind could easily have had the most devastating effect. At the very least, she would have been, and must still be, sunk in a misery like his own. And she had no Jack Chetwynd to distract her for a few hours with extravagant lunches.

For his aunt and uncle's sake, he tried to shake off his anxieties, and talked animatedly about his luncheon and all that Jack had said, and the proposed visit to the theatre on the morrow. But eventually he stopped. He looked directly at Frances. 'It's no use, I keep thinking of Mary the whole time . . . wondering how she is. I'm so worried about her. I realise that it's right for me not to see her, but I just wish I

76

could find out how she is. Do you think . . . do you think you could write to . . .' He hesitated, not wanting to say Richard's name. '. . . to Wensham?'

'I am already part way through a letter,' Frances said. 'It will be posted tomorrow, and I'll let you know as soon as I hear.'

*   *   *

The following evening was a considerable success. Nothing could entirely drive the thoughts of Mary from Edward's mind, but Jack was the most pleasant of companions, and, even if it was not as memorable as the earlier Savoy Operas, *The Grand Duke* had sufficient charm in its music and its nonsense to distract Edward for a while. Afterwards, at the Café Royal, he met some of Jack's bachelor friends, and ate with them and lingered over the coffee and port and brandy, and made the effort to join in their frivolous, witty conversation.

He was appalled when he realised how late it was. 'My aunt and uncle will be waiting up for me,' he said.

'It's barely midnight,' Jack protested.

'No, I must go. I hope I can get a cab.'

'Of course you can. They don't all turn into pumpkins at midnight. But this really won't do, my dear chap. If we are to repeat this kind of evening, you can't play at Cinderella every time. I know. You must come and live in my place. I mean it.'

Promising to consider the proposition, Edward hurried off. The cab seemed to take an age to get to Battersea, but Edward was relieved to see a light still on in his aunt's house.

Alfred Bunn let him in, smiling indulgently, and would hear none of Edward's apologies. 'You must treat this as your own home,' he said, 'but I shall give you a door-key. Then we old fogies can go to bed at what we consider a reasonable hour.'

As he prepared for the night, Edward thought seriously about Jack's offer. It would mean that he was even more beholden to him, but at least he would be on hand if Jack should suddenly decide to start some kind of business in which Edward might become involved. More importantly, it would relieve his aunt and uncle of the burden of his presence. Even if he had a key to the door, he would not be able to come home too late, for fear of disturbing them, whereas at Jack's he would have total freedom.

'You must do as you think best,' Frances said in the morning. 'You know you are very welcome to stay here, but I can understand your wish to go to your friend. When did Mr Chetwynd speak of it?'

'After supper last night.'

'Then do make sure that he remembers doing so, and that he really wants you there, before you take your luggage round. Gentlemen often say things late at night and forget them in the morning. And promise me that you will come back and see us from time to time.'

'I'm sure he meant it. And as for coming to see you, of course I shall. In any case, I shall call here tomorrow, to see if there is any word from Wensham.'

As Edward told her later that morning, they were both right. Jack had totally forgotten his offer, which proved Frances' point, but once reminded of it had positively insisted that Edward should come to stay with him. 'An extended visit, old chap—extended indefinitely.'

The next day, Edward again visited the house in Battersea.

Frances waved a letter at him. 'It came this morning. It says very little about Mary—indeed, it is mainly filled with apologies for not having informed me of the facts of your parentage. Though why he thinks I should have been told, I don't know. If he and your mother decided to keep it a secret, that was a matter for them, and no one else.'

'And for me!'

'Yes, of course. Your uncle—your father, I mean—is most contrite about you, and very concerned.'

Edward made no attempt to disguise his bitterness as he said, 'That's *very* good of him.'

Frances put her hand on his arm in a gesture of sympathy. 'Try not to think that way, Edward. Your father is human, and like all humans he makes mistakes.'

'Oh, I understand that. I know that to err is human—the trouble is that I'm not divine enough to forgive. Actually, I don't think it's him at all—it's that old gorgon, his wife—my dear stepmother.'

78

The corners of Frances' mouth twitched. 'Perhaps.'

'She really is a frightful old battleaxe, and she's got him under her thumb, hasn't she?' Frances did not reply, and he went on, 'What does he say about Mary?'

'Simply that Louisa and Mary were both extremely shocked—so much so that the doctor had to be called—but that they are both much recovered now. That is all.'

'I ought to go there, whatever he says. I ought to see her.'

'It really wouldn't be wise, my dear,' Frances said. 'It would do neither of you any good.'

'I'd know whether he is speaking the truth in that letter—whether she is really recovering. I beg you at least to write again—ask him to tell you exactly how Mary is.'

Frances nodded slowly.

*   *   *

Jack Chetwynd was far from insensitive, and it had not escaped him that Edward was unhappy. Over the next few days he did his best to distract him. They went to the theatre twice, to a ball, to the races, and although Jack employed a manservant who was a passable cook, the only meal they ate at home was breakfast. Suspecting that Edward's trouble was an affair of the heart, especially since, when he probed a little in that direction, Edward immediately changed the subject, Jack made a point of introducing him to a number of young ladies of his acquaintance. They were attractive, poised, intelligent women, and Edward enjoyed their company, and made amusing contributions to the conversation, but his interest was never really engaged.

One evening, as they returned to the Albany, Edward said, 'You haven't anything special planned for tomorrow, have you?'

'Nothing much. Up at the crack of dawn—not a minute later than half past ten—because I want to go to Tooth's—he's got a Constable sketch for sale. Luncheon at Rule's with Percy, and on to Mrs Prior's At Home—those delicious daughters of hers will be there. An early dinner with some friends of Percy's, then the concert, and supper at Romano's. That's all.'

Edward laughed. 'Sounds like a dull, quiet sort of day! Would you forgive me if I did not join you for it?'

'Why ever not?'

'I've got to go to Wensham. Family business.'

'You didn't mention it before.'

'No, but I really must go.'

'It's damned inconvenient,' Jack grumbled. 'I promised Mrs Prior to take you along, and now I'll have to make your excuses. I wish you'd try not to let it happen again without giving me fair warning first.'

That, thought Edward, was the price he had to pay for Jack's generosity towards him. He was to be at his beck and call. Well, perhaps it was fair. Anyway, he was determined to go to Wensham the next day. Aunt Frances had had a reply from her brother, but it added little to his knowledge of how Mary was, saying merely that though the doctor had feared a decline, it had not materialised, though Mary was still much distressed 'She is now taking a little exercise,' the letter continued, 'a short walk most days, whatever the weather, and is feeling strong enough to do so on her own. She seems to prefer her own company most of the time. I believe she prays a great deal.'

'You have no idea what damage it might do to Mary to see you at this stage,' Frances had said.

'I cannot hurt her any more than she has been hurt already,' he told her. 'A meeting, however brief, might be the best thing for both of us. I must see her—just once—or I shall never have any peace of mind. I shall not go to the house—I shall hope to meet her on one of her walks.'

'I still think it's unwise.'

'I've made up my mind, Aunt. I must go.'

'Very well, my dear. Very well. I'll say no more.' Then, after a moment, she asked brightly, 'Have you written to your mother?'

'She has nothing to do with it.'

'I didn't say she had, and I wasn't talking about Mary. I simply mean that you cannot leave your mother without news of your whereabouts. Supposing she has sudden need of you.'

That made Edward laugh. 'Mama? Have need of me? That's not very likely. Anyway, I did write to her a couple of days ago, and told her she could reach me either through you or Jack.' His expression changed. 'But she won't need me. I don't think she's ever needed me. Or cared very much for me.'

'I'm sure that's not true.'

'You don't know her well enough, Aunt. I do.'

His harshness distressed Frances, and later she spoke to Alfred about it. 'I hated hearing him speak like that of his mother.'

'He's been badly hurt,' Alfred said. 'Give him time. You can't put an old head on young shoulders, but that boy's got plenty of character, and it'll pull him through. Sooner or later he'll get his sense of humour back, and his tolerance, and he'll be back to his old self. My heart goes out to him now, but he'll be all right, in the long run.'

*   *   *

When Edward reached Wensham, he had little idea of what he was going to do. He could not be in so small a place for long without the Goodwins becoming aware of his presence, and then any chance of meeting Mary would immediately vanish. And supposing she chose that day to ask her mother to accompany her, or had caught cold, and would be confined to the house. The more he thought about it, the more he realised how ridiculous his scheme was; almost certain to fail from the very start.

Nevertheless, he was here now, and he could only trust to luck. He turned up his coat collar, pulled his hat well down over his eyes and set off towards the Goodwins' house. He would have to pass the gate, but just beyond it on the other side of the road was a small copse, where he could conceal himself and still be able to watch the house.

Feeling like a criminal, he reached the copse, and settled himself down beside a large oak. One root had been partially exposed, and it made a rough seat. He had remembered to bring with him an apple, and a sandwich hastily made from his breakfast toast. He could, of course, have asked Jack's manservant to provide a picnic, and would no doubt have been given a hamper with caviar and *pâté de foie* and a galantine of game, and wild strawberries, and three kinds of wine including champagne. That was the way Jack lived, and he had been happy enough to share Jack's expensive

81

tastes, but he wondered why he was thinking now of such extravagance with a kind of contempt.

He allowed his thoughts to wander on. It was time he found employment of some kind. After only a few days of Jack's hospitality, he knew he would not be content to live in that idle style for long. He wondered how his mother was. Despite what he had said to Aunt Frances, he had no wish to cut her out of his life. Perhaps he had been wrong to leave Brentfield. He could have given up any idea of working at Harcourt's, but stayed on in the house, and found employment elsewhere in the neighbourhood. And if he left Jack and found a job, somewhere in London, where would he live? He could hardly impose upon Aunt Frances again. He had been wrong to go there when he first came to London—it was a burden for them, and created obligations for him. Oh, Lord, so many mistakes he had made and was still making. His mind was awhirl with questions to which there were no answers and guilty feelings and vague, undefined longings.

And then his heart leaped; he saw her. She was coming down the path from the house. Alone. Which way would she turn? Towards him and the fields, or back to the village?

He had to attract her attention. He called, as softly as he dared, 'Mary! Mary!'

She turned, curious, and he called again. 'Mary, it's Edward. Let me talk to you, please. Just for a minute. I promise not to . . .'

For a moment he thought that she was going to walk away from him, but then, slowly, she began to move in his direction.

'I daren't be seen, Mary,' he hissed, thinking how ludicrous the whole scene was. 'Come into the copse. I *must* speak to you.'

The expression on her face was apprehensive—he could see that even at a distance—but as she approached he noticed, too, her pallor, and the dark rings beneath her eyes. She was still beautiful, but the beauty was tarnished with tiredness and pain. His heart bled for her.

She stopped, facing him, but made no move when he held out his hand towards her. Nor did she smile, but he sensed that the fear had gone from behind her eyes.

'How are you, Mary?'

'All right.' Her voice was a whisper. 'And you?'

'Never mind about me. I heard that you had to have the doctor, but that you are better now—is that right?'

'Yes.'

'I'm sorry about . . . about everything.'

'It wasn't your fault, Edward. It wasn't anybody's fault. I hope you carry no rancour in your heart. If you do, you must root it out. Take it to the Lord, Edward. He will forgive, and teach you to forgive.' Her voice was still very quiet, almost a monotone. 'It was He who stayed my hand when I tried to kill myself.'

'To kill yourself?'

'Didn't they tell you that? When I first knew about you and me, I wanted to die. Especially since they had sent you away so that we couldn't even say goodbye. But God had other plans for me, and I survived. It was while I was ill that God spoke to me and told me that I must live, and work for Him.'

He stared at her, knowing that he must accept her words as seriously as she herself did. 'What sort of work?'

'I am not sure. Papa and Mama won't hear of my doing anything until the doctor is perfectly satisfied. But I think I may become a nun.'

'A nun!'

The faintest hint of a smile touched Mary's lips, the first sign of animation he had seen in her expression. 'There *are* Anglican nuns, you know. But I am not certain yet of God's intention for me. Sometimes He just puts ideas in your mind, you know, so that you can think about them and decide whether they are right for you. If you ask Him, He helps you to make the right decision. He helped me just now. I wasn't sure whether to speak to you or not, but He told me it would be right. He told me something else, Edward—that I must speak to you of Him, persuade you to offer your pain, too, on the altar of His compassion. Give yourself to Him, body and soul. Will you do that, Edward?'

Something about her voice, her eyes, her attitude was hypnotic. Edward heard himself saying, 'For your sake I will do anything.'

'Not for my sake, for His. Promise me.'

'I promise.' And then he came to his senses, and said, 'No,

Mary, I am wrong to say that. I cannot make such a promise, especially to you of all people. I am not sure that I can even pray for myself.'

'Then I will pray for you,' she said, and her eyes lit up suddenly with a kind of radiance. 'I do already. Every day I pray for you, Edward.'

'Then you truly forgive me?'

'Truly.'

'And you are not unhappy?'

'No, Edward. I was, but I am not now.'

'Swear that you are not.'

'I swear.'

He believed her, and realised that this above all was what he had wanted to hear. 'Thank you,' he whispered. And suddenly he longed desperately to take her in his arms again, to taste the sweetness of her lips, to forget all that he had learned of his parentage and to go back to the days when they believed that they would marry and be happy together for the rest of their lives. 'I must go,' he said roughly, to break the spell. But he did not move. 'Will you tell them that you have seen me?'

'No. Mama has forbidden even the mention of your name.'

He shook his head sadly.

After a moment she went on, 'I must continue my walk. Thank you for coming, Edward. But please, please do not try to see me again. It will only cause heartache for us.' Suddenly her voice trembled and there were tears in her eyes. 'Close your eyes, Edward. Don't look at me. Please, please, close your eyes. Keep them closed until I have gone.'

He obeyed her. He sensed her moving close to him, and for the briefest moment her soft cheek brushed against his. 'God bless you, Edward,' she whispered, and then he heard her footsteps moving slowly away.

It was a long while before he dared or wanted to open his eyes. Then he walked slowly back to the station. He was glad that he had come to Wensham. He was not sure whether she had really retained her sanity, or whether the devotion to God she expressed was a kind of madness. But at least her mind had not been so turned that she had lost all touch with reality, and at least she had said that she forgave him, and at least she had sworn that she was no longer unhappy. That would lift the burden of guilt which he had been carrying, the belief that he had betrayed her.

He caught the next train back to London, but for all his relief, he was haunted by the figure of Mary, standing before him. Fate's tragic victim. He found himself able to pray—for her happiness, for her continued belief in all that she heard her God say to her.

*　　*　　*

Returning to London, Edward went first to Battersea.

'I'm glad I did go,' he told Frances. 'At least I know that Mary's over the worst of it.'

'This religious obsession sounds unhealthy.'

'Perhaps. But she seems to be finding comfort in it.'

'You didn't see any others of the family?' Frances asked.

'No, and just as well, I gather.' Edward spoke with bitterness. 'Apparently, my dear stepmother has forbidden my name even to be mentioned in the house.'

Alfred Bunn, so often silent, suddenly intervened. 'She is wise. It may seem harsh to you, Edward, but it is better that you and Mary should forget each other completely. Even the mention of names can keep old wounds open.'

'I shall never forget her.'

'Perhaps you should try. Your aunt and I were apart for many years, but we always kept our memories fresh, because we cherished the hope of being able one day to come together again. Where there is no such hope, then to forget may be the kindest thing for everyone.'

Edward was not sure that he agreed, but there was no point in arguing.

'Changing the subject,' Frances said brightly, 'you know Mr Leroy, the silk merchant?'

'I have never met him, but his name's very familiar. My mother was going to send me to see him, as part of my education in silk.'

'All three of us are invited to dinner with the Leroys next Tuesday. What do you think of that? I gather your mother told Mr Leroy that you are in London, so the party is really in your honour. Now, don't tell me you can't come. If you

85

have another engagement, I shall . . . oh, I shall be so disappointed, I shall be absolutely horrid to your Uncle Alfred for weeks.'

'I must certainly save him from that fate,' Edward smiled.

*　　*　　*

When they arrived at the Leroys' house in Spitalfields, and were shown into the drawing-room, Edward was surprised to recognise the imposing figure of James Prideau, and, beside him, his granddaughter, Alice Ouvray. He hoped that he would not have to sit next to her at dinner. He was introduced to his host and hostess, who in turn presented him to their elder daughter, Miss Isabelle Leroy; she was a cripple, confined to a wheel-chair, and as thin and pale as her parents were plump and rosy-cheeked.

'Of course, I know your mother, Mr Harcourt,' she said. 'And your uncle, too. In fact—'

'Later, Isabelle, later,' Mrs Leroy interrupted. 'You can talk to Mr Harcourt at dinner. Let me introduce you to Miss Ouvray, Mr Harcourt.'

'We have met before. How do you do, Miss Ouvray.' It was a cool greeting.

'I am well, Mr Harcourt. And you?'

Edward was surprised. Her voice was lower-pitched and much more musical than he had remembered. He bowed. 'Thank you, yes, Miss Ouvray.'

'I will leave you two young people together,' Mrs Leroy said. 'You already know Miss Ouvray's grandfather, I believe, Mr Harcourt?'

'Yes, indeed, ma'am.'

As Mrs Leroy moved away, Alice Ouvray said, 'I am glad to see you, Mr Harcourt. I feel I owe you an apology. I thought of writing, but it seemed difficult to phrase.'

'I cannot think why I deserve an apology,' Edward said.

'Oh, our last meeting—I blush when I think of it—the way I chattered at you, endlessly. And then I fear I was quite abrupt . . . What you must have thought of me, I don't know.'

'I thought you were very charming, and I was certainly not aware of anything of which the most critical person could complain.'

'Polite, Mr Harcourt, but perfectly untrue. Be honest now. I insist.'

The intensity of her gaze reminded him of Mary. It was difficult to lie. 'There is a time and place for honesty,' he said, 'but only the oldest and most solid of friendships should ever be exposed to it.' He laughed. 'Oh, my goodness, how pompous that must have sounded!'

'Not at all.'

'Now *you* are being polite.'

She smiled. 'Pompous or not, Mr Harcourt, since we are scarcely old acquaintances, let alone old friends, it amounted to a confession that your earlier words were no more than flattery. Is it not so? And is not honesty always the best policy?'

'No, I do not think it is.'

'Oh, I challenge you to prove that!'

'All right. Take my late grandmother. In her latter years, she frequently gave in to the temptation to be perfectly honest, and as a result became an extremely rude old lady.'

She laughed then, and it was again a more pleasant sound then he had remembered. 'Clever, Mr Harcourt, clever. I concede the point. And, whatever you say, I insist on asking your pardon for my behaviour the last time we met, and you will please me by accepting the apology.'

'Then I do so, but under protest that it was not necessary.'

She held up two crossed fingers. 'Pax, Mr Harcourt?'

'Pax, Miss Ouvray.' Edward smiled at her, and then said, 'Are you staying long in London?'

'We go home tomorrow. But, oh, what an exciting week it has been!'

She spoke amusingly of the theatres she had been to, the dinner parties she and her grandfather had attended, and the shopping she had done. 'It is a perfect arrangement— Grandpapa goes to his business meetings, and I go to the shops. And since he makes much more money at his meetings than I spend in the shops, everyone is happy.'

Edward enjoyed listening to her, and was quite sorry when he saw Mr Leroy advancing towards them with obvious intent. 'I fear we are to be parted, Miss Ouvray,' he said. 'I hope only temporarily.'

For reply, she opened her fan and looked at him, with

laughing eyes, over the top of it. Then she snapped it shut, and said, 'I am never sure about the language of the fan, Mr Harcourt, but you may take it that I intend to indicate that I share your hope.'

Mr Leroy stood in front of them. 'Mr Prideau tells me he is eager for a word with you, Mr Harcourt,' he said. 'He is waiting for you over there. And I myself have many pleasant things to say to Miss Ouvray.'

Reluctantly, Edward bowed to Miss Ouvray, and went to the settee where Mr Prideau had planted himself. Even seated, he was a striking man. He was tall and could carry his ample corporation without loss of dignity, and the shock of white hair and his aquiline features gave him a commanding look. He could have been a general, an emperor . . . Did looks like that predispose a man to a position of eminence, Edward wondered, or was it that exercise of power left its mark upon the face?

'Don't look so disappointed, Mr Harcourt,' Prideau said. 'I know I am hardly a fair exchange for my granddaughter, but I expect you will get another chance to talk to her later this evening.'

'I am sorry, sir,' Edward said hastily, 'if my expression . . .'

'Enough!' Prideau laughed, good-humouredly. 'The fact is, Mr Harcourt, I really do want to speak to you. Your mother tells me that you have left the silk business. Is that true?'

'Yes, sir.'

'For good?'

'I think so.'

'H'm. I will come back to that. Now, why have you left not only your family firm, but also, as I understand it, your uncle's concern?'

Edward stiffened slightly. 'Personal reasons, sir.'

Prideau looked at him closely. 'Shall I tell you my own theory? I think you wanted to modernise Harcourt's, to make it more efficient, to expand its interests so that it is not entirely dependent on crape. And your mother, admirable woman though she is, refused to accept your recommendations. Whether that also applies to your departure from your uncle's firm, I don't know. Perhaps that's where the personal reasons come in.'

Edward was irritated. He bowed his head slightly. 'It

would be useless to deny the accuracy of your assessment, sir. Miss Ouvray has just been insisting that I should be honest with her. It must run in your family.'

'There is no need to be testy, my boy. I have good reason for my curiosity.'

'I apologise.'

Prideau lowered his voice. 'You know that I have long wanted to purchase Harcourt's Mill. I am eager to do so now while there is time to save it. The business is in no immediate danger of collapse, but action must be taken soon. Your mother consistently refuses to sell, and—'

'I think she is right in that, sir.'

'Stop being so prickly, young man, and listen to what I have to say. My business is a large one, and there is always room in it for men of ability, and excellent chances of promotion. I have been wondering whether I could kill two birds with one stone . . . Suppose I were to employ a young man who might one day bring about the amalgamation into Prideau's of a smaller mill, which has great potential still, if only it could be brought under modern and progressive management.'

'You mean when my mother dies, and Harcourt's Mill passes to me?' Edward laughed. 'But that is a long way off.' He was enjoying fencing with the old man.

'No, no. I was thinking that if your mother were to see you in a position of some importance within my organis-ation, then she might be much more willing to sell Harcourt's. In a year or two's time, perhaps.'

'I beg leave to doubt that, sir.' The amusement in his voice made Prideau look up sharply. He was not used, Edward guessed, to being taken so lightly, or indeed, to anyone who did not immediately fall in with his plans.

The corners of Prideau's lips tightened for a moment. Then, as though he had been telling himself to remain unruffled, he smiled. 'Maybe that's just a pipe-dream. But the offer of a position in my firm is not.'

Edward, feeling in command of the situation, said more seriously, 'Forgive me if this sounds impertinent, Mr Prideau, but it seems to me that you have few grounds for making this offer. You scarcely know me, and can have no idea of whether or not I would be suitable for the responsibilities you have in mind.'

Prideau smiled again. 'I know that you have a degree, which speaks of some intelligence. And you forget, young man, that you called on me once and quizzed me about my business. Not much to go on, perhaps, but I *was* impressed. We should soon find out, however, how well you would fit in. Think it over, talk to others, if you wish. There is no immediate hurry. If you are interested, visit me in Franton, and we will discuss the matter in detail, including, of course, the salary, which you would not find ungenerous.'

'Thank you. I will indeed think about it.' Edward was saved from having to say any more by Mrs Leroy's announcement that dinner was served.

The ceiling and walls of the Leroys' dining-room were panelled in dark oak. It gave the room a sombre atmosphere, except on an occasion such as this, when the table was laid with snowy cloth and gleaming silver and sparkling crystal, and lit with the branched seventeenth century candelabra which Mr Leroy's Huguenot ancestors had brought from France when they fled to avoid persecution.

Edward was seated between Mrs Leroy and her daughter, Isabelle.

'It is strange that we have not met before, Mr Harcourt,' Miss Leroy said. 'I know your mother well, and your uncle, too, of course. I first met him many years ago. We kept silk moths in those days, on the big mulberry tree in our back garden, and I remember your uncle coming here and watching me as I showed him how the silk is unravelled from the cocoon.'

Her voice went on, and Edward found his attention wandering. He looked at Miss Ouvray, seated opposite him and engaged in a lively conversation with Uncle Alfred. She was making him laugh, and that, Edward thought, was quite an achievement. He remembered, wryly, hoping that he would not be seated next to her.

'The silkworm takes two or three days to make its cocoon,' Miss Leroy was saying. 'Such prodigious labour from so small a creature.'

'Indeed?' For the sake of politeness he needed to show greater interest. 'Do go on,' he said. 'I come from a silk-manufacturing family, but this is new to me. Silk has been simply something which arrives in packets, with the name Leroy printed, of course, on the wrappings.' It was a prevarication. He knew exactly how silk was made, and had listened innumerable times to the legend of its discovery by the Chinese Empress Si Ling more than four thousand years ago, and had indeed watched the silk being unwound from the cocoons.

Edward had hoped to be able to talk to Miss Ouvray again when the gentlemen rejoined the ladies after their port and cigars, but Mrs Leroy buttonholed him, and soon Aunt Frances was preparing to leave, and clearly, although he would take a separate cab back to the Albany, he would have to go, too.

Saying goodbye to Miss Ouvray, he added, 'The pompous young gentleman dares to hope that he may meet Miss Ouvray again before long.'

'The apologetic lady would be delighted, Mr Harcourt. If you are ever in Franton, you must call upon us.'

Her grandfather overheard. 'I have already extended a similar invitation to Mr Harcourt. I trust you will not forget, young man.'

'No, sir. I shall write with the promptitude that I am sure you expect.'

If Mr Prideau recognised any irony in the reply, he ignored it, and they all parted amicably.

Edward thought about his earlier conversation with Mr Prideau as his cab took him back towards Piccadilly. He would have to find something to do soon—he could not remain idle for ever. But, whatever it was, it certainly would not be working for Mr James Prideau, even if that meant forgoing the opportunity of another meeting with Miss Ouvray.

*   *   *

As the days passed by, pleasant thought they were, Edward realised that he had no hope of finding gainful employment through Jack in the immediate future. From time to time, Jack would talk of various possibilities, even reverting to the plan of starting a publishing house, but it was quite plain that none of the ideas appealed to him sufficiently to make him abandon his present way of life. 'I know you think I'm a frightful wastrel,' he said once to Edward. 'No, don't deny it. But I do want to be sure that what I eventually do is right, and meanwhile, since I've got the money, I might as well spend it.'

Edward became increasingly unsettled—the more so because he was well aware that the solution lay, to some extent at least, in his own hands. There was no point in waiting, Micawber-like, for something to turn up. He had to make it happen. He **had to** create his own opportunities.

As he sat opposite Jack at the breakfast table one morning, he decided that he would give himself just a few more days of leisure, and then would start hunting seriously for work. If he had found nothing within a week, then perhaps he would write to James Prideau and ask whether the position was still open, or he would even return to Brentfield and eat the humble pie that his mother would so lovingly prepare for him.

'Oh, my God!' Jack exclaimed, staring with horror at the letter he was reading. 'The old man wants to come here on Friday. This is dreadful! What on earth can we do?'

'Why shouldn't he come here?'

'My dear good idiot, because this place will drive him absolutely berserk. He'll go on and on about my extravagance, and the need for thrift, and the way I'm wasting my inheritance, and that sort of thing, and it will turn into the most frightful row, and we shall both say things we regret, and . . . Oh, my God!'

'Put him off.'

'How can I? He's coming to London on business—he wouldn't postpone his trip on my account.'

Jack looked so downcast that Edward began to laugh. 'Honestly, Jack, your father can't be all that much of a monster.'

'He isn't. He's quite a decent sort, really. I hate rowing with him, but put us together, and the sparks start flying. What on earth am I going to do? Oh, come on, Edward, think of something. Why do I have you here, if not to be as brilliant as you always were at Cambridge?'

Edward thought for a while. 'If it's just a question of keeping him away from here,' he said at last, 'why not tell him that you've discovered a very good new restaurant, and you'd like to meet him there?'

'He *wants* to come *here*.'

'Well, take him out first, and wine him and dine him, and then he'll be a bit mellower.'

'I suppose it's worth trying. Which restaurant?'

'Someone at Mrs Prior's the other day was talking about a place in Soho called the Silver Fountain.'

'Right, old chap. We'll dine there this evening, and see if it's any good.'

*　　*　　*

On Friday evening Edward sat alone at a table for two in the Silver Fountain. He and Jack had eaten there, and found the food and service excellent, and a telegram had been despatched to Shropshire to advise Mr Chetwynd that he should meet Jack at the restaurant.

But that morning, Jack had called Edward into his room. 'I say, old chap, I feel absolutely awful. I'm burning hot, and I keep shivering, and I ache all over.'

'Influenza,' Edward said. 'I'll get the doctor.'

The doctor confirmed the diagnosis, prescribed some medicine, and told Jack to stay in bed.

'What are we going to do about the old man?' he said, miserably.

'He'll just have to come here,' Edward said.

'I don't want him here. Especially not the way I feel now. You'll have to meet him at the Silver Fountain.'

'I can't do that, Jack,' Edward protested.

'Oh, yes, you can. It isn't much to ask. Take a fiver out of my jacket pocket, and make sure he has everything he wants. Give him a good meal, get him a bit tipsy if you can, and then try to steer him back to his hotel. At all costs, stop him from coming here.'

'He'll probably want to come and see you.'

'No!'

'All right. I'll tell him you've got the plague.'

'Tell him anything. Lay it on as thick as you like.' He groaned. 'Oh, Edward, be a good chap and tell Templeton to make me a hot toddy—a strong one—and then both of you leave me alone.'

Edward looked up from his table in the Silver Fountain, and saw the headwaiter conducting towards him a portly, silver-haired man, walking slowly with a stick. His complexion was ruddy, and his earlobes stuck out from his plump cheeks like two scarlet buttons. Edward thought he could detect some family likeness to Jack, especially about the eyes and mouth. Perhaps Jack would look just like his father when he was old and very much overweight.

Edward rose. 'Mr Chetwynd? Allow me to introduce myself, sir. I am Edward Harcourt, a friend of Jack's.'

'Yes, I think he has mentioned you.' Mr Chetwynd shook his hand, and sat down heavily, puffing and wheezing to get his breath back.

'I'm afraid he has been unable to come this evening. He is not very well.'

'What's the matter with him?'

'The doctor says it's influenza—quite a mild attack, but he's got to stay in bed for a day or two.'

'I see. Well, I'd better go and see him. If you will forgive me, Mr Harcourt, I will deny myself the pleasure of dining with you.' He began to struggle to his feet again.

Edward decided that the only course of action was to be blunt. 'He asked me to prevent you from going to his apartment, sir.'

Chetwynd sank back into his chair. 'Yes, that sounds like Jack,' he said, harshly. 'And I suppose you have been told to wine and dine the old man, and then see that he goes safely back to his hotel, eh?'

Conscious of the hurt in Chetwynd's eyes, Edward found it impossible to deny the charge. 'Something like that,' he mumbled, and then added hastily, 'but he is not himself. He is unwell, and . . .'

'You needn't try to defend him, young man. Did he say why he did not want me to visit him?' Without waiting for an answer, he went on, 'No doubt he fears a lecture on his extravagance. Is that not it?'

'Yes, sir.'

'If only he would understand. He can do what he likes with his money. My only fear is that he will find himself set upon by leeches who would drain him dry. But when I try to warn him of that danger . . .' He sighed. 'Take my advice, Mr Harcourt—when you marry, think twice before starting a family. The joys of parenthood are sometimes notable chiefly by their absence. He is not seriously ill, you say?'

'No, sir.'

94

'Then I will wait a little before I decide what to do. When you are faced with a problem, young man, always push it to the back of your mind for a short while, if that is possible. Then, when you consider it again, the sensible course of action often becomes obvious. So, in the meantime, perhaps I will dine with you after all, if it will not prove too much of a penance for you. And have no fear—I shall not spend the entire time in burdening you with unwanted advice.'

'I am sure it will be a pleasure, sir,' Edward said, deciding that he rather liked Mr Chetwynd.

'It will, of course, be at my expense.'

'Oh, no, sir. Jack insists on paying for the meal.'

'He does, does he? Well, he is not going to take every trick in this game of cards. Now, we shall order our food and some wine, and then, while we eat, you must tell me about yourself.'

Despite the blandishments of the headwaiter, they both eschewed the more exotic dishes on the menu, and settled for asparagus soup, a grilled sole, and a bottle of Chablis.

'Tell me, Mr Harcourt, are you as much of a good-for-nothing as Jack?' Mr Chetwynd asked then.

It was a disconcerting question, and Edward did not know how to answer. 'I don't know, sir,' he said.

'Yes. I suppose that was the only reply you could make. You met him at Cambridge, I believe.'

'Yes, sir. And whether or not I'm a good-for-nothing, I'm certainly one of the leeches, I'm afraid.'

'Indeed?' The grey eyes looked at him with interest.

'I am presently his guest, and he is a more than generous host. He insists on paying for everything. I could not afford myself to live as I have been doing, which is why I describe myself as one of the leeches. But Jack is difficult to resist. I am very fond of him, of course—we were good pals at Cambridge—and perhaps that's why he is so generous towards me, and why I find it possible to accept his generosity. But I sometimes think he has a need . . .'

'Go on.'

'A need for someone like me, to be the object of his . . . charity.'

'That is very perceptive,' Mr Chetwynd said. 'And if I am

not mistaken, you are somewhat unhappy about the situation. Am I right?'

'Yes, sir.'

'Then tell me how you got into it, and why you do not extricate yourself.'

George Chetwynd was easy to talk to, and Edward found himself relating in detail the events of his life since leaving university. He spoke fluently and amusingly, and now and then Chetwynd chuckled at his self-deprecating humour. Edward concealed only, as he had done from Jack, the reason why he had left his employment at the Goodwin Mill, and his relationship to Richard Goodwin and to Mary.

Chetwynd seemed to understand that he should not probe that part of the story, and returned to the subject of Edward's investigation into the affairs of Harcourt's Mill, showing particular interest in the methods Edward had used to get his information, and asking exactly how he would have implemented his plans.

'Your mother rejected *all* your propositions? She has not followed any of them up since you left the company?'

'I do not think so. She is no doubt right. She has far more experience than I.'

'The sentiment is admirable, but do you really believe that your ideas were mistaken?'

'With respect, sir,' Edward said, 'You cannot expect me to answer that.'

'Because your reply would reflect either on your mother's judgement or your own. Yes, I understand.'

'It is not entirely that, sir. If I may say so without offence, you have subjected me to something of an inquisition, and I am beginning to feel a little uncomfortable under such dissection.'

'I apologise, my boy. I am afraid I have let my curiosity get the better of me. You are quite right. There comes a point where a man must keep his own counsel. But, Edward—may I call you Edward?—there is one more question which I must ask. Why have you not found yourself employment since you came to London? Is there nothing that you could do? You are not making any use of your degree?'

His interest seemed so genuine that Edward could not resent the further cross-examination. 'There are two reasons for my idleness. Firstly, when I arrived in London, I was somewhat ... distressed, as a result of a family upheaval of which I am not free to speak, but which had particular significance for me. Secondly, I suppose the problem is that I don't know what to do. As for my degree, I am not sure that I see a future for myself in mathematics. I don't regret going to Cambridge—I am sure it was of great value to me, as it was to Jack, too. But ...' Aware of Mr Chetwynd's steady gaze, Edward felt a need to defend himself. 'I was offered a position only the other evening with Prideau's.'

'The silk makers?'

'Yes.'

'It did not appeal to you?'

'My mother has always looked upon Prideau's as the enemy. On a personal basis, she and Mr Prideau get on quite well, but for me to work for him would have seemed like a betrayal of the most heartless kind.'

Chetwynd nodded. He was silent for a while as he finished the last of his sole and leaf spinach. He wiped his lips carefully, took a long sip of his wine, and then said, 'How would you like to work in cast iron?'

The question was so unexpected that Edward laughed. 'Cast iron? But I know nothing about it. Oh, forgive me, but you might as well ask me why I don't become a—' He looked at his wine-glass. '—a vintner, for instance.'

'I've no doubt that wine-making is a highly skilled business. So is the manufacture of silk. And the production of cast iron is not without its need for expert knowledge. But skills and knowledge of that kind can be acquired. What cannot so easily be learnt are the qualities which I am looking for. Do you know why I am in London?'

'No, sir.'

'I suppose the situation as far as Jack and I are concerned is similar to that between you and your mother—with the striking difference that you were prepared to take an interest in your mother's business. Anyway, since Jack has no desire to join me, I have to look elsewhere. I arranged to interview candidates for the position this week, and a more namby-pamby lot of young men I have not seen in all my years. My business needs new blood, and probably changes which I am too set in my ways to envisage. Not one of these candidates would have had the imagination to see any need for change, nor the courage to stand up for himself if I happened to disagree with anything that he said. I really don't know what England is coming to! If you ask me, it is people like Oscar Wilde who are responsible.'

With a slight smile, Edward said, 'Surely, sir, he must be forgiven a great deal for the brilliance of his writing. Artists are a very special breed, and—'

'Stuff and nonsense!' Chetwynd said, loudly enough that some of the other diners turned to look in his direction. He was about to go on, when he caught Edward's glance. 'You are provoking me deliberately, are you not?'

'Yes, sir,' Edward said. 'Sorry.'

'Young puppy!' But there was no anger in his voice. He took another sip of wine. 'How would you like to work for me, Edward?'

Startled, Edward looked up. 'Work for you?' He paused briefly, and then said, 'I find that difficult to answer, sir. I confess to being caught completely off balance.'

'No doubt you are thinking that I am acting on impulse. But I count myself an experienced judge of men. I have learnt as much about you in the last hour as I learned about any of those young men I interviewed—more—and I believe you have the qualities I have been looking for.'

It was just like his conversation with Mr Prideau, Edward thought, except that Mr Chetwynd seemed more approachable, and he had no ulterior motive, like Prideau's determination to acquire Harcourt's Mill.

'What position are you offering me?'

'Initially, that of my assistant. Later, we shall see. Are you interested?'

'I don't know,' Edward said guardedly. He found himself grinning. 'Perhaps.'

'Ah.' Mr Chetwynd signalled for a waiter. 'Pudding? No? Then coffee, and brandy, and a cigar.'

For a long while Edward said nothing more, and Chetwynd seemed content to leave the silence unbroken. Eventually, drawing appreciatively on his half Corona, Edward said, 'I'm not even sure, sir, where your business is.'

'Foolish of me not to mention it. Rudleigh, in Shropshire. Quite near to the Iron Bridge over the Severn.'

'The Iron Bridge?'

'Surely you have heard of it? What on earth do they teach in the schools nowadays? It is famous everywhere—the first iron bridge in the world, built just over a hundred years ago. There's even a town there now, called Ironbridge—all one word. Some say it's the birthplace of the industrial revolution.'

Edward glanced at his host. 'I hope I'm not being impertinent, sir, but you look prosperous enough, and Jack was always flush, even before his inheritance. So I presume the business is flourishing.'

Chetwynd nodded approval of the question. 'You're right to ask. And I will be honest with you and say that the company is sound, but its profits badly need to be increased.'

'And what rewards would my employment entitle me to?'

'Accommodation would be provided—there is a small furnished house available. Your salary would be commensurate with your responsibilities.'

Edward was silent.

'You do not ask how much that would be,' Mr Chetwynd said.

'I assumed fair treatment, sir, so I saw no need to press you for details, which you seemed, if I may say so, slightly reluctant to give.'

Nettled, Chetwynd said quickly, 'Bearing in mind that you would be living rent-free, your salary would be ten pounds a month. I think that is not ungenerous.'

'Neither is it a fortune.'

'But fair for someone starting without experience. There is no reason why it should not increase substantially in due course.'

Edward smiled to himself. That little duel had given him at least a couple of hits. 'What about the people who work for you already?' he asked. 'Will they not resent the advent of a newcomer who knows nothing about cast iron? Is none of your existing employees suited to the job?'

'I want a fresh pair of eyes. I know the business too well, and so do all my senior employees. "It's always been done that way," we say, and that is the curse of British industry today—the refusal to face the fact that progress is achieved by change, not by . . . But this is not a lecture.'

99

They sat for some minutes, avoiding each other's eyes, smoking and sipping at their coffee and brandy. Then Chetwynd turned to Edward again. 'I do not expect an immediate answer. This is far too important a decision to be made hastily. Take your time.'

Edward laughed. 'Sorry again, sir, but that's exactly what Mr Prideau said to me.'

'No doubt. Here is my card. If you are interested in joining me, then send me a telegram.'

'And when would I start, sir?'

'As soon as possible. The end of next week, perhaps.' He paused, and then said, a little hesitantly, 'Tell me, Edward, is there any lady with whom you will wish to discuss this matter?'

'Lady?' Edward repeated blankly, and then realised what he meant. 'Oh, no. Not at the moment.'

'Ah. Well, so much the better. Not that I am against matrimony—far from it—but at your age freedom of movement can be important, and there is plenty of time for you. How old are you, by the way?'

'Coming up to twenty-three, sir.'

Chetwynd nodded, as though to approve. He placed his napkin on the table. 'When you are ready, young man, I shall call for the bill. And then we shall take a cab to the Albany, in the hope that Jack is sufficiently awake to receive his father.'

*　　　*　　　*

Templeton, the manservant, let them in. 'The master is asleep, sir. At least, he was a few minutes ago. Should I wake him?'

'No,' said Chetwynd. He turned to Edward. 'I shall not stay. I have enjoyed our conversation, Edward, and I shall hope to hear favourably from you. You can tell Jack that his father sends his kind regards—no, his *affectionate* regards.'

As he left the room, leaning heavily on his stick, Edward thought he seemed almost pathetic, vulnerable. It was odd that he and Jack should get on so badly. Mr Chetwynd appeared to be exactly the sort of father that any boy would be fortunate to have. But if he took the job, perhaps he would discover a very different man.

The next morning, Jack wanted to hear every detail of

100

the evening. He listened with amusement as Edward told him of the offer of employment. 'You're not going to take it, are you?'

'Yes,' Edward said.

Jack laughed then, and went on laughing. 'You're mad,' he gasped. 'Working for the old man? Absolutely mad. Besides, you don't know anything about cast iron, and if you've any sense you won't want to. Mucky stuff, cast iron.' He laughed again. 'Where are you going to live? Has he offered you my old room perhaps?'

'He talked about a house being available.'

'Did he, by Jove! A house!' For a moment, Jack seemed quite taken aback. Then he laughed even louder, and, when he could eventually speak, said, 'The old devil! He's planning to marry you off to Beatrice.'

'Beatrice?'

'My stepsister, old chap. I told you about her. She's frightfully old—an old fright, in fact—and desperate to get a man. Rather like Katisha in *The Mikado*. You're mad, I tell you. Mad.'

Edward's determination was strengthened, rather than diminished by Jack's continued mockery. He sent his telegram, and then went to see the Bunns, who were both delighted with his news.

When he returned to the Albany, Jack was dressed. 'You know what, Edward? Either that whisky I had last night has special curative powers, or it wasn't flu after all. I've still got a bit of a headache, but I feel heaps better. Tonight we shall celebrate.'

'Tonight we shall stay in. You may feel better, but you look ghastly, and you'll go to bed early and not dream of going out until tomorrow, and only then if you're really recovered.'

'You're just being beastly to make up for me saying you're mad.'

'Someone's got to look after you. You ought to have a wife.'

Jack shook his head. 'No. I ought to have a mistress. We ought both to have mistresses. Perhaps, once you've gone, I'll take one. A bit awkward while we're both in the flat. And you can find yourself one in Shropshire, if you're really going.'

It was not until the Tuesday morning that Jack was really better, which meant that they had three days before Edward was due to leave for Rudleigh, days which Jack insisted on filling with a seemingly unending round of meals and visits and entertainments, including a party in his rooms on the last evening.

With his intended early departure in mind, Edward contrived to be comparatively abstemious, but Jack imposed no such restriction on himself, and as Edward was about to leave the next morning, he appeared, still in his nightshirt and dressing-gown. 'Oh, God!' he said. 'I feel awful, and it's surely not morning yet.'

'I didn't think you'd be up.'

'Couldn't let you go off without saying a fond farewell, old chap.'

'That's good of you. I'm glad, because—well, I wanted to say I owe you an awful lot, Jack. It's been marvellous to be here. You know I can't do much about it now, but I'll make it up to you one day.'

'Nonsense, old boy. Nothing to make up. What are old friends for, eh? And we are old friends, aren't we? Listen, I still think you're mad, absolutely mad, and I'll go on saying so, but . . . well, I hope it works out for you, Edward. But watch out for Beatrice, and don't let the old man put anything over on you.'

'I don't think he's that sort,' Edward said.

'Oh, my head!' Jack groaned again. 'No, I don't think he is, either. He'll treat you fairly enough. And we'll meet again before long, eh? Here . . . here's my hand, Edward. But for God's sake, don't squeeze it too hard. I'm far too delicate for that this morning.'

102

4

Jack's words rang in Edward's ears as he sat in the train taking him to Shropshire. Jack was right, he thought—he *was* absolutely mad. He had no idea what lay ahead of him, and whatever Mr Chetwynd said, it was surely madness to go into a business of which he knew nothing. When he worked in his mother's mill, at least he had, as it were, been brought up in silk.

He did not even know much about what sort of cast iron he would be concerned with. In reply to his question, as they were finishing their coffee in the Silver Fountain, Mr Chetwynd had said only, 'Decorative stuff, decorative. We don't make machinery, or anything on that scale.'

Yes, he was mad. An even more alarming thought was that Mr Chetwynd himself might be off his head. He wasn't all that old, but could it be—what was it they called it?—senile dementia? Surely no sane business man would offer a position of responsibility to an inexperienced young man about whom he knew virtually nothing.

Knowing that he ought to be feeling increasingly apprehensive, he was filled with excitement instead. What an adventure! And after all, he was under no obligation to Mr Chetwynd, who had not even offered to pay his train fare. If the situation turned out to be unsatisfactory, he would return straight to London, and look for employment elsewhere.

He changed trains at Shrewsbury. It was a short journey to Ironbridge, but the scenery was interesting, soon changing from a plain with wide vistas to steep hills and deep valleys through which the track twisted and turned, so that every minute a new picture was revealed. Here and there in the woods bluebells carpeted the ground, and on the banks beside the railway the yellow gleam of late-flowering primroses could occasionally be seen.

Outside the station at Ironbridge stood a pony and trap, an old man in the driving seat.

'From Mr Chetwynd?' Edward asked.

'Aye.'

Edward hoisted up his bags, and climbed into the trap. 'Is it far?'

'No,' the man replied, as he tugged on the reins and the pony began to amble out of the station yard.

'My name is Harcourt, Edward Harcourt. I have come to work for Mr Chetwynd.'

The man merely grunted, and Edward abandoned any further attempt at conversation. It was near to dusk, and to the left of the road he could see the glow of fires, and rising sparks against the darkening sky. In the distance there was a roaring sound, and the air smelled of burning coal and acrid gases. Smelting furnaces, he guessed.

Soon they were clip-clopping steadily along beside the Severn. There was just enough evening light to see how beautiful it was, flowing in a gentle curve, the opposite bank steep and wooded. And then he saw the Iron Bridge—a vast tracery arch bearing the carriageway across the river. It rose towards the middle and then sloped down to the other bank, and in the very centre, at the top of the arch, the bridge looked, from a distance, delicate, almost fragile. Yet it had stood for more than a hundred years, a much-used crossing.

Edward was pleased—almost excited, like a little boy—when the driver turned the pony to go over the bridge. It seemed very high, as they crossed, and had to be, of course, to allow passage for the tall-sailed boats which Edward had seen upstream. On the far side, the driver halted the trap, and burrowing into his pocket, extracted a sixpence, which he handed to the toll-keeper.

Once across the river, they drove perhaps three miles along a fairly wide road, and then arrived at a large, early Georgian house. A flight of steps led up to the front door. A plaque on the wall was inscribed 'Rudleigh House'.

The driver said nothing as Edward climbed down and took his luggage, and then moved off.

Mr Chetwynd himself answered Edward's knock. 'Ah, you got here. Good. Have a good journey?'

'Yes, thank you, sir.'

'Wait just a minute, and I'll show you where you'll be living. Nothing grand, you know—it's not a mansion.'

The effort of putting his coat on, even with Edward's help, made Mr Chetwynd wheeze.

'I am sure I could find it, sir,' Edward said, 'if you give me directions. I don't want to make you . . .'

'Nonsense! The doctor tells me I ought to take more exercise. The walk will do me good. And it is not far.'

It was certainly no mansion, Edward thought as, some three hundred yards away from Rudleigh House, they came to a small cottage. Chetwynd struck a match, and lit an oil lamp, by the light of which Edward could see a narrow room, dominated by its wide, open hearth. It was simply furnished with a table, a couple of rough wooden chairs, and one padded chair which looked both ancient and uncomfortable, but the smallness of the room made it seem crowded. There were two doors, one leading to a bedroom containing a single bed, a chair and a small washstand, and the other to a tiny scullery. There were no taps over the sink.

'The well's in the garden,' Mr Chetwynd said. 'Good, clean water. And the privy's over there.' He pointed to a shed. 'I've arranged for the Widow Woodham to come in every morning. She'll get your breakfast, pack you bread and cheese for you to take with you for your midday meal, and leave something for you to eat in the evening. She'll do your washing, and keep the place clean. You'll pay her twenty-two shillings a week, and she'll see you well-fed and looked after. I trust that's acceptable.'

'Yes, thank you, sir.'

'Now, do you think you can find your way back to my house?'

'Yes, sir.'

'Then I'll leave you to tidy yourself up. Join us for dinner at half past eight. No need to dress—we're very informal here in the country.'

When he had gone, Edward examined his domicile more carefully. The rooms were bare, but spotlessly clean. In the cupboard set into the wall of the bedroom, he was surprised to see a small pile of clothes. They looked worn, but they, too, seemed clean. Perhaps the previous occupant had left them behind.

It did not take him long to survey his domain. He would not have called it a house, but this tiny cottage was in fact quite attractive, and if Mr Chetwynd felt it necessary to give it a grander description than was justified by reality, perhaps that was an indication of his real desire to have Edward on his staff.

*　　*　　*

'Emily, my dear, and Beatrice, may I present Mr Harcourt?' Chetwynd paused to get his breath. 'My wife, Edward, and my step-daughter, Miss Unwin.'

Mrs Chetwynd and her daughter were sitting side by side, and very upright, on a sofa. As Edward bowed, they inclined their heads, Mrs Chetwynd gravely, but Miss Unwin with a smile which revealed large projecting teeth. Jack had been unfair, Edward thought, in describing her as a fright, but he had to admit that she was no beauty, with a long, narrow face, dominated by a bony nose. Inexpertly applied rouge made two patches of colour on her high cheekbones. He was conscious that her eyes were fixed on him unblinkingly, and later he realised that this stare was in fact her habitual expression. He was not sure how old she was—in her mid-thirties, he guessed.

'Come closer, Mr Harcourt,' Mrs Chetwynd said, in a high, almost child-like voice. 'I am very short-sighted.'

Both ladies had on their laps what Edward had taken at first to be furry muffs. As he stepped closer, these revealed themselves as small, but very fat, lap-dogs, which raised their heads and yapped in unison.

'Be quiet, Prince!' said Mrs Chetwynd, at the same time as her daughter was issuing a similar command to Fido.

The dogs took no notice, but gradually subsided into a discontented snuffling.

'I hope you like dogs, Mr Harcourt.'

Edward nodded and smiled.

Meanwhile, Mrs Chetwynd had produced a pair of lorgnettes, and was peering at him through them, while Miss Unwin's unwavering gaze was still fixed on him, and he began to wonder whether perhaps he had failed to tie his cravat correctly, or perhaps left an embarrassing button undone. At length, Mrs Chetwynd seemed satisfied. 'I must apologise, Mr Harcourt, but it is so confusing when one is not sure what one's visitors look like. Now, do sit down.'

When he first came in, the room had struck Edward as being strange in some way, and it was only now that he realised that he had felt this because all the many pieces of furniture were so formally arranged. One sofa faced another, easy chairs were ranged in a straight line at right angles to the sofas, occasional tables and pouffes and whatnots were not scattered about haphazardly, but placed so that each one complemented and balanced another on the opposite side of the room. Edward wondered which of the ladies was responsible for the careful arrangement.

He decided that he would have to sit on the sofa where Mr Chetwynd was already sitting. Only in that way, with the two gentlemen exactly facing the two ladies, could he maintain the symmetry. But before he could sit down, a maid knocked and entered and announced that dinner was ready.

'Ah, good,' Mr Chetwynd said. 'Come, my dears. Edward must be starving.'

The meal was simple but plenteous. Mrs Chetwynd and Miss Unwin plied Edward with questions about Jack's health, and his own journey, and whether he had been to Shropshire before, and if he had admired the Iron Bridge, stopping only to feed titbits from their plates to the little dogs on their laps.

Edward answered their questions as politely as he could. It was all rather like a comical *viva voce*. He hoped he would pass.

Mr Chetwynd had remained silent, but once a maid had cleared their pudding plates and brought a pot of coffee, he said, 'We have many things to discuss, my dears. Be so good as to leave us.'

Obediently, the ladies rose and went to the door. Miss Unwin turned and gave Edward her toothy smile. 'I shall look forward to working with you, Mr Harcourt.'

When the door had closed, Chetwynd gave Edward a strange look. It was almost defensive, as though he were expecting some adverse comment on his womenfolk.

'I must compliment you, sir, on the ladies of your family,' Edward said. 'Most charming.'

'Yes,' said Chetwynd drily. 'Now, you must have a thousand questions. Ask away.'

Miss Unwin's parting remark had lingered in Edward's mind. 'Miss Unwin said something about us working together . . . ?'

'Yes. She keeps my books for me. You will need to familiarise yourself with the accounts. I have already informed her that she is to open the ledgers to you, and answer your questions freely.'

'I see. I am sure I shall enjoy working with her.'

Again Chetwynd looked at him, sharply this time, as if to check whether the words were meant ironically.

'I think the first thing I need to know, sir,' Edward went on, 'is a little more about your business. You told me that you were concerned in making decorative cast iron—could you be more specific?'

'We manufacture a very large range of goods—grates, chairs, tables, figurines, hat-stands, gates, bird baths—anything in the ornamental line.' He pushed his chair back. 'I'll get you a catalogue.' A moment or two later he returned to the room with a thick booklet.

The products were indeed immensely varied, and included many items which Chetwynd had not mentioned. Edward realised that the company must be larger than he had expected. 'Do you employ a large staff?' he asked.

'Two dozen.'

'Is that all? To produce all this? Is it economic to have so large a range?'

'When we have made the prototype of a design, it is easy enough to repeat it, and we have felt a need to maintain as many lines as our competitors. Nevertheless, you are right to suggest that it strains our resources. Storage itself is a problem.'

'Who are your main competitors?'

'The Hancocks at the Ironbridge Works are the leaders in the field. They have a very much bigger catalogue than ours, and the volume of their business enables them to undercut us on some lines. Their stranglehold on the market has increased over the past two or three years, and while our own sales have held up reasonably well, I have to

108

admit that the figures show a slight decline—a trend which must be halted.'

Edward chose his words carefully. 'I remember you saying that you wanted a pair of fresh eyes to look at your business, presumably with a view to reversing that decline. But it seems to me an almost impossible task for someone with no experience of the trade.'

'You sound as though you regret having come here, Edward. Do you?'

'No, sir.' He went on, smiling, 'On the other hand, I hope you will pardon me if I say that I am still not certain that I want to make a career in cast iron.'

'You may not do so,' Chetwynd said. He wheezed for a moment, and then went on, 'It will all depend on you. You are here on trial, as it were. I may not have made that clear to you—in which case I apologise—but you can surely not have expected otherwise. My expectations of your ability might be wrong, or you could decide after a time that you did not want to make a career, as you put it, in cast iron. To that extent I do not guarantee your future here. As for knowledge of the business, as I am sure I told you, I am looking for intelligence, not experience.'

Edward remembered his thoughts on the journey. If Mr Chetwynd were suffering from senile dementia, he was showing no signs of it. 'I appreciate all you say, sir,' he said. 'It still bothers me that I don't even know how cast iron is made.'

'You will learn. Let me tell you exactly what I have in mind for you. I want you to study every aspect of my business—spend some time in the foundry, examine the accounts, study the market and the way we distribute our goods, look at our competitors. Take as much time as you need—two months, three months, more. Then make your report. I shall be greatly surprised if you do not have useful recommendations to put forward.'

'You are expecting a lot of me, sir,' Edward persisted.

Chetwynd smiled. 'Perhaps I am. But unless you are intending to pack your bags and leave, which would not be easy at this time of night, let us talk a little of cast iron. People often confuse it with wrought iron. Do you know the difference?'

'No, sir.'

'To put it simply, when making wrought iron, most of the natural impurities, including carbon, are removed during the smelting process, and the metal will then bend under pressure, so that it can be worked, or wrought. Cast iron, on the other hand, does not have those impurities taken out, with the result that it is very strong, but breaks if you try to bend it. It melts easily, and is therefore ideal for casting in moulds. You will see exactly how it is done tomorrow. A model of whatever we want to produce is carved in wood, and then pressed into sand to form a perfect impression of it. Pig iron is melted and poured into the mould, producing a cast iron copy of the wooden original.'

'I don't understand, I'm afraid. How can you make a firm enough impression in sand for it to stay when you take the model out? Surely even damp sand would run here and there, especially when molten iron is poured in.'

'It is not the same kind of sand as you see on a beach. We use grains of silica, bonded together by clay, with small amounts of coal-dust, sawdust and horse manure added.'

'Horse manure?'

'It helps to bond the sand together. It's even more essential in loam-moulding, which is used for heavier castings than we produce. Mixing the sand is a highly skilled job, and the end result is a mould that will keep a clean impression of the pattern. It is then baked hard, so that it will receive the molten iron without altering its shape in any way.'

'Can I learn how to do it?'

'Mix the sand, you mean, and form the mould, and pour in the iron? Oh, it takes years to become a skilled foundryman.'

'I presume that you can do all those things, sir.'

'I have not worked in the foundry for a very long time, but, yes, if need be I could do it all still. Anyone who aspires to manage other men should understand their work and at least know the rudiments of it.'

Edward smiled. 'Exactly, sir. That is why I should like to learn how.'

'You shall. You can begin tomorrow. I'll have a word with the overseer, and make sure he looks after you.'

'I'd prefer not to have any special treatment. And I'd like

to work in all the departments—I mean, not just walk in and look around, like an inspector, but actually work there.'

'Are you an artist, too?' Mr Chetwynd asked drily. 'Will you expect to design new artefacts for us, and carve the models?'

'Hardly that, but I can surely do something to help in that department, even if it's just carrying lumps of wood about. I'd like to see just how the models are made, so that I understand the possibilities and the limitations.'

'There are very few of those. Work of considerable delicacy can be produced in cast iron.'

Edward thought of the illustrations in the catalogue. Almost all the designs had been very elaborate, sometimes lace-like, often extremely heavily ornamented. 'Do you employ many artists?' he asked.

'Two. Sam Nightingale and Walter Sales. They have been with us for many, many years. Sam is responsible for such things as gates, tables—mostly comparatively flat articles of formal design—while Walter produces our figurines and similar more free-style objects, if you understand the distinction I am making. And of course they carve replacements for worn or damaged models.'

'They have been with you for many years, you said?'

Chetwynd smiled. 'No doubt you are thinking that perhaps they are old-fashioned, and their designs no longer popular. It is not so, I assure you. Sam and Walter are among our greatest assets.'

Edward promised himself a close look at Messrs Nightingale and Sales and their work.

Outside in the hall a clock chimed. 'Half past nine,' Chetwynd said. 'We have talked long enough, I think. I like to be in bed by ten, for we rise early here. I trust you are no lie-abed, Edward. I want you to report to me here at six-thirty. Mrs Woodham will prepare your breakfast in good time. You'll need suitable clothing. The men usually provide their own, but I doubted you'd have anything suitable, so I've left some things in your house. They're clean, and I hope they'll fit.'

'I saw them, sir. Thank you.'

'I think we should now join the ladies. Mrs Chetwynd and Miss Unwin will take it ill if you do not spend a few minutes in their company.'

111

'I would not wish to deprive myself of that pleasure,' Edward said politely.

'At least I shall not have to do any more talking,' Chetwynd said. 'And you shall be released before you are overcome by weariness, especially if those damned dogs start their infernal yapping again.' He rose and went slowly towards the door. 'Don't tell me you like Pekinese.'

'No, sir,' Edward grinned. 'I won't.'

*　　*　　*

After Edward had left, Mrs Chetwynd said, 'A pleasant young man.'

'Very pleasant indeed,' Miss Unwin added.

'Don't you go setting your cap at him,' Mr Chetwynd said.

Mrs Chetwynd gave a little shriek. 'Oh! How can you say such a thing? As if such a thought had entered Beatrice's head!'

'I know her too well.'

Beatrice rose. 'I will not stay here to be insulted.'

'None of your hoity-toity airs with me, miss,' her step-father said. 'Sit down. I simply want to make it clear to you that pleasant though he may be, and rather more intelligent than his friend, my son and heir, I see no prospect of young Mr Harcourt remaining here for very long.'

'I thought you intended making him your deputy,' Mrs Chetwynd said.

'A boy who knows nothing about iron and is also quite inexperienced in the business world . . . ? No. I was a fool to offer him employment, but I was impressed when I met him, and disappointed that I had found no other candidate. He will stay for a month or two, write me a report which will tell me little, if anything, that I don't know already, and then return to London. Of course, *he* doesn't know that—I did my best to reassure him on that very point—but that's what will happen.'

'None of that is any reason,' said Miss Unwin with some asperity, 'why I should not set my cap at him, as you so vulgarly put it. Not that I have any intention of doing so.'

'You are not to distract him from such work as he does do for me. When he comes to you for financial information,

112

pray restrict your conversation entirely to matters of business.'

With a furious look, Beatrice rose and swept out of the room, carrying a protesting Fido with her.

'Really, my dear,' Mrs Chetwynd said, 'I cannot think what gets into you to talk to poor Beatrice so.'

Chetwynd shook his head. 'Neither can I. There is something about her—I don't know what it is—that makes me want to wound her. I shall apologise in the morning.' He paused. 'Nevertheless, I fear that she does view every new young man that she meets as a possible husband.'

'So do most young women.'

'Yes, but not with such obvious determination.'

'You are impossible, George.' And in her turn, Mrs Chetwynd, with an angry toss of her head, gathered up her Prince and hurried out.

Chetwynd was annoyed with himself. He had upset both the women in his household quite unnecessarily. He asked himself again what it was about Beatrice that irritated him so, and found no answer, beyond the feeling that beneath that bony exterior something lay concealed. He knew all about the mental breakdown she had had, though it had happened years before he met her mother. It had apparently been a very trivial matter, and he had certainly seen no sign of instability since, unless you counted her obsessive tidiness. Nevertheless, perhaps what was concealed was some kind of imbalance which might one day surface. But there was certainly no cause to be unkind to her. He vowed to be kinder to her in future, and went to bed.

*　　*　　*

Edward was suddenly wide awake. Inches from his eyes was a face which seemed, in that moment of confusion between sleep and the return to full consciousness, as if it could belong only to a witch in a fairy story. In the flickering candlelight he could see a hooked nose and pointed chin, and little glittering black eyes . . . And then he realised that this must be Mrs Woodham, and that she had just shaken his shoulder, which was just as well, for in the warmth and comfort of the old-fashioned feather bed, he might easily have slept on and on.

113

She was saying something, but whether because of the thick dialect or because her toothless gums made articulation difficult—or perhaps a combination of the two—he could not understand her. He nodded, and said loudly and slowly, as though talking to the deaf, 'Thank you. Yes. I'll get up straight away.'

A can of hot water stood on the washstand, and by the light of a candle he quickly washed and shaved, and dressed in the flannel shirt, moleskin trousers and heavy boots that Mr Chetwynd had left for him. The trousers were far too big around the waist, but there was a stout belt which kept them from falling.

From the scullery came the appetising smell of bacon frying. While he was washing and dressing he could hear Mrs Woodham talking. She was speaking quite loudly, and he felt that he was expected to reply, but he still did not understand a word.

When he sat at the table in the living-room, Mrs Woodham placed before him a plate of two fried eggs, three thick rashers of bacon and a slice of fried bread. A loaf stood on the table, too, and a block of butter, still criss-crossed with the design to indicate which of the local dairymaids had churned it. The breakfast was completed by a pot of strong tea, and a jug of milk so rich that it was almost cream.

While Edward ate, Mrs Woodham went on talking, mostly with her back to him. Sometimes it sounded as though she were asking a question, and if she paused slightly, he would say, 'Very good, thank you. Just what the doctor ordered,' or something similar. She seemed satisfied with this, and nodded her head, and resumed her incomprehensible litany.

Carrying the lunch packet she had prepared, Edward set off though the dark, and arrived at Rudleigh House at twenty-five past six. Mr Chetwynd looked at him approvingly. 'Good man. Mind you, I knew Mrs Woodham would get you up in time.'

'Does she always talk as much as that?'

'Who? Mrs Woodham? Oh, yes. Don't take any notice. Just tell her anything you want done or want to eat, and you'll get it.'

'Is it some kind of dialect?'

Chetwynd laughed. 'Yes. Don't worry—you'll pick it up. Now, come on, young man, and see what casting iron is all about. We'll start with a tour through the works, and then I'll hand you over to Thomas Yardman, the senior foundry-man.' He looked Edward up and down. 'Clothes all right?'

'Yes, sir, thank you.'

'Good. It's a dirty job, you'll find.'

He led the way slowly along a rough path through the trees until they came to a small road or lane. Once they were out of the wood, Edward could see a faint orange light rising into the sky. He guessed that it came from a furnace. 'Is that your foundry, sir?'

Chetwynd stopped and fought for his breath. 'That's right,' he said at last. 'The glow comes from our furnaces—we keep the fires going day and night. You'd have seen it yesterday evening if it hadn't been for the trees.'

Edward could make out the shape of two long, low, shed-like buildings. The light from the furnaces seemed to rise directly from their roof. 'Are the furnaces set down deep in the ground?' Edward asked.

'No.' Chetwynd sounded surprised. 'What made you ask that?'

'I thought furnaces were huge constructions—great towering monsters. The ones I saw at Ironbridge last night were enormous.'

Chetwynd laughed. 'We'd have no use for that kind of furnace. We don't to our own smelting, you understand—I mean we don't take the iron ore and process it from the beginning. We buy pig iron from the Ironbridge Works and then melt it down in small cupola furnaces.'

'I'm afraid you need to start at the beginning, sir. What exactly is pig iron?'

'Iron comes out of the ground as rock—iron ore, we call it—and is put in a blast furnace with coke and limestone. Coke is almost pure carbon, and that's needed to convert the ore into iron, while the limestone is there to get rid of impurities. The coke they use is a special kind—silvery, almost metallic to look at—and when it burns it gives off a very intense heat. Clear so far?'

'Yes. Except that you talked of a cupola furnace and a blast furnace.'

'In essence, the fire in a blast furnace is constantly

115

fanned by air pumped in through a tube called a tuyere. That's what raises the heat sufficiently to melt the iron ore. The impurities rise to the top in a liquid that we call slag, and the molten iron is at the bottom of the furnace. Open a tap and it flows out into moulds, which are arranged in the form of a central channel and arms leading off it on either side. Someone, somewhere, thought it looked like a sow and her sucklings—hence the name pig iron. Fanciful, but that's why they call it that. And a cupola is simply a small blast furnace used for remelting pig iron.'

'I see. Thank you. There's iron ore in these hills, is there?'

'Yes, and coal. That's why people like the Hancocks started up here. And my father, who founded our business, came because the Hancocks were here to supply pig iron, and the coke was here, too. And of course the river was another factor.'

'Water-power to drive the bellows?' Edward guessed.

'No. A sensible suggestion, but you don't need a river for that. You can use steam, or if you want to use water-power, you'll probably do rather better with a hill-stream than a river. No, the Severn provides transport. That's something you can look into later.'

By this time they had reached the first of the sheds. Edward's first impression as they entered was of heat and steam and noise. The air was heavy with a strange, almost sour smell, compounded of hot metal and something redolent of a stagnant pond. As Chetwynd led the way, Edward saw that the floor was covered in black sand. At one end of the shed was a kind of tapering brick cylinder, about seven feet tall, and perhaps two and a half feet in diameter at its base, attached to which was a huge bellows, worked by means of a crankshaft, the handle of which a man was turning. This, Edward guessed, was the cupola furnace, and it was the source of the noise, for the fire within was roaring fiercely.

'Very old, this furnace,' Chetwynd shouted to him. 'The blast is still worked manually. In the other shed, the bellows is powered by steam. I shall convert this one when I can.'

From the furnace a gutter ran towards a deep trough. 'The molten iron will run into that,' Chetwynd said, 'and from there it can be ladled into the flasks.' He indicated a number of iron-bound boxes standing on the floor in neat rows.

'Flasks?' Edward queried.

'Sand-boxes are known as flasks. Here, look.' He led the way to the far end of the room, where two men were working. 'Ah, Yardman. This is Mr Harcourt. He'll be coming to learn something about foundry work, and you'll look after him.' He turned to Edward. 'You couldn't have a better teacher than Thomas Yardman,' he said.

The man grinned with pleasure. He was short and stocky, with grizzled hair. 'Pleased to meet you, Mr Harcourt,' he said. 'When will you be starting, sir?'

Edward looked inquiringly at Chetwynd.

'Later today,' Chetwynd said. 'You see, Edward, the flasks are in two halves. The bottom half's called the drag, and the top, the cope. I won't go into all the details now, but the two halves are filled with green sand—so called not because it's green, but because it's wet—and the pattern is pressed into the sand, so that when it's taken out, the hollows form in contra-relief the shape of whatever it is that is to be cast.' He picked up a wooden carving of a cat, sitting upright, its tail curled about its feet, the surface finely grooved to give the appearance of fur. 'That's what we're doing now. Ornaments. One of our very successful lines. Very life-like, very delicately carved.'

'And the casting will come out exactly like this?' Edward asked.

'Yes. Very slightly smaller, because the iron shrinks as it cools—an eighth of an inch in every foot. It's not crucial in an ornament, but for some work, of course, the shrinkage has to be carefully calculated, so that the casting is the exact size intended.' He handed the model back. 'The two halves of the flask are bound together, after tubes have been inserted to lead the molten metal to the pattern, and to allow gases to escape, and those tubes are connected to others in the flask above, and so on, so that with one pouring we can produce several castings. That's what those piles of flasks are doing over there. You understand?'

'I think so,' Edward replied, a little doubtfully.

Yardman smiled encouragingly. 'You'll soon pick it up, sir.'

'Right. Let's go and look in the other shed,' Chetwynd said.

117

In the wall of the room opposite to the furnace were two doors. 'What's in there, sir?' Edward asked.

'The fettling room—that's where the castings are finished off—polished, and so on. And the other room's an office. You'll see them later.'

The next building was larger than the first, as was the cupola furnace, and the bellows attached to it were worked by a steam engine, resulting in a more continuous blast of air.

'We do the bigger work here,' Chetwynd explained.

As he and Edward entered, the workman in charge of the furnace was just about to open the trapdoor to release the molten iron. White-hot, it ran down into the receptacle. One after the other, half a dozen workmen stepped forward, and dipped their long-handled ladles into the metal. Some part-filled a kind of bucket, suspended between two long arms, which two men could then carry.

'Why are some taking more than others?' Edward asked.

'They know how much will be required for different mouldings—a good workman will take out exactly the amount he needs. Like most skills, it's a matter of experience.'

Carefully, slowly, the men carried the molten metal to the stack of flasks, and poured it slowly into the feeder cups. Edward watched in fascination. This, too, was clearly skilled work; not a drop was spilled.

'What are they making here?' Edward asked.

'Garden furniture,' Chetwynd replied. 'It's made in sections, which are welded together after. And then, of course, it has to be enamelled. The paint shop is in this building, and so is the pattern department. But I really haven't the time to show you them now. We'll go back to the other shed, and I'll hand you over to Yardman.'

*　　*　　*

Edward spent several weeks in the foundry, at the end of which time, although he could not have claimed to be more than the most junior of apprentices, he had learnt sufficient of the various processes to begin to understand them, and to know something of the methods used in making various kinds of castings, and what could go wrong.

He had been allowed, under supervision, to tend the furnace, and to carry the ladles of molten iron and pour it into the flasks. And he had spilt the metal, and been cursed for so doing, and had realised why the foundry floor was covered in sand, which prevented the liquid iron from burning the floorboards.

The most skilled work was the making of the moulds, at which he had little success. The sand had to be rammed into the boxes around the pattern. Old sand came first, dampened and shovelled from the floor, black because of the coal dust mixed with it and the burning it had endured in previous castings; this would not come in direct contact with the molten iron. Then facing sand was used, a mixture of old and new sand and coal dust, into which the pattern would be set. And there was plumbago, to stop the two halves of the flask from sticking together. The sand had to be rammed so that it was neither too tightly packed nor too loose, and, however hard Edward tried, he never managed it to Thomas Yardman's satisfaction.

The overseer gave him some comfort. 'You don't learn moulding in a few days,' he said. 'You're doing better than most. I reckon I could make a foundryman of you.' He laughed. 'Given twenty or thirty years! Besides, those tools of yours are no good. Not smooth enough.'

'But they're new,' Edward protested.

'Ah, trowels are no use until they're nearly worn out. Look at mine—smooth as a baby's bottom. It's use that's done that. And you needn't think you can borrow 'em, because I don't lend 'em to no one, see? Nothing personal, mind—a foundryman never lets anyone else use his tools.'

Yardman had been a friendly and patient teacher. He often laughed at Edward's clumsiness, but there was never any malice in his joshing. At first, the others had treated him with suspicion, mocking his 'la-di-da' accent, sending him on absurd errands—'Go and ask the gaffer for a piddling flask!'—and watching as he struggled by himself and in vain to lift a sack of sand which would normally be hefted by two men. Despite aching muscles, he had tried to do everything that was asked of him—they admired that—and he had accepted their mockery and their teasing good-humouredly, and joked with them, and quite quickly they had accorded him a measure of comradeship. They reminded him of the workers in his mother's mill, where he had learnt to accept the rough ways and the constant mindless cursing of men who had had none of his own advantages of upbringing and education. They might be lacking in manners, they might care little for cleanliness, but those were unimportant things. They were honest, and they took a pride in their work, and if they were sometimes surly, they often laughed, too, and there was between them a camaraderie to which he warmed.

The longer Edward worked in the foundry, the more he enjoyed it. There was something quite fascinating in the way that the dull pig iron could be turned into objects of beauty, and the skills of the moulders and the finishers gave him an almost physical pleasure.

Only Sam Nightingale and Walter Sales were at all off-hand with him. The workers in the fettling shop, removing any rough edges from the castings with emery wheels, and in the paint shop, where hard-wearing enamel was applied to many of the artefacts, were a kindly, amiable lot, but Nightingale and Sales seemed to treat him as an unwelcome interloper. A silent pair, even when he tried to win them over with open and genuine admiration of their skills, they would cut him off in mid-sentence, telling him that he was not there to interrupt their work with his chatter.

'Trouble is they're carvers,' Yardman said. 'Always think they're the only craftsmen in casting. Anyone could do *our* jobs, according to them.'

During Edward's first week, he was so tired at the end of the day that he could only walk slowly home, eat the supper that Mrs Woodham had left for him, and then fall into bed, asleep as soon as his head was on the pillow. Gradually, however, he became used to the physical work, and was able, after his evening meal, to write letters, or to go, as the evenings grew longer, for a stroll. He had grown almost to like the dirt and all-penetrating smell of the foundry, but it was good to wash, and change into his ordinary clothes, and walk through the woods to the river bank. Sometimes he would sit there, looking across the water to the hills, green in the mantle of early summer, curving away until, in the distance, they turned purple and blue. Often he would stroll on as far as the Iron Bridge, and pay his halfpenny toll for the pleasure of watching the river slip by below, and the ships loaded with iron sailing gently down stream from the warehouse serving the Ironbridge Works, and the tiny coracles, deftly paddled by fishermen in search of eels and other fish.

He saw very little of his employer, and on the few occasions when they met, Mr Chetwynd would simply ask if he was getting on all right, in a rather absent-minded way, almost as though he had forgotten that Edward was anything other than a young apprentice from the nearby village.

Edward knocked one day at the door of his office.

'Ah, Edward. Good to see you. Come and sit down. I've been expecting you to come. Yardman tells me that you have made good progress. No doubt you feel now that it is time to move on from the foundry and look at other aspects of the business. Is that it?'

'Yes, sir.'

'Let's see what you've learned. What happens if a mould is not properly dried?'

'It could cause blow-holes, sir, and if it's really moist and the molten metal comes in contact with water, it could explode.'

'Good. What if the sand in a mould is rammed too hard?'

'Scabs on the casting, where parts of the mould have flaked.'

'And if it's too soft?'

'The sand may give way, and there'll be lumps on the casting.'

'Called?'

'Swells.'

The inquisition went on for some time, and Mr Chetwynd's smile grew broader. 'Excellent, Edward,' he said at last. 'Do you want to ask any questions?'

'I'd like to know something of our distribution methods, sir.'

'We have a warehouse in Bristol. All our goods go there.'

'Why Bristol?'

'It goes back to my father's time, before we had the railway. All the iron makers in this area used the Severn to

121

send their products to Bristol. It was easier to distribute them from there to other part of the country.'

'But why do you continue? Surely rail transport is better.'

'The boats are quite fast, and cheap, and Bristol is still an excellent centre. Besides, if we gave up the warehouse there, we should have to build one here. We also have to think of the men who work there. Many of them are long-serving employees, and one cannot just dismiss them.'

'But on economic grounds—'

Chetwynd cut him off. 'You can study the economics of it, if you like, when you take a look at our accounts. I'd suggest you do that next. I shall want your solemn word as a gentleman that you will regard all the figures you see as strictly confidential and will not divulge them to anyone unauthorised under any circumstances.'

'You have my word, sir.'

'Right. Then come to Rudleigh House tomorrow morning at eight thirty. I shall be away for the day, but I will warn my stepdaughter, and she will be expecting you.'

*　　*　　*

When he arrived at Rudleigh House, on the dot of half past eight, he was shown at once into a downstairs room where Miss Unwin was waiting.

She greeted him warmly. 'Mr Harcourt, how pleasant to see you again. I have been hoping for your presence at dinner, but you have not been near us since your arrival.'

'I fear I have been in no state for visits at the end of the day, Miss Unwin.'

'My stepfather tells me that you have shown considerable dedication during your time in the foundry. It must have been most distressing for you.'

'Distressing?'

'The smell, and the noise, and the dirt, and the confusion. I can't bear confusion; I like things to be tidy and in their place. And of course it cannot have been pleasant for you to be thrown constantly into the company of our workmen. They are hardly of our class.'

'I have enjoyed it in the foundry. And I think the workmen are jolly good chaps.'

122

Miss Unwin gave him a curious look. 'Indeed? Well, I am sure it will be more pleasant for you to work here.'

'Yes,' he said, not wishing to argue.

The room, used as an office, was airy and light. Miss Unwin sat on one side of a large partners' desk, on the other side of which was a chair in which, Edward guessed, Mr Chetwynd would take his place when he was working here. The remaining furniture consisted of two upright chairs, and two tables covered in piles of neatly-arranged papers, but there were also shelves on two of the walls, holding numerous leather-bound account books. Everything was tidy and balanced and symmetrical. It was obvious who had been responsible for the arrangement of furniture in the drawing-room of Rudleigh House.

'May I ask how you came to assume your responsibilities as accountant for Mr Chetwynd's business?' Edward asked.

Miss Unwin looked down her nose. 'I hope you are not one of those gentlemen who think that a lady should never occupy herself with anything but needlework and water-colours and playing the piano.'

'I could hardly think that, Miss Unwin, when my mother runs the family mill at Brentfield, and has done for many years.'

'Indeed? Tell me about it.'

Edward naturally did not reveal any of his reservations about his mother when talking to a stranger. He painted a glowing picture of her, and the warmth in his voice communicated itself to Miss Unwin. She favoured him with a toothy smile. 'I should like to meet her, Mr Harcourt—a lady after my own heart. And I would venture to suggest that she has lost none of her femininity despite playing what many would regard as a man's part in the world. Am I not right?'

'Indeed. She has always retained a most womanly nature, a tenderness, a charm . . .' Edward hesitated for a moment, thinking that he was doing his mother a little more than justice. 'And she is a beautiful woman still.'

'Ah,' said Miss Unwin, 'brains and beauty—a combination which is far more frequent in the fair sex than you gentlemen will normally allow. My stepfather was gracious enough to recognise that my own intellect, weak though it

123

is, cannot be content with trivialities. I have always had a mathematical bent. Yes, Mr Harcourt, I flatter myself that I have the necessary brains, and . . .' Her voice trailed off, and she looked at him from under her lashes.

'And beauty, too, Miss Unwin,' Edward said, since it was clearly expected of him.

She smiled broadly, obviously pleased, leaning slightly towards him, so that her large teeth seemed more prominent than ever. 'Pardon my blushes, Mr Harcourt. I am not used to such compliments. But I know that you are merely being polite.'

'How could you think it?' Edward mentally crossed his fingers.

She favoured him with another looming smile. 'Enough of this idle chit-chat. We must get to work. My stepfather wishes me, I understand, to open all our books for your private and confidential inspection. Apart, of course, from his personal ledger. Where do you wish to start?'

'My first interest must be the general profit and loss account.'

'I am working on the quarterly figures now. Perhaps, while I am completing them, you would wish to glance through our sales ledgers.'

Edward was indeed eager to do so, for he intended, as he had done on his mother's behalf, to call upon the major customers to discover exactly what they thought of Chetwynd's products and their various views of market trends. He took the heavy ledger that Miss Unwin indicated, and sat on a chair in a corner of the room.

As he leafed through the pages, he was aware from time to time that Miss Unwin's stare was fixed on him. If he looked up, she quickly averted her gaze, but their eyes met once, and then she gave him a half smile and blushed, before lowering her head. She really was excessively plain, he thought, and her drab olive-green dress did not help, accentuating the flatness of her chest and the boniness of her frame.

He felt something touch his ankle, and looked down. Miss Unwin's lap-dog was snuffling at his foot, and looked as though it were about to cock its leg. He jerked away from it.

The sudden movement drew her attention. 'Something wrong, Mr Harcourt?'

124

'It's quite all right, thank you. I didn't realise that your dog . . .'

'Fido always comes to the office with his Mama, don't you, Fido? He has a little walk before breakfast, and then he usually sleeps the morning through in his basket here. Your being here has disturbed him, but he likes you, I am sure. He always knows who are my friends. Back to your basket, Fido, there's a good boy. Basket!'

Fido took no notice, but after a final sniff at Edward's boots, waddled over to another corner of the room, and with a great deal of snuffling and snorting, settled down to resume his morning's sleep.

Looking at the ledger, Edward found with interest that there appeared to be no really large accounts. Chetwynd's customers were numerous, but all seemed to deal in small quantities. He asked Miss Unwin about it.

'That's the problem we face, Mr Harcourt,' she replied. 'We just cannot compete with the Ironbridge Works.'

'Why not? Because their goods are cheaper, I suppose. Or are they also of better quality? Or do the Ironbridge people have more salesmen, or more effective salesmen? Or is there some other reason?'

'Oh, so many questions, Mr Harcourt! Our products are just as good, but our prices are a little higher. But I don't think that is the main trouble. Ironbridge have recently adopted undesirable methods to sell their products. They maintain a large staff of salesmen, who receive no payment other then commission on sales, and who are under constant threat of dismissal if they fail to achieve the sales targets they have been set.'

'It sounds a very sensible way of improving one's business.'

'It is unfair, and quite unmannerly,' she replied stiffly.

'And how then do we sell our products?'

'Mr Chetwynd visits many of our customers from time to time, and we send out our catalogue regularly. That is the way it has always been done, Mr Harcourt. It has been a gentlemanly trade, until recently.'

'I see,' Edward said. He was conscious that Miss Unwin was looking at him with some hostility. 'I beg you to believe that I have an open mind, Miss Unwin. I am very conscious of being a new boy, and I shall need a great deal of help from

125

you before I can make any judgements.' Seeing that she looked a little mollified, he asked, 'May I look at some of your other ledgers? Do you keep a separate book for purchase of raw materials?'

'Everything is there,' Miss Unwin said, waving a hand towards the shelves, and then added a little primly, 'Please be sure to replace them in the correct order.'

She bent back to her figures as Edward studied the ledgers. The problem was that he had no criteria for judging the cost of the pig iron purchased from the Ironbridge Works, or the sand or coke, or any other raw materials used.

'May I interrupt you again, Miss Unwin?' he asked.

She smiled and nodded graciously. 'I had quite resigned myself, Mr Harcourt, to several days in which I should achieve little of my usual work.' She lifted one hand. 'No, pray don't apologise. Indeed, it is a welcome break. What is your question?'

'The price you pay for the pig iron you buy from the Ironbridge Works—since you are in direct competition with them, is it possible that you are charged over the odds for it?'

'We pay the same as anyone else. The price is more or less standard throughout the country, only varying because of transport costs.'

'Ah, transport—I wanted to ask about that, too.'

'Yes, I'm sure. I've nearly finished these figures. Bring your chair round here, Mr Harcourt. Then we can go over everything more easily.'

They sat together for the rest of the morning, going over many of the financial details of Chetwynd's business. There was no more coldness from Miss Unwin, and indeed she beamed at him constantly, even when he ventured to suggest that the firm's net profits were far too low when expressed as a percentage of turnover. He began to realise that, though she was a more than adequate bookkeeper, she had little understanding of the overall financial situation. 'You'll have to ask my stepfather about that,' she kept saying.

He had expected to leave for a brief period at midday, to eat the bread and cheese which Mrs Woodham had supplied for him, but Miss Unwin insisted that he should

126

have luncheon at the house. The meal consisted mainly of roast mutton, cold and tough. Mrs Chetwynd, in her high little voice, asked an unending series of questions about his family and background. Edward would have much preferred to enjoy his solitary bread and cheese.

After luncheon, he and Miss Unwin returned to her office, where once again he found himself sitting next to her. He was certain that she was attempting to establish some kind of intimacy between them. It was embarrassing, and he decided that as soon as he had most of the information he wanted, he must make his escape. If only she would not lean towards him so often, and smile her ghastly smile.

*   *   *

For the next two weeks Edward spent his days at Rudleigh House, finding out everything he could about the firm's finances. It was soon obvious that the business was less profitable than it should have been, but he was careful not to make critical remarks which might upset Miss Unwin. Although she complained from time to time that she was unable to get on with her regular chores, she clearly enjoyed her role as teacher, insisting always that he should sit beside her while she explained the accounts to him, and breathing her admiration at his pertinent questions as he analysed the costs, and worked out profit percentages, and gradually gained an overall view of how the business was run. 'Oh, you're so clever, Mr Harcourt!' she would say, smiling toothily at him.

And then he had a moment of compassion for her. Poor lady—she had a good brain, but that might be more of a hindrance than a help in attracting a husband, and with her looks, and her age, she must feel well and truly condemned to an unwanted spinsterhood. Stuck here, in the middle of nowhere, with few chances of meeting eligible young men of her own class, no wonder she was attempting to engage his interest.

He thought of Jack's warnings, which he had pooh-poohed. He grinned to himself. Maybe Jack was right, after all. And then his smile faded. The thought of Beatrice Unwin setting her sights on him as a marriageable target

127

was amusing indeed, but she could land him in a very embarrassing situation, and he would have to take care that she had little opportunity to do so. Well, he thought, grinning again, it certainly added a little spice to the situation.

5

When Edward arrived home one evening, a letter from his mother was waiting. It was brief. 'My darling Edward, I should welcome a visit from you as soon as possible, if your employer will consent to release you for a few days. I wish to discuss with you a matter of great importance. In haste, but with great affection, your loving Mama.'

The only matter of considerable importance that it could possibly be, Edward thought, was that somehow she had found out that he knew about his parentage. Perhaps Richard had told her.

He ate his supper, and then returned to Rudleigh House, hoping that Mr Chetwynd would be willing to see him.

'Couldn't it wait until the morning, Edward? We are just about to dine,' Chetwynd said.

'I won't keep you long, sir.' He explained about his mother's letter. 'I thought perhaps I could kill two birds with one stone, sir, and take the opportunity to call on some of our customers, which in any case is something that I should now like to do.'

'As a salesman, you mean?'

'No, sir.' He smiled. 'I shall say that I am considering taking employment which you have offered, and want some advice as to whether yours is a suitable business for an ambitious young man.'

Briefly, Mr Chetwynd looked angry. Then he laughed. 'An impertinent young man, I would say.'

'I think I might pick up far more useful information that way about what our customers really think of us.'

Chetwynd pondered. 'Very well,' he said at last. 'You may go. But I do not expect you to be away for longer than a week in total. If your family situation should require your presence for a longer period, you will send me a telegram. It must be quite clear, however, that I may not in that case be able to keep your job open for you.'

'I understand, sir.'

'And another thing—you will pay all your own expenses.'

*   *   *

When he arrived in Brentfield, Edward was afflicted, as always when he came home, by a sense of nostalgia. The village was so pretty with its higgledy-piggledy thatched cottages and the green, and the old bridge across the gently-flowing river. Shropshire was charming, and its old black and white houses picturesque, but this part of Essex would always have the special feel of home to him.

Sarah was pleased to see him, in a somewhat off-hand way, as though it were no more than a casual visit.

'What is it you want to talk about, Mama?' he asked, with some apprehension.

'It can wait until after dinner.'

She asked about his employment and listened, at first with distracted interest, but later, as she heard the enthusiasm in his voice, with more attention, and even, he thought, approval.

'And how's the mill?' he asked, wondering if that could, after all, be what she wanted to discuss. 'Are you thinking of making some changes?'

'Certainly not. Please don't start on that again, Edward. I know what is best for Harcourt's.'

As they sat in the drawing-room drinking their after-dinner coffee, Edward tried again. 'Why did you send for me, Mama?'

'I wanted to see you. There seemed to be no possibility that you would ever come here unless I sent for you. So I did. I am your mother, Edward, and I expect you to visit me from time to time.'

'Do you mean that there's nothing to discuss?'

'Nothing special. But I wanted to hear how you were getting on.'

'Really Mama! I had to beg Mr Chetwynd to let me come.' He laughed in exasperation. 'Oh, it's too bad of you.'

'Oh, Edward, now you're spoiling everything. I thought you'd be glad to be home again.'

'I am. But I shall leave first thing in the morning.'

'You will do no such thing. Apart from anything else, I thought you would like to go to Wensham while you're here.'

'To Wensham?'

'Yes. I'm sure your uncle will be pleased to see you.'

Then she did not know. 'I don't think so, Mama,' he said carefully. 'We did not part on the best of terms.'

'Really? He didn't tell me. What was it all about?'

'Just a row. I'd rather not go into it now.'

'Oh, Edward!' she said. 'You quarrel so easily. You really must control your temper.'

It was unjust, but he merely smiled at her.

'Anyway, you can't leave tomorrow,' she continued. 'I'm giving a dinner party in the evening. I've asked the Ashtons—young Roderick is home on leave, so there'll be four of them—and Mr Prideau and Miss Ouvray. I arranged it specially for you, Edward.'

Edward had often thought about Miss Ouvray since their last meeting. He could not really remember what she looked like—dark hair and brown eyes, yes, but whenever he tried to summon up a complete picture, it would dissolve into a cloudy vagueness—but he could recall every word of the short conversation they had had at the Leroys' house. If he indicated his interest to his mother he would never hear the last of it, so he tried to look indifferent, and only with apparent reluctance allowed himself finally to be persuaded to stay another night in Brentfield.

In the morning, Edward suggested tentatively that he might accompany Sarah to the mill, if she were intending to spend the day there.

'Of course I shall spend the day there!' she flared at him. 'I have to. There is no one else to run the mill, no one to assist me. As for coming with me, we have decided that issue once and for all—at least, I thought we had, and since it is quite clear that you are determined on a career with Mr Chetwynd, then it is completely pointless for you to accompany me now. You would only be in the way.'

Edward was taken aback by the bitterness of her tone. 'Very well, Mama,' he said, trying again to avoid a quarrel. 'I'll find something to occupy myself with. I might even go into Great Luckton. There's a big ironmonger's there

—one of Mr Chetwynd's better customers, I think.'

It turned out to be a strange morning, both frustrating and interesting. Since a visit to the shop would take comparatively little time, he decided not to hurry himself, and did not reach Great Luckton until nearly twelve. The shop was empty of customers. Behind the counter was a lad of perhaps eighteen, wearing an apron several sizes too big for him. His face looked well-scrubbed, and his hair was neatly combed. 'Morning, sir,' he said, and grinned.

'Tell me, do you stock any of Chetwynd's products—cast iron, that is?'

The lad looked at him quizzically. 'You a traveller?'

'No,' said Edward hastily. 'No. But I am particularly interested in cast iron from Chetwynd's.'

The boy looked doubtful. 'There's that lot, over there,' he said, pointing to a display of grates, 'and then we got all sorts of other things in cast iron. But where they come from . . . I know the prices, 'cause they're marked on. You'll 'ave to arst Mr Jarvis.'

'Is he available?'

'No, sir. 'E's not 'ere.'

'Do you know which of these goods sell the best?'

'Not really, sir. I ain't been 'ere no more 'n a couple o' weeks. I been concentrating on nails, sir. Sixty-three kinds of nails we keeps—that's a lot to remember, sir.'

'When will Mr Jarvis be back?'

'Not till termorrer, sir. Only just missed 'im, you did. 'E left not five minutes afore you come in.'

Annoyed with himself for having dallied half the morning away, making this a useless expedition, Edward asked pointedly, 'Does he often leave the shop without anyone competent to run it?'

The boy smiled and said amicably, 'Lor' bless you, no, sir. 'E ain't never done it afore, an' I don't suppose 'e'll do it again. But, you see, sir, 'e knows three things: 'e knows I can count, so's I'll get the right money, and give the right change. 'E knows I won't run off with none of it. And 'e knows I'll remember any messages what the customers give me, and'll pass 'em on to 'im. Nails is one thing, messages is another—much easier to remember, they are. So if you'd like to leave me your name, sir, I'll see as Mr Jarvis 'ears all about it.'

His pleasant manner restored Edward's good humour. 'What's your name?' he asked.

'Beeson, sir.'

'Well, Beeson, you may tell Mr Jarvis that Mr Harcourt called—Mr Harcourt from Brentfield.' It might be worth letting the ironmonger think that his call had some connection with the mill. 'Tell him I shall come again tomorrow morning.' He took a threepenny bit out of his pocket, and put it on the counter. 'However, I should prefer it if you would make no mention of my enquiries today. I am sure I can trust to your discretion.'

The boy looked at the threepenny piece, and frowned. 'Well, there you puts me in what you might call a quandairy, sir.' He scratched his head. 'On the one 'and, the customer's always right, Mr Jarvis says, so I ought to do like what you say. On the other 'and, 'e expects me to tell 'im everything what 'appens in the shop—everything. I wouldn't mind taking thruppence off o' you, sir, but it's Mr Jarvis what pays me wages every week.' He smiled, rather shyly this time.

'A nasty dilemma, Beeson,' Edward said, with grave humour. 'You are quite right—your prime loyalty belongs to your employer, and I shall immediately withdraw the cause of any temptation to betray him.' He picked up the threepence, aware of a tinge of disappointment in the lad's eyes. 'Tell Mr Jarvis everything. Will he be here at nine o'clock?'

'Sure to be, sir.'

'I shall call then.' Edward went to the shop door, the boy following and bowing him out. On the pavement outside the shop, Edward stopped and turned. 'Here! Not a bribe—just a tip!' He tossed the coin to the boy.

Beeson caught it deftly, and touched his forelock in gratitude. 'Ta very much, Mr 'Arcourt! I'll exercise me discretion, sir.'

Edward laughed to himself as he walked away. It had been a wasted morning, and yet . . . He took out his pocket watch. Almost half past twelve. He decided to treat himself to a meal at The Green Man, where there was usually a good roast joint to be had. As he ate, he thought again of young Beeson. He was amusing, and he liked him, and maybe Mr Jarvis was not after all such a fool to leave him in

133

charge of the shop. He remained in high spirits for the rest of the day, deciding to forgive his mother for her absurd summons, and to enjoy the dinner party.

* * *

The guests arrived promptly and all greeted Edward warmly. He had eyes only for Miss Ouvray, who looked entrancing, he thought, in a gown of white silk with a bodice of crimson velvet.

When sherry had been served, Mr Prideau said, 'I am eager to hear, young man, what you have been doing. Your mother tells me you are working in a foundry. You surely do not intend making a career in cast iron.'

'I am not sure, sir, but I find it very interesting.'

'Do tell us all about it,' Mrs Ashton chimed in. 'Why, in the carriage as we came here, Edith was saying how much she longed to hear your news.'

Edward smiled. 'I am quite tongue-tied,' he said. 'I had not expected such eagerness for what is really a very dull story.'

'I am sure it is not,' said Miss Ouvray.

He began to talk, and perhaps because everything he said was intended for Alice Ouvray alone, the elated mood which had begun in Great Luckton that morning stayed with him and grew, and he spoke with such enthusiasm and wit that they listened with genuine pleasure, laughing often. His description of the witch-like Mrs Woodham was so alarming that Miss Ashton, in mock horror, gave a series of little shrieks.

'What did she give you for your luncheon each day?' Mrs Ashton asked.

'Bread and cheese mostly—but home-baked bread and good strong cheese with a bite to it.'

'And is that what your fellow workmen had?'

'Some brought sandwiches. Imagine slices an inch thick. Doorsteps are nothing to them.'

'And what would be in the sandwich?'

'Cast iron, ma'am.' Edward answered gravely and with such apparent sincerity that for a moment they all seemed to accept the absurdity before laughing again.

Sarah watched her son with pleasurable surprise. As

134

they went into dinner, she whispered to him, 'What has happened to you, Edward? I have never known you in such sparkling form.'

'I don't know, Mama, but I'm sure I inherited it from you.'

She smiled again, and took Mr Prideau's arm and went into the dining-room.

Edward was delighted to be sitting next to Alice Ouvray. She told him that she was now running her grandfather's household for him. 'Do you enjoy that?' he asked.

'Yes. Grandpapa has a beautiful house, and I enjoy being its mistress.'

'He should be very grateful.'

'Oh, he is.' She lowered her voice. 'In fact, he worries constantly that I am doing too much.' She gave a little laugh. 'Mind you, he still wants me to do it all, but he keeps telling me that I should get out more and meet young people.'

'But surely you have many friends of your own age, Miss Ouvray.'

'Of course, but Grandpapa—'

'Grandpapa is hoping that you will find yourself a husband,' Edward whispered, feeling that he should run the risk of offending her. Surely she would recognise that he was trying to find out only whether or not her heart already belonged to someone else.

'That is a most indiscreet remark, Mr Harcourt,' she told him sternly. 'I am sure that such an idea has never entered his head.' Then she smiled. 'Neither has it entered my own.'

'I am very glad to hear that, Miss Ouvray,' Edward said.

She blushed, but was saved from replying, for at that point Sarah called the ladies to leave the gentlemen to their port and cigars.

Mr Prideau began a long political argument with Mr Ashton, and Edward was left to entertain Roderick Ashton, a young Guards officer, who appeared to be possessed of remarkably little brain.

Edward was not really listening to him. 'Alice,' he said to himself. 'Alice.' What a delightful name it was.

'I say, did I say something witty?' Roderick Ashton asked.

135

'Er . . .'

'You were smiling, old chap. Demned if you weren't smiling.'

'Was I? Then you *must* have said something witty, mustn't you?'

'What was it?'

Edward hesitated. 'Awfully sorry—it's gone right out of my head.'

'Oh, I say, that's a pity. Don't think I've ever said anything witty before. Would have been nice to remember, what?' Roderick went into the series of convulsive brays that passed with him for laughter.

Soon after, the gentlemen joined the ladies, the older people began to play whist, and the four younger ones sat together at the opposite end of the large sitting-room.

'Shall we have some music?' Edward asked. 'Miss Ouvray, would you play for us?'

'Oh, no music, please,' Edith Ashton said. 'No offence to you, Alice dear, but I get so tired of hearing the same pieces over and over.'

Alice caught Edward's glance, and her right eyelid flickered in the hint of a wink. 'Oh, but I have just learned several new pieces,' she said.

'Oh, now I've offended you,' Miss Ashton wailed.

'Not at all. I was teasing you. I quite agree with you. No music.'

'Then let us just talk,' Miss Ashton said. 'Mr Harcourt, you have so many splendid tales to tell.'

'I think I have exhausted my repertoire, Miss Ashton. No, wait. Let me tell you the story of the strange encounter that I had today.' And he related his conversation with the young lad in Mr Jarvis' ironmongery.

When he had finished, he saw that both the Ashtons were looking puzzled.

'If you will forgive me for saying so, Mr Harcourt,' Miss Ashton said, 'I cannot understand how you could have allowed him to talk to you in that fashion. A common tradesman.'

'Impertinent, by Jove!' her brother said.

'Alas,' said Edward, 'then I have failed entirely to convey to you the flavour of the encounter.'

'I think not,' said Miss Ouvray. 'He sounded amusing

and, above all, honest, and that quality seemed to me to remove all possible offence from his remarks.'

'That is exactly it, Miss Ouvray,' Edward said. 'I did not think him in the least impertinent, and indeed look forward to seeing him again when I return to Great Luckton tomorrow.' She was so intelligent, he thought, and her perceptions and likes and dislikes coincided with his to perfection.

'He is your inferior,' Miss Ashton said, 'and should know his place. He had no right to speak his mind with such familiarity. Besides, the boy is a fool—you might well have reported his insolence, and that could have cost him his job.'

'Since you and I were not there, Miss Ashton, we would surely both be wiser to make no judgement,' Alice Ouvray said, gently. 'For my part, I am willing to accept Mr Harcourt's assessment.'

'Oh, indeed, and so am I,' Miss Ashton said hastily, in some embarrassment. 'I did not mean . . . Oh, Mr Harcourt . . . !'

'Of course you did not mean it. And I am sure that Mr Harcourt will forgive me if I change the conversation, because I am eager to hear all about your visit to London. Last week, was it not?'

Miss Ashton seized the opportunity eagerly, and as she prattled away, Edward caught Miss Ouvray's eye, and thought he saw in her expression a smile of complicity. She had been very clever, he thought, to put Miss Ashton so neatly in her place, and then to give her a chance to redeem herself and become the centre of their attention.

He kept stealing little glances at Alice Ouvray, noting to himself the enchanting curve of her neck, the delicate outline of her lips, the liveliness of her eyes, in which he could read both compassion and laughter. It was her eyes that you noticed first, he thought, not just because they were so bright, but because when she fastened them upon you, you felt that you were the only person in the world who mattered to her. Was that just a trick? No, he was sure it was genuine—she was truly interested in other people. And he knew, with all the certainty of his instincts, that she was especially interested in him.

Suddenly, he found himself thinking of Mary, comparing

137

Alice with her. That had just been calf love, he told himself—and immediately his heart cried out, 'No!' It had been a deep, abiding and adult passion. But why think of Mary? Why think of love? He had not fallen in love with Alice Ouvray, and had no intention of doing so. He was attracted to her, and it would be very pleasant to see her again, and . . . For a moment he was lost in fantasy, imagining the touch and taste of her lips, the entrancing curves of her breasts and hips, the joy of caressing her naked body.

That was lust, not love. He banished the thoughts, and glanced at her again. She turned her head, her eyes meeting his, and blushed and lowered her gaze, but not before he had seen and read the clearest of messages in her look. Somehow he would have to arrange to see her again. Perhaps he could stay another two or three days at Brentfield, even if it meant visiting more customers in East Anglia than he had intended, and fewer in London.

Miss Ashton was still monopolising the conversation. He heard little of what she said, but contrived to smile and nod in what appeared to be the right places.

As the guests were preparing to leave, he seized an opportunity when Miss Ouvray was standing momentarily on her own. 'I shall be staying in the neighbourhood for a day or two longer, Miss Ouvray. May I call upon you?'

'Certainly not,' she whispered back, smiling, 'but there is every reason for you to call on Grandpapa. He has told me that he has not abandoned hope of persuading you to join Prideau's. And I am sure that what he has heard this evening has only increased his interest.'

As soon as the guests had all gone, Edward feigned tiredness and said that he would go straight to bed. He had no wish for a long heart-to-heart talk with his mother. He was sure that Sarah had noticed his interest in Alice Ouvray.

Sarah looked at him as he left the room, and smiled. It really had been a most successful evening. He had been quite brilliant, which was not only unexpected, but very gratifying since both Mr Prideau and the Ashtons had complimented her on having such a handsome, intelligent and charming son. And she and Mr Prideau had won decisively at whist, and he had had no opportunity to pester her with his ever-repeated suggestions of buying-out or merging.

She rose and poured herself a large glass of brandy. Yes, a delightful evening. And, though she had not been able to keep too close an eye on the young people, she was almost certain that Edward was developing an interest in Edith Ashton. Whenever she had glanced across, Miss Ashton had seemed to be talking, and Edward had been looking at her with the sort of foolish smile on his face that men put on when they have fallen in love and are worshipping at the shrine of the adored. Edith would be much more satisfactory than Alice Ouvray, Sarah thought—an ideal bride for him —well-to-do, not ill-favoured, and stupid enough to be no match for herself.

She refilled her glass. The first lot had not tasted of much—or was it that she had drunk it almost absent-mindedly while thinking about Edward? She took another mouthful, and swallowed slowly, making sure that her tastebuds had time to register the full flavour.

'I shall be a model mother-in-law,' she said aloud. 'I shall start by being sweetness itself. Once the girl has been won over, and is eating out of my hand, we shall see what we shall see. Oh, yes, Edward, my darling, your mother will win yet.'

A trifle unsteadily, she put the empty glass down, and went up to bed.

*   *   *

Mr Jarvis was delighted to see Edward. 'Very pleased to make your acquaintance, Mr Harcourt. Young Beeson told me you called yesterday. Sorry I missed you.'

'He's a bright lad.'

'Beeson? All right, I suppose. Always dropping things. But he tries. Now, what can I do for you, Mr Harcourt?'

Edward told him the story about considering employment with Chetwynd's.

'But you're from Harcourt's Mill, aren't you?'

'Yes. But I do not work there.'

'Ah. I see.' Jarvis was plainly puzzled, but when Edward did not volunteer any more information, he said, 'Ah. Well, you'd be all right with Mr Chetwynd. A gent—yes, a gent.

139

One of the old school. Mind you, the firm's a bit stick-in-the-mud. Yes, a bit stick-in-the-mud, I'd say.'

'Do you sell many of their products?'

'A fair number. I'd sell more, probably, if I had a traveller calling on me regularly. Now, Ironbridge—they're always in here, and I give 'em my order, and the goods come quickly. With Chetwynd's I have to post the order, and then the delivery's very slow. Yes, very slow. Of course, everything has to come from Bristol.'

'Does no one ever call on you?'

'Oh, Mr Chetwynd himself comes once in a blue moon. That's the way it was always done in my father's time. The only person who ever came was the owner, or one of the partners. I'm always pleased to see Mr Chetwynd, very pleased, but times are changing, Mr Harcourt. You can't do business that way nowadays. Chetwynd's need waking up, Mr Harcourt—that's what they need.'

'What about quality?'

'Not bad. Not bad. And the prices are reasonable. Bit more expensive than some, but not bad. Not bad.'

At that moment, Beeson appeared from the back of the shop. ''Allo, Mr 'Arcourt. I give Mr Jarvis your message. "Mr 'Arcourt from 'Arcourt's Mill," I says. "Coming back termorrer," I says. That were all, weren't it?'

'That'll do, Beeson,' Mr Jarvis said. 'You mind your manners, and get on with filling the nail boxes.'

'Yes, sir, Mr Jarvis.' He disappeared again.

'Cheeky young devil,' Jarvis said, without anger. 'Sorry, Mr Harcourt. Where were we?'

'I think you've told me most of what I want to know. Which of Chetwynd's lines sells best?'

'Oh, their figurines. They're different, you see. Nothing quite like it from their competitors, if you follow me. I always try to keep some of them in stock, but, like I say, it isn't always easy when the delivery's so slow. Those animals they make—very droll. Yes, very droll.'

'And what about the other items in their catalogue? A bit too ordinary, perhaps?'

'You might say that. Yes, a bit on the ordinary side. Nothing to make you stop and look, you might say. That's what the public wants—something new. Always something new.' He sighed and shook his head. 'Still, I reckon you'd

140

be all right working there. What job are you after with them, if you don't mind my asking?'

'Oh. Oh, I'm not sure. Something in the office.'

'Ah. Well, that's where they need bucking up, if you ask me.'

'Yes, I see. Well, thank you very much, Mr Jarvis. You've been very helpful.'

'Not at all, sir. Always pleased to oblige.'

*   *   *

As he sat in the train on the way back to Shropshire, Edward worked on the report that he intended to make to Mr Chetwynd. Although his knowledge might still be no more than superficial, he felt capable of presenting a useful statement. During the time that he had spent with Miss Unwin, he had discovered a great deal about the business, and his visits to retailers during the past week had been very instructive. Most of what he had to say was already in his mind, and the only difficulty was that thoughts of Alice Ouvray kept coming between him and his work.

He had spent a very pleasant evening at the large house in Franton. Mr Prideau had given his opinion that Edward was foolish not to accept his offer of employment, but had not pressed the point, and after dinner had had the good sense to drop off to sleep, leaving Edward to talk happily to Miss Ouvray. They laughed a great deal, and were serious, too, and the longer they talked, the more he admired her. She was well-read, and well-informed, and was ready, in amicable argument, to allow herself to be convinced by him on some matters and to stick resolutely to her guns in others. Inevitably, they discussed Miss Ashton, and her discomfiture.

'I suppose it is unfair to laugh,' Edward said.

'No, because she is a bigot, and bigots deserve to be scorned. Miss Ashton has no tolerance. I often think that tolerance is the quality I most admire—tolerance of the points of view and beliefs of others.'

'Bigots have points of view.'

'No, one only. They're intolerant of all ideas other than their own.'

'So you are tolerant of anything but intolerance.'

141

'And a few other things like cruelty and vice. But even those, I try to remind myself, are relative. What is cruel to us may not be to another culture in some other part of the world, and before we condemn anyone, we have to be sure that he has had the opportunity of acquiring the high moral standards by which we judge him.' She laughed nervously. 'How terrible of me to burden you with these opinions. Who is being pompous now?'

'Certainly not you, Miss Ouvray.' He was tempted to say that he could listen to her views all day, because he admired her independence of thought, and because he agreed with her, and especially because he thought her enchanting. 'I am flattered that you should confide in me.'

'I did not mean to become so solemn, Mr Harcourt. Tell me, have you seen that young man again—what was his name?—Beezer?'

'Beeson. Not to speak to. I saw Mr Jarvis.'

'And did you learn what you wanted from him?'

'Yes. And from others. I've been trying to get some idea of the general trade opinion about Chetwynd's.'

'And what have you discovered? Or is it secret?'

'I doubt it would interest you, Miss Ouvray.'

Anger flashed in her eyes. 'Because I'm a woman, you mean, and therefore extremely limited in intelligence!'

Edward held up a hand, a half-smile on his lips. 'I apologise, Miss Ouvray, I apologise. I assure you that I said that only because I thought the subject would bore you. The problems of a small foundry are not exactly exciting.'

'That depends.'

'On what?'

'On who is speaking of them, Mr Harcourt. Perhaps you do not realise it, but when you talk of your business, your enthusiasm for it becomes contagious. You have found your niche in cast iron, have you not?'

'I suppose so. I have been fascinated by it since the first day I stepped into the foundry. It is an interesting process—so simple, and yet so complex. Yes, indeed I am enthusiastic about it.'

'So pray continue. Have you been to many shops?'

'I have covered about a dozen retailers in the last two days. And I shall go to more, mostly in London, on my way back to Shropshire.'

'And is there a consensus of opinion so far?'

'Indeed. They all agree that the quality is good, though some think our prices are a little high, but there are two main complaints: that our sales and delivery methods are old-fashioned; and, perhaps the most important, that our designs are not original enough.'

'So you will be telling Mr Chetwynd that he needs new designers?'

'That among other things.'

'And how will he react?'

Edward laughed. 'I don't think he'll like it at all. His carvers, who prepare the patterns from which the castings are made, have been with the firm since before he began to work in it himself. No doubt he'll ask me where he is to find new designers, and I can't answer that.'

At that moment Mr Prideau awoke, and launched into a monologue about the iniquities of the government, and the threat to employers in the increasing activities of trades unionists, and the appalling fecklessness of the younger generation. Soon after, it was time for Edward to leave to go to his hotel. Mr Prideau, complaining of his gout, asked forgiveness for not coming to the front door to see him off, which delighted Edward, for it meant that he would, after all, have the opportunity of exchanging a few further words with Miss Ouvray.

He thanked her warmly for her hospitality, and then said, 'May I write to you, Miss Ouvray?'

She smiled. 'I should welcome it, Mr Harcourt.'

'And may I presume to call you Alice?'

She blushed, and dropped her head. 'If you wish.'

'And my name is Edward.'

'Yes.' She looked up, and the brown eyes were twinkling at him. 'I was aware of that.'

Greatly daring, he took her hand and kissed it. 'Goodbye, Alice.'

'Goodbye, Edward.' She waved as he walked quickly down the drive.

*　　　*　　　*

On his way to London from Essex, Edward had thought

happily of the previous few days. He should really have been worrying about his mother, he supposed, but she obviously did not welcome or seem to need his concern. Absurd though her summons had been, he was glad now that she had sent it, and that he had been persuaded to stay for the dinner party. Alice! He had smiled to himself, thinking how pretty and elegant she was, and how genuine her interest had seemed in all that he had told her about Chetwynd's. And what a delightful sense of humour she had!

Suddenly, he had felt guilty. He had really done little work since leaving Rudleigh. Originally, it had been his intention to stay with the Bunns while he was in London, but he had decided instead to put up in a hotel and spend the rest of the week visiting as many ironmongers as possible, without anything to distract him, apart from calling on Jack, so that he could tell Mr Chetwynd about him.

Now, in the train that was carrying him back to Shropshire, he considered that his absence from the works could truly be justified. Altogether, he had called on nearly fifty retailers, and had built up a substantial dossier of their opinions of Chetwynd's.

He put his notes away, and gave himself up to thoughts of Alice Ouvray. And suddenly, as he recalled their long conversation for the hundredth time, the answer to one of his problems came to him. Of course! Why had he not thought of that before? He would put it to Mr Chetwynd, who surely would agree.

*   *   *

Arriving back in Rudleigh, he went straight to the foundry, knowing that Mr Chetwynd would be there.

'Ah, the wanderer returns,' Chetwynd wheezed. 'I trust you managed to solve your family problems.'

'Yes, sir. Thank you.'

'And did you visit many of our customers?'

'Quite a number, sir. And I saw Jack, and he sent his kind regards.'

'How is he?'

Thomas Yardman came up, touching his forelock.

144

'Begging your pardon, sir, I'd like you to look at this lot of pig iron. Looks poor quality to me, sir.'

'Don't go away, my boy,' Chetwynd said to Edward, hauling himself with difficulty out of his chair. 'I want to hear about Jack.'

As he limped away, Edward thought that he could hardly report that Jack had spent most of their brief time together in mockery of his family. 'How's the old man?' he had asked. 'As much the autocrat as ever? Knows what's best for everybody, don't he?' And he had made fun of his stepmother, imitating her little-girl voice. 'And what about the man-eating Beatrice? What a fright, eh?'

'She's very clever,' Edward replied. 'She keeps your father's accounts meticulously.'

'Ah, you're smitten, I can tell,' Jack laughed. 'Watch out, Edward, old boy! She'll get her hooks into you, and then, poor fellow, you'd be my stepbrother-in-law!'

Leaving the Albany, Edward had gone, after all, to the Bunns, who had been far more interested than Jack to hear of all that he had been doing.

He asked whether they had news of Mary.

'Yes,' Frances said. 'That visit of yours, Edward, seems to have had strange results. I gather that my sister-in-law found out that you had come to Wensham, and was furious. It has turned her even more strongly against you, I fear. But as far as Mary is concerned, her health is much improved, and seeing you apparently finally made her mind up for her. My brother says that she went to an Anglican convent near Norwich, determined to enter and to become a nun, and then . . . Wait a minute, I have his letter here.'

Frances found the letter, and began to read. 'He says, "I understand that the Mother Superior said she believed Mary was trying to escape from the world, and that she should seek some other form of service. Mary was heart-broken. For three days she stayed in her room, praying, I believe, but when she came back to us, she said she had come to see that the Mother Superior was right, and sought my permission to become a nurse. She has written to the Norwich hospital, asking if she may join the staff."'

Frances folded the letter and put it back in its envelope. 'I have since had another letter—Mary seems to be happy in

145

the work, and much more like her old self. So your visit has had both good and bad effects.'

Mr Chetwynd's return dragged Edward back to the present. He seemed to have forgotten about Jack. 'Those damned people at Ironbridge,' he grumbled, 'trying to foist us off with third grade iron. I'll have a word or two to say to them about that.' He turned to Edward. 'I'd like to hear about your visits to our customers, but it will have to wait a bit. I've no time today.'

'By tomorrow, sir, I hope to be able to give you a complete report on the business as a whole.'

'Do you, indeed?'

'There's just one more bit of information I need from Miss Unwin, and I can get that in the morning.'

'H'm. You think you know it all already, do you?'

Edward smiled. 'No, sir. But I can at least give you my preliminary views.'

'I shall be away tomorrow until the evening, but you can come to dinner then, and afterwards I'll listen to what you have to say.'

*   *   *

Miss Unwin greeted Edward with a toothy smile, and held out her hand to him. 'Oh, Mr Harcourt,' she cried, 'I am so delighted to see you again. Everything has been at sixes and sevens since you left. I have been in such a state.' Her face was flushed, and she seemed to be in an excitable mood.

'Why, what has happened?'

'What has *not* happened? The figures won't balance, and a number of invoices got muddled up, and altogether I have never known such a time. Now that you're here, perhaps you can help me to sort it all out. I really am pleased to see you, Mr Harcourt. We've missed you, haven't we, Fido?' She bent to pat her little dog, flashing Edward coquettish looks. She straightened up. 'Have you had a good journey?'

'Yes, thank you. It is kind of you to ask.'

'I have thought of you so much. I trust that you thought of *us* now and then.' She fluttered her eyelashes at him.

For reply, Edward simply smiled. Her behaviour could only be described as flirtatious. Had his absence really made her heart grow fonder? It was an alarming thought. 'I

146

saw your stepbrother,' he said, hoping to change the direction of the conversation, 'and we talked of you.'

The foolish smile left her face. 'Nothing good, I'll be bound, if Jack had anything to do with it. No doubt he maligned me as usual. He has a wicked tongue, Mr Harcourt, wicked. But let us not talk of him. We have work to do.' Suddenly she turned back to him, and spoke almost wildly. 'No, I must tell you. I must speak to someone—I *must*. When my mother told me that she was to marry Mr Chetwynd, my heart was filled with happiness, not only for her, but because the thought of having a brother—a stepbrother, that is—gave me great joy. But from the very start he has tormented me.' Tears formed in her eyes. 'And I have done nothing to incur his displeasure, I assure you. I have tried my best, my very best, to be a loving sister to him.' She began to sob.

Fido, the Pekinese, who had been lying in a corner of the room, came over to his mistress, yapping and jumping up at her.

Edward watched in consternation, wishing he had not mentioned Jack. This was even worse than the flirtation. 'But Jack spoke of you with great affection,' he said, hoping that he sounded convincing.

'It is kind of you to say so,' she said jerkily, between sobs, 'but, alas, I cannot find it in my heart to believe you. I know Jack only too well, as his father does, too.' For a few moments, she struggled to overcome her emotion. Then she whispered, 'Oh, pray forgive this exhibition of feminine weakness, Mr Harcourt.' With her fingers, she wiped the tears from her eyes. 'I would not have exposed you to it were it not that you are so understanding, so gentlemanly. Indiscreet though it may be, I feel I can open my heart to you. We are friends, are we not, Mr Harcourt? Good friends.'

'Why, yes, I am sure we are.'

She smiled at him a little tremulously. 'May I . . . ? Have you a handkerchief that you could lend me?'

'Of course.'

As he passed the handkerchief to her, she seized his hand. 'Such a fine hand you have, Mr Harcourt—so strong, so manly.' To his horror, she suddenly pressed his fingers to her cheek, then kissed them. Her cheeks flaming, she dropped his hand, and turned away. 'Oh, I do not know what I am saying! I do not know what I am doing! What will you think of me?' She blew her nose loudly and, sobbing, ran to the door. 'I must . . . I must compose myself. Please wait. I shall not be long.'

Edward wondered what to do. The whole scene had been embarrassing in the extreme. She was obviously in a highly emotional state—almost unbalanced. He remembered Jack saying that she had once had a mental disturbance of some kind. First his mother, and now Miss Unwin—was he to be plagued with irrational women?

A quarter of an hour passed, and he had just decided to leave, when Miss Unwin reappeared, carrying Fido. Her eyes were red-rimmed, but she held her head high. She crossed to the corner of the room, put the dog down, and turned to Edward. 'I ask your forgiveness, Mr Harcourt.' Her voice was strained, and she was speaking in almost a monotone. 'I was not myself. And I beg you to forget what transpired just now.'

'It is already forgotten, Miss Unwin.'

'Thank you. Now, may I ask you to check these figures for me? Normally it is child's play to me, but for some reason I just have not been able to get them right, however often I go over them.'

Edward spent the next hour adding up columns of figures. The task was not made easier by Miss Unwin hovering over him, darting forward every now and then to explain, for the most part unnecessarily, various entries in the ledger. She seemed irritable, but perhaps, he thought, it was a mask for her continuing embarrassment. Despite her interruptions, before long he had found the errors and managed to make all the figures agree. He pointed out to her, without any hint of criticism, where she had gone wrong.

'Oh, what a fool!' she said, glaring at him. 'How stupid!' The mistakes might have been his, rather than her own. When he had finished, she said, perfunctorily, 'I am glad that is out of the way. Thank you.' Then she went on, still in an apparently offhand way, 'Now, I am sure that you must have questions for me, following your trip.'

Edward was not at all certain that this was a good time to try to obtain useful information from her. 'Well,' he said, doubtfully, 'I would like to check again on those customer accounts which have been outstanding for more than three months, together with a note of the date on which statements were sent. But if you would prefer—'

'May I ask why you require that information?' she asked stiffly.

'A number of the retailers on whom I called seemed to regard us as somewhat lax in the collection of moneys due to them.'

'Indeed? As I seem to remember telling you when you first asked about the statements, ten days or so ago, I send them out as and when necessary, and my stepfather has never complained.'

'I have no intention of questioning your ability, Miss Unwin.' He smiled at her in a conciliatory way. 'It is simply that I did not make a note at the time of how many overdue accounts we have, that is all.'

'It will take me a long time to extract all the relevant figures. Are you sure this information is essential?'

'Perhaps I could do it myself.'

'Certainly not! Since you insist, I will do my best to produce the figures quickly. But you may prefer to come back later.'

'I thought perhaps I might be able to offer you some assistance.'

In contrast with her previous attitude, the look she shot him seemed to be one of strong dislike. 'I am quite capable of preparing the figures on my own. If you do not wish to go, then you may sit and wait.'

It was incredible, Edward thought. One minute she was leering at him sentimentally, the next she was wildly amorous, and now there was anger. Was that because she had humiliated herself in front of him?

Miss Unwin turned the pages of one of her ledgers impatiently, now and then noting a name and an amount in slashing strokes of her pen. When she had finished going through that ledger, she shut it, lifted it and banged it down on the side of her desk. The Pekinese awoke at the sound and began yapping. 'Quiet, Fido!' Miss Unwin shouted, with such ferocity that the dog was startled into silence.

The list was as long as Edward had feared, and the

149

lengthier it became, the more obvious was her annoyance. Finally, she slammed the last ledger shut, gathered together the lists she had made, and stood up. 'Here you are then, but I deliver these details to you under protest. Apart from anything else, you should know that immediately after you left, I prepared and despatched statements to all customers who owe us money. I have been a slave this past week.'

'I am sorry, Miss Unwin. And I should like to assure you again that I am making no imputations against your efficiency.'

'Oh, spare me these protestations! Here is your list.'

Edward rose. Miss Unwin came out from behind her desk towards him, and at that moment, for some inexplicable canine reason and with unaccustomed swiftness, Fido ran across her path. She tripped and fell against Edward, her outstretched hands thudding into his belly. Winded, he fell back on the floor, and Miss Unwin landed on top of him. She made no effort to get up, but began laughing and crying hysterically. Fido circled them, yapping furiously.

'Are you all right?' Edward panted. 'If you could just move off me.'

But Miss Unwin made no attempt to move. Edward was reluctant to lay his hands on her, but had to do so to free himself. As he grasped her, Fido, yapping at Edward's leg, decided that the best way of helping his mistress was to bite.

Edward's shout of pain coincided with the arrival in the room of Mrs Chetwynd, who looked in horror at the couple on the floor, gave a little scream and swooned. She had of course been accompanied by Prince, who now joined Fido in frenetic barking.

Edward managed to clamber off the floor, and helped Miss Unwin to her feet. He supposed that he should slap her face to stop the hysterics, but she gave him no chance to do or say anything, and ran from the room. That left Mrs Chetwynd for him to cope with. As he bent over her, Fido snapped at his trousers, while Prince pranced—as well as a very overweight lap-dog can prance—at him. Edward was normally very fond of dogs, and abhorred ill-treatment of animals, but before he could stop himself, he seized Fido and Prince each by the scruff of the neck, and threw

150

them into the corridor outside, quickly shutting the door.

What should he do for Mrs Chetwynd? Pat the wrists, he remembered ... and, of course, smelling salts or sal volatile. He opened the door again—fortunately the two dogs had gone—and shouted for help. He was patting her wrists, when a maid knocked on the open door. 'Salts! Sal volatile!' he shouted at her. The girl gaped at him. 'Go on, girl! Your mistress has fainted.'

He turned back to Mrs Chetwynd, who was regaining consciousness. She made a number of small, incoherent sounds, and then her eyes peered short-sightedly at him. 'Mr Harcourt!' she said, in her little girl's voice. 'Mr Harcourt!'

He helped her to her feet and took her to a chair. 'Are you all right?'

Angrily, she brushed his hand away from her arm. 'Pray do not touch me. Yes, I am all right—but small thanks to you! Where is my daughter?'

'She ran out, Mrs Chetwynd.'

'I am not surprised. You had better explain yourself, Mr Harcourt.'

'It was an accident, ma'am. Miss Unwin fell against me and knocked me over, and she became a trifle ... well, hysterical, if you will pardon the word, and—'

'And what occasioned this ... this *fall*?'

'Miss Unwin tripped—she tripped over her dog.'

'Fido? But how extraordinary!' She obviously did not believe him. 'That does not explain what I saw, Mr Harcourt. I saw you struggling on the floor with my daughter, while she tried to free herself from your embrace, screaming for help, poor child.'

It was so ludicrous an interpretation that he could not help laughing. 'But I assure you, Mrs Chetwynd—'

'It is disgraceful, sir. An abuse of our hospitality, of my husband's generosity! And you have the impertinence to laugh at it!'

'I am sorry. I agree it is not a laughing matter, but on my word of honour, ma'am—' A stinging sensation on his leg reminded Edward of the bite that Fido had inflicted. He drew up his trouser leg. His long underpants had saved him from much harm, but the dog's sharp teeth had broken the skin in a couple of places, and the wounds were bleeding slightly. Damn the little tyke! he thought.

'Serves you right,' said Mrs Chetwynd vindictively. 'Brave little Fido.'

He felt for his handkerchief, and remembered that Miss Unwin had it. He shrugged, and pulled his trouser leg down, hoping that the bite would carry no infection.

At that moment, the maid ran into the room and thrust into Mrs Chetwynd's hands a small, silver-topped bottle of smelling salts.

Mrs Chetwynd sniffed at them, shuddered, and then, standing, drew herself up to her full height. 'I shall speak to my husband, and you will hear from him, I have no doubt. In the meantime, leave this house, sir!'

Edward had no option but to obey. He snatched up the papers that Miss Unwin had been about to hand him, and left the room.

What an absurd, farcical situation it was! He did not know whether to laugh about it, or be angry. He walked slowly back to his cottage. Well, that obviously put paid to his employment in the cast iron business—at least at Chetwynd's. And if Mrs Chetwynd and Miss Unwin had anything to do with it, he would probably be blackballed throughout the industry. Moreover, looking to the immediate future, he would hardly be a welcome guest for dinner that night, so there would be no opportunity of going over his report with Mr Chetwynd. His report! He need not have saved that list of outstanding accounts; there would be no need of a report now. 'Damn that blasted dog!' he thought. 'And those weeping, hysterical women!' He could almost weep himself, at the thought that all his labours were never to come to fruition.

No, dammit, they should not go for naught. He would write his report, and send a note to Mr Chetwynd, excusing himself from dinner, protesting his innocence, and promising to deliver the report at dawn, before leaving Rudleigh for good. 'At dawn' sounded over-sensational, he thought—'at 7 o'clock' would be better. But, no—why not a touch of melodrama? It would go well with the absurdity of the rest of the day's events. And then it occurred to him that if he were no longer employed at Chetwynd's, he need not concern himself with niceties. He could be as critical as he liked in all that he wrote, with no fear of the consequences.

In the cottage, he examined his wounds, washed them, and decided that, if left alone, they would probably heal without trouble. He penned his note, walked back to Rudleigh House to deliver it, and then returned to the cottage and began to work. He broke off in the early evening, suddenly conscious of not having eaten since his breakfast. While he was chewing a sandwich, there was a knock at the door.

It was one of the Chetwynds' maids. She said nothing, but thrust a letter into Edward's hands, and was gone in an instant.

It was less of a letter than a hurried note. 'Harcourt. I forbid you to leave until I have read your report and discussed it with you. Attend me in the main foundry at 10.30 a.m. Geo. Chetwynd.'

Edwards's first thought was to ignore it. He had no wish to be put through the hoop, and no doubt accused of ignorance and vindictiveness. He returned to his writing, grinning with pleasure as he pinned down every little deficiency which, in his view, was preventing the greater prosperity of the firm, which failings included Miss Beatrice Unwin.

In the morning, he changed his mind. If Chetwynd wanted to pull his report to pieces, he would not let him get away with it unopposed. He had to stay, to defend what he had written—and, by God, he would!

After he had delivered the fat envelope, he decided that he would fill in the time by taking a walk. He would climb up one of the hills, feast his eyes for the last time on the beauties of the Shropshire countryside, and let the wind blow away the last regrets that he had at leaving. But first he decided to return to the cottage.

His relationship with Mrs Woodham had hardly developed since his first days in Rudleigh. Still unable to understand much, if any, of her constant monologue, he had taken to smiling and nodding at her, and when he spoke, did so slowly and loudly. She did not seem to mind. She had worked well for him.

When he got back to the cottage, he pressed a sovereign into her hand. 'Thank you, Mrs Woodham,' he said, 'for all you've done.'

The response was amazing. Total silence. She was gazing at him, open-mouthed, her eyes two round saucers. Then she spat on the coin, and buried it in some recess of her clothing beneath her apron, and the avalanche of words began again.

Hastily, Edward left the cottage and went for his walk. It was a brilliant, clear day and even the distant purple hills were sharply defined against the bright sky. He climbed so that he could see the Severn winding its way slowly southwards, on towards Worcester and eventually the Bristol Channel. It gave him a strange sense of excitement, this natural waterway which man exploited for his transport and his trading, and used as a source of food, and could feast his eyes on without ever tiring of its beauty.

He was in a happy, almost exalted mood as he made his way back to Rudleigh, but his elation faded as he approached the main foundry. The next hour or so was not going to be pleasant.

Mr Chetwynd looked at him without smiling. 'Follow me,' he said, and led the way into his office. It was tiny, cluttered and far from clean. There were two rickety chairs on either side of a desk. Mr Chetwynd sat with his back to the window, and motioned Edward to the other chair.

'You're given me all kinds of trouble,' he said. 'I'd like to hear your side of the story.'

'The story?' Edward said stupidly.

'Whatever it was that went on at my house yesterday morning.'

Edward gave as accurate an account of what had happened as he could, apologising, and doing his best not to malign Miss Unwin. 'She was . . . well, in a somewhat excitable mood, sir.'

'Yes,' said Chetwynd. 'So I believe. Well, go on, go on.'

Edward completed his narration.

'H'm,' said Chetwynd. 'Exactly as I thought. I heard, of course, what my wife had to say, but it was difficult to get much sense out of Beatrice, especially since her mother was fussing over her the whole time. Beatrice was in a very distressed state, so much so that we called Dr Bellamy. I was able, before he arrived, to have a few words alone with her. She could not tell me much, but she kept repeating, "It was Fido. I fell over Fido." Her mother persisted with her

154

own version, but I had my doubts about it from the beginning. Dr Bellamy examined Beatrice carefully, but could find no cause for alarm. It happens to be that time of the month when ladies . . . You understand? That may have been the cause. Anyway, he gave her a mild sedative, and sent her to bed, saying that she should rest for a few days. But this morning she appears to be perfectly all right, and absolutely insists on working as usual.'

'Is that wise, sir?'

'Wise or not, she refuses any advice to the contrary. Perhaps it may prove the best medicine. Anyway, I am glad to know the truth of the matter. She sent you her apologies, by the way, and I will add my own, especially since you were done out of your dinner yesterday evening. Not that it was a very good dinner . . . Well, it is all over and forgotten, I hope. Now, this report of yours.'

Edward braced himself.

'I must admit,' Chetwynd continued, 'that when I first asked you to carry out an investigation, I did not expect that much worthwhile would come out of it. How could someone new to the trade learn enough in a few short weeks to be able to make useful judgements?'

'I said as much myself,' Edward said, 'but you brushed that aside. I consider that you hired me under false pretences, sir. I am not sure that I should have come here at all if I had known from the start that you were not serious about the enterprise.'

'Hold your horses, my boy. I was serious enough—it was simply that my expectations were not high. And I am confounded. I find this report quite remarkable, and all the more so since it has been completed in less time than I had expected.'

'I have not done all I intended,' Edward said. 'I should have visited far more shops, and I wanted to go to the warehouse in Bristol, and I think there is much to be checked in cost of materials.'

'I appreciate that, but the scope and depth of your comments are most impressive, and support my belief that an eye new to the business will see much that is obscured by custom and familiarity. Familiarity does not only breed contempt, it breeds blindness. In particular, I am pleased that you have been unsparing in your criticisms—a bland report would have been useless. I am grateful to you, Edward.' He paused. 'You seem surprised. Were you not aware of the value of what you had written?'

'I believe my ideas would improve the firm's fortunes considerably.'

'Then your surprise can only mean that you expected me to reject all that you had to say.'

A little uncomfortably, with the feeling that he was being led into a trap, Edward said, 'I hoped that it might meet some measure of agreement, sir, but, yes, I did expect you to find most of it unacceptable.'

'And that, Master Harcourt, suggests that you do not have a high regard for my business acumen, nor for my general intelligence. There can be two reasons only for rejecting a report of this nature. Either it is composed of rubbish, or the person to whom it is made is too stupid to see its value. Will you deny that the second proposition was the one you believed?'

Edward hesitated for a moment. There was a certain amount of truth in what Chetwynd said. He found he was enjoying the skirmish. The antagonism he had felt disappeared, and he went on easily, 'I expected you to reject my report, not because of stupidity, but because of the blind familiarity to which you referred earlier. I underestimated you, sir, but I would point out that you did your best, by your talk of a fresh pair of eyes, and that kind of thing, to make me believe you to be far more hidebound than in fact you are.'

'A very good answer,' Chetwynd said. He got up and peered through the grimy window of the little room, staring out for a long time, though Edward had the impression that he was not really looking at anything. When at last he turned round, he said, 'Are you willing to continue working here?'

'In what capacity, sir?'

'As my assistant, my right-hand man.'

Edward smiled. 'It depends, sir, firstly on what duties will be expected of me, secondly on what rewards will come my way, and thirdly on what my future prospects will be.'

Chetwynd chuckled. 'And fourthly, fifthly and sixthly on all sorts of other questions that you will wish to ask! I can see that we have a great deal to talk about.' He laughed again. 'Now, I can spare an hour or so this morning to begin with, and I have arranged that a simple meal will be served to us this evening in the dining-room, while my wife and stepdaughter eat elsewhere. I think that will be as well—less embarrassing for all concerned. And it means that we can talk from then until midnight or longer. Does that suit you?'

'My plans for today, sir, included only a long journey by train.'

'By train? Where to?'

'Back to London.'

'Ah, yes, I see. Well, Edward where shall we begin?'

Edward laughed, 'I think,' he said, 'we should start by talking about me.'

It took them nearly an hour to reach agreement, but Edward then accepted the position of Assistant Manager at a starting salary of two hundred and fifty pounds a year, which sum would be swiftly increased if his plans produced greater profits.

'Well,' said Chetwynd, 'that is settled. This evening we will get down to your report.' He saw that Edward was frowning. 'What's wrong?'

'I was thinking, sir, about Miss Unwin. I gather that you have not been in the habit of involving her in policy decisions, but she will certainly be concerned in most of my proposals.'

'And so?'

'Well, I was wondering, sir, whether she should not be present this evening after all. If, of course, she feels up to it.'

Chetwynd considered for a moment. 'I am sure it would be better for her to rest, but I take your point. I will ask her if she wishes to join us, and I will give her your report to study beforehand. You still look worried.'

'If I had known that she would see the report, I would have worded it somewhat differently, in certain places.'

'Oh, come, Edward!' He laughed. 'My stepdaughter is an intelligent woman, quite able to take justifiable criticism. She may be a little upset with you on a personal basis, but it will not cloud her business judgement, of that I am sure.'

Edward hoped he was right.

157

6

'The firm began here in Rudleigh,' Edward said, 'because iron ore and coke were readily available, but chiefly because of the river, which in turn dictated the maintenance of a warehouse in Bristol. There is no good reason why it should remain here, and every reason for going somewhere else, so that foundry and warehouse can be together in one location.'

He and Mr Chetwynd and Miss Unwin were seated at the dinner table, and had just finished their meal, eaten largely in silence. It had been an uncomfortable hour for Edward. Miss Unwin had barely greeted him on his arrival, and had responded curtly to his enquiry about her health, saying that she was perfectly well. Every time since then when he had caught her eye, she seemed to be gazing at him malevolently. Mr Chetwynd had made it plain that he preferred not to talk while dealing with the beef, watery cabbage and overdone roast potatoes, but had finally suggested that they begin with the most radical proposal in Edward's report.

'A single site,' Edward continued, 'would clearly be more economical, with greatly reduced transport costs. We should be able to dispense with river transport altogether, and our deliveries could be greatly speeded, especially if the business were sited within easy reach of a major rail junction. Moreover, we should escape from the shadow of the Ironbridge Works, and—'

Miss Unwin interrupted. 'You quite forget, Mr Harcourt, that this happens to be our home. Would you uproot us all? As for the matter of using the river for transport,' she went on with an air of triumph, 'Ironbridge still use the barges.'

'Less and less.'

'And what about our workers, both here and in Bristol, who have been loyal to us for generations? You have no thought for them.'

'Indeed, I have, Miss Unwin. Ironbridge is always advertising for more hands, foundrymen and warehouse-men alike. They would find employment without difficulty.'

'Don't you realise that they stay with us precisely because they do not want to work for a large concern, and at a distance from their homes?' When Edward did not immediately reply, she went on, 'And pray explain what you mean about escaping from the shadow of Ironbridge.'

'I believe our proximity to them leads naturally to comparisons, which are rarely in our favour.'

'Oh, nonsense, Mr Harcourt!' She glared at him for a moment. 'I am most strongly opposed to the whole idea.'

George Chetwynd had listened to the argument with a slight smile of amusement. 'Set your fears at rest, my dear,' he said. 'I have no intention of moving the business from Rudleigh. On the other hand, the closure of the Bristol warehouse makes sense, though we shall have to ensure that the warehousemen do not suffer. Fortunately, as Edward points out in his report, we have ground available here to build a new warehouse—otherwise I might have been forced to accept the validity of his arguments for moving, lock, stock and barrel. Do you wish to argue further, Edward, in favour of that cause?'

'No, sir,' Edward said. 'The proposal may have been the most radical, but it was also the one about which I felt least strongly.'

'Good. Then let us look at output and sales.' He turned to Miss Unwin. 'Mr Harcourt is correct, Beatrice, in saying that our foundries do not run to full capacity, and, to solve that problem, we need to increase our sales.'

'Stupid though I am, that is obvious, even to me,' she said.

She clearly expected some kind of protest from Edward, but he decided it would be best to make no comment, and went on smoothly, 'It is essential that we should visit our customers regularly. Our catalogues are well produced and presented, but by themselves they clearly do not produce the volume of orders we should like.'

'Of course, I call on the larger customers from time to time,' Chetwynd said. 'I can remember as a youngster going round with my father, as he introduced me to them. Now it's often their sons that I talk to.' He sighed, wheezily. 'But,

159

as your report says, my visits are not very frequent. I find it difficult to get away from the administrative work here, and as you know my health has not been of the best recently.'

'I believe we need a team of salesmen, sir—but I suggest we begin modestly, with just one.'

'Where do we find him?' Chetwynd asked.

'I have someone in mind,' Edward replied. 'His name is Beeson, and he is presently employed in Mr Jarvis' shop in Great Luckton. He struck me as an exceptionally bright lad, with the kind of ability we need.'

'But no experience,' Miss Unwin said.

Edward smiled, 'No, but he will learn, and learn quickly, I think. My idea would be to tour the country myself, taking Beeson with me. If he turns out to be less useful than I think, then he can be discharged. If not, then eventually he would take over, working on commission.'

'Well, I will think about that,' Chetwynd said. 'Go on, Edward.'

'Secondly, we must lower our prices, so that we are directly competitive with Ironbridge.'

'Our quality is higher than theirs,' Miss Unwin said. 'But if we cut our prices, we should be selling at a loss, especially if we are paying this man of yours commission. Really, Mr Harcourt, your views are naive.'

'Perhaps, Miss Unwin,' Edward said pleasantly. 'But by becoming competitive, I am certain that we should increase our output sufficiently not only to afford a salesman's commission, but substantially to increase our profits. And if, at the same time, we could improve our delivery time, and the collection of overdue accounts—'

'Yes, I was waiting for that,' she interrupted, spitting the words out venomously. 'I take the strongest exception to your comments on our accounting procedure. Much of our business is achieved precisely because we do not dun our customers. You forget that we are an old-established firm. We are far from being as stupid as you suggest throughout this—this report. Our methods, including the running of our accounts, are tried and tested.'

'And what do you say to that, Edward?' Chetwynd asked.

'That I believe your customers take advantage of your generous credit terms, without increasing the business they do with you in exchange. That list of outstanding accounts proves my point. But I would repeat, Miss Unwin, that I mean nothing personal by my comments.'

'They are inevitably aimed at me, Mr Harcourt. It is most provoking.' She turned to her stepfather. 'Perhaps, if you have so much faith in Mr Harcourt's judgement you would prefer me to give up my work.'

'I have not said so, Beatrice,' Chetwynd replied mildly, 'and I beg you to retain your sense of proportion. Edward's report gives you every credit for the excellence and accuracy of your record-keeping. He merely suggests the employment of assistance for you, and a prompter collection of our debts. I am certain that he is right.'

'You have never said so before,' Miss Unwin protested. 'I fail to understand. If all that he says is so obvious and sensible, why was it not apparent to you, and why did you do nothing about it?'

'Really, Beatrice, you forget yourself! However, I will answer you, once and for all. My preoccupations have made me remiss, I confess, in putting off until tomorrow many things which should have been done today. Some are those which Edward has pinpointed, but he also makes suggestions which had not occurred to me, or had not appeared to me to be of sufficient moment to be dealt with immediately. If perhaps I had found the time to visit more of our customers, I should have been more aware of what needed to be done. And it is only recently, once Doctor Bellamy pronounced his Jeremiads, that I have felt the situation to be one of urgency.' He paused, gazing at her sternly. 'Now, let us have no more carping. You and Edward will have to work together in amity, and I am sure you can do so.'

Miss Unwin lowered her head. 'Yes. I am sorry.'

'Go on, Edward,' Chetwynd said.

'The third point about the way we sell,' Edward continued, 'is the size of the catalogue. It is well organised and printed, but there are far too many items in it, including many which have little, if any, sale. Apart from anything else, they give the list an old-fashioned look.'

'Ironbridge have a much bigger catalogue than ours,' Miss Unwin said.

'With respect, Miss Unwin,' Edward said gently, 'I do not

think we should continue to compare ourselves with Ironbridge. Theirs is a very large concern, and what suits them may not necessarily suit us. In some respects, we should follow their example, but not, I believe, in this case. If we eliminated from the stock-list all those items which we no longer sell in any but the smallest quantity, then we could concentrate on the more successful lines, and we should also save valuable warehouse space in Bristol, and storage of the patterns here in Rudleigh.'

'I think that makes sense,' Chetwynd said, 'and it brings us to the crucial question of our designs. I note your recommendation that we should produce a special line for the Jubilee next year—I had of course planned to do so—but we shall have to be very careful over the quantities we produce. You realise that anything labelled "Queen Victoria's Diamond Jubilee, 1897" will be totally unsaleable six months later.'

'My main point there, sir, is that we should always take advantage of any outside circumstances which may boost our sales, even if only on a temporary basis.'

'Agreed. Have you anything else you wish to add to what you have already written?'

'I'd simply like to emphasise, sir, that the comment I received most often from the retailers I visited was that there is nothing in our catalogue, apart from the figurines, which is really innovative or so attractive that it will outsell our competitors' designs.'

'And it is for that reason that you suggest the dismissal of Sales and Nightingale.' Chetwynd shook his head. 'I must confess that this proposal gives me great concern. They are excellent craftsmen, who have served us for very many years, and are still capable of fine work.'

'You will think that I am venting my spite again,' Miss Unwin said, 'but I cannot remain silent in this matter. Why, it would kill them, Mr Harcourt, to be dismissed. You cannot be so cruel. They are the salt of the earth, and everyone respects them.'

'We have to consider the good of the firm and all its employees,' Edward said patiently. 'Perhaps it would be possible to offer them a pension.'

'A pension? When we are already committed to your own employment, plus an assistant for me, to say nothing

162

of lowering our prices and paying commission on them?'
Her mouth clamped shut in disapproval.

'Then perhaps we could simply pension off Nightingale.
He is the older of the two, and could not in any case
continue working much longer.'

'And Sales?'

'He could be retained on a part-time basis—to continue
to design and carve the animal statuettes.'

'We can postpone a decision on that subject,' Mr
Chetwynd said. 'I don't think that even Edward would
propose that we should change all our designs overnight.
No, any new designers and carvers will have to work
alongside Sales and Nightingale for a period, at least until
we can judge the quality of their work. But where are we
going to find the right men, Edward?'

It was time to produce the inspiration which had
suddenly come to him on the train. 'I believe I know two
people who would be suitable, sir. My aunt is an artist.'

'Oh, so is mine,' Miss Unwin said, sarcastically. 'We all
have relations who dabble in water-colours and the like.
Indeed, I have some skill myself. Perhaps I should give up
the accounts and become our chief designer.'

'Beatrice, Beatrice!' Mr Chetwynd said, gently. 'You do
not help by these comments. Your aunt is experienced in
this field, Edward?'

'Not exactly, no, sir. But she has worked commercially,
designing silk fabrics for my . . . for her brother, my uncle,
for many years. And her husband is an engraver. Together I
am sure that they could provide what we need.' He waited
expectantly for Chetwynd's approval.

But his employer shook his head again. 'It sounds most
unlikely, Edward. Designing silk fabrics, and engraving—
these are hardly the same as carving our patterns in wood.
Where do they live? Near here?'

'In London, sir.'

'London! Would they be willing to move to Shropshire?
And what sort of salaries would they want?'

'I would offer a token fee, and then a small commission,
so that their rewards would come only if they were
successful. As for moving here, I am not sure. But I think I
could persuade them. I should certainly like to ask them.'

Mr Chetwynd interlaced his fingers and considered. 'No,

163

I think not, Edward,' he said. 'We must look nearer home, and for someone with proven ability in this kind of work.'

Edward tried to hide his disappointment. 'Yes, sir.'

There was a silence, and then Miss Unwin asked, 'Is this boy that you mentioned—what was his name? Beeson?—is he a relative, too?'

'No, he is not!' She had commented adversely on every point he had made, and Edward was close to losing his temper. Remembering that she had been unwell, he made an effort and said, as calmly as he could, 'And I did not suggest my aunt and uncle out of nepotism, I assure you.' He turned to Mr Chetwynd. 'It was a very foolish idea, sir, and I apologise.'

Irritated by the unfairness of his stepdaughter's question, Chetwynd decided, after all, to give Edward his support. 'Virtually everything else you have put forward is eminently sensible, so I suppose you are entitled to a little foolishness, if it *is* that. All right, Edward. Ask them. But you must make it clear that there is no commitment on our part at this stage.'

'Of course, sir. Thank you.'

Miss Unwin sniffed.

*   *   *

Two days later, Edward travelled to London. He felt pleased with life and with himself. Mr Chetwynd had accepted most of his suggestions, at least for an experimental period, and he had not expected more than that. And after a brief stay in London, he would be going on to Essex to see young Beeson, and that would give him the chance of fitting in a visit to his mother, and also perhaps another meeting with Alice Ouvray.

When he arrived at the house in Battersea, Alfred Bunn was out. Aunt Frances received Edward with delight, and fussed around him with cups of tea and a newly-made seed cake. 'Such a surprise!' she kept saying. 'Now, tell me, what are you doing in London again so soon?'

Edward explained his mission.

'Me? Designing cast iron?' she said in astonishment. Then she began to giggle. 'Oh, Edward, how could you think of anything so hare-brained? I know nothing about

164

cast iron, and I've never done any three-dimensional work. I wouldn't know where to begin.'

Edward laughed with her. 'Oh, it's very simple, Aunt. You simply have to make sure the work tapers, so that when you press it into the sand to make the mould, you can remove it without damaging the impression, if you see what I mean.' She looked puzzled, so he went on to describe how the moulds were produced. 'The only other thing you need to worry about is that no thin part of the design is right next to a thick part, because the rate at which the two bits cool would differ, and that might cause problems.'

'Oh, it's ridiculous, Edward. You can't be serious. You'll have to ask your Uncle Alfred yourself, but I'm pretty sure that he'll think the whole idea is as nonsensical as I do.'

He produced one of Chetwynd's catalogues. 'Just to please me, have a look through our catalogue, and tell me what you think of the products. Don't just turn the pages, please—have a really good look.'

Edward had time for a second slice of seed cake as Frances leafed through the stock-list. 'Well?' he asked when she had finished.

'Fussy,' she said. 'Oh, I know it's fashionable to have a great deal of ornamentation, but so many of these things look fiddly. It's partly a question of the suitability of the material. I see that quite tiny details can be reproduced satisfactorily—those animals seem very lifelike, and indeed are the most admirable of the items in the catalogue—'

'They are our most successful line,' Edward interrupted.

'I am not surprised. But the question remains whether cast iron is an ideal medium for intricate designs which demand great delicacy. And what about the weight? Look at this cake-stand, for instance.' She turned to the illustration in the catalogue. 'Why, it makes my wrist ache just to think of handing it round. It would be difficult to simplify, too, because the plate has to be almost solid, so that you could cut a cake on it. And then this garden furniture . . .' She paused, as she turned to the appropriate page.

'People like garden furniture to be heavy.'

'I'm sure they do, but not so heavy that they can't lift it. Just look at all those little curlicues and bumps on the legs, and the back of the chair has such a heavy pattern. I'm sure it could be made much simpler, and lighter, and still be entirely functional.'

'Draw it, Aunt Frances.'

'Oh, no! You don't catch me that way! I am quite willing to give you my opinion—not that I think it amounts to much—but that's all. Besides, you must have people to do this sort of work already. Why can't you simply tell them to do whatever it is you want.'

'Partly because I'm no artist, and don't *know* what I want, and partly because I don't think they're capable of really imaginative work. They pinch their ideas from our rivals at the Ironbridge Works, making small alterations to avoid infringing their patents. The most creative work we produce is those animal statuettes. They're designed by an old fellow whom Miss Unwin insists on calling "the salt of the earth". He likes making animal figures, but apart from that I don't think he's got an original idea in his head, however salty he may be.'

Frances smiled. 'Miss Unwin? Oh, I remember—you told me about her last time you were here. How is she?'

'Ghastly.'

'Edward! Whatever do you mean?'

'Let me tell you what happened the other day.' With one or two minor embellishments, designed to make his aunt laugh all the more, he described the absurd contretemps as Miss Unwin tripped over Fido and landed on top of him. 'And then her mother ran in,' he went on, 'and fainted neatly on to a convenient rug. When she came to, I had finally struggled free from Miss Unwin's grip, and she had fled the room, wailing at such a pitch that all the workers in the foundry downed tools, believing the end of the world had come. Mrs Chetwynd, on the other hand, was convinced I had inflicted all kinds of wrongs, of a nature which I am far too delicate to mention to a lady, on her defenceless daughter. Defenceless, indeed! She'd knocked all the breath from my body. I was quite helpless beneath her onslaught.'

'Oh, poor Edward!'

'I thought my career was in ruins. Fortunately, Mr Chetwynd got the truth out of his stepdaughter, so all was well in the end. Mind you, Miss Unwin does not look upon me with favour, I'm afraid, and when I am with her, I feel as though I were a prisoner in the dock, and she the Counsel for the Prosecution.' He drained the last of his tea. 'And talking of trials, you have passed yours, my dear Aunt Frances, with the most triumphant of flying colours.'

'I haven't been on trial, have I? Dear me!'

'All I mean is that you said exactly the sort of thing I wanted to hear about that catalogue. I'm sure you're right, and—'

'There's Alfred,' Frances interrupted happily as they heard the sound of the front door. 'I must make another pot of tea. You haven't eaten all the seed cake, have you, dear?' She hurried out.

After Alfred Bunn had welcomed Edward, and been plied with tea and seed cake, and had answered Frances' questions about his expedition, the midday meal he had bought himself, and whether he was now exhausted by his exertions, he looked at Edward. 'You're bursting with something,' he said. 'What is it?'

Edward repeated his story concerning Chetwynd's need for new designers. Although Alfred listened attentively, he showed no reaction at all, and this disconcerted Edward, who found himself over-emphasising in an effort to convey his own enthusiasm. 'When you came in,' he finished, 'I think I had just persuaded Aunt Frances to prepare some designs for me, which I hope you will agree to carve.'

'No.' The negative was quietly spoken, but very definite.

'Why not, Uncle Alfred?'

'For a very simple reason. Your aunt succeeds with anything she puts her hand to. But I can only engrave metal, and that's not the same as carving wood—different material, different tools, different techniques.' He paused for a moment, and then went on gently, making the reproof as mild as he could, 'I would have thought that you might have realised that.'

Edward grinned ruefully. 'I think I did, but I had to try.' He turned to Frances. 'Dare I beg yet another slice of seed cake, Aunt?' When she had cut it for him, and he had thanked her, and had swallowed the first mouthful, he went on, 'It seemed such a good idea to have you both working for the same business. I even hoped you might

167

come and live in Rudleigh—we could have shared a house.'

'I have a strong suspicion, my dear,' Frances said to Alfred, that it's not us he wants, it's my seed cake.'

'I bet men kill each other for it,' Edward laughed. 'But seriously, Aunt, it may have been daft to think that Uncle could have become a wood-carver, but I still believe that you could draw some splendid designs for us.'

Frances shook her head.

Edward turned to Alfred. 'She could, couldn't she?'

Alfred smiled. 'Undoubtedly. Whether she will is a different matter. And it would be more than my life is worth to try to persuade her. She'd have my head off in a trice. A terror with a meat-axe, is Mrs Bunn.'

'Oh, what a one for nonsense!' Frances said. Then she turned to Edward. 'I'm sorry, my dear, but I know nothing about cast iron, and—'

'I'd be delighted to show you,' Edward said. 'You could both come to Rudleigh. It's beautiful country, and I know you'd enjoy it, and while you were there you could come to the foundry and see how everything is done, and then . . .' He became aware that they were both looking at him with an amused, gentle tolerance. 'All right,' he smiled. 'I give in.'

'Thank you for asking us,' Frances said. 'We appreciate it, don't we, my dear?'

They passed the evening in inconsequential chatter, until it was late enough for Edward to make his escape to his hotel. How strange, he thought, that he should think of it as an escape. Perhaps it was because his failure to persuade them to work for Chetwynd's lingered somehow in the air, and left them all feeling vaguely unsettled.

Arriving in Chelmsford the next morning, he hired a pony and trap and drove first to Franton, where he called at the Prideau residence, spoke briefly to Alice Ouvray, and shamelessly procured himself an invitation to dinner that evening. Then he went on to Brentfield. Inevitably, his mother was still at the mill, so, leaving a message that he would be spending the night there, he continued to Great Luckton.

He glanced through the shop window. Mr Jarvis was serving a customer at the counter, but there was no sign of young Beeson. Edward was in a rather difficult position. Mr Jarvis was hardly likely to be pleased if he seduced his assistant away from the shop, and his aim was to make friends, not enemies, of the retailers who sold Chetwynd products.

As he entered the shop, the customer was being seen to the door by Mr Jarvis, an operation which appeared to demand a great deal of bowing, and repeated thanks for the much esteemed order.

Jarvis eventually resumed his place behind the counter. 'Why, Mr Harcourt. What can I do for you, sir?'

'You remember I asked your advice about joining Chetwynd's. Well, I have done so.'

'Ah. Come for an order, have you? I don't usually see anyone in the mornings. But it's about time someone came from Chetwynd's. Yes, about time.'

'I hope to make sure that you are called upon regularly, Mr Jarvis. That is, if you are not so angry when I tell you the reason for my visit here today, that . . . You see, Mr Jarvis, I find myself on the horns of a dilemma. If I conclude the business I came for without a word to you, I shall certainly incur your most serious displeasure. And so I thought, "Why not confess what you are about? Mr Jarvis may still be upset, but there's just a chance that he'll appreciate being taken into your confidence and will respect you for it. And if he's still upset, you've lost nothing." That's what I said to myself.'

Jarvis looked at him in bewilderment, and then shook his head. 'I'm sorry. I don't get your drift, not at all I don't.'

'I'm talking about Beeson, your young assistant.'

'What about him?'

'I want to offer him a job.'

'What? Freddie Beeson?' He looked even more puzzled. 'Here,' he said, 'is this some kind of a joke?' Then he turned his head so that he was looking at Edward almost from the side, and there was grave suspicion in his eyes. 'You're not . . . you're not one o' them . . . ? What sort of job did you have in mind? Nothing immoral, I hope. I wouldn't be a party to nothing immoral.'

'Immoral? Good Lord, no! It's employment with Chetwynd's. I want to train him as a salesman.'

Jarvis stared at him. 'A salesman?' he said. 'Freddie Beeson a salesman? Oh, that's a good one!' He laughed loudly. 'Now, come on, Harcourt—what's it all about? I like

169

a joke as much as the next man, but this beats the band. Yes, it beats the band.'

'I am quite serious,' Edward said. 'I take it that your opinion of Beeson is not as high as mine. However, I'll take my chance on that, though I'd welcome the opportunity of a few minutes' conversation with him, before I finally make up my mind up. But the question is, what is your reaction going to be if I take him away from you?'

'My reaction? Good riddance to bad rubbish—that's what I'd say. No, that's unfair, the lad's not all bad. He's honest, and he knows his figures.'

Edward decided to probe a little. 'Lazy, is he?'

'No-o-o,' said Jarvis, rather grudgingly, 'I wouldn't say he was lazy. No, not lazy.'

'Forgetful, habitually late, slow?'

'No, none of those—no more than any other youngster, that is.'

'Then what is wrong with him, Mr Jarvis?'

'Clumsy. And cheeky. That's the main thing. Cheeky. The way he talks to the customers. Familiar, much too familiar.'

'Have there been complaints?'

'No-o-o, not actually complaints—not in so many words. In fact, some customers seem to quite like the lad. But you can't have a youngster talking familiar to customers, now can you? It's not right. It's not what customers expect. You'll be doing me a favour if you take him off my hands. It'll save me from having to give him the sack, sooner or later.'

'I see.' Edward was beginning to suspect that Mr Jarvis' view of young Beeson was coloured by more than a little jealousy. Perhaps some of the shop's customers had made it plain that they preferred to be served by the cheerful young assistant. 'As I say, I'd like a word with him. But first, perhaps I could go through the Chetwynd catalogue with you.'

'I don't usually see anyone in the mornings,' Jarvis said. 'Not in the mornings. I'll give you five minutes.'

It did not take even that long. Jarvis ordered a couple of mincing machines, among the smallest items in the catalogue, but that was all.

'Thank you very much, Mr Jarvis,' Edward said. 'I will

170

see that the order gets prompt attention. By the way,' he went on, almost casually, 'there are going to be some changes at Chetwynd's. Next time I call I hope to have a new range of goods on offer, and some very competitive prices.'

'Ah. That's what's needed. Yes, that's what's needed.'

'And now, would you mind if I had a word with Beeson?'

'I can't spare him for more than ten minutes. And if he takes your job, he can't leave before the end of the week.' He shouted for the lad, and when he appeared, said, 'Fellow here wants to talk to you. Take him into the paint room, out of the way.' Grumbling to himself, he turned to greet a customer.

'This way, Mr 'Arcourt,' said Beeson.

'You remember me.'

'Course I do, sir. You come in last week.'

'Do you always remember people's names?'

'Most of the time, yes, sir. Soon as I see someone, up pops a name in me 'ead, and nine times out o' ten, it's the right one.'

That ability would be very useful, Edward thought. They had reached the paint store, thick with the smell of turpentine and white lead. 'Do you also remember the name of the company for which I work?' he asked.

'To be honest with you, no, sir,' Beeson replied, 'but I'd guess that it's . . .' He paused long enough to grin. '. . . Chetwynd's.'

'How did you know that?'

'A lucky guess, sir, seeing as you got a Chetwynd's catalogue in your 'and, an' it's got yer name on it.'

Observant, too. This was better and better, Edward thought. The lad was a paragon. Surely there must be some fault in him, apart from Jarvis' accusations of clumsiness and cheek. Of course he did not speak a word of the Queen's English, and the mangled vowels and dropped aitches and chaotic syntax might irritate some of the grander buyers who preferred to be called upon by salesmen with pretensions to education. 'Listen, Master Frederick Beeson—'

'Frederick *William* Beeson.' He grinned again.

Edward curbed an inclination to grin back. 'That, young man, was damned near impertinence, and you'll have to

171

learn pretty soon how far is far enough and how far is too far.'

'Yes, sir. Sorry, sir.' The apology was a genuine one, yet not overdone.

'I was about to ask if you've lived here all your life.'

'Lor' love you, no, sir. Born and bred in London, I was—a Cockney, from me 'ead to me 'eels.'

'What family have you got?'

'Live with me aunt and uncle, sir.'

'Your parents are dead?'

'Yes, sir.'

'And are you fond of your aunt and uncle?'

'Fond of 'em, sir?' Again there was laughter in his eyes. 'Not always, but most of the time. Like other fam'lies.'

'So how would you feel about leaving Great Luckton? I am looking for someone to train as a travelling salesman for Chetwynd's, and I thought the position might suit you.'

The young man's dark eyes, always lively, seemed to light up. 'Reelly, sir? And you come all this way just to talk to me about it?'

'Yes, Beeson, I did. I hope it wasn't a fool's errand.'

'If you ask me, sir, there's two answers to that question. The first is what you might call the 'ere-and-now of it. An' I got to ask a question before I can give that 'ere-and-now answer.'

'Ask away.'

'What wages do I get?'

'To start with, while you're being trained, you'll get whatever you get here. Which is how much?'

'Five shillings a week, sir. Pitiful, ain't it?'

'Pitiful or not, that's what you'll get from Chetwynd's, too—until you're trained.'

'And then, sir?'

'Nothing.'

'Nothing?'

'No wages, just commission on your sales. You'll be making a lot more than five bob a week—if you're any good, you will.'

'Ah, that's the second answer, sir—the this-time-next-year answer, you might call it.'

'What do you mean?'

'Well, the question was, 'ave you, or 'ave you not come on a

172

fool's errand? And the 'ere-and-now answer is, no, you ain't, seeing as 'ow I'm accepting the position offered. But then there's the this-time-next-year answer, and that depends whether I'm any good at the job or not, don't it?'

'Yes,' said Edward, after taking a moment to work it all out, 'I suppose it does. All right, Frederick William Beeson, I'll take you on. Mr Jarvis says that you will be able to leave at the end of the week. I shall expect to see you in Rudleigh on Monday.'

'Yes, sir. Where's Rudleigh, sir?'

'Find out, my enterprising young friend. I'll send you a railway ticket, but the rest is up to you.'

'Righto, Mr 'Arcourt. Suits me.'

'And now you had better get on with whatever it is that you should be doing for Mr Jarvis.'

'It's nails, sir. Mr Jarvis is very fond o' nails, and expects me to be fond of 'em, too, sir. I do me best.'

'I'm sure you do. Remember, next Monday. Come to the foundry. I expect you there no later than five o'clock in the afternoon. Understood?'

'Yes, sir. And thank you, sir. I won't let you down.'

Edward went back into the shop, and waited as Mr Jarvis finished packing a parcel for his customer. The counter was covered in various brands of mincing machines, including one made by Chetwynd's, of the kind that Mr Jarvis had re-ordered.

When the customer had gone, Edward said, 'I've offered him the job. Beeson, I mean. He's to start on Monday, if that's all right with you.'

Mr Jarvis nodded, and began to put the unsold mincing machines away. 'Couldn't sell your model,' he said, with some satisfaction. 'Too dear, the lady said. Yes, too dear. Next time you call,' he went on, his voice quite sharp, 'I expect a card first. And I do not see commercials until the afternoon. Remember that, Harcourt. Good morning to you.'

Perhaps it was a sort of revenge for stealing Beeson, Edward thought. Or maybe the ironmonger was simply making it clear that from now on he was in command, like a Roman emperor against whose thumbs-up or thumbs-down there was no appeal. Well, let him enjoy his moment of superiority. Edward was pleased with himself, convinced that Beeson was going to be worth his weight in gold.

And he was not the only gain from this journey to Great Luckton. He had suddenly realised from Jarvis' final comment that he had almost as much to learn as Beeson would have about the life of a salesman, the conventions and etiquette of the business. For a start, he decided, he would compile a card index of all Chetwynd's customers, noting their peculiarities and interests and likes and dislikes. 'And,' he thought, 'I'll record their orders on these cards, and get Miss Unwin to let me know how much they owe, and when they pay, and so on. And every time I visit them, I'll look at the card beforehand, so that I know what to say, and then I'll put the new details on afterwards. And I'll teach Beeson to do the same.'

*   *   *

His evening with the Prideaus followed the same delightful pattern as on the previous occasion. Alice was eager to hear of what Edward had been doing since their last meeting, and had stories of her own, too. She had been to London with a Mrs Gage, a friend of her mother, and Mrs Gage's bachelor son, Wilfred, had insisted on taking them to the theatre and then to supper at the Trocadero.

'And what do you think?' Alice went on. 'The next morning, the most enormous bunch of roses came.'

'Indeed?' Edward exclaimed, painfully aware of jealousy eating into his self-satisfaction.

'So kind. He's such a gentleman.'

She did not mention him again, but Edward did not forget him, and as he drove his hired trap to Brentfield he wondered whether Alice had been attracted to—what was his wretched name?—Wilfred Gage. Surely not, or she would have spoken of him at greater length. Or was that because she wanted to hide her feelings for him?

Anyway, he told himself firmly, he had no right to feel jealous. He had not declared himself to her. Marriage . . . It had not entered his mind seriously before this. How could it, when he had no wealth, no position, no house, to offer any girl?

Sarah greeted him somewhat absently. She asked a few perfunctory questions, but when he answered at some length, describing his life at Rudleigh, and the events of this current trip, he soon realised that she was not really listening. She sat facing him, still an attractive woman, with her head held at a listening angle, her eyes fixed upon him, and whenever he paused for breath she would make a little sound to indicate her interest; it would have deceived many, but he knew her too well: her eyes were empty, and her thoughts were miles away. No, not miles away—as always she was thinking of Harcourt's Mill.

He wondered what she would say if he were suddenly to announce that he was engaged to marry Miss Alice Ouvray, and that he needed her financial assistance. She would undoubtedly greet the news with genuine interest, but she would be careful to avoid making any comment about the money. Sarah Harcourt, as long as he could remember, had been adept at ignoring totally those things which she did not want to discuss.

He noticed that the look in her eyes had changed suddenly, as though she had made her mind up about something.

'Now, do stop talking for a moment, my dear,' she said. 'I love listening to you, but so far I haven't been able to get a word in edgeways. And I do want to talk to you, Edward. I'm so glad you came today. I have been considering very seriously the points you made before you left home, and I have come to the conclusion that you were justified in many ways, and that I was . . . let us say . . . over-cautious in my response to your suggestions for change.'

Edward stared at her, trying to hide his astonishment. He could not remember ever having previously heard his mother admit that she was wrong.

'In short,' she continued, 'I have decided that Harcourt's should enter a wider market. I have been thinking that we might produce a very simple silk fabric, set up a sewing shop, and then sell the garments we make to the retail trade.'

'Ready-made dresses, you mean? I wouldn't have thought that ladies who can afford silk would be interested in something not made for them personally.'

'Nor would they,' Sarah said, 'but I was not thinking of dresses so much as . . .' She coughed delicately. '. . . under-garments. There is an increasing tendency, even among the

175

well-to-do, to purchase such necessities direct from a ladies' outfitters, though in my young days a well-brought up girl always made her own.'

'Bravo, Mama! It sounds like just the kind of expansion that the mill needs.'

'The credit is really yours, dear boy—you were the one who made me look at the whole position seriously. And I am so pleased that you like the idea.' She rose, and came to sit beside him on the sofa. 'I have listened to you very carefully this evening, my dear, talking about Chetwynd's and cast iron and Rudleigh and goodness knows what, and doing your best to sound enthusiastic about it all. But you cannot deceive your mother, my darling. I could tell that it was all pretence.'

'But, Mama—'

'And I know what is at the back of it. Your pride, my dear—it won't let you admit that it was a mistake to leave here. You cannot be happy in a Godforsaken place like Rudleigh, and you surely cannot have any feelings for anything as dull as cast-iron. No colour, no texture, no delicacy—nothing to please one's aesthetic senses.'

Edward could not believe his ears. He laughed at her. 'This is ludicrous, Mama.'

'I am serious, Edward. Please do me the favour of being serious yourself.'

'I am sorry, Mama,' Edward said solemnly. 'But I am truly happy at Chetwynd's. I beg you to believe me. As for cast iron being dull, you can't be aware of what can be achieved with it. Let me show you our catalogue.'

'I have no wish to see it. I don't want so much as to *think* about cast iron, let alone discuss its artistic failings. I want to talk about silk—and about you. I need your support in this new venture, Edward. I cannot undertake an enterprise of this kind on my own. I want you to come back, back to Harcourt's. The mill needs you. I need you. Now, what do you say?'

Edward hesitated. Was she as serious as she said, or was this all some kind of trick? Had she really been thinking about it, or had she invented the whole idea on the spur of the moment? He said, carefully, 'We didn't get on all that well the last time we tried to work together, did we?'

'Oh, but that was just a silly quarrel—only because we

176

had not decided properly how to handle our various responsibilities. Perhaps I was thinking of you still as a little boy, instead of as a man with an ability and a need to shoulder responsibility. It would be different this time. I promise I would not interfere—you would have complete control of the new department. Of course, I would remain head of the company, but otherwise . . . Oh, what do you say, Edward? Wouldn't it be fun? Wouldn't it be wonderful to work together again?'

When he came home to Brentfield, or indeed whenever he thought of his mother, Edward tried to suppress the feelings of guilt—guilt because he had deserted her, and run away from his duties towards the family firm; guilt because his lack of interest in silk was a betrayal of both his parents; and even guilt because of Mary. Again the thoughts haunted him, and it was difficult to chase them away. And if he did come back, he would be near to Franton, and Alice Ouvray . . . He was tempted to give in, but something told him to be cautious, to remember what had happened before. His mother's sweet and reasonable attitude seemed genuine, but she had always been good at dissembling.

His thoughts went on. Was he really wedded to Chetwynd's, or was it simply the excitement of the opportunities he was being given there? And had he perhaps bitten off more than he could chew?

Sarah was watching him closely, guessing at what was going through his mind. 'There's nothing to beat flesh and blood to make an effective, lasting partnership, Edward.' Her eyes were shining. 'Harcourt's rose from the ashes before—it could do so again, if you and I set our minds to it.'

She was playing every possible card, a cynical voice in his mind told him. But if she were really convinced of the need to look for new business and bring the mill back to life again, perhaps it *would* be possible for them to work together amicably and effectively. 'Have you worked it all out, Mama? The costings, the likely size of the market, the profit margins?'

'No. But I know the demand is there. All the other details would be for you to discover, and the decisions for you to make. You get on so well with the retailers—in no time at all, you could build up the business. And it would be *your*

177

business. We could even set up a subsidiary company, with you as its manager. Doesn't that all sound interesting?'

'Yes. Yes, it does. But I need time to think about it.'

'Of course you do. Sleep on it. Take longer than that. There's no rush. We'll talk about it again tomorrow, and then you can think about it, and I'm sure the more you do, the more you'll see how wonderful it would be.'

'I'm going back to Rudleigh tomorrow. I want to catch the early train.'

'Why go back at all? What does it matter? You won't be working for that tinpot little iron foundry any more! You'll be working for Harcourt's, and for me.'

The danger signals flashed in Edward's brain. 'And for me'—the words which he knew showed her once again in her true colours. It was all a trick, and he doubted whether she had ever thought before of this scheme to manufacture undergarments. Why had she proposed it? Why did she want him back in Brentfield? Simply, he told himself because she could not bear to think that he could be successful and happy away from her. And if he did come back, it would be just the same as it had been before. Even if she did mean to give him more responsibility, she would do so reluctantly, and the situation between them would be fraught with uneasy antagonism, which would soon develop into open warfare.

He stood up. 'I think it's time to go to bed, Mama.'

Sarah saw that his face had changed, and realised that somehow she had lost. 'You're going to refuse, aren't you?' she said bitterly. 'I suppose it's because I called it a tinpot little foundry.'

'It isn't that at all, Mama.' He laughed. 'Of course not.' But there was no point in telling her the real reason.

She rose, and went to pour herself some brandy. 'Go on, then—go back to your precious foundry! I'll do it without you—you'll see. It'll be easy enough, and God knows I've never been afraid of tackling something new.'

*   *   *

The next morning, driving towards Chelmsford, Edward relived the scene in his mind, wondering yet again whether his mother was really serious about this new project. She

178

was so mercurial that it was difficult to tell. It suddenly occurred to him that it was his own presence which brought on her extravagant tempers and the rapid changes of mood. He had never heard anyone else even hint at the slightest eccentricity in her. Perhaps she needed him as the catalyst who could release her pent-up emotions.

Well, he thought, harshly, she would have to cope with them on her own. But there was a lingering uneasiness in his mind, and he decided that he needed someone who could let him know if . . . well, if things started to go badly wrong at Harcourt's. Richard Goodwin could have done it, but he could not ask him. And then he thought of the perfect answer. Alice Ouvray was kind and sympathetic, she would hear any gossip in the trade, and she met Sarah socially from time to time. Edward resolved to write to her as soon as he got back to Rudleigh.

He was looking forward to his return. Whatever doubts his mother had put into his mind were swiftly dismissed. His future lay with Chetwynd's, and it would be exciting and rewarding. To have engaged Frederick Beeson might not be much to crow about now, but it would be, he was sure, some day in the future. As for his failure with Aunt Frances and Uncle Alfred, perhaps that would turn out not to be a bad thing; both Mr Chetwynd and Miss Unwin had been opposed to the idea, and now they could enjoy their triumph. And ahead of him lay so many other challenges to be met . . .

He thought of Alice Ouvray.

*   *   *

As he got out of the train at Liverpool Street, Edward decided on the spur of the moment to go and call on Jack Chetwynd.

'Come in, old chap,' Jack said. 'Let me guess. Driven to breaking point by the importunate advances of my step-sister, to say nothing of the dulcet tones of her Mama, and the yapping of those disgusting dogs, you have come to ask my help in disposing of the lot of them, by fair means or foul.'

'A reasonable guess—but wrong,' said Edward.

'Don't tell me you are still happily employed by that impossibly bigoted tyrant, my old man.'

'I find him neither impossible nor a tyrant, and I hate to hear you talk of him in that way.'

'Oh, Edward, don't be so priggish. Anyway, you know I don't mean half I say. Oh, for God's sake, laugh, my dear boy. You take everything so seriously.'

'Everybody else tells me the exact opposite. But I do take some things seriously, and you don't, do you?'

'No,' said Jack happily, and then went on in more sober a tone, 'That's the trouble. I'm just not the sort of person the old man hoped for as a son, whereas you are. You've got a sense of humour, but you're also serious and industrious, and, in an extraordinary way, quite likeable at the same time. I bet you're his blue-eyed boy.'

'Hardly,' Edward said. And then, as pride overcame modesty, he added, 'But he seemed pretty pleased with the report I did. He's offered me a proper job, as what he calls his right-hand man, and he's going to put into practice all sorts of things that I suggested in my report.'

'I say! That's good going, old chap—you've only been there five minutes.'

'I know. I worry about that; whether I'm trying to run before I've learnt to walk, and all that sort of thing.'

'Don't give it another thought. The old man's got far more sense than you're giving him credit for, and he's never wrong in his judgements of people. If he thinks you're capable of doing this job, then, by God, you are! I say, this needs celebrating! Let's go and have oysters and champagne, and this evening we can have a quiet little dinner here in the flat, and a good old chat.'

'No, I've got to get the afternoon train.'

'Nonsense!'

'But your father's expecting me.'

'Send a telegram. I've got lots to tell you, and some of it I want you to pass on to the old man. He might even be pleased, and with any luck it'll stop those infernal letters of his. Do you know he writes to me every week, exhorting me to be a good boy and do something useful?'

'And do you write back?'

'Good Lord, no!'

'Perhaps you should.'

'Don't you start lecturing me, Edward—it's bad enough from my elders and betters, and I'm certainly not going to

180

take it from my youngers and worsers. Now, don't argue, there's a good fellow. We're going to spend the rest of the day together, and you can catch the first train in the morning.' While he was talking, he had seated himself at his desk, and scribbled a few words on a sheet of paper. He crossed to ring the bell by the fireplace. 'I've written a telegram for the old man. "Essential business delays return until tomorrow. Have good news. Harcourt." All right?'

'No,' said Edward. 'I can't send that. Honestly, Jack!'

'What's the matter with it?'

'Well, it's so abrupt.'

'Telegrams usually are. We can put in "kind regards", if you like.'

There was a knock at the door.

'Come in,' Jack called. 'Ah, Templeton. I want you to send a telegram. Just hang on while we sort out the wording. Now, seriously, Edward, what's wrong with what I've said?'

'What was that bit about good news? I'm not sure whether or not I've got good news. Some of what I've got to report is disappointing.'

'I'm not talking about your news, idiot! I'm talking about mine.' He handed the paper to his manservant. 'Oh, go on, Templeton, take it. Here's half a crown.' Then, as Templeton left the room, he said, 'Come on, old boy, luncheon!'

Edward abandoned all resistance, and laughed. Jack was sometimes infuriating, but it was just impossible to remain angry with someone whose joie de vivre and enthusiasm were so infectious.

Over their oysters and champagne, Jack brought Edward up to date with the latest gossip, and then reverted to the subject of Edward's new position at Chetwynd's. 'I'm delighted for you,' he said, 'and for the old man, too. You really are just the sort of fellow he's needed. He's not had much luck, you know—my mother dying, getting caught, poor chap, by my unrevered stepmother, and having to take the dreaded Beatrice into the bargain, and then the business slipping downhill a bit. Poor old chap!' He laughed a little ruefully. 'And all that's on top of his disappointment in me.'

Edward suddenly felt much, much older than Jack. He

181

could see that, despite his mockery and his refusal to make
the slightest concession in his behaviour, Jack longed for
his father's approbation and even love, while Mr Chetwynd,
claiming to see no vestige of good in his son, was searching
desperately for something which would allow him to reveal
his own affection. Perhaps Jack's new venture, whatever it
was, would prove the needed catalyst. 'Tell me about this
exciting news of yours,' he said.

'Guess.'

'You're going to run a high-class bordello.'

'No,' said Jack doubtfully. 'I suppose that might be
described as faintly warm, but it's also a gross slander.'

'You're going to be a publisher, after all.'

'Oh, don't be a fool, Edward—that was all over long ago.'

'Then you're going to be a . . . a publican. An explorer. A
keeper at the zoo. A politician. A stockbroker.'

'Getting colder with each of those.'

'Then I give up.'

'I've gone into the theatre.'

Edward was flabbergasted. 'Acting, you mean?'

'Good Lord, no! That's a dreadful life; touring the
country, staying in frightful digs . . . Bored stiff if you're in
a hit, and out of a job if you get in a flop. And unless you're
terribly successful and go regularly to Windsor, like the
pussycat, to look at The Queen, you're an outcast in most
decent society.' Jack nonchalantly knocked the ash from his
cigar. 'No, I've gone into the management side. I've bought
a theatre.'

'Where? Which theatre? What on earth made you go in
for that? You don't know anything about it, do you? When
did it all happen?'

Jack held up his hand. 'Peace, my dear chap, peace! All will
be revealed in due course. Let me just pay the bill, and we'll
procure a cab and I'll take you there.' He signalled to a
waiter.

'It's not within walking distance, then.'

Jack ignored him. 'The bill, waiter, if you please.'

'Is it a West End theatre?' Edward asked.

Jack laughed briefly. 'It is no use, Edward, I am not going
to say another word. No more questions until we get
there.' Pleased at Edward's impatience, he sat smiling to
himself as he paid the bill, adding a generous tip. When the

doorman had found them a cab, he insisted that Edward should get in it while he whispered their destination to the driver.

The hansom turned left along the Strand, and then down Whitehall. Reaching Millbank, where there was less traffic, the horse trotted smartly along beside the Thames in the direction of Chelsea.

Edward had been doing his best to stay silent, but as they crossed Chelsea Bridge, he said, 'South of the river, then.'

'Quite remarkable, your powers of observation,' Jack laughed. 'Yes, south of the river, like Shakespeare's Globe.'

'Not in Battersea, where my aunt and uncle live?'

'No, but not far from there. Oh, I'll give in, Edward, and tell you—it's at Clapham—the Grenville, Clapham.'

'The Grenville. Never heard of it.'

'No reason why you should have,' Jack said blandly.

Soon after, Edward was gazing at the façade of the Grenville Theatre. A rather forbidding-looking building, badly in need of redecoration, it seemed, from the evidence of the tattered posters pasted on its walls, to have been shut for a very long time.

Jack took a key from his pocket and unlocked a side-door. 'I'll lead the way.'

Edward could see nothing in the pitch-black interior, but was acutely aware of the smell of stale beer and oranges, and an underlying mustiness.

'Stand still,' Jack said. 'I'll light a lamp or two.'

Before long a gas lamp flared, and then another, and Edward realised that he was standing at the back of one of the circles. The light shed by the two lamps was dim, but he was able to make out below him the stalls—or at least, where they should have been, for there were no seats there—and the empty stage beyond. Everything looked worn and dirty. His gaze travelled over the proscenium arch, decorated with cupids and cornucopias, chipped and filthy. Above it stood two statues of females in Grecian robes. One, he could just see, was labelled 'Melpomene', and the other 'Thalia'. How many of the theatre's patrons had ever heard of the Muses?

Jack rejoined him, carrying a candle. 'Marvellous, isn't it? Come on, I'll show you the rest of it.' With bubbling enthusiasm, explaining where they were, what this room

183

was used for, how many of the audience could be accommodated in this part, he led the way up and down stairs, along corridors, through subterranean passages.

Edward followed miserably. He found the all-pervading odour of dirt and decay half-stifling, and was relieved when at last they returned to the dress circle.

'Seen enough?' Jack asked.

'Yes, I should think so.'

'Well, what do you think?'

Edward avoided a direct answer. 'You'll never get the fashionable world to come all the way out here,' he said.

'Who said anything about the fashionable world? I'm going to do for the people of Clapham and Battersea and Wandsworth and Balham what Emma Cons has done for those around Waterloo and the Elephant and Castle. The Grenville's been a music hall, with none too savoury a reputation. I'm going to bring top actors here, in the best plays.'

'Will they come? Top actors, I mean.'

'They'll come anywhere, provided they're paid.'

Edward could no longer restrain himself. 'But, Jack, the whole place is filthy, and decrepit, and . . . and horrible!'

'Of course it is, old chap,' Jack said. 'I wondered when you'd notice. You don't think I'm going to let it stay like this, do you? Try to imagine it cleaned and redecorated and re-equipped.'

'That's going to cost a fortune.'

'I can afford it.' Jack looked at Edward seriously. 'I've taken professional advice, and I know just what it's going to set me back. Let's go back home, and I'll tell you all about it.'

For the next few hours, Edward listened as Jack talked without pause about his theatre, and produced the plans, and explained every detail. This was a Jack he had never seen before—no dilettante, but a man of enthusiasm who seemed to have considered every aspect of the project from a sensible and practical viewpoint. 'I'm very impressed, Jack,' he said. 'It's a huge undertaking.'

'Not all that big,' Jack said. 'Much of what you saw this afternoon can be repaired and renovated. A lick of paint, some new upholstery on the seats—the whole place will be transformed at far less cost and time and trouble than you might imagine.'

'What about that space where the front stalls should be?'

'Yes, I've got to get new seating to go there. That used to be the promenade, when the Grenville was a music hall. And you know what the promenade was used for.'

'No.'

Jack laughed. 'Even you can't be that innocent, Edward. It's where the prostitutes went, and the pimps, and the pretty boys, too. You could find anything you wanted in the promenade.' He smiled. 'So they tell me, of course. I don't speak from personal experience. But the Grenville's going to be respectable—the sort of place the family can come to.'

'It all sounds wonderful, but—'

'But . . . ?'

'I'm afraid it's going to be much more difficult than you think. A theatre can't work without an audience, and Clapham's such an out-of-the-way place to get to. The Old Vic's just over the river at Waterloo. This is miles away.'

'Emma Cons didn't rely on people coming over the river. She brought the locals in, and if she could do it, so can I. Dammit, Edward, I'm *going* to do it. Raise your glass, old boy, and I'll give you a toast. The Grenville Theatre!'

'The Grenville Theatre, and your success!' Edward sipped his brandy. Then he asked, 'What made you so enthusiastic about this?'

'I'm not sure. When I heard about it, it suddenly seemed . . . well . . . worth doing. I've always loved the theatre, and I think other people—people who wouldn't ever go to a West End theatre—ought to have the chance of enjoying it, too.'

'Yes,' Edward said. 'I can understand that.'

'Can you, Edward? Can you really?' There was great intensity in the way Jack put his question.

Edward considered carefully. He had drunk a great deal, and his mind felt a little fuddled. 'Yes,' he said. 'Yes, I can. I've just said so.'

'Then join me, Edward. I can do with your brain—with all the qualities that my father's recognised in you.'

Edward gave a little laugh, and shook his head. 'Everybody wants me to join them. It's very flattering. But, Jack, the theatre's not for me. It's good of you to ask, and I appreciate it. But, you see, I don't feel about it the way you do; I don't love it. I mean, I enjoy it, and . . . and everything, but . . .'

'You can't love cast iron more than the theatre. That doesn't make sense.'

Edward laughed. 'No, it doesn't, does it? But I do. At least, I don't know whether I *love* it, exactly, but I'm fascinated by it. Besides, I can't leave what I'm doing, all that I've started at your father's firm. "No man, having put his hand to the plough," and all that sort of thing.'

There was a long silence before Jack spoke again. 'I suppose you're right, Edward, old boy. Anyway, tell the old man, will you? Tell him Idle Jack has found himself something worthwhile to do at last. Have some more brandy.'

'Yes, I will,' Edward said. 'Tell your father, I mean, not have more brandy. I think I'd better go to bed.'

'Nonsense! There's still half an inch left in the bottle. I can't drink all that by myself.'

'Well, only a little,' Edward said.

Jack poured some of the brandy into Edward's glass, and the remainder into his own. He held the bottle up and peered at it. 'That's funny,' he said, 'I gave you a little, and me a little, and I thought there'd be a little left. But since there isn't, no heel-taps, Edward. Here's to us!'

But Edward was already asleep.

7

Edward did not enjoy his journey back to Shropshire. His head was throbbing, and though he managed to doze, the jerking and the noises of the train soon woke him up again, and each time he felt worse than before. The fact that his own stupidity was to blame did not help. He should have refused most of the liquor—he did not have Jack's head for it. But he was glad he had had that conversation, and looked forward to relating it to Mr Chetwynd.

Arriving in Rudleigh in the early afternoon, he decided to wash and change before going to report. A sponge-down, and then a clean shirt might make him feel better. He was surprised to find Mrs Woodham waiting for him in the cottage. He was able to understand her better these days, and gathered from the usual flow of words that Mr Chetwynd had warned her of his return, that she had heated water for him to wash, and that she would have a meal ready by the time he came out again.

When he emerged, having washed away the grit of the train journey and changed his linen, Mrs Woodham brought in a large pot of stew, and ladled a generous portion on to his plate.

He had not eaten all day, but the smell of the stew, appetising though it might have been, was too much for him. He smiled at her apologetically, and pushed the plate away, closing his eyes and resting his head in his hands. He was vaguely aware of her leaving the room, and a few moments later felt her touch his sleeve. When he opened his eyes, the pot and his plate had gone, and she was offering him a glass containing a dark brown liquid.

'What is it?'

The reply was beyond comprehension. He swallowed the concoction, which had an unpleasant bitter taste. Putting the glass down, he closed his eyes again, nauseous from the relentless pain of his headache. But after a few minutes, he realised that the throbbing in his temples was slightly less intense. Cautiously, he opened his eyes. There was no blinding agony, and the pressure in his head was slowly disappearing. Mrs Woodham was gazing intently at him, like a witch casting a spell. 'What on earth was in that drink, Mrs Woodham?' he asked.

'Herbs,' she said, for once quite clearly. 'Wormwood, mostly.'

'You should put it on the market. You'd make a fortune with that.'

He felt less of an invalid with every moment that passed. He thought about the stew, and realised that he could do so without nausea. Perhaps if he had something to eat, he would finally lose that unwelcome taste of brandy which had been in his mouth all day. After a while, he smiled at Mrs Woodham. 'I wonder . . . I feel so much better, I think I could manage that stew now.'

She shook her head. 'Not yet,' she said. 'In a minute.'

He nodded, accepting that she knew what was best, and leaned back in his chair, closing his eyes again. He must have dozed, because once more Mrs Woodham touched his sleeve, and the piled plate of stew was in front of him again, and this time he felt as fit as a fiddle, and ravenous.

As he finished his second helping, he noticed a small packet, lying on the chest in a corner of the room. 'What is that, Mrs Woodham?'

She bustled over and brought it to him.

He opened the envelope and pulled out a sheaf of papers. On the first sheet was written, 'My dear Edward, I kept thinking of your requirements, and could not stop myself from committing a few thoughts to paper. They are very rough, and may not be at all what you had in mind. I could do more, if you want me to, but shall take no offence if you consider them worthless. N.B.: No cake-stand!!! Your affectionate Aunt Frances.'

The drawings were little more than sketches. There were designs for gates and garden furniture and an arch which might lead to a rose walk, and another clearly meant for the roses themselves to climb upon; Frances had also drawn some smaller objects—a book-trough and a little stand to carry a pocket watch when it was not in use and a candlestick. The designs all had considerable simplicity and whenever it was suitable, made much use of slender fluted columns; it was this element which gave them a common identity and an elegance which quite delighted Edward. He leafed through them again, with growing excitement.

She must have drawn them that very night after he had left, and posted them first thing in the morning. Dear Aunt Frances! He could have hugged her, if she had been there to hug.

Hastily he finished the stew, thanking Mrs Woodham again, gathered up Aunt Frances' designs, and ran out of the cottage and towards the foundry.

Mr Chetwynd greeted him warmly, and asked, 'How is Jack?'

'Very well, sir, and I have much to tell you about him. How did you know I'd seen him?'

'Easy, Edward. Your telegram was something of a surprise, since I knew no reason why you should wish to spend an extra night in London. And then I guessed that it must be at Jack's behest.'

'Yes, the good news the telegram mentioned is about him.'

Chetwynd looked at him sharply. 'Indeed? What's he been up to now?'

Edward began to explain.

'A theatre!' Mr Chetwynd exploded, going into a paroxysm of coughing and wheezing. 'What sort of theatre?'

Edward explained, doing his best to understate the dilapidated condition of the Grenville Theatre and its previous history.

After a while, Mr Chetwynd stopped him. 'The boy is mad,' he said, grimly. 'There is no quicker way of losing his money. Well, it may bring him to his senses. He'll discover that it's no good playing at life, or at being the manager of a business—especially not a theatre.'

'I don't think he *is* playing at it, sir. I've never seen Jack so determined about anything. And all the plans he's making —he's going into everything in the greatest detail, and taking advice, and . . . He showed me all the papers, and he has all the information at his fingertips.'

'It doesn't sound at all like Jack.'

Edward smiled. 'I thought the same, sir. I think . . . well, you might say he's turned over a new leaf. And I'm sure it's because he's taking it all so seriously that he said it would be good news for you.' When Chetwynd did not reply immediately, Edward said, 'Jack cares a great deal about your opinion, sir.'

'Nonsense! He has never cared twopence for it.'

'I assure you he does, sir.'

'Did he tell you so? Perhaps he instructed you to say as much.'

'No, sir. I doubt if he would ever do that. But I'm certain that it's true. He wants your approval. I know it's none of my business, but you might drop him a line, and—'

'I write to him regularly.'

'I know, sir. But . . .'

'Well? Spit it out!'

Edward drew a deep breath, took his courage in both hands, and said, 'When you write next, sir, don't tell him all the things that worry you about this project of his—just tell him how pleased you are.'

'I am *not* pleased. It's the last thing he should be doing.'

'You could pretend, sir. You could wish him luck.' Chetwynd's face was getting redder by the minute, and Edward hastened to apologise. 'I'm sorry, sir. I'm afraid I have been impertinent.'

'Yes, perhaps you have.' He thought for a moment. 'It is not like you to forget your manners, Edward. Just what is your concern in this?'

'He's my friend, sir.'

'Is that all?'

Edward smiled. 'Isn't it enough, sir?'

For a moment or two Chetwynd held Edward's gaze, the muscles in his cheeks flickering. Then he looked away, and said, a little gruffly, 'I shall think about it. Now tell me *your* news.'

'I've engaged Beeson, sir. The more I talked to him, the more I felt sure he was the right chap for the job. Mr Jarvis doesn't seem to mind the thought of him leaving, but wants him to work out the rest of the week. He should arrive here on Monday.'

'He doesn't mind him leaving? That isn't much of a recommendation.'

'I think he gets on with the customers too well for Mr Jarvis' liking.'

'H'm. Well, we shall see. And how about your aunt and uncle?'

'When I spoke to them about it, they both turned me down flat.'

'I'm not surprised. Silk is not cast iron, and engraving is not wood-carving. Well, I have some news for you on that score. After you had left, I had what I think is a good idea. Why not retain Sales and Nightingale as carvers, but use freelance designers? I mentioned the idea to my step-daughter, who recalled an acquaintance of hers, a Mr Ralph Quennell. You may have heard of him. He is an artist—a celebrated artist, one might say—who has exhibited at the Royal Academy and who lives not far from Shrewsbury. She has been to see him, and secured his agreement to draw up some designs for us. Sales and Nightingale have been informed, and though their noses are a bit out of joint, naturally they will do as they are told. What do you say to that?'

'Excellent, sir. And perhaps my aunt could work on a similar basis, too. You see, although she turned me down when I talked to her, she must have had second thoughts, because when I got home today a package was waiting for me with a batch of drawings that she's done. I've got them here, sir. I think they're just what we need.' He drew out the sketches that Frances had sent him, and handed them across the desk.

Chetwynd glanced at the top drawing, and then quickly leafed through the rest, frowning as he did so. 'Nothing there,' he said, dismissively. 'You cannot seriously be suggesting that we should use these.'

'Why not?'

'Why not? Because they're amateurish, and out of fashion, which is worse. We used to have a line with this same sort of crude simplicity, but it didn't sell. People like cast iron to be embellished. After all, we are manufacturers of *decorative* cast iron.. It's a matter of the dictates of the material, you see. Cast iron is solid and perhaps a little lacking in—what shall we say?—in romance, if that is not too fanciful a word. It needs embellishment, decoration, fancy work, particularly in a period like this, when the

191

richness of the age is reflected in popular taste. These drawings of your aunt's have an austerity, a lack of imagination which would make them virtually unsaleable.'

Edward could not hide his disappointment as he gathered up the drawings. 'Yes, sir.'

'It's no use looking like that, Edward,' Mr Chetwynd said. 'I know you think I'm wrong, but you must simply accept that I know a great deal more about this subject than you do. I am sure that Mr Quennell will produce designs about which we can both feel enthusiastic.'

'Yes, sir.'

*　　*　　*

Edward quickly recovered his good humour. In any case, he had no time to brood. There were long consultations with Mr Chetwynd and Miss Unwin, and many hours of figure work, concerning the changes to be put into effect in accordance with Edward's report. The most time-consuming business was the assessment of all items in the stock-list to decide which should be deleted, and the repricing of those that were to remain, in order to make them competitive with Ironbridge's products. Each catalogue entry had to be considered separately, and Beatrice Unwin, apparently fully recovered, but still unconvinced that the scheme would not ruin the firm, argued interminably, particularly about the reduction of the prices. She gave in eventually, but only when Edward suggested that any losses might be recouped by increasing the prices on their most successful lines, such as the animal figurines.

On the Monday, Frederick Beeson arrived, looking rather bedraggled and extremely young.

'What on earth's that?' Edward asked.

'What?'

'On your upper lip.'

'That's me moustache,' the boy said, with some indignation.

Edward hid his smile. 'Oh, is it? Well, my friend, I wouldn't have recognised it as such, and it's going to have to go. I suppose you think it makes you look older.'

'That's right.'

'On the contrary, it makes you look absurdly young. You

192

just wait a bit before you start growing a moustache. You found Rudleigh all right, then.'

'Easy, Mr 'Arcourt,' Beeson said. 'But it ain't 'alf a long way from Great Luckton.'

'Yes, you look a bit travel-stained. We'd better go to my cottage before I introduce you to Mr Chetwynd, and tidy you up. And I expect you'd like a cup of tea.'

'An' a bite to eat wouldn't do no 'arm, Mr 'Arcourt. Sort of reward for givin' up me moustache.' He grinned. Then he said, rather uneasily, 'What's 'e like—Mr Chetwynd? Sounds a bit of a tartar.'

'Oh, he is! He'll have you quaking in your shoes,' Edward said solemnly, and then relented. 'No, he's all right. A real gentleman, you'll find.'

Despite that reassurance, he was amused to see that the young man remained apprehensive. However, a wash and a few strokes of his cut-throat razor left Beeson looking more respectable, and a cup of tea and several slices of bread and jam seemed to restore his self-confidence. By the time he was taken to meet Mr Chetwynd and Miss Unwin, he was his normal chirpy self again.

Though Edward had decided not to offer any advice about his conduct, Beeson gave an excellent account of himself. His manner was deferential, but at the same time he managed to convey that he was not over-awed by his employer. With Miss Unwin, he was even more successful, though when he thought about it afterwards, Edward could not see exactly how Beeson had achieved it. Again he was respectful, but it was almost as though he were subtly flirting with her.

'You work well for me, young man,' Mr Chetwynd said sententiously, 'and I'll work well for you.'

'I'll do me best, sir,' Beeson said.

'Good. Good. Now, just wait outside for a moment. I want a word with Mr Harcourt.'

'Yes, sir. Thank you, sir.' He turned to Miss Unwin. 'Thank you, too, ma'am.'

She nodded to him graciously, as though she were Queen Victoria herself, Edward thought, and suddenly had to fight to keep from laughing.

'That boy's got character,' Chetwynd said when Beeson had gone.

'He'll be an asset,' Miss Unwin said.

'I'm glad you approve,' Edward said.

'Yes, a good choice, Edward. He'd better start off in the foundry—the same as you did.'

'If he's as good with figures as you say, Mr Harcourt, he might be able to help me,' Miss Unwin put in.

Edward was again forced to conceal his amusement. 'I was hoping that he might spend some time in your office later, Miss Unwin, familiarising himself with the names and details of some of our customers.'

'And I was thinking,' she said tartly, 'of your insistence that I should have an assistant, and as the advertisement does not appear until next Friday . . .' She gave him one of her hostile looks, and then said, 'If you will excuse me, I will get on. There is a great deal to do.' She left the room.

Chetwynd turned to Edward. 'We're advertising for a female assistant. Obviously, that's better for Beatrice, and since the advent of the Board Schools one can be reasonably certain that even girls of the lower classes will be able to do their sums.' He mused for a moment. 'I wonder if universal education will really mean the end of the class system, as some people say. What do you think, Edward?'

'If we have to have a class system at all, it ought to be based on intelligence rather than on ownership of property and on whether you're a business man or a worker in a factory.'

Chetwynd laughed. 'The trouble with that theory is that intelligence very often leads to ownership of property, and to being what you call a business man. Ah, well, we've no time to solve the problems of the world this morning. Tell me, has your young man got suitable clothing for the foundry?'

'No, but I'll see he's fixed up,' Edward said. 'Incidentally, I'd like to be able to call him out of the foundry when I go through our customer accounts, and plan our journeys.'

'All right. Where's he sleeping?'

'He's lodging with Mrs Woodham.'

'You seem to have thought of everything.' He sounded almost disappointed, as though he had hoped to catch Edward out.

Dressed in ill-fitting old clothes, Beeson cut a slight and

194

almost pathetic figure, but, trotting along by Edward's side, he was as happy and excited as a child on an outing. Edward delivered him to Thomas Yardman, asking for a report on his progress at the end of the day, and then busied himself with other chores. Absorbed in his work, he had quite forgotten Beeson until, early that evening, Yardman knocked at his door.

'I sent him off to Mrs Woodham, sir. Bit fagged out, 'e was.'

'How did he get on?'

'Nice enough young chap, 'e is. Friendly, and full o' fun. All the men took to 'im. But I'll tell you this, sir, 'e'll never make a foundryman, not in a month o' Sundays, 'e won't.'

'Why not?'

'All thumbs, sir. Not to mention two left feet. Never known anyone as clumsy as 'im.'

'I was warned he was like that. But he was probably a bit overawed.'

'Not the way 'e was laughin' and jokin', 'e wasn't.'

'Well, he may improve. Try him again tomorrow, Yardman, if you can put up with him. Don't let him do anything that he can spoil. All I want is that he should understand the processes.'

'Aye, sir.'

When Yardman had gone, Edward decided that he had done enough work for the day. It was nearly nine o'clock. By candlelight he ate the cold supper that Mrs Woodham had left for him, and decided then to write some personal letters.

First, a brief but dutiful note to his mother to say that he was well and busy. She would not want to hear more than that. It was soon done, but about to fold it, he realised that he had not enquired after her health or that of the business and her new project, and added a long, concerned and affectionate postscript.

The words of the next letter flowed easily—writing to Alice was almost like talking to her—and he included, because he knew she would be both interested and amused, the story of Beeson's first day in Rudleigh. 'I must admit,' he wrote, 'to being rather pleased that at least one of Mr Jarvis' strictures proved justified. It is something of a relief to find a flaw in my paragon (apart, that is, from his

195

inability to grow a moustache, and even that, I suspect, will come to him in time).'

He hesitated over his previous decision to tell her of his anxieties about his mother, and to ask that she should keep her eye open for anything strange at Brentfield, but the more he thought about it, the more reluctant he felt to make the implied criticism of Sarah, or indeed to involve Alice in what was really no more than a family quarrel.

He sealed the letter in its envelope, drew another sheet of writing paper towards him, and almost without thinking began to write, 'My dear Mary . . .' He had not written to her since seeing her that day in Wensham—indeed, he suddenly realised, he had never corresponded with her before—and there was so much to tell her, and then so many pleas for a response, that it was late when he finished. And he had still not written the letter which really should have taken priority over the others.

He got up and stretched, and decided to make himself a cup of tea. The kettle was steaming gently on the edge of the hearth, and as he waited for the brew to mash, he worked out what he would say in the letter. The plan had been at the back of his mind for several days. It was undoubtedly disloyal to Mr Chetwynd, and might even lead to his dismissal, but he was determined now to go ahead with it.

The candle was beginning to gutter. He lit a new one, poured his tea, and took up his pen.

Dear Aunt Frances (he wrote), I cannot thank you enough for the designs you sent me. They are quite beautiful, and exactly the kind of artefacts, I believe, that Chetwynd's should be producing.

Unfortunately, however, Mr Chetwynd does not share my enthusiasm. I greatly regret this, but you will understand that I cannot contradict him, especially since he invokes his long experience of the trade. He had commissioned a certain Mr Quennell, an artist whom he describes as "celebrated" (though I have never heard of him!—perhaps you have), to prepare a series of designs for us, and is confident that they will be excellent. For my part, I doubt whether Mr Quennell, however 'celebrated' he may be, will show a tenth of the originality and elegance which are the characteristics of your own work, my dear Aunt.

In the next few days, I am to undertake a journey to visit some of our larger retailers. Before my departure, Mr Quennell's drawings should have been delivered. Assuming them to be acceptable to Mr Chetwynd, I intend to take them, or copies of them, to show to some of our customers in order to hear their comments and, I hope, to accept their orders. I shall also take with me your own designs, Aunt, and we shall see whether the trade has more appreciative eyes than Mr Chetwynd (who in other respects is a most admirable gentleman).

I shall of course inform you as to the outcome, and I have no doubt that if the trade receives your work with warmth, Mr Chetwynd will be generous in his admission of error and in the reward which he will grant you.

With my kindest regards to you, my dear Aunt, and to Uncle Alfred,

I remain your affectionate nephew, Edward.

*   *   *

Edward took an instant dislike to Mr Quennell. A small man, he had made himself into almost a caricature of an artist, with long hair, and an outfit—velvet jacket, enormous drooping bow of silk at his neck, loud-checked trousers—which even Oscar Wilde might have considered *de trop*. He exuded self-satisfaction, but at the same time looked at everyone around him with suspicion in his hard little eyes, as though he felt they might attempt at any moment to expose him as a charlatan.

However, there was no doubting his talent, and Edward joined Mr Chetwynd and Miss Unwin in sincere admiration of his designs. They were quite unlike those which Aunt Frances had prepared, being much more in the tradition of the existing Chetwynd products, but, although Frances herself might well have condemned the intricacies and elaborate ornamentation of Mr Quennell's work as 'fussy', there was no denying that they were attractive and, which was more important, distinctive.

197

'An artist's work,' Mr Quennell pronounced, 'must have a leitmotiv. I have taken two basic shapes, the diamond and the shell. These are my leitmotiv, and all my designs are variations upon that theme. Even in those items designed to commemorate the Jubilee, where I have used the Imperial Crown, the diamond and the shell still make their presence felt.'

'Yes. Yes, I see,' Chetwynd said.

Quennell was not to be stopped. 'The work therefore has a coherence,' he went on, 'and it is this, Chetwynd, which transforms it from a utilitarian product into art. Art, moreover, I flatter myself, of the highest order. I am not given to blowing my own trumpet, but I venture to suggest that you would have to go a long way, a very long way, to encounter originality, coupled with beauty of conception, to that degree.'

'I am delighted, Mr Quennell, delighted,' Chetwynd said. 'You see, Edward? This is what I meant when we were discussing the matter the other day—*decorative* cast iron.' He turned back to the artist. 'I trust that you will be willing to design other articles for us, Mr Quennell. No doubt Beatrice has told you that our range has to be extremely wide.'

'I will see whether I can find the time for it, Chetwynd,' Quennell drawled. 'Of course the fee would have to be negotiated. Far too many so-called artists nowadays believe that they demean themselves by designing for commercial purposes, whereas in my view, to bring art to the public at large is the worthiest of missions. But you would no doubt agree that the labourer, especially in so exalted a field, is worthy of his hire.'

Chetwynd bowed. 'We can discuss that in due course.'

'Might I have a private word with you, sir?' Edward asked.

'Beatrice, my dear,' Chetwynd said. 'Do offer Mr Quennell a glass of cordial, or indeed whatever refreshment he desires. Mr Quennell, would you excuse me for a brief moment?' He drew Edward over to the window. 'What is it, then?'

'I was simply going to suggest,' Edward whispered, 'that before we commission any more designs from Mr Quennell, we ought to see how the trade reacts to those

198

we've got. I could take the drawings, or copies of them, when I begin calling on our customers.'

Chetwynd looked impatient. 'But of course, Edward. That was my intention. I'm certainly not going to pay Mr Quennell a penny more than his already excessive fee until we see how the designs go. But I am confident that they will be very well received. Now please don't interrupt again unless you have something important to say.'

Yes, Edward thought, he had deserved that, and made a mental note never to underestimate Mr Chetwynd.

*   *   *

Edward had hoped to begin his travels almost at once, but when the thinning out and repricing of all their products had been completed, the catalogue had to be reprinted, which took time, and there was a further delay because the proofs arrived while Mr Chetwynd was away, visiting the Bristol warehouse and making the preliminary arrangements for its closure, and he had left strict instructions that they were not to be passed for press in his absence.

Fortunately, there was plenty of work to keep Edward occupied, including the preparation of costings for the new designs from Mr Quennell, and here Miss Unwin agreed that their originality and attractiveness justified, at least initially, a fairly high price. Edward also took it upon himself to order trial mouldings to be made of a couple of the Quennell pieces—items small enough for him to carry on his journey.

Beeson, meanwhile, was still working in the foundry most of the time. It was apparent from Thomas Yardman's reports that his practical ability had not improved, but he had quickly assimilated the theory of casting iron. 'An' 'e's picked up all the terms we use, and says 'em the way we does, too,' Yardman said. 'You'd think 'e'd been born and bred in Rudleigh.'

Finally, at the beginning of September, 1896, all was ready, and Edward and Beeson set off, full of high expectations. This, the first of their trips around the country, was to set the pattern for the firm's new prosperity. They left on a Tuesday morning, and were to be away for the rest of the week, but the distances they travelled were to be kept to a minimum, and they would visit only Shrewsbury, Stafford, Wolverhampton and Bridgnorth. Edward had no worries. Given the new prices, the new designs, and the fact that their customers had not been called on regularly, he expected something of a triumphant progress.

When they got back to Rudleigh on the Saturday afternoon, although he refused to be totally downcast, still convinced that Chetwynd's was working on the right lines, he had to admit to a considerable disappointment. The journey had not been wasted, and, indeed, he had brought back many orders—sufficient to justify the expenses he and Beeson had incurred—but nothing like the growth in business that he had envisaged. Few of the retailers had seemed at all impressed by the price cuts—'Trying to get rid of your old stuff, eh?'—and seemed in no hurry to add to their existing stocks by more than small quantities, even though the prices were more competitive.

The new designs had been rather more successful, but although Quennell's drawings had been much admired, most ironmongers seemed to think that the products were too expensive, and their orders were cautious. The Jubilee designs received some approbation, but it was too early for much response for them.

The reports which Edward had written at the end of each day made no mention, of course, of the fact that everywhere he went he had shown the designs drawn by his Aunt Frances, though he had had to let Beeson into the secret. Few retailers had expressed much interest, and only one had been willing to give an order if Chetwynd's should decide to begin manufacture.

To Edward's surprise, Mr Chetwynd was not at all dismayed by the other results. He studied Edward's reports, and said, 'Not too bad, Edward. Not too bad at all. You can't expect much more from these people—after all, they're all on Ironbridge's doorstep—in their pockets. Next time you can go a bit farther afield.'

'I'd thought that the Quennell designs would do much better.'

'It's a conservative trade. We'll see how well the line does on your next trip, but it's my guess that we'll soon be able to start manufacture.'

'I'm relieved to hear you say that, sir. I was afraid you might be on the point of regretting everything that we're trying to do now.'

'Or that I might think it was all your fault, that you were not much of a salesman. Well, I don't. I have every confidence in you, Edward, and in our new approach. You still believe we're right, don't you?'

'I've no doubts at all, sir.'

'Good. How did Beeson do?'

'Extremely well. After we'd made three or four visits, I let him try on his own, and he got some of the best orders we had.'

'Good.' Chetwynd paused. 'Beatrice has at last found her assistant. I was giving up hope that we'd ever get anyone suitable. A young woman from Shrewsbury applied— name of Nancy Huggins. Used to be a housemaid.'

'A housemaid? But we wanted someone good at figures.'

'Wait, wait. Her parents put her into service, but she's always hated it, and she claimed to be a dab hand with her sums. So we gave her columns of figures to add up, multiplication of pounds, shillings and pence, and so on, and she got it right every time. Besides which, she's a nice girl, well turned out, and quite a looker. I don't mind telling you, Edward, if she were a maid in my parents' house and I were a boy again I'd be looking to roger her before you could say knife.' His laugh turned into wheezy splutterings.

Edward was inevitably reminded of Tessie, and somehow expected Nancy Huggins to look like her. But Tessie had been big and blowsy and no one would have called her pretty, while Nancy was beautiful, Edward decided. Not very tall, and slight of build, she looked like a delicate piece of porcelain. Her face was enchanting, elfin, with wide green eyes, and a pretty little nose, and full, almost pouting lips.

Edward could fully understand Mr Chetwynd's feelings. If his own thoughts had not been so filled with Alice, he could have fallen for Nancy himself. Beeson was obviously knocked, as he might have expressed it, into the middle of next week, and could not take his eyes off her.

Beatrice was naturally aware of the effect that Nancy was having on the two young men in her office, and acted

201

quickly, sending the girl on what Edward thought was almost certainly a totally unnecessary errand.

When he got back to his cottage, he was delighted to find a letter from Alice waiting for him. 'I wonder whether, since you are intending to travel quite widely in England, you will soon be coming to this part of the world again. I know that your mother will be pleased to see you—she said as much when we dined at Harcourt Place a few days ago (she is in the best of health, by the way, which I am sure you will be gratified to hear)—and of course there is always a welcome for you in Franton. It seems a very long time since we saw you here.'

Edward promised himself that he would visit East Anglia as soon as he could. But, much as he wanted to see Alice again, there were other areas of England which were of greater importance to the business.

During the autumn and winter of 1896, and on into the spring of 1897, he and Beeson travelled up and down the country. Mr Chetwynd's optimism was entirely justified, and orders began to creep up in size and frequency. The more compact catalogue proved to be a useful sales tool, and more and more retailers decided to stock the Quennell line. Quite early on, Chetwynd started manufacture, and also commissioned Mr Quennell to produce additional designs.

The time eventually came when Edward travelled to East Anglia, and while Beeson visited his aunt and uncle in Great Luckton, was able to make a brief call on his mother.

She was in the sitting-room when he arrived, sitting at her desk, working on various papers. A glass of brandy was by her side. 'Edward!' she exclaimed. 'You didn't let me know you were coming.'

'No. I'm sorry, Mama.'

'You're staying the night, of course.'

'No. A very short visit, I'm afraid. I'm going on to Franton and putting up at the hotel there.'

'And what's wrong with your home?'

'Nothing, Mama,' he said patiently. 'But I have to be in Franton early tomorrow.'

'I thought you must be dead,' she said. 'I never hear from you.'

It was quite unjust. He wrote to her regularly, but rarely

received a reply. He did not acknowledge the accusation. 'How is everything, Mama?' he asked pleasantly. 'You never told me what happened to your plan for manufacturing silk undergarments.'

'What? Oh, that was never more than a wild idea. As soon as I thought about it properly, I knew it wouldn't work. I've quite enough problems, without adding to them. Pour me another drink, will you?'

'A bit early, isn't it, Mama?'

'Edward, really! You're not in the house five minutes before you start criticising.'

They spent an uncomfortable hour before Edward could make his escape. Dinner with the Prideaus was much more pleasant, and Alice Ouvray listened sympathetically as despite his previous resolutions, he poured out his anxieties about his mother.

'I know I can trust you not to let it go any farther, Alice,' he said. 'I don't even want your grandfather to know. But she's drinking a great deal, and . . . Every time I see her, it's the same old story—she needs me at the mill; she can't carry on by herself; if only I understood the burdens she has to carry, and so on and so on. The time before this when I saw her she was talking about branching out into the manufacture of clothing, and I was to be in charge of it, but it was just a trick to try to get me back. She doesn't really want me there anyway, and if I went back, we'd be at each other's throats in a matter of hours.'

'It is very difficult for you, Edward,' Alice said. 'We always feel guilty if we believe that we are neglecting the duties which our relationships impose upon us. But I think sometimes that those duties have to be ignored. From all you tell me, there is really nothing that you can do to help your mother, and you have your own life to consider. You are making a success of your work, are you not?'

'I think so.'

'And you enjoy it?'

'I love it,' he said, smiling for almost the first time in their conversation.

'Then you must continue with it, and not let your concern for your mother deflect you from it.'

As he went back to his hotel, Edward felt much happier. It had been a relief to share his problems with Alice, and it

203

was wonderful to have her support. She was so understanding and level-headed.

Beeson was waiting for him at the hotel, and before going to bed, they discussed their plans for the next day, and went through the customer record cards which they now kept. Then Beeson said, ''Scuse the liberty, Mr 'Arcourt—are you goin' to marry 'er, this lady you been to see?'

Edward laughed. 'That's none of your business, Beeson. But while we're on the subject, don't you get any ideas in your head about Nancy Huggins. You're far too young to settle down to being a family man.'

'Yes, sir.' Beeson paused, and then asked innocently, 'When shall I be old enough, sir? When I'm as old as you?'

Edward laughed again. 'You know what, Beeson? You're a cheeky young bugger!'

'You still 'aven't answered me question, sir.'

'What question?'

'Whether you're going to marry the young lady.'

It was impossible to be angry with him. 'I told you, it's none of your business. I'm not ready for marriage yet.'

'I see,' Beeson said, giving him an amused look.

'And what are you grinning about?'

'Well, Mr 'Arcourt, I notice as you didn't say you *wasn't* going to marry her—only as you wasn't ready.'

'Same thing, Beeson, same thing,' Edward said, still smiling. 'And now back to business, if you don't mind. Have you done your reports on today's calls yet?'

But Edward did not listen to the reply. Was it really true, he wondered, that he was not yet ready to marry?

*   *   *

When he arrived back from that trip, a message was waiting for him, telling him to report immediately to Rudleigh House.

Chetwynd's face was grim. 'I am very disappointed in you, Edward, very disappointed indeed. In fact, I have been considering whether simply to pay you what I owe you and tell you to pack your bags and go.'

Edward stood in front of him, white with shock.

'You know what I am talking about, don't you?'

Chetwynd continued. 'You have disobeyed my express orders, and it is only because of all the excellent work you have done that I do not dismiss you out of hand. While you have been away, I have received an order from Kay's in Chelmsford which refers to some designs done by that aunt of yours. I forbade you to show those designs in the trade, did I not?'

'Yes, sir.'

'And you have disobeyed me.'

'Yes, sir. I am very sorry.'

'I take it you have shown the designs everywhere you have been.'

'Yes, sir.'

'Then the fact that this is the only reference to them that we have received bears out my original belief that they would not prove acceptable in the trade. You can only have diminished our reputation.'

Edward looked him straight in the eye. 'No, sir,' he said. 'I recognise that I have been very wrong and foolish, but I never in any way committed the firm to supplying any of the articles. I have shown them, and asked for opinions, but I've made no attempt to sell them, or even to argue with those who disliked them.'

'Which most of them did.'

'Most of them, but not all. Some have been very interested. Not enough to warrant going into production, but . . . The only thing I wanted to do, Mr Chetwynd, was to widen our line with something different from what our competitors produce. I assure you, sir, I acted in only what I thought to be the best interests of the firm. And again I apologise.'

Chetwynd considered. Edward had spoken fearlessly and openly, explaining but not really trying to excuse his conduct. 'If that is all,' he said at last, 'I suppose no great harm has been done. But the fact of your disobedience remains. I find it very hard to forgive, Edward. It will be a long while before I feel I can wholly trust you again.'

'Perhaps I should resign, sir.'

Again Chetwynd did not reply at once. 'No. No, I intend to put this down to the folly of youth. But never, never do such a thing again. If you had told me in advance what you intended to do—'

Edward permitted himself a slight smile. 'You would have forbidden me to do it.'

'Perhaps. Perhaps not. You have very persuasive ways, young man. But the point is that honesty, Edward, really is the best policy—especially towards me. No, I do not wish you to resign.'

Edward remembered his conversation at the Leroys' with Alice Ouvray. Somehow, he had let her down, he felt, as well as Mr Chetwynd . . . and himself. 'I am very grateful, sir' he said, 'and I promise that nothing of the sort will ever happen again.'

Chetwynd was still unsmiling. 'What happened in East Anglia?'

'We took a lot of orders, sir, and young Beeson is doing better and better. He got the biggest order out of Mr Jarvis that we've had for years. And since you know about it now, I must tell you that I had quite a lot of interest in my aunt's designs.' He paused. 'Forgive me, sir, but may I not go on showing them? The customers seem flattered when I ask for their reactions, and, as I say, that is all I do. Only the other day, one of them said, "Now that's the right idea. *We* know what sells, and if more manufacturers would ask our opinion . . ." He didn't like them, actually, but he gave us a good order for our other lines. And if we could arouse enough interest, it might give us entrée into some of the shops who don't stock us at present.'

Chetwynd listened impassively. He sighed heavily. 'As I say, you can be very persuasive, Edward. Well, I will consider it. But never ever take advantage of me again. Very well, we will say no more about it. Sit down, and tell me what else you have to report.'

*　　　*　　　*

Trade reaction to Aunt Frances' drawings continued to be lukewarm, until it occurred to Edward that, since he called the other new designs 'the Quennell line', it might be worth giving a similiar title to Aunt Frances' work. 'The Bunn line' had a slightly comic ring to it, he felt, but why not 'the Frances line'? The new designation did not bring about an overnight success, but seemed to arouse greater interest, and he thought that before long he might

206

even be able to persuade Mr Chetwynd to start casting.

The last of his journeys, before the cycle would begin again in Shropshire, was to London. He had postponed an earlier visit, because expenses would undoubtedly be high, and the capital had never provided any of Chetwynd's larger customers—another weakness he had pointed out in his original report. But now, in late April 1897, the Londoners were preparing for the excitement of the Queen's Jubilee celebrations in June, and trade was buoyant. Big orders were given for all the souvenir items in Edward's stock list, but what really delighted him was the enthusiasm shown almost everywhere for the Frances line. Perhaps Londoners were more sophisticated in their tastes, but it was likely that the rest of the country would gradually follow the capital's lead, and that meant that manufacture should undoubtedly begin.

Edward had been reluctant to visit the Bunns, conscious that he had given his aunt no news of her designs since his first letter to her, and since Beeson was with him he had not thought it reasonable to ask her to put them both up. But now, near the end of the London trip, there was nothing to stop him. Leaving Beeson tucking into a large supper at the Bell at Spitalfields, he headed for Battersea.

As always, the welcome was unstinted, and Frances set about preparing a meal, refusing to allow Edward to consider going back to the Bell to eat.

'One of the things I never understand, Aunt,' Edward said, 'is how you can always provide such a spread when I haven't even had the courtesy to let you know I'm coming.'

'It's soup, cold meat, pickles and bread—that's all. Your uncle drinks soup by the bucketful, loves cold meat, and dotes on pickles, and I bake my own bread, so I've always got them in the larder.'

'But you'll both go short.'

'Nonsense! Anyway, it would do your uncle good to go without for once. Look at him—simply bursting out of his clothes!'

Edward glanced at Alfred Bunn, so thin that he seemed little more than skin and bones, and laughed.

'I do my best,' Alfred said modestly.

'I pour food in,' Frances said, 'and it never puts an ounce of flesh on him. I wish it would. Now, Edward, tell us all you've been doing. You're a naughty boy, you know—you haven't written to me for ages.'

'No, I've been putting it off.' Edward told them everything that had happened, including an account of how he had nearly lost his job, and then said, triumphantly, 'But it's all come right. When I get back to Rudleigh, I'm going to tell Mr Chetwynd to start manufacturing from your designs straight away. The demand is there.'

'Good,' Frances said. 'I'm so pleased for you, Edward.'

'For me? What about for you?'

'Oh, yes, I'm pleased, but it doesn't make any difference to me.'

'It certainly does. You don't think we'll use your designs without paying you for them, do you?'

'How much?' Alfred Bunn asked.

'Now isn't that typical of you?' Frances said. 'You don't ask questions like that, my dear. It's not polite.'

Alfred grinned at Edward, and shook his head. 'Women!' he said. 'Of course you ask. I don't work unless I know what they're going to pay me. So, how much, young Edward?'

Edward suddenly realised that he had never found out how much Ralph Quennell had been paid. 'I'd better confess that I have no idea what we pay for this sort of work. I'll have to discuss it with Mr Chetwynd when I get back.'

'What your aunt wants,' Alfred said, 'is a down payment —it needn't be much—say five guineas per drawing, plus a royalty on every article sold.'

'Yes, I see.' Edward turned to Frances. 'I'll remember what Uncle Alfred says when I talk to Mr Chetwynd.'

'I'm sure anything you say will be fair. And you needn't take any notice of your uncle. I don't, do I, my dear?'

'No,' said Alfred. 'That's why we're so happily married, I suppose. Come, give me a kiss, my love.'

Smiling, Frances went to him, and exchanged kisses. 'You see, Edward, we're a foolish old couple.'

'That, my dear,' said Alfred, 'is simply an invitation for flattery. Take no notice, Edward.'

Edward laughed, and then found himself saying, 'Have you heard from Wensham recently?'

'Yes,' Frances replied. 'Everything is much the same there.'

'I wrote to Mary some time ago—quite a long letter, telling her all that I was doing, and so on.'

'And did she reply?'

'Oh, yes. She said she was well, and enjoying her work as a nurse. She sounds happy, and there was none of that over-emphasis on religion. But then—I've read her letter so often I know it by heart—she went on, "Mother would prefer us not to correspond. She is still bitter towards you, but, dear Edward, I am hopeful. I showed Father your letter, and I know from the way he read it that he was deeply interested, and, I believe, pleased for you. But then he told me that I could reply only to say that you must not write again." So that's my Father for you. Still under Aunt Louisa's thumb. I call him the Cast Iron Man—he can't even move unless she lifts him up and puts him down again like a doorstop.'

'Oh, Edward, my dear, I'm sorry.'

'Let's talk about something else. I hadn't really finished about your designs. Do you think you could do some more?'

'Yes, of course. If you'll tell me what you want.'

'She won't put pen to paper,' Alfred said smiling, 'until the matter of her payment has been settled to my, that is, to *our* satisfaction.'

'Oh, you be quiet, Alfred Bunn!' Frances said. 'You're as sour as all those pickles you like so much. And in any case, I prefer a pencil to a pen, so there!'

'Talking of pickles,' Alfred said, 'when's supper going to be ready?'

Frances gave a shriek. 'Oh! The soup! It must be boiling over.'

*　　*　　*

Edward had so many calls to make that he had no time to go to see Jack until his last day in London. With a couple of hours to spare before their train went, he said to Beeson, 'You'd better come and meet Mr Chetwynd's son.' But Jack's manservant, Templeton, told them that they would find his master at the theatre. Edward calculated that they would just have time to get to Clapham, have a few words with Jack, and hurry back.

The Grenville Theatre looked a great deal smarter than

last time he had seen it. The building had been decorated and was glossy with new paint. A score of posters announced: *Grand Jubilee Re-Opening June 26th*—THE GREAT MACDERMOTT, MARIE LLOYD, ALBERT CHEVALIER, LITTLE TICH, *and full supporting company.*

'Well, I wasn't expecting that,' Edward said.

Beeson's eyes sparkled. 'Cor!' he breathed. 'Wish I could be 'ere then.'

'I didn't know you were a devotee of the music hall,' Edward said. 'You should have said. We could have gone to a show one evening.'

'I already did, Mr 'Arcourt. When you went to your relatives, I gobbled down me supper, and 'igh-tailed it to the old Bedford. Proper treat it was! Dan Leno, and Eugene Stratton, and 'Arry Champion, and Kate Carney—cor, she ain't 'alf a girl, she ain't!'

'How did you develop a taste for music hall?' Edward asked. 'You wouldn't have had much chance in Great Luckton.'

'Lor' bless you, I didn't live there all me life, sir. Me Ma was on the 'alls. I used to go round with 'er.'

'What, all over the country?'

'No. Only in London. She wouldn't take no provincial bookings.'

'And your father?'

'Didn't 'ave no father, sir. Not that I know of, that is. And then me Ma died when I was nine, and I went to live with me uncle and aunt in Great Luckton. I did all manner of things, and ended up with Mr Jarvis. Now you know the story of me life, sir.'

'You don't hanker to go on the boards yourself?'

'I've thought of it, once or twice. I can still do the old soft shoe me Ma taught me. But I like this job, sir. A bit like acting, ain't it? Sort o' puttin' on a show for the shopkeeper. And getting orders is a bit like getting applause, and not getting orders is like getting the bird.'

'Yes, I suppose it is.'

The inside of the theatre had also been decorated, and the workmen were laying a thick new carpet in the lobby and on the stairs and along the corridors that led to the auditorium. One of the men directed them to Jack's office, at the very top of the building.

'Come in,' he called in answer to their knock. He was sitting in his shirt sleeves, his feet on his desk, smoking a large cigar, idly leafing through a magazine. 'Edward, my dear chap! How delightful to see you. Just when I was working myself into a frenzy. Sit down, and we'll have a long chat. I've nothing on this evening, so we can dine together, eh? How's the old man? D'you know, Edward, there's been a miracle? His last letters have been positively friendly. Mind you, he may not approve quite so much when he finds I've gone for music hall rather than the dear old Bard.'

'Yes, I thought you were going to bring culture to this part of South London. Like Miss Emma Cons, remember?'

'I did a bit of checking, old chap, and it seemed as though the natives might be a little more amenable to the likes of Marie Lloyd than to Irving or Tree or any of those. But maybe one day . . . I'll tell you all my plans this evening.'

'No, we've got to leave in a minute or two, or we'll miss our train. And this time I really must catch it, Jack, so don't try and persuade me not to.' He had almost forgotten Beeson, who was standing shyly in the doorway. He beckoned him in. 'Jack, this young man goes by the name of Frederick Beeson. He's working for me—well, for your father really—Chetwynd's first regular salesman, when he's finished his training. He'll be coming to London every so often, and, unless I miss my guess, whenever he does, he'll be patronising your theatre. He's a fervent music hall supporter.'

'Ah, that's what I like to hear. I need people like you, Beeson. Next time you come here, ask for me. You can have my box—compliments of the management.'

'Very kind, sir, but I couldn't do that. I'd feel out o' place in a box. Up in the gallery, that's where I go.'

'Choice or necessity?'

'Well, sir, it's friendly up in the gods, but I'd rather go in better seats if I could afford 'em.'

'Then have a seat in the pit or the upper circle if you prefer. Up to you.'

'Ta very much, sir. Ta very much indeed. Upper circle, if you don't mind. Nearest thing to the gallery, sir. Reckon I'd feel more at 'ome there.'

'All right,' Jack said, smiling.

He had clearly taken a liking to this young man, Edward thought, just as nearly everyone did. The only customers who had not accepted him were the few who clearly thought it beneath their dignity to talk to so young and junior a person. Even those would probably be won over in due course. What a pity it was that Beeson was not better educated—he could go right to the top if he spoke a little better and learned a few social graces.

Jack was still smiling at Beeson. 'There is a condition,' he said.

'Yes, sir?'

'The old man—my father, that is—if he finds out you've seen me, will ask you for a report. Mind it's a good one.'

Beeson grinned. 'Rely on me, sir. I know just the way to do that—sort o' realistic, so 'e don't think it's all a put-up job. And some of the best bits thrown in casual-like.'

'All right, Beeson,' Edward said warningly. The lad had really gone a bit far. 'That's enough.'

'Yes, sir.'

'There's one other thing you can do for me, Beeson,' Jack said. 'Listen to what the audience is saying, and come and tell me. I want to know whether they like the theatre, what they think of the acts, everything.'

'A pleasure, sir.'

'Now, wait a minute, Jack,' Edward said, for once unsmiling. 'He's my employee, not yours.'

'For two pins I'd take him away from you.'

Irritated, Edward said, 'We must go. Good to see you, Jack. Come on, Beeson, before Mr Chetwynd puts any more wild ideas in your head.'

Still annoyed at Beeson, Edward was silent as a cab took them to the station, and once in the train, he worked on his papers for a while, then put them away, and stared out of the window, still without speaking.

'You overstepped the mark, Beeson. You know that, don't you?' he said at last.

'Yes, sir,' Beeson said unrepentantly. 'Sorry, sir.'

Edward thought for a moment. Perhaps he was being unreasonable. After all, Jack had not seemed put out. 'I want you to do something, Beeson,' he said.

'Yes, sir?'

'Listen. Have you ever read any Shakespeare, or Milton, or Keats, Shelley, Tennyson?'

'Poetry, sir?' Beeson sounded outraged.

'Yes, poetry. Prose, too—Dickens, Scott, Jane Austen, the Brontës.'

'No, sir. I don't go much on reading.'

'Well, you're to do so. That's an order, Beeson. The next sales trip you can do on your own.'

'Reelly, Mr 'Arcourt?'

'Yes, really. And when you've finished for the day, and have written up your orders and your report, you can jolly well sit down and start improving yourself by reading.'

'Well, if you say so, sir,' Beeson said doubtfully.

'I do say so. Reading is the best form of education you can find. Tell me, can you speak without dropping your aitches?'

''Ow d'yer mean, sir? Speak proper?' There was the suspicion of an ironic smile on Beeson's lips. 'Oh, Ai could speak ever so naicely if Ai rahlly traid, sir. Or if you won't think me rude, sir, I could talk like Mr Chetwynd—Mr Jack, I mean. "The old man—my father, that is—when he finds out you've been here, he'll ask you for a report. Mind it's a good one."' The tones and the emphases were exactly Jack's.

Edward looked at him in amazement. 'That's incredible. Can you do it again?'

'"I want to know whether they like the theatre, what they think of the acts, everything",' Beeson said, in Jack's voice.

'Can you do me?'

'"That's incredible. Can you do it again?"'

'That doesn't sound in the least like me,' Edward protested.

'Everybody says that about theirselves,' Beeson said, in his normal voice. 'Be just the same if you was to 'ear yourself on one o' them gramophone cylinder things.'

'"One of those gramophone things",' Edward corrected, 'and it's "themselves", not "theirselves". If you can talk decently when you're imitating other people, why can't you do it all the time?'

'Because I don't think of it, I suppose.'

'Well, you jolly well start thinking about it, and learn a bit

213

of grammar, and read some of those books I told you about.'

'Yes, sir, Mr 'Arcourt—Harcourt, I mean.'

'That's better. What are you grinning about, you young scamp?'

'Well, I was just thinking I ain't—I 'aven't—I *h*aven't seen you as worked up since you was trying to sell them 'alf dozen sets o' fireirons to that old geezer in Cheapside.'

'I wasn't worked up. I simply knew that if I persevered I'd get the sale. And I did. Perseverance, Beeson, that's what it takes. That's what you need.'

'Yes, sir.'

It was Edward's turn to grin. 'As a matter of fact, you're right. I *was* worked up. I never thought the old geezer, as you call him, would give in.'

*   *   *

The months slipped quickly by. Chetwynd's was changing rapidly from a sleepy, almost moribund concern into a successful, expanding company, and Edward was kept so busy that he barely noticed the passage of time.

The Bristol warehouse was eventually closed, Mr Chetwynd insisting first that new employment should be found for the younger warehousemen, and *ex gratia* payments made to those of retiring age, and a loan was obtained from the bank for the erection of a new warehouse, built close to the foundry at Rudleigh. When completed, it seemed absurdly large, but its size was soon justified by the firm's increased business.

Ralph Quennell continued to produce a flow of new and successful designs, while a modest but satisfactory sale developed for the Frances line. By the middle of 1898, the Chetwynd catalogue contained no items, other than the animal figurines, which had been in it when Edward first came to Rudleigh; everything else was new, and more popular, and more profitable.

Beeson proved a first-class salesman, and was now quite well-to-do as a result of the commission he earned. Whenever he returned to Rudleigh, he spent as much time as he could in the accounts department, flirting with Nancy Huggins, until Miss Unwin would indignantly turn him out.

214

She, Beatrice Unwin, was a source of some embarrassment to Edward. In terms of the business, she still treated him with suppressed hostility, which sometimes flared into open opposition, but when they met socially, she would fawn on him, smiling toothily, and beg him to sit next to her and would speak to him with the intimacy that might have been reserved for an old, old friend.

She had pressed Edward to spend the Christmas of 1897 at Rudleigh House, but he had pleaded the necessity of visiting his mother, and had escaped for a couple of days. It had been a somewhat reassuring visit. Sarah had behaved more normally than for some time, neither attempting to persuade him to return to Brentfield to work, nor putting forward wild plans for the future of the mill, nor even complaining overmuch of the burdens she had to carry.

He had been disappointed during this visit not to see Alice, who had been spending the festive season with cousins, but he now wrote to her at length and regularly, and she matched him with her replies. As their friendship developed, he came to rely on her as a kind of sounding-board for any problems he encountered, and he could always be sure that her opinion would be carefully considered, to the point, and always leavened with a touch of humour.

One matter in which she could not help him was his concern for his employer's health. Mr Chetwynd, more florid than ever, constantly fought for his breath, and could walk only the shortest distance without a pause for recovery. Though there was no question of relinquishing command of the business, and indeed he made all major decisions, he left more and more of the routine work to Edward, and since he could no longer travel, also depended on him to make any journeys to see important customers or suppliers.

It had become Edward's habit, on his return from one of these business trips, to dine with the Chetwynds that same evening, so that he could make his report and hear of any developments at the foundry.

On one occasion, in December, 1898, he was pleased, when he arrived at Rudleigh House, to find Mr Chetwynd in better health than he had been for some time. He seemed to be breathing much more easily, and even moving with rather less effort.

Now that Chetwynd's was prospering, the food at Rudleigh House had become rather less plain, and the drink flowed, if not like water, at least a little more liberally than at the time of Edward's first visit to the house, as instanced by the glass of sherry which was now regularly offered before dinner.

'Very successful, very successful,' Mr Chetwynd beamed, when Edward had told him of the results of his journey. 'I think we should indulge ourselves—drink to your health, Edward.' He turned to Mrs Chetwynd. 'Ring for the maid, Emily. We'll have another bottle of sherry.'

'No more for me, my dear,' piped Mrs Chetwynd. 'And you shouldn't. Remember what the doctor said.'

'Oh, piffle!' Mr Chetwynd got up, and rang for the maid himself.

A little later, as they were all enjoying the excellent saddle of mutton and were in the middle of a conversation initiated by Miss Unwin about the need for a campaign to introduce some of the villagers to the admirable properties of soap and water—in the midst of this, Mr Chetwynd suddenly rose from his seat, made a strange noise which was half way between a belch and a word of some sort, and pitched forward on to the table.

For a moment there was a stunned silence. Then Mrs Chetwynd cried, 'Oh, no!'

George Chetwynd's head, slightly twisted to the left, rested on the remains of the saddle of mutton. Gravy had splashed everywhere, and little globules of fat were beginning to congeal where they had fallen in his side-whiskers. Blood was running from a wound in his cheek, caused by the protective prong on the carving fork, which seemed in fact still to be slightly embedded in the flesh. His one visible eye was open. He was quite dead.

8

'You're obviously the man for the job,' Jack Chetwynd said.

He and Edward were sitting in the dining-room of Rudleigh House, on the day after George Chetwynd's funeral. The church had been packed, with a great many local dignitaries, business friends and acquaintances of the deceased, and all the foundrymen, uncomfortable in their best clothes. The vicar's obituary remarks had lasted a full hour. The widow, weeping copiously, was much gratified.

After the reception which followed the service, the will had been read to the family, and Jack was now in process of acquainting Edward with its main points. Mrs Chetwynd and Miss Unwin were suitably provided for, and would suffer no real change in their circumstances, especially as Jack was enjoined to allow them to live in Rudleigh House for the rest of their lives, if they so wished, or until one or other of them married. There were no restrictions, on the other hand, on his ownership of the foundry and the business.

'Aren't you going to take over yourself?' Edward asked now.

'Me?' Jack laughed. 'Are you off your head? I couldn't, and I wouldn't if I could. No, I need someone to run the business for me, and you're the obvious candidate.'

'I couldn't either,' Edward said. 'I've been working closely with your father, but he made all the important decisions. I'm still learning. I haven't nearly enough experience.'

'You've got more than most.' Jack looked hard at him, and said, tauntingly, 'Afraid of it, are you? The responsibility beyond you?'

Edward considered. 'Yes. I *am* afraid of it. You can't take a job like this lightly. There are too many other people depending on you—the men at the foundry for a start, and Mrs Chetwynd and Miss Unwin, and young Beeson—everyone.'

217

Jack laughed again. 'Good old Edward! Do you always reply so sensibly to questions like that?'

'But I mean it, Jack. After all, I'm only twenty-five.'

'What's that got to do with it? So am I. Listen, you may not trust my opinion—I'm not sure that I do myself—but it's the old man's judgement I'm going on. He thought highly enough of you to make you his right-hand man. If you were good enough for him, you're good enough for me. And he's not the only one; my dear stepsister is full of your praises.'

'Miss Unwin? But she's opposed me at every step.'

'She thinks you've done splendid work for the firm. She told me she'd been against the changes you'd suggested at first, but that you'd been proved right. But perhaps she's prejudiced in your favour; she's got her eye on you, as I've told you before, and now that you're to run the firm, she'll be keener than ever to be Mrs Edward Harcourt.'

Edward smiled. 'I'm sure you malign her. But in any case, I still think you ought to bring in someone with more experience.'

'Oh, for heaven's sake, Edward, old boy, I want you to run the place for me. How many more times do I have to say it?'

'And supposing I make an awful mess of it?'

'You won't. I don't expect you to be perfect—you'll make a mistake or two. But nothing major. Besides, you won't be operating in complete limbo. You can write regular reports, and we'll see the figures, and if anything starts to go wrong . . . well, we'll have to do something about it.'

'Reports? What sort of freedom would I have?'

'I've got far too much to do to want to interfere with you, old chap. The theatre's not doing too badly, by the way, though things have dropped off a bit since the start. You'll have total freedom. I want you to run the business for me, not pester me about everything. After all, I know nothing about cast iron. And when I talk of reports, all I really want to know is that you're making good profits. Now, do stop arguing, Edward, old son. Accept your fate. Listen to Gipsy Jack, even if you haven't crossed his palm with silver. And talking of money, what was the old man paying you?'

'Four hundred a year. He increased it to that last July.'

'Is that all? Right, we'll put it up to seven hundred and fifty.'

'Wait a minute,' Edward began.

'Plus a share of profits. I'm not sure how much, but we'll work that out later. I believe in incentives. I'd never have got to Cambridge if the old man hadn't bribed me. Love makes the world go round, they say, but incentives give it a little extra push now and then. Does that tempt you?'

Edward was silent for a long time, thinking. He would be a fool to refuse the opportunity, but it was a major responsibility. He looked up almost shyly. 'Well, I'll try,' he said, 'but let's say that it's on a temporary basis to begin with, until—'

'Until you've proved to me that you can do it,' Jack prompted.

'No,' Edward said. 'Until I've proved to myself that I can do it.'

* * *

Miss Unwin had already confirmed her willingness to continue to work under his direction, and Mrs Chetwynd accepted Jack's decision without comment, still preoccupied with her grief. But how would the foundrymen and warehousemen react? They had been friendly enough over the past two years, but it was all very well to have a young live-wire bringing in his new ideas while the old master was still in control; might they not fear that, given his head and with no restraints, the new broom would sweep too clean and push them all to disaster?

Edward and Jack walked together to the foundry. 'I'm going to say as little as possible,' Jack told him, 'and leave the speech-making to you.'

The men had gathered together, solemn and a little apprehensive.

'I have only two things to say,' Jack told them. 'The first is that Chetwynd's will continue. Your jobs are safe, and I look for the business to grow and prosper. The second is that, since I have a concern of my own to run, I have appointed Mr Harcourt to be Manager of the company, in sole control of it. I need not tell you that my father held him in high regard. I now expect you to give to Mr Harcourt the

219

loyalty that you always showed towards my father. That is all, and I will hand you over to Mr Harcourt.'

Edward had been watching their faces. Relief had shown when Jack had spoken of the continuation of the firm, but the announcement of his own appointment had been greeted with little expression, though he was sure that he detected surprise and even some alarm in their eyes.

'My friends—if I may call you that,' he began, 'I am very grateful to Mr Chetwynd for offering me the position of Manager. He has told you that I shall be in sole control of this business, empowered to make all decisions. But I intend to consult you regularly, to inform you of developments or changes, to seek your advice. Normally I shall do so through the person of Thomas Yardman here, who will speak for you, but any one of you may come to me at any time with your problems, whether personal or to do with your work, or to give me advice.' He paused, and grinned at them. 'I cannot promise that I shall always follow what you say. You might suggest that I should double all your wages!' There was a little ripple of amusement, and he waited for it to die down before continuing. 'I'm sorry to say that I'm not going to do that. But I promise that I shall listen carefully to what you have to say, and if there is a decision to be made, and it goes against you, I shall always explain my reasons.'

The men seemed to approve of that, and he went on confidently. 'As you know, our business has been highly successful recently. If our order books continue to fill, then I foresee expansion, enlargement of our works, with perhaps the building of a new foundry, additional employment. And I want you to share in the firm's prosperity. I said just now that I did not intend to double your wages, but I expect to be able to give an extra ha'penny an hour to the lowest paid—that's two shillings and ninepence a week—and more for those on higher wages, beginning in April.'

He raised his hand to still the pleased murmur. 'But none of this, I repeat, will be possible without your help. I trust I can depend on it.'

There was a brief pause as the men waited to see whether he was going to continue, and then several of them said, 'Aye!' and others nodded their approval. Edward

220

stepped forward and offered his hand to Thomas Yardman, who, after a moment's hesitation, wiped his own hand on the seat of his trousers and then gripped Edward's. Someone at the back called out, 'Three cheers for Mr 'Arcourt!' and the response was enthusiastic.

As they walked back to the house, Jack said, 'Well done, Edward. I knew I was right to give you the job.'

'There's a lot of eating to be done before the pudding is proved,' Edward replied.

'Well, you've made a good start. Can we afford those extra wages? What are you going to pay the most senior men?'

'Maybe fourpence an hour more.'

'What's that a week?'

'Twenty-two shillings.'

'What? That's a bit steep.'

Edward sighed. 'Look, Jack, we've got to keep our workers satisfied. The competition from Ironbridge is going to get fiercer, and it's my guess that one of the ways they'll try to beat us is by hiring our best people. We could easily afford to pay the extra now, but by delaying until April, I've dangled a carrot—you remember what you said to me about incentives.'

'Well, all right. As long as you know what you're doing.'

He sounded just like his father, Edward thought.

Jack was silent for a few moments. Then he said, 'You've been going out selling with Beeson from time to time, haven't you? You won't be able to do that so easily now. Are you really satisfied that he can cope on his own? It's a lot of responsibility, and he's very young.'

Edward laughed. 'So am I, and so are you, Jack. And I thought you were happy to leave all the decisions to me. That's two things you've questioned in as many minutes.'

'Touché, old chap, touché. If Beeson's really trustworthy, you can use him as a messenger. Between us, I mean. Tell him to come and see me when he's in London, and he can report on your behalf.'

'I thought you said he was too young for responsibility.'

'Oh, do shut up, Edward!' Jack smiled, and clapped his friend on the shoulder. 'Listen. You made a promise to the men, and I'll make one to you. Keep up the orders, expand the company, and I'll make you a director, and give you a real share in it.'

*　　*　　*

It was finding the house which finally made Edward's mind up for him.

The tiny cottage, though he had grown quite fond of it, was hardly a suitable residence for the Manager of Chetwynd's, and at Jack's suggestion, supported by Miss Unwin, Edward had moved temporarily into Rudleigh House.

During the next weeks, he worked as never before, rising early, taking little time for meals, and stopping only when the chimes of Mr Chetwynd's long-case clock told him that it was midnight. There was no sense in continuing later than that—he would have to leave his bed at five-thirty—but often he failed to hear the twelve chimes, having fallen asleep over his work. Eventually he would stir and work on until the clock struck again at one, or two, or three in the morning.

There was so much to do: keeping watch over the orders as they came in by each day's post; controlling the daily output of the foundry and the stocks in the warehouse; ensuring that supplies of sand and pig iron were on hand; and a hundred other routine matters. There were daily conferences with Miss Unwin, and with Thomas Yardman, and consultations with Ralph Quennell, and occasional visits to important customers, and Beeson's reports to be read and his expenses to be checked. And taking advantage of his promise, some of the men came to him from time to time with their troubles—a request for an advance of wages, or for leave of absence, or other such minor matters.

He began to have a greater respect for the late George Chetwynd—no wonder, even when he was fit enough, he had neglected his regular sales trips, when there was so much to be done here in Rudleigh.

When, after Jack had first offered him the position, it began to sink into Edward's mind that he could make any changes at Chetwynd's that he wished, a little rush of power went to his head, and he spent a happy hour or two

222

dreaming of all that he would do—the extra employees he would take on, the construction of a new, large foundry, additional ranges of goods, and different prices and discounts. And then he thought again, and decided that he would initiate no changes at all for at least six months, so as to be sure of not making foolish mistakes.

But one thing did need to be done straight away. The quality of the pig iron supplied from the Ironbridge Works varied in quality. He knew that Mr Chetwynd had complained on this score, and in the files found a careful letter from Ironbridge, which regretted 'the very occasional lapse', explained that it was almost impossible to maintain an unvarying standard of manufacture (Mr Chetwynd had written 'Rubbish!' against this paragraph), promised an improvement in future, and assured him of their best attention at all times.

When Yardman complained of yet another faulty batch, Edward asked, 'Why do we go on buying from Ironbridge when we get this sort of stuff?'

Yardman considered. 'We always 'ave,' he said at last, and then, as an afterthought, he added, 'They was friends of Mr Chetwynd's.'

'Yes, I saw them at the funeral. But they're a fine lot of friends if they're sending us poor quality pig. I can only assume they're doing it deliberately, because of the inroads we're making into their decorative castings business. What about getting iron from Ellerdine's?'

'Ellerdine's?' Yardman stared at him in astonishment. 'But they're miles away!'

'Yes, but I believe they can still deliver cheaper than Ironbridge, and they're said to produce the best pig iron in Shropshire.'

Yardman shook his head. 'Matter of opinion,' he grumbled. 'You want my advice, Mr 'Arcourt—like as you said you would ask it—my advice is stay with Ironbridge.'

'No, I'm going to give Ellerdine's a trial. We can hardly do worse than at present, and there's every chance we can do better.'

Yardman went away muttering to himself. Edward realised that his opposition did not indicate any lack of respect for himself, nor a genuine doubt about the validity of the new proposal, but was simply due to his belief that the old ways were best and should be adhered to.

He drove to the Ellerdine Company, sought an interview with the manager, and gave a trial order for pig, making it clear that he would take regular supplies only if satisfied that Ellerdine's could maintain their quality, deliver promptly and keep their prices down.

On the way back, he called at the Ironbridge Works. He had hoped to see Mr Hancock himself, but could get no farther than the manager, a Mr Pickering, who clearly had nothing but contempt for young men elevated to positions beyond their competence.

When Edward presented his catalogue of complaints, he was treated condescendingly to a lecture on the difficulties of iron production. 'Had you been in this business as long as I have, Mr Harcourt, you would know that it is inevitable that some batches shall be of a very, very slightly sub-standard quality.'

'I would not complain so forcefully if they were merely very, very slightly sub-standard. The lot you have just delivered is useless. But let me come to the point, Mr Pickering—I have today arranged for the delivery of a quantity of pig iron from Ellerdine's. They have guaranteed the price, the quality and the speed of their delivery.'

'I am sure they have, Mr Harcourt.'

'Why do you say that?'

'Obvious, my dear young sir. They will do everything they can to impress you—until you've signed a contract. Thereafter . . .' He gave a short laugh.

'A contract? Now, that is interesting,' Edward said, pleasantly. 'I do not believe there has ever been a contract between Chetwynd's and Ironbridge.'

'No, there has not. It has not been thought necessary.'

'Ah. Because a contract suggests a more favourable purchase price perhaps? But I was about to say that, in view of our long association, I will cancel my order to Ellerdine's and allow you to continue to supply Chetwynd's, provided that you will guarantee to match Ellerdine's for quality, speed of delivery, and, of course, whatever price they are prepared to offer to anyone who signs a contract with them.'

'There is no question of our reducing our prices,' Mr Pickering said stiffly.

Edward picked up his hat. 'Then there is no further need of discussion. If you will see that we are sent your invoice, less a suitable allowance for the faulty batch of which I have just complained, it will be settled at once. It will, of course, be your final invoice as far as Chetwynd's is concerned. I bid you good-day, sir.'

Edward had been back in his office at the foundry for no more than half an hour when a letter was delivered by hand. It was from Mr Josiah Hancock himself, regretting that Edward should have had cause for complaint, and assuring him that future deliveries of iron would be of the expected quality. 'I understand from Mr Pickering,' the letter continued, 'that you ask us to match the prices submitted to you by the Ellerdine Company, but we would point out that our prices are standard throughout Great Britain.' Mr Hancock ended by assuring Edward of Ironbridge's best attention at all times.

Edward smiled to himself. It was quite obvious that Mr Hancock did not really care whether or not he retained Chetwynd's custom.

From that time on, all their pig iron was supplied by Ellerdine's. Even Yardman found nothing to complain of, and Edward felt that he had gone up in the overseer's estimation—not so much for having had the courage of his convictions as for turning out to be right.

In those early days of his appointment as Manager, Edward had little time to think of himself, but was eventually forced to consider the question of where he should live. To remain in Rudleigh House would be an imposition upon Mrs Chetwynd and Miss Unwin. He must have a house of his own—large enough to be in keeping with his present standing, and yet not so imposing and expensive to run that it would be a financial burden.

He remembered having seen a very pleasant house for rent, situated about a mile outside Rudleigh. On enquiry, he discovered that it was modest enough, consisting of three reception rooms, five bedrooms and two attic rooms for the servants, but nevertheless suitable for a person of some consequence, and the rent was reasonable.

And it was then, while he was thinking about the house, that those memories and longings and hopes, which had lingered at the back of his mind, were at last released, and

225

he knew what he was going to do. It would mean at least two days' absence from the business, he thought, and he could barely afford to be away for as long as that at this juncture. But nothing would stop him from going.

He sent a telegram. It would arrive later in the evening, and give them time to reply before he set off in the morning, if his visit were inconvenient.

He smiled to himself, and began to hum 'Dashing Away with the Smoothing Iron'. It was not very appropriate, but its jaunty rhythm seemed to suit his mood.

*   *   *

'Mr Prideau,' Edward said, 'I am grateful to you for seeing me at such short notice. I am not sure whether you have heard of my recent appointment as Manager of Chetwynd's.'

'Indeed, I have. My congratulations. I am not surprised, Edward. I flatter myself that I saw your potential before anyone else did.'

'I fear you overestimate my abilities, sir, but your good opinion encourages me to continue with what I wish to say. My appointment has resulted in a substantial change in my financial position. While not wealthy, I can claim to be comfortably off.'

'Quite right. I am sure you deserve whatever you earn.' His eyes were twinkling as he looked at Edward.

'I suspect you have already guessed what I am going to say, sir.'

'You seek my permission to ask my granddaughter for her hand in marriage, is that not it?'

'Yes, sir, but—'

'My dear boy, I am delighted. Have you spoken to Alice yet?'

'No, sir, but—'

'I think she's very fond of you. Well, you have my blessing, Edward, and you may tell her so. Not that I would expect her to take much notice of her old grandfather. She has an independent mind, and always has had.'

'Yes, sir, but—'

'What are all these "buts", Edward? You surely have no reservations?'

Edward had spent hours on the journey debating with

226

himself, first deciding to say nothing, and then resolving to reveal the whole story. 'I should have told you right at the beginning, Mr Prideau,' he went on unhappily. 'There are certain facts which you are entitled to know.'

'Facts? What sort of facts?'

'Concerning my . . . concerning myself, sir.'

'Bless my soul, boy, what are you trying to say?'

'It is very difficult, sir. Forgive me. I thought I had prepared myself fully for this, but now I find . . .'

Prideau looked at him in a kindly way. 'Take your time, my boy, take your time. Remember that, whatever these facts are, you are telling them to a friend.'

Edward nodded gratefully. 'Thank you. You will understand my hesitation when I say that what I have to tell you concerns my parentage.' He paused yet again, and then, gazing almost defiantly into Prideau's eyes, blurted out the words he had prepared. 'Although you know me as the son of Mr and Mrs Thomas Harcourt, in fact I am of illegitimate birth.'

The encouraging smile dropped from Prideau's lips. 'Illegitimate?' He drummed his fingers on his desk. 'What are you saying, Edward? That you were adopted?'

'No, sir.'

'No?' It was obvious that the thoughts were whirring through his brain. 'Are you telling me that you are Mr Thomas Harcourt's natural son, born out of wedlock?'

'Not that either, sir.'

'Then what the devil *are* you saying, Edward?'

Edward lowered his head again, and did not reply.

After a moment, Prideau went on, his eyes wide with dismayed astonishment, 'You mean it was . . . your mother who . . . who was at fault?'

Edward nodded miserably.

Embarrassed, Prideau did not know what to say. 'Are you sure that you should be telling me this at all, Edward?'

'How can I do otherwise, sir? What would you think if I were to conceal the truth, only to have it come out later, perhaps when Alice and I were already married? Oh, I fully realise that I am destroying my mother's reputation, and branding myself a bastard, but I have no choice.'

Prideau sat in silent thought for a while. 'Are you certain of this?'

'Yes, sir. It was my father—my real father—who told me.'

'Then you know who he is?'

'Yes. I would prefer not to reveal his name, but he is considered, by those who know him, to be a gentleman of honour, well-to-do and respected.' He raised his head and gazed unflinchingly into Prideau's eyes. 'I am proud to be his son.'

'Has your mother confirmed what you were told?'

'No, sir. She has always brought me up as her late husband's son. And my father . . . my real father . . . has forbidden me to speak of the matter to her. Neither he nor she intended that I should ever know. It came out . . . by accident.'

'I see. Has it changed your feelings towards her?'

Edward gave a little sigh. 'As you know, sir, she and I do not always get on, but I am equally proud to be her son. My mother is a very remarkable woman.'

'Indeed, she is.'

There was a long silence. Prideau went over to the window and gazed out. It seemed an age before he turned, and said, 'Your revelation has been a considerable shock to me, Edward. However, I am glad that you have confided in me. I am even more glad to have heard you express pride in your parents. Tell me, who else knows these facts?'

'No one outside my immediate family, sir.'

'Then, as far as I am concerned, it shall remain a secret. I have never believed in judging a man by the accident of his birth, but rather by his character and his behaviour. Alas, however, there is no denying the stigma attached by present-day society—and by the churches—to those born out of wedlock.' He went back to his desk and sat down. 'I shall endeavour to put the whole matter out of my mind, Edward.'

'Thank you, sir.' Edward's hopes had been alternately rising and falling while Prideau spoke. The words had been encouraging, but the stern, unsmiling way in which they had been spoken seemed to indicate that bastardy might well be a barrier to marriage to Alice.

As if echoing his thoughts, Prideau went on, 'Of course, it is easy to say that, but harder to do, especially as my own interests, and those of my granddaughter, are touched. I will confess that there is a war in my mind. One side of me sees no reason to withdraw my blessing, while the other trembles at the thought. But the fact that you saw fit to tell me frankly of the position, and above all, your attitude towards both of your parents, coupled with my own high regard for you . . . In short, I shall not withhold my consent.'

Edward sighed with relief. 'I cannot thank you enough, sir.' He stood up, and leaned over the desk to shake the old man's hand.

'I would not, however, have my granddaughter enter into this match unaware of the facts. You must tell her, as frankly as you have told me; my consent is dependent upon that. You may be confident that, whatever her decision, neither she nor I will ever reveal your secret. I say "whatever her decision" because you must be prepared for the possibility that your disclosure will change her attitude towards you. I don't suppose it will, but it is a possibility.'

Edward nodded unhappily.

Prideau smiled. 'Cheer up, my boy. Faint heart never won fair lady, and Alice is not only fair, but remarkably sensible.' He leaned back in his chair, as if to relax after a difficult negotiation. 'Now, before you rush off to see her, a few other matters have to be discussed. If she accepts you, there are other conditions that I must put upon your marriage. First, I wish to be reassured that you have suitable accommodation for a wife, and eventually, perhaps, a family.'

'Yes, sir. I have in mind the renting of a property, presently on the market, suitable both for my position and for hers.'

'In Shropshire?'

'Yes. A short distance from Rudleigh.'

'Ah, but a very long distance from Franton. That is my second condition, Edward. Somehow or other you must contrive it that I see my granddaughter regularly. I am too old to go gallivanting about the country, so you must bring her frequently to Essex, or release her from her wifely duties so that she can come on her own to see me. Is that agreed?'

'With all my heart, sir.'

'Then go and find her, and put your question to her.'

229

Edward rose. 'Yes, sir. Thank you very much.'

'Just one other thing,' Prideau said, as Edward reached the door. 'Don't rush her, Edward. Give her time. I have no real doubt of her answer, despite what you have told me, but women are strange creatures, Edward; they like to savour a situation such as this, to linger over it. Do not be surprised if she begs for time to consider your proposal, especially in view of the information that you have to give her.'

'No, sir, I won't.'

'Off you go, then. Good luck.'

'Thank you, sir.'

Edward went in search of Alice. A maid told him that she was in her little private sitting-room. He knocked, and at her command, entered. She put down her sewing and rose to greet him. 'Edward! How good to see you again. How are you?'

'Thank you, I am well. And you? Am I disturbing you?'

'Not in the least,' she said, resuming her seat. 'I am bored. I put on this dress to cheer myself up.' She laughed. 'But it hasn't worked. At least, not until you came.'

The gown was of deep blue, its leg-of-mutton sleeves decorated with a trimming of miniature flowers.

'It's charming,' Edward said.

'You're very kind. Won't you sit down?'

'Not yet. I have been talking to your grandfather.'

'Yes, I know.' She gave a half smile, waiting for him to go on.

Despite having rehearsed what he was going to say, the words stuck in Edward's throat. He swallowed. 'I . . . I . . .' He stepped nearer to her.

'Yes, Edward?' she prompted gently.

'I begged his permission to . . .' He dropped on one knee beside her. 'Will you marry me, Alice?' He saw that she was smiling, but that could mean anything, and there was so much more that he had to say. He hurried on, pouring out the words in one breathless rush. 'It will mean moving away from here to live in Shropshire, but I've promised your grandfather that you shall come back here often to see him, and we shan't be rich, but I will do anything to make you happy, Alice, dear Alice, because I love you more

230

than life itself, and I shall be the happiest man in the world if only you will say "yes". Will you, Alice? Will you marry me?'

She began to laugh, and he looked at her anxiously, realising suddenly how ridiculous he must have sounded.

'Oh, Edward, my darling fool!' she said. 'Of course, of course I will.'

Edward rose and stood gazing at her, thinking of the confession that he now had to make.

Her smile faded for a moment, and then she said lightly, 'It is usual, I believe, for a newly affianced gentleman to kiss the lady of his choice. And to look less solemn.'

'Alice, please sit down again. There is something I must tell you. If, when you have heard it, you wish to change your mind, I shall understand.'

'Why, Edward, you sound so serious.'

'It is a very serious matter.' He began the story, telling her far more than he had told her grandfather, omitting nothing—neither Richard's name, nor even his involvement with Mary.

*　　*　　*

'You have told her, Edward?' Mr Prideau asked, an hour or so later.

Alice squeezed Edward's hand. 'He has told me everything, Grandpapa, and I said it makes not the slightest difference to me.'

'Good. I am glad, and we shall not speak of the matter again. Come and give me a kiss, my dear. I wish you both every joy.' After he had embraced Alice, he asked, 'When's the wedding to be? I have never been in favour of long engagements. What about next month?'

'Impossible, Grandpapa,' Alice laughed. 'There's far too much to do. I thought of April.'

'And what are all these things that have to be done?'

'There's an engagement ring to be bought,' Edward said.

'That won't take till April!'

'And I want Alice to see the house in Rudleigh. And we shall have to see my mother, and some of my other relations.'

'And Edward has to meet *my* relations,' Alice said.

'And I can't ignore my new responsibilities at Chetwynd's. I can't get away just when I feel like it.'

'Nonsense!' Prideau said. 'You're the Manager, you can decide when you'll take leave.' He chuckled, and then added soberly, 'No. I understand your position, my boy. All good businesses derive their success from the man at the top, so you must devote your energy and determination to your work. But never become its slave, Edward. Find yourself a competent man who can take charge in your absence, and everything will continue to tick over happily enough for a few days—even for a week or two.' He paused. 'Ah, but there I go, giving a lecture again. April, is it, then?'

'Yes, sir.'

'Very well. Now, you two young things had better start drawing up a list of wedding guests. As many as you like.'

'But we want a quiet wedding, Grandpapa,' Alice said, 'with just our relations and a few of our very closest friends.'

'It's nothing to do with what you want, Miss. It's for me to decide, and I decide here and now that we shall have a large wedding, a grand wedding, so that everyone can share in the joy, and in *my* pleasure. And you two are going to enjoy it just as much as anybody else, and don't you dare to argue with your grandfather!'

*　　*　　*

Sarah was delighted, in a somewhat absent-minded way, when Edward and Alice travelled to Brentfield to give her their news. The engagement did not surprise her. She had long ago realised that Edward was not drawn, as at one time she had thought, to Edith Ashton.

'You're not taking on an easy man,' she told Alice once when they were alone for a few minutes. 'He's stubborn.' She smiled. 'So am I, if the truth is known, and of course Edward takes very much after me. However, I have no doubt that you'll be able to wheedle him. Men are remarkably easy to manage, my dear. You probably know that already, but you will find it even truer once you are married.' Her brow clouded at a distant memory. 'You are fortunate, of course. Edward has never been attracted to the bottle or to low women.' She raised an admonitory

232

forefinger. 'But make sure that you and your home always provide him with more attraction than he might find elsewhere.'

Alice later related the conversation to Edward, to their shared amusement. But neither expressed to the other the irony which they both saw in such a little homily from Sarah, when they had so recently been concerned with the circumstances surrounding Edward's birth.

Edward would have liked to take Alice on to Wensham, so that she could meet Richard and Aunt Louisa—he could still not think of her as his stepmother—and Mary. But that was impossible. Instead, he wrote to Richard, not only announcing his engagement, but explaining why he had felt it necessary to reveal the truth of his parentage. 'I could not enter upon married life with such a secret between myself and my future wife,' he wrote. 'As for Mr Prideau, he stands *in loco parentis* to Miss Ouvray, and I felt it essential that he should be informed of the facts before I sought his permission to propose marriage to his granddaughter.' He went on to say that he had concealed from Mr Prideau his true father's identity, that Miss Ouvray would not reveal her additional knowledge to her grandfather, and that neither of them would speak of the matter to anyone else.

'I would like to bring Alice to Wensham to meet you and Aunt Louisa and Mary,' he continued. 'I am sure you will like her, and consider me to be the most fortunate of men. There shall not be the least embarrassment for you or for any member of your family. I leave for Shropshire next Wednesday, and beg for the favour of a reply before then.' In a postscript he told Richard of the date of the wedding, and hoped with all his heart that the Goodwins would attend. An official invitation from Mr Prideau would follow in due course.

He did not receive a reply until he was back in Rudleigh.

My dear Edward (it said), I acknowledge receipt of your letter announcing your engagement to marry Miss Alice Ouvray.

I wish you had not felt it necessary to reveal any details of your parentage either to your fiancée or especially to Mr Prideau. I cannot agree that it was essential—surely you should have considered your duty to protect your mother's reputation as of greater importance than the revelation of secrets which are not yours alone. Moreover, it could prove of great embarrassment to my wife and myself. However, it is done, and now I can only hope that no further word on the subject will be divulged to anyone. In particular, Miss Ouvray must not reveal the additional information you have seen fit to give her. I beg you to ensure that she and Mr Prideau both keep their promises of silence.

I pray that no further distress will be caused to your mother, or to my family, or indeed to your future wife by your hasty and ill-considered action in this matter.

I have discussed the matter of the wedding with my wife, and we are agreed that it would not be appropriate for us or Mary to attend.

Yours most sincerely, Richard Goodwin.

It was like a blow in the face to Edward. Even though he could read Louisa's influence in every line, there was not even a word of congratulation to soften the cold, angry tone. The Cast Iron Man, indeed! He wrote a furious reply, but tore it up. That would do no good. He had simply to keep the hurt to himself, trying to forget about it as soon as possible. He would have to tell Alice the gist of the letter, but decided that he would certainly not show it to her.

*   *   *

The news of his engagement was received with apparent pleasure in Rudleigh. Even Miss Unwin was ready to congratulate him, and when he said that he hoped to bring Miss Ouvray to Shropshire before the wedding so that she could look at the house he proposed to rent, Mrs Chetwynd at once offered a room for her stay.

In some mysterious way, the men in the foundry had heard about it before Edward entered the building, and as he did so, they gave him a cheer. He had occasion to visit the foundry several times that day and the next, and each time he was aware of some kind of conspiracy afoot. Men who were talking together would scatter at his approach, looking faintly guilty. On the second day, shortly before

234

knocking-off time, Thomas Yardman came into his office.

'Could the men 'ave a word, sir?' the overseer began. 'Out in the foundry. Won't take a moment, sir, an' it's important.'

Curiously, almost apprehensively, Edward followed him out into the foundry, where the men were gathered.

Among them was Walter Sales, who was carrying something wrapped in paper. He thrust the parcel into Yardman's hands. 'You do it, Thomas.'

Yardman came forward. 'Excuse the liberty, Mr 'Arcourt. Me and the lads, we made this for you—or rather for the lady who's done you the honour, as they say.' He thrust the parcel into Edward's hand.

Edward undid the paper carefully, to reveal a small plaque of polished wood, on which was mounted a delicately moulded piece of cast iron in the shape of a true lover's knot, on which had been superimposed the initials E and A.

'Oh, that is charming,' Edward said. 'Thank you very much. Miss Ouvray will be delighted, I'm sure. You made it very quickly.'

'Started as soon as we heard the news, sir,' Yardman said. 'Old Walter carved it out, we made the mould yesterday, cast it, polished it and mounted it this morning.' He grinned. 'You see, sir, we can work like lightning when there's really good cause.'

'The money, Thomas,' one of the men whispered hoarsely.

'Oh, by gum, I nearly forgot. We all put a 'a'penny in, sir, to pay for the materials, and also so's everybody could be a part of it—even them 'oo didn't do anything to its making. It's 'ere.' He pulled a small packet from his pocket.

Edward was deeply touched. He turned slowly before he spoke, looking each one of them in the eyes for a brief moment. 'I thank you all very much,' he said. 'I know that Miss Ouvray, my fiancée, will treasure this very beautiful example of your craft. It is our first joint present, so it will always be especially precious to us. As for the money, I should like to hand each of you his contribution back, because the skill that has gone into the making of this is sufficient, but, as Yardman has said, not all of you helped in the manufacture, so I accept it gratefully on behalf of

Chetwynd's, and I would ask you, Yardman, to give it into the hands of Miss Unwin.'

'I'll do that, sir. Right, lads, back to your work. There's still ten minutes to go.'

Happily the men turned away.

'Yardman,' Edward called, going into his office. 'I'd like a word.' He indicated the lover's knot. 'Tell me, is it usual to produce something of this sort when one of the men gets engaged.'

'No, sir. Not as I'm aware.'

'You don't usually mark the occasion at all? Then I'm very honoured.'

'What we do is go down the pub and commiserate with the poor bugger, and tell him what 'e's got coming to 'im.'

'That sounds like the stag night before the wedding.'

'Oh, no, sir,' Yardman said seriously. 'Stag night's for getting drunk. This is for having a joke or two.'

'I see. But you didn't think I'd take kindly to the idea of going to the pub, eh?'

Yardman looked uncomfortable. 'Not usual, sir—you being the gaffer, like.'

'How do you think the men would react if I said that I'd be in the Chequers ten minutes after knocking-off time here, and that the first round would be on me?'

'I reckon they'd be right mazed,' Yardman said, grinning. 'Shall I tell 'em, sir?' He went towards the door.

'Yes. But there's something else I want to ask. This present you gave me today—we could sell a design like that. Made to order, with the appropriate initials. Do you see any obection to that?'

'Objection?'

'Well, it was made especially for me and my fiancée. I thought you might not like the idea of turning it into a commercial proposition.'

Yardman looked at him uncomprehendingly. 'You're the master, sir. It's up to you.'

'Yes, but what I want to know is whether anyone will feel upset.'

'More like proud, I'd say.',

Later that evening, Edward met his workers in the Chequers, and supped a couple of beers with them while they joked that his wedding day would mark the end of his freedom, and how you could always tell a married man by his hang-dog expression, and so on. And with each joke they hastened to assure him that nothing personal was meant, and that they were sure that he would be very happy with his chosen lady. And Edward laughed heartily, and pulled their legs in turn. Before he left, they drank his health and that of his wife-to-be, and sang 'For He's a Jolly Good Fellow'.

As Edward walked back to Rudleigh House, he thought that this modest little entertainment, which he had begun simply as a means of expressing his gratitude, had turned into something more. The bonds of friendship had been strengthened, without any loss of respect on either side.

The next day he told Yardman to cast and mount a large number of the lover's knots, still with his and Alice's initials. He would send them out to retailers all over the country, with a note saying that they could be made to order, with any initials. And he called Walter Sales into his office and instructed him to make some other designs—a heart with an arrow through it, or two hearts entwined— all the symbols of affection which could be made personal by the addition of appropriate initials. 'And different sizes, too,' he said, 'so that we've got a whole range. We'll call them "Mementoes of Love", and if they catch on there'll be a special bonus for you, Sales.'

Edward was eager to return to Franton and Alice as soon as possible, but there were many problems which demanded his attention. The pig iron from Ellerdine's continued to be of good quality, but Yardman complained that the latest delivery of sand contained too many impurities, and no sooner had that been put right, than Nightingale and Sales began grumbling that the wood from which they carved the patterns for the moulds had not been properly matured. And Miss Unwin wanted to discuss various slow-paying accounts with him, and Quennell constantly delayed the delivery of new designs, with a succession of specious excuses, and a mild epidemic of influenza swept through the workers and disrupted production for a week. And always at the back of Edward's mind was the question of whether, if there were a sudden surge in orders, they would be able to cope with the extra work in the present foundries. But if he built a new, large, modern foundry, would there be sufficient business to make it economically viable?

He knew that Alice was planning to introduce him to various cousins and friends, while for his part he wanted very much for her to meet Aunt Frances and Uncle Alfred Bunn, especially since it seemed that he had no other near relatives to offer her. And there was Jack Chetwynd, too. A great flurry of letters passed between them as they tried to arrange their travels and visits so as to cause the least possible disruption to Edward's work. Each letter seemed to demand others to the friends and relations involved, and their plans had constantly to be revised.

It was finally agreed that Edward would make the journey to Franton on a Saturday in late March, when the Prideaus would give a dinner party for a dozen relatives and friends. On the Monday they would go to London, visit the Bunns that evening, and travel on to Shropshire by an early train the following day. The following Saturday they would return to London, take luncheon with Jack, and Edward would see Alice safely on to the train for Chelmsford, before returning to Shropshire. He would be away from the business for no more than three and a half working days.

'Thank goodness it's all settled,' Alice wrote, 'after so many seemingly insoluble problems. No wonder people get married—if only so that they may make such arrangements sitting comfortably in their drawing-room instead of having to rely on the postal services. What should we have done without Sir Rowland Hill and the penny post? And what a fortune the Post Office must have made from us! They will surely notice the sharp decline in their income over the next few days!'

*   *   *

The dinner party was very successful, and Alice's cousins seemed pleasant enough. 'They're very quiet, though,' Edward said to her as they walked together to attend Evensong at the nearby church.

'Oh, yes,' she said. 'Very nice, very quiet and very boring. I'm quite fond of them in a funny sort of way, but I'm glad I

238

don't have to see them more than once a year. But they'd have been mortally offended if they hadn't met you.'

'And now that they have?'

'Oh, they're all very impressed.' She giggled. 'I don't want to disillusion them, so I haven't told them the truth about you!'

'Alice!' Edward stopped and turned her sharply towards him.

The laughter faded from her eyes. 'Oh, not *that*!' she cried. 'I wasn't even thinking of that. It was just a silly joke, Edward. I was going to say that I hadn't told them all about—well, silly things, like pretending you're conceited and rather too fond of whisky, which you're not, and nonsense like that.' Her eyes began to fill with tears. 'It was just a joke. Oh, Edward, I'm sorry. Please say you forgive me. It was so thoughtless.'

'There's nothing to forgive. Indeed, I should ask your forgiveness for even thinking that you might mean anything else. Come, dry your tears, my darling, and give me a kiss.'

But it was difficult to put the episode out of his mind, and during the Vicar's sermon, his thoughts wandered back to it. He remembered that his father, in his letter, had said he hoped there would be no further distress arising from Alice's knowledge of the facts. Would they both be able to live with the secret without ever referring to it, without ever thinking of it? Was it going to spoil all their jokes together?

The subject came up again when they were on their way to London.

'Your Aunt Frances knows about you?' Alice asked.

'Yes.'

'But she does not know that you have told me. Perhaps it would be better if she continued to believe that I am ignorant of it.'

'Yes,' Edward said, 'perhaps it would.' And then he changed his mind. 'No. The Bunns have an absolute knack of worming the truth out of you. It's not that they dig away with questions, it's just that when you talk to them you find yourself telling them whatever it is. And if you manage to deceive Aunt Frances, there's Uncle Alfred looking at you with those gently enquiring eyes of his—not accusingly, you understand—and before you know where you are, you're confessing everything.'

'They sound terrifying.'

'Oh, they're not. They're gentle and kind. It's just that they're . . . well, more honest than most people I know.'

*   *   *

Alice was enchanted by the Bunns, and they by her. Before long, Alfred Bunn was showing her his work, and she was commenting on it in terms that obviously pleased him. No doubt, Edward thought, he was used to being told how beautiful it was, but Alice seemed to understand how the chasing was patterned and formed by the material involved and its shape, and the use to which the article would be put. Her comments were those of one artist to another.

She was equally successful with Frances, praising the composition, and the chiaroscuro and the balance of the colours of her paintings.

Edward was amazed. 'I never knew you were such an artist, my dear.'

'Oh, but I'm not,' Alice cried. 'I only wish I were. I couldn't paint to save my life, and as for doing anything like your work, Mr Bunn . . . But I've always tried to see what the artist is aiming at, and to judge how far he has succeeded. I admire your work very much indeed, Mrs Bunn. And yours, too, Mr Bunn.'

'I think you should call us Aunt and Uncle,' Frances said.

'You are very kind.'

'My dear wife has not shown you her real forte,' Alfred Bunn said. 'No doubt you are aware that she designs brocades for her brother, who is a fine silk maker. Whenever he makes a brocade from one of her designs, he sends her a sample. Perhaps she will show them to you.'

'After we've eaten,' Frances said, a little shortly.

'Have you met my brother-in-law?' Alfred asked.

'No,' Alice said. Although it was no more than one short syllable, it was difficult to say it, she thought, without an intonation which would reveal more than she wished. She glanced quickly at Frances, and thought that she was looking at her husband in a warning way.

Edward caught the look, too, and decided that now was

240

the time to come out into the open. 'You needn't worry, Aunt Frances—I have told Alice everything. She's been marvellous—a real brick.' He smiled happily. 'She didn't think it was a good enough excuse for turning me down.'

'I'm glad,' Frances said. 'And are you taking her to Wensham?'

'No. My father has made it very clear that he and his wife do not want to see me.'

'Really? Oh, he can't mean that! Not now that Mary's settled down, and you've got engaged.'

'I'd rather not talk about it, if you don't mind. It's very distressing to me, and I see no reason to inflict it on Alice.'

But later, since Alice was happily engaged in conversation with her new uncle, Edward followed Frances into the kitchen. 'Is there anything I can do?' he asked.

'Of course not, Edward. Just because we have no servants, you needn't think I feel hard done by when I have to prepare a meal. I enjoy it. It only needs a little bit of organisation—like a painting, in a way.' She chattered on for a while, and then stopped and looked at him. 'You came out here because you wanted to tell me something, didn't you?'

'Yes. When I became engaged to Alice, I wrote to Wensham, and explained why I had revealed the truth about myself to Alice and Mr Prideau. This is the answer I got.' He handed her his father's letter.

Frances read it through quickly, and then again. Folding the paper, she handed it back to Edward. 'Oh, dear,' she said. 'I can see why you're feeling hurt. He is, too, you know. He doesn't mean it, Edward.'

'Well, I know it's all Aunt Louisa's doing, but if he doesn't mean it, why doesn't he stand up to her?'

She spoke emphatically. 'I am quite sure that my brother does not mean to write so coldly, so angrily.' She sighed. 'Oh, dear, oh, dear! What a mess we humans make of our lives! Why doesn't he stand up to Louisa? Because he's loyal to her. But that isn't all. You know, of all the deadly sins, I always think pride is the worst. Richard always had a great deal of pride, and I think it's very difficult for him to alter the position he's got himself into. It's not just Louisa—he was hurt and shocked by the whole business. He may suspect now that he has treated you badly, but his pride

241

won't let him admit it. Now what can we do about it? Oh, do go away, there's a good boy. Go back and talk to your fiancée, and let me think.'

As she dished up the supper, Frances made no mention of the subject, but when they had finished the meal, she said, 'I've decided what you should do, Edward. You must take Alice to Wensham, and the pair of you go and see your father and Louisa.'

'They wouldn't let me in the door.'

'Write to him first.'

'And get another letter like the last one? Even if he wanted to, *she* wouldn't let my father see me. Why should he agree, when he has never done so in the past?'

'Partly because you'd be taking Alice with you, but chiefly because he feels guilty, that's why. Guilty about you, and guilty about your mother, and guilty because he's allowed himself to be swayed by . . . by other people. Your going there would give him the opportunity to make amends.'

'You don't know that, Aunt Frances—you're just guessing.'

'I've known him a great deal longer than you have, Edward.'

'But—'

'Don't argue, Edward,' Alfred Bunn put in. 'Your aunt is bound to be right. She always is in such matters. It is one of her most irritating traits.'

'Oh, you!' said Frances affectionately, wrinkling her nose at him.

'What do you think, Alice?' Edward asked.

'I think we must take your aunt's advice. Surely if there's any chance of a reconciliation we must do everything we can to bring it about.'

'Quite right,' Frances approved. But Edward still looked doubtful, and she went on, 'At least try it. It can do no harm, and it might do a lot of good.'

'You understand your brother so well, Aunt Frances,' Edward said, with some bitterness, 'perhaps you should come with us, and plead on my behalf.' He checked himself. 'I'm sorry—that was rude. But, seriously, would it be a good idea for you to come, too? You and Uncle Alfred. If we all went, then surely they couldn't refuse to see us.'

'That's a good idea,' Frances said. 'At least, I think it is.' She gave a half-smile, and looked at Alfred. He gazed back at her calmly, without changing his expression, which meant that he was leaving the decision to her. 'All right,' she said, 'we will. When? Tomorrow?'

'No,' Edward said. 'I have to get back to Rudleigh tomorrow, and Mrs Chetwynd is expecting Alice. I can't take another day away. What about next Saturday? We were coming back from Shropshire that morning to have lunch with Jack Chetwynd. But we can easily cancel that engagement—you can meet him any old time, can't you, Alice? Are you sure you don't mind, Aunt?'

Frances held up her hands in smiling protest. 'Wait a minute, Edward, wait a minute. First of all, is next Saturday all right, Alfred?'

'I think so, my dear.'

'You sound very doubtful.'

'It is just that it will mean staying overnight in Wensham, and . . . well, that raises a question or two, does it not? Quite apart from whether Richard will be at home next Saturday.'

'I shall write to him,' Frances said. 'If he's not away, undoubtedly he will wish you and me to stay with him, but until he has seen Edward . . .'

'I shall take rooms in an hotel for Alice and myself,' Edward said.

'Then that is settled. But remember, Edward, I am not going to plead for you, as you put it just now. It may help that I am there, and it will help even more that you will have Alice with you, but—'

'One of the best things about marriage,' Alfred broke in, 'is having a woman behind you at difficult times. They may seem frail creatures, but they're a match for any man—any group of men. I'd rather have your Aunt Frances behind me than a whole legion of Roman soldiers.'

'Oh, do be quiet, Alfred,' Frances said, smiling. 'I am talking very seriously, and if you have nothing useful to say, it were best that you kept out of it.'

'What I said may not be useful,' Alfred commented unrepentantly, 'but it's still true.'

'I understand the point you are making, Aunt,' Edward said. 'I shall be happier with you there than going to my father alone, but I know that this matter is between him and me. It is my fight, and in the end I must fight it alone.'

For a moment or two solemnity fell upon them all. Then Alfred Bunn asked, 'Is there any more of that delightful figgy duff that you gave us, my dear?' He turned to Alice. 'Always make sure that Edward gets plenty of suet puddings—there's nothing else so guaranteed to keep a man happy in his marriage, is there, my dear?'

'You're impossible, Alfred,' Frances said, shaking her head, 'quite impossible.'

*　　　*　　　*

When the letter from Frances arrived in Wensham, Richard read it through, and then turned to Louisa. 'Frances and Alfred propose to visit us on Saturday,' he said.

'How nice. Are they going to stay?'

'They are going to bring Edward and his fiancée with them.'

'Then they must certainly not come,' Louisa said vehemently. 'I will not have that young man in my house.'

'Let me remind you, my dear, that it is *my* house.'

'Of course it is, but you will surely not go against my wishes.'

'I never do, do I, my dear?' Richard said. He rose. 'I am going to my study.'

There was something strange in his expression, and Louisa watched him leave the room with puzzlement. She hurried after him, but he had shut his study door, and it had been an inviolable rule in their household that when he did so, he was not to be disturbed.

He emerged an hour later, and went to his wife, who was sitting in their drawing-room. He had a letter in his hand. 'I have written to Frances,' he told her, 'and I have said that she and Alfred, *and* Edward and Miss Ouvray, will be most welcome on Saturday.'

'Richard!'

'My mind is quite made up. I do not say that Edward and I will be totally reconciled—I have said as much to Frances in this letter—but I am conscious that I have behaved very badly towards him. He is my son, and I owe him at least the

244

chance of talking to me. As for you, my dear, I cannot expect you to greet him with affection, but you will do me the honour of behaving towards him with the politeness due to a guest in our house.'

'In *your* house.'

'If you wish to put it that way, yes. You will be spared the necessity of preparing rooms for the young couple—Frances and Alfred will spend the night here, but my son and his fiancée apparently intend to put up at the Wensham Arms.'

'But—'

'I will have no arguments, Louisa. You will obey me in this matter, if in no other.'

Louisa stared at him open-mouthed, and then took refuge in tears. 'You have never . . . you have never spoken to me like that before,' she said.

'No. I have never previously felt the need. Perhaps I should have done so.' He turned, and left the room.

*　　*　　*

On the following Saturday, Edward and Alice caught an early train from Shropshire, and by midday they and the Bunns were on their way to Norwich.

Frances had not told Edward the contents of Richard's letter, merely saying that he was willing for the four of them to pay their visit. She did not want to raise Edward's hopes, since Richard had made it clear that this was no more than a truce—the family hostilities might easily be resumed afterwards.

'Are we all going straight to the house?' Edward asked his aunt. He looked very tense.

'No. I think it best if you and Alice book in at the hotel, and then come on a little later. I would like to have time to talk to my brother first.' She felt as nervous as he obviously did, and turned to Alice to change the conversation. 'Now, my dear, tell me about your stay in Rudleigh.'

Alice chattered gaily, trying to hide her own fears about the forthcoming visit. The house was perfect, she said—exactly the right size for a couple starting out on married life, and in a beautiful position, too. 'It is perched on a hillside, and there is the most marvellous view, and you can see the river winding away into the distance.' And she had

245

been quite enchanted by the wood-covered hills and the deep valleys and the twisting roads of Shropshire, where none of the scenery was predictable and every turn brought a new surprise. Mrs Chetwynd and Miss Unwin had been charming, and she had thoroughly enjoyed her stay with them, despite the presence of those dreadful little dogs.

'Do you not care for dogs?' Frances asked.

'On the contrary, I shall be very unhappy if we do not have at least one dog when we are married—'

'As many as you like, my dear,' Edward said indulgently.

'—but I hope they will be proper dogs, not snuffly little lap-dogs. A Saint Bernard, perhaps, or an Irish wolfhound, or a Great Dane—that's my idea of a dog.'

'On second thoughts, perhaps one will be enough,' Edward laughed. But the smile soon faded from his face, and he sank back into thought.

Only Alfred Bunn seemed unconcerned. 'Courage, my dears,' he said. 'Richard is no ogre, and though Louisa may be somewhat more in that line, she is not invulnerable.'

'Oh, Alfred!' Frances said irritably. But she took his hand and squeezed it in thanks for his encouragement.

Arriving at Norwich, they split up, taking separate flies. Edward and Alice booked into the hotel and unpacked their bags, and set off for the Goodwin residence only after allowing Frances a full hour in which to talk to her brother.

As they approached, Alice put her hand in Edward's. She could feel his slight trembling. 'You are nervous, dearest?'

'Terrified.'

'So am I. But we mustn't be, Edward. Remember, *he* is probably as alarmed at the prospect of this interview as you are—if not more so.'

'It is not only him that I'm afraid of meeting. There is the dreaded Aunt Louisa, and especially Mary. What will she think of . . . of me and of you?'

'When she sees your contentment she will be happy for you, as any sister would be. As for me, I shall offer her my warm affection, and from all you have told me I am sure she will accept it as readily as I offer it.' Alice spoke as confidently as she could, knowing that Edward was in desperate need of her support, but in her heart she was almost as apprehensive as he.

246

When they reached the house, the maid took their coats and hats and conducted them to the drawing-room, which was occupied only by Louisa and Alfred Bunn.

Louisa greeted them coldly, barely acknowledging Edward. She made a little more effort towards Alice, saying that she was happy to meet her, but there was a lack of sincerity in the words. 'My husband is with his sister,' she told them. 'He will no doubt be out directly.'

'Yes, of course,' Edward said. 'And Mary?'

'She will be down soon, too. Your Aunt Frances thought that perhaps it would be better if she came down later.'

The four of them sat in silence. Alfred tried to begin a conversation about the weather, but received no response and soon gave up. He did, however, unseen by Louisa, give Edward a wink, as if to bolster his confidence.

The door opened and Frances came in. There were two bright spots of colour on her cheeks. 'I'm glad you've arrived, Edward,' she said. 'My brother is ready to see you, but he insists that, to begin with at least, it shall be alone. He is in his study.'

As Edward went to the study, he remembered the previous times he had been there, first when there had been the trouble over Tessie, and then later with Mary. The room was associated with anger. He knocked on the door.

'Come in.' Richard was seated at his desk. He looked up as Edward came in, but did not smile. 'Ah, Edward. Sit down. I trust you are well.'

'Yes, sir. And you?'

'Yes.' He paused. 'I have spent a rather difficult half hour with my sister, who has accused me of acting unjustly against you. I cannot entirely agree. She seems to think that I have been unduly influenced by your Aunt Louisa, but I have to tell you that the harsh words which have passed between us expressed my own views as well as hers. I have been disappointed in you, Edward. It was not honourable of you to seek that interview with Mary behind my back, just after she was so ill, and I was extremely distressed that you should more recently have revealed certain secrets, and by so doing exposed your mother to the possibility of great damage.'

Edward wondered unhappily whether there had been any point in coming to Wensham. He was tempted to

247

counter his father's harshness with accusations of his own, but said, with an effort, 'I am very sorry. I would not ever wish to do anything to offend you, but in both cases I could see no other course of action.'

'I shall say no more of it. No doubt there have been faults on both sides.' Richard paused again, for a long time. Then he said, 'I wish to apologise to you, Edward. I believe my sister is right, and that I have behaved extremely badly towards you, whether there was any justification or not. I hope that you can find it in your heart to forgive me. Is it . . . is it your wish that we should be reconciled?'

Edward could hardly speak for the lump in his throat. His father's apology had caught him completely off balance, after the way the interview had begun. 'It is indeed, sir,' he managed at last.

'Very well. Then it is mine also.'

Edward waited for a moment, then stood up and held out his hand. 'Thank you . . . Father.'

'For your mother's sake you must never call me that!' Richard said vehemently. 'You will address me, as you always did before, as "Uncle Richard".'

'Yes. Yes, of course.' There was an awkward pause. 'My fiancée is here and she is very much looking forward to meeting you.' There was no response, and Edward went on uncertainly, 'Now . . . now that we . . . you will be able to come to our wedding now, sir.'

'I . . . am . . . not sure.'

The voice was strange, and Edward peered at his father. Sitting with his back towards the light, his head tilted downward, Richard's face was shadowed. A little desperately he said, 'Won't you please shake my hand?'

Slowly Richard pulled himself to his feet. Briefly he shook Edward's hand. Then he said, 'Go back in to the others. I shall join you shortly.' He sat down, and turned his face away.

Again his words sounded strained, and then the light caught the trail of moisture on his cheek, and Edward realised that his father was weeping. He stood for a moment awkwardly, and then something told him that, though deep inside himself Richard wanted his son's forgiveness and comfort and embrace, his pride would not yet let him confess such weakness. Softly he left the room.

The sitting-room was silent as he entered, and they all turned anxiously towards him. He nodded. 'It's all right. At least, I think so.'

'Oh, Edward, I'm so glad!' Alice said. 'Come and sit down. Are you going to tell us about it?'

'No, I'd rather not. My . . . my *uncle* will be joining us shortly. If there is to be any explanation, it should be left to him.' He was aware of Louisa gazing at him angrily, her lips clamped together, but he ignored her and went over to Frances. 'Thank you, Aunt,' he said. 'You said you wouldn't plead for me, but I think you did. And your pleading seems to have worked.'

'I'm very glad,' she said.

Edward went back to sit next to Alice. She squeezed his hand, smiling at him.

Almost immediately, the door opened and Richard appeared. He stood there, looking at them all. They waited, frozen into immobility, almost as though time had stopped, and the silence seemed to last for ever. 'I am happy to tell you,' Richard said then, his voice barely under control, 'that Edward and I have agreed to . . . to reconcile our differences.' The others, apart from Louisa, smiled, and began to express their pleasure, but Richard held up his hand. 'There is something else which I must say.' He paused. 'This is . . . I do not find this easy, as I am sure you will appreciate. But . . . You all know that Edward is my son. You also know that I must deny myself the pride of acknowledging that relationship publicly, for I will do nothing to impugn the honour of Edward's mother. Nevertheless . . .' He stopped again, and lowered his hand. 'We have therefore agreed,' Richard continued, 'that he will continue to address me, as in the past, as his uncle, and I should be grateful if you would all think of him, and refer to him if the occasion arises, as my nephew. He knows, I believe, how very much I regret the necessity for this.'

Edward found himself grinning, and went over to Richard, shook his hand again, and stood beside him.

The others in his audience seemed to be stunned. Richard himself had to struggle to retain his composure, but then went over to his wife. 'Louisa, my dear, you will rejoice with me that the rift in our family is mended.'

'Yes, of course,' she said, her face like stone.

Richard turned to his brother-in-law. 'Alfred, how good to see you.' He shook hands with him, and then looked back at Edward. 'And now I hope I may have the privilege of meeting your fiancée.'

'Yes, sir. Alice, may I present my uncle, Mr Richard Goodwin? Uncle, this is Miss Alice Ouvray, who has done me the honour of promising to become my wife.'

'How do you do, Miss Ouvray?'

'How do you do, Mr Goodwin? I am delighted to make your acquaintance. Edward has always spoken of you with such high regard.'

'Indeed? I am afraid he has had little cause.'

'But he understands, I am sure, and your reconciliation is more important than what has happened in the past.' She turned to Edward, and said, lightly, 'Go away, Edward. I wish to talk to your uncle about you, and cannot do so with you listening to every word.'

He hesitated for a moment before obeying, but she nodded and smiled at him encouragingly. As he moved away, he heard her say, 'Even in moments of bitterness, and I will not conceal from you that he has experienced them, his affection—no, his love—has always been plain to me.' He glanced back. Richard was not smiling, but there was a look on his face of . . . it was almost, he thought, of peace.

The door opened and Mary entered. She looked thinner than the last time he had seen her, but the dark patches beneath her eyes had gone, and there was a healthy glow in her cheeks. She came to Edward and kissed him on the cheek. 'I am so happy for you, Edward. I could tell as I entered the room that this visit, which I expect you dreaded, is going to be a happy occasion. And I am so looking forward to meeting your fiancée. Aunt Frances has told me how much she likes her.'

'Yes, I'll introduce you in a moment. First, tell me how you are.'

'I am well, Edward, and happy.'

'Really?'

'Really. It is a wonderful thing to feel that your life has purpose.'

'It's not the life you would have chosen, is it?'

'You're blaming yourself, aren't you? Don't, Edward,

250

don't. My way was chosen for me, and it is right for me, and I am happy to accept it. Truly happy.'

'You have no regrets, Mary?'

'None, except for the distress that has been caused. I have prayed that it should pass, and I believe that now it may do so.'

'Yes. I wish . . . your father would agree to come to the wedding, and bring you and Aunt Louisa.'

'I hope so, too.'

'And what about you, Mary? Is there no young man . . . perhaps a doctor at your hospital?'

She laughed. 'I shall never marry, Edward. Oh, don't look so solemn. Not all of us are made for matrimony, you know.' She patted his arm. 'Dear Edward. Now, introduce me to your fiancée.'

Richard and Alice were deep in an animated and happy conversation, but they broke apart as Edward and Mary approached.

'Excuse me, Uncle,' Edward said. 'My cousin wishes to meet . . . Alice, dearest, this is Mary.'

The two girls looked at each other for a moment, instantly liked what they saw, and without hesitation embraced.

Richard went over to his wife. 'What a charming girl,' he said. 'It really seems quite ridiculous that she and Edward should be staying at the hotel when we have rooms here, don't you agree, my dear?'

Louisa smiled thinly. 'As you wish, Richard,' she said submissively. She went back with him to Edward and Alice. 'Your uncle and I would like you and Miss Ouvray to stay here for the night,' she said to Edward. 'Or indeed for as long as you can.'

Aware of the effort that it was costing her, Alice smiled warmly. 'We accept with much pleasure, don't we, Edward? You are most kind.'

'Before I tell Violet to get the rooms ready, I must compliment you, Miss Ouvray, on that charming dress, and indeed, if you will allow me to say so, on your entire person. I think Edward is a very lucky man.'

'Why, thank you.'

Richard smiled, and patted his wife on the shoulder in approval.

'Now, if you'll excuse me,' Louisa went on, 'I'll go and give the maid her instructions. When she's finished preparing your rooms here, she can go over to the hotel and collect your luggage.'

'That is kind, too,' said Alice, 'but I think it might be better if we went there ourselves. I have left everything in such confusion that I could not expect anyone else to pack for me.' It was not true, but she wanted an opportunity to speak to Edward alone.

As they walked to the hotel, arm in arm, she said, 'Tell me what happened.'

Edward reported the conversation with his father. 'It was strange,' he said. 'It began as cold and angry as you like, and then at the end I think he was crying.'

'He's a darling. He's been as unhappy as you have, Edward.'

'Did he say so?'

'Yes. And that he's been very unfair to you.'

'I think you've won Aunt Louisa over, too.'

'It almost killed her to say those nice things, but I think we shall get on together all right.'

'I asked my . . . Uncle Richard if he would come to the wedding. He said he wasn't sure.'

Alice laughed. 'Oh, he's coming all right.'

'Has he said so?'

'Not in so many words, but he asked me twice what date it was, and the time, and whether there was to be a reception afterwards, and where, and would there be many guests.'

'He might just have been making conversation, or perhaps he simply wanted to know for interest's sake.'

'Edward, my darling, if it had been your aunt, I might have agreed with you, but men don't ask that sort of question out of idle curiosity. I'll have a bet with you, if you like. Before the day is over, he'll have said outright that they're all coming.'

'You've enchanted him. I'm not surprised—you've enchanted me. I think I ought to take you on some of my sales trips. If you can do that to Uncle Richard, *and* Aunt Louisa, you could probably at least double all our orders! I'll think about that, once we're married and you've promised to obey me.'

Alice laughed.

252

9

Mr Prideau had arranged a wedding breakfast which left his hundred and twenty guests speechless with admiration. Several different soups and bisques were followed by lobster and salmon in aspic and huge hams and turkeys and barons of cold roast beef, with every kind of salad to accompany them, and then a magnificent array of elaborate desserts and sorbets and fresh fruit and cheese. Each guest could make his or her selection and eat as much as the stomach could hold, while the score of waiters filled and refilled their glasses with the finest champagne, until it was time for coffee and liqueurs—brandy for the gentlemen and Kummel and Cointreau and Benedictine for the ladies. And all the while a little band played softly as a background to the babble of happy chatter. Later, when the meal was over and the speeches had been made, the tables were moved back, and everyone applauded as Edward led Alice out to begin the dancing.

Prideau turned to the mother of the groom, resplendent in the purple of a long-time widow. 'Well, Sarah?'

'Magnificent,' she replied. 'It must have cost you a fortune.'

'It has. But only the best is good enough for Alice. She's all that I have left, you know.'

'And now you're losing her.'

'Oh, no, I don't look upon it like that. Her happiness is the main thing, and I believe she will be happy with your Edward. He's a fine young man, and you should be very proud of him.'

'Yes,' Sarah said. 'There have been disappointments, but we cannot always expect our children to turn out exactly as we should like.'

'Oh, come, dear lady, you can be more generous than that. He is all that any parent could wish—upright, considerate, ambitious—he seems to be making a great

253

success of his business—and good-looking into the bargain.'

'You flatter me in saying so. I am sure I did my best to bring him up properly, and it was not always easy without a father's guiding hand. Yes, I am proud of him. It is just that . . . I can speak frankly to you, James, can I not? I ask you, why cast iron? I just do not understand why he should have chosen to leave the family business, especially when he knows that I need him.' She was aware that she was embarrassing her host, but could not stop herself. 'I am no longer a young woman, James, and it is not easy. It is not easy at all.' She took out a handkerchief, and dabbed at her eyes.

'Why don't you give up, Sarah? Let me buy Harcourt's. I will not be ungenerous, and I will make sure that none of your workers suffers.' He held up his hand. 'No, let me finish. I know that you are proud of Harcourt's—perhaps, if you will allow me to say so, more proud than you are of your son. Well, I will keep the name. "Prideau and Harcourt"—how does that sound?'

Sarah put her handkerchief away, and gave a short laugh. 'Never, James! You and I are friends, but Prideau's is my competitor. I shall never sell. Do you remember how I answered you when you came to me all those years ago, and threatened me because we were encroaching on your markets? I told you that if you sought war, we would defend ourselves, and that we were capable of doing so. That is still my answer today.'

'Sarah, you are incorrigible!' Prideau said with a smile. 'Well, I will not persist, but remember that my offer still stands. Come, dear lady, we should circulate among the guests. There are the Leroys sitting by themselves. Let us start with them.'

They began their slow progress round the hall.

Jack Chetwynd turned to Mary. 'There, Miss Goodwin! They're playing a waltz.'

'No, I beg you to excuse me.'

'But the best man always dances with the chief bridesmaid, and people will think it most strange if we do not take the floor. I do not believe that you cannot dance. Come!' He rose, and held out his arm for her.

It had taken all Alice's powers of persuasion to convince Mary that she should be her sole bridesmaid. Reluctantly she had agreed, and had regretted the decision as soon as she had learnt that Jack Chetwynd was to be the best man. All that she had ever heard of him led her to fear that he was a spendthrift and a rake, and had been the despair of his poor late father. When they first met, she behaved distantly towards him, warning him by her manner that she would brook no liberties, but during the wedding breakfast he had been so courteous and attentive, and had spoken with such sensibility, that she had been forced to concede that he seemed nowhere near as black as he had been painted.

He had asked her about her work, and unlike most who spoke to her of nursing, made it plain that he saw it not simply as a noble vocation. 'There must be a great deal of drudgery,' he said, 'and much that is distasteful. Are you not sickened by some of the things you have to do? And is it not exceedingly painful to watch the dying?'

'You are right,' she replied. 'But I am given strength from above to perform the many unpleasant tasks that come my way. Death is distressing, yes, but there is usually a sense of peace, and I am sustained by the knowledge that the suffering is over and that a better life awaits in Heaven.'

Jack was tempted to ask how she could be sure that many of her patients were not on their way to a hotter destination, but he restrained himself. Her sincerity was so patent that flippancy would have been out of place. In any case, much to his surprise, he felt a great sympathy for her, and no embarrassment at the frank expression of her piety.

'Are you a religious person, Mr Chetwynd?' she asked.

'Alas, I cannot claim that, Miss Goodwin.'

'That makes me very sad.'

'If I may say so, I am grateful for people like you, who take the sins of the world, including mine, upon their shoulders.' As he said it, Jack was astonished at himself. What an extraordinary girl she was! Who would have believed that he, a wealthy young sophisticate, should be saying such a thing, and meaning it, too?

'I shall pray for you,' she said.

'Thank you.'

She smiled. 'I am afraid I have disconcerted you.'

'No, not at all.'

'But tell me about yourself. You own a theatre, I believe.'

'Yes, a music hall.' He looked at her. 'You do not approve.'

'Oh, I . . . I'm sorry. I am prejudiced, no doubt, but the music hall is usually so . . . so vulgar.'

'Perhaps. But it is an honest vulgarity, Miss Goodwin, and vulgarity is part of life, is it not? I would hazard a guess that you encounter it frequently among your patients.'

'That is true. But there is a difference between meeting it in the course of duty, and deliberately seeking it in a place of entertainment. Oh, you will think I am a prude, and I am not. The music hall is a place of laughter, is it not? Laughter is good.' She smiled. 'Believe it or not, Mr Chetwynd, I am not all seriousness—I can laugh, too.'

'I know you can, and I am glad. Do you ever come to London, Miss Goodwin?'

'Rarely.'

'I wish you would. I should like to take you to my theatre. I doubt if its vulgarity would bring a blush to your cheek, and I am sure you would find much to laugh at.'

'The only times I have been to London have been with my father, and now that I am working at the hospital it is unlikely that my free times will coincide with his visits.'

'You could arrange it, surely. Promise me you will try. And of course your father could come, too, and your mother, if she is with him.'

Mary smiled. He really was a most charming man, and she was very tempted to accept his invitation. 'I'll think about it,' she said, and then felt the blood rise to her cheeks. 'You make me blush, Mr Chetwynd.'

'And very prettily, too.'

It was then that he had first tried to persuade her to dance, but at that time the band was playing a polka, which she felt to be a little unseemly. Now she was enjoying herself as they swept around the floor in the waltz, conscious of the light pressure of his hand at the back of her waist, and of his eyes constantly on her.

'You dance beautifully,' he said.

'Oh, no. I am very clumsy.'

As if to prove it, she tripped and fell against him, and both his arms tightened around her to prevent her from falling, and for a brief moment she surrendered to the pleasure of being held in this tight embrace, her head against his broad chest. She felt her heart beating, and knew that she was blushing again. Almost at once, she regained her footing and he released her, apologising.

'It is I who should apologise, Mr Chetwynd. It was my fault entirely. But, if you will forgive me, I would rather . . .'

'Of course.' He escorted her back to her seat. 'May I get you something?'

'A glass of water, perhaps. Thank you.'

He went to get it, but when he came back she had disappeared. She did not return for some time, and then seemed subdued, giving his questions and remarks only the minimum of response which politeness required. He persisted, however, and eventually achieved at least some of the animation of their earlier conversation.

Meanwhile, the bride and groom had gone to change their clothes. When they returned Alice's outfit was admired by all the ladies present. A three-quarter length coat, with a high collar and leg-of-mutton sleeves, gave way to a long, full skirt, all in a brilliant shade of turquoise blue. Velvet bows and ostrich feathers on her wide-brimmed hat were dyed to match.

She and Edward moved swiftly round the room, speaking to the guests and accepting again their congratulations and best wishes.

Richard and Louisa Goodwin and Alfred and Frances Bunn were together. Edward shook hands with Alfred Bunn, and kissed his Aunt Frances. He hesitated when he came to Louisa, but she proffered her cheek, so he kissed her, too. He drew Richard aside. 'Thank you for coming,' he said. 'It would not have been the same without you. I hope that we shall be able to see you more often in future.'

'I hope so, too, my boy. You will always be welcome in Wensham; you and Alice.'

'Thank you.'

Richard stepped forward and embraced his son. The hug was brief—no more than might have been expected from an uncle towards his nephew on such an occasion. For Edward, however, it was a moment that he would never forget—an additional blessing on this day of joy.

Then it was time to say goodbye to his mother, who unemotionally allowed him and her new daughter-in-law to kiss her cheek, and to Alice's grandfather, who seemed

257

reluctant to let either of them go, holding Alice in his arms for some minutes, and then shaking Edward's hand in an equally long grip.

'Take care of my little girl, Edward. Take care of her.'

'I will.'

At last they were able to make their escape.

'Well, Mrs Harcourt?' Edward said, as the carriage took them to the station.

'Very well, my dear, dear husband.'

Gazing fondly at her, Edward saw that there were tears in her eyes. 'What is it?'

'Nothing. Nothing. I'm just so happy. Oh, Edward, we shall always be happy, shan't we?'

'I doubt it,' he said, laughing. 'We shall probably start fighting like cat and dog before long, and then I shall take to beating you, and . . .'

'Don't!' she cried. 'Not even in fun.'

'I'm sorry. I didn't mean it.'

'I know you didn't, and I know we're going to be the happiest couple that ever lived, but . . .'

'I swear I'll never do anything to hurt you. I love you far too much.' And he put his arm about her and drew her towards him, and kissed her, not caring whether anyone could see them.

*　　　*　　　*

Arriving in London, they went to their hotel, and having seen their room and left their luggage there—trying all the while to look like an old married couple—took a cab to the Silver Fountain restaurant in the heart of Soho.

From the confident way in which Edward had given the cabbie the name of the restaurant, Alice had expected that he would be greeted there as an old and valued customer, and was surprised when this did not happen. Indeed, Edward had to protest before they were moved from the badly positioned table to which they were first shown.

'Why have we come here?' she asked. 'Is there a special reason?'

'I've been here once or twice with Jack, and I've always liked it, but the real reason I chose it is because it was here that I first met Mr Chetwynd, and that meeting changed my life. Now my life is changed again, so it seemed appropriate.'

'Changed for the better, I hope.'

'How many more compliments are you going to fish for?' Edward laughed. Then in all seriousness he said, 'Changed not just for the better, but for the very best, and—'

'Oh, look,' Alice interrupted. 'Isn't that Sir Arthur Sullivan?'

'I told you we should quarrel before long,' he said, indulgently. 'There was I, right in the middle of a declaration of my undying love, and you interrupt to ask me about some composer, whom I certainly do not love, even if I like his music. You really must have a little more respect for your husband.'

'I have,' Alice said, 'but I still want to know whether or not it's Sir Arthur.'

'I'm sure it is. I remember Jack telling me that he and Gilbert used to dine here regularly until they quarrelled. Now Gilbert goes elsewhere.'

'And who's the woman with him?'

'I've no idea. Possibly his lady friend—what's her name? Mrs Roberts? No—Mrs Ronalds, that's it. This is a great place for people in the Arts. If we were to stay here until very late, after the theatres finish, you'd be able to see any number of actors and actresses. But we're not going to stay very late, are we?'

He had expected that she would blush at such a reference to the night ahead. Instead she looked squarely into his eyes, smiling gently, and slowly shook her head.

Edward ordered a light supper of *crêpes aux crevettes*, served with a mixed salad, and lemon sorbet to follow—all they needed after the wedding feast.

They arrived back in the hotel just before ten. As Edward shut the door of their room, he held out his arms. Alice came to him, and he kissed her tenderly. 'I do love you,' he whispered.

'And I love you.'

'Are you frightened?'

'No,' she laughed. 'Should I be?'

He was a little disconcerted. 'Well, I thought . . .'

'Why should I be frightened of my husband? Oh, I know men are supposed to be brutes, but I've seen too many of my married friends come back from their honeymoon as though they've been in paradise. There isn't anything to be frightened of, is there?'

'I may hurt you.'

She came back to his arms. 'I know, but it's a hurt I want, Edward.'

'I promise I'll be gentle, my sweetheart.'

'The only thing I'm frightened of is that I may not please you.'

It was Edward's turn to laugh. 'Not please me? Oh, my darling, I adore you.' He looked into her eyes. 'Shall we . . . shall we get undressed? I'll turn my back, shall I?'

Suddenly shy, she nodded.

He sat for what seemed an age, staring at the pattern of twining roses on the wallpaper, and hearing the soft rustle of silk as she removed her garments.

At last she said softly, 'Edward?'

She was wearing a nightdress of cream-coloured silk, heavy with embroidery. It was fastened high at the neck with a bow, and the cuffs of the sleeves were buttoned, and its fullness concealed her figure. It made her look small and vulnerable, and his heart went out to her. He reached for her hands and kissed them softly. Then he crushed her to him, and this time the kiss was passionate, and desire rose in him as his hands smoothed the silk of the nightdress, conscious of the naked flesh beneath.

She whispered to him, 'The bow—untie the bow. Here.'

He looked at her with astonishment and delight, and undid the bow at her neck. She stepped away from him slightly, and unfastened the buttons at her wrists, and then, her face flaming in a blush, wriggled her shoulders, and slowly at first, and then in a rush, the silken material slipped loose and cascaded around her feet.

She was more beautiful than all his imaginings—the small, firm, pink-tipped breasts; the softly curving hips; the shapely legs; and that sweet triangle of dark hair. Into his mind flashed the words of Solomon—'thy belly is like an heap of wheat set about with lilies'. It had always seemed an absurd description, and yet suddenly now its poetry seemed to be apt and true.

'I am a wanton, Edward,' she said, almost breathlessly, in a strange, strained tone. 'Your wife is a . . . a wicked woman. No doubt you are already ashamed of her.'

Edward knelt before her and looked up at her with adoration plain in his eyes. 'So beautiful,' he murmured, 'so beautiful. Not wanton, not wicked. Oh, my darling, "with my body I thee worship".'

She pressed his head against her belly, caressing his hair.

After a few moments, he rose. 'Now it's your turn to look away.'

'No,' she said. 'I want to watch you. I told you you had a wanton for a wife. I want to see you.'

He laughed nervously. 'A woman, when she takes off her dress, is still beautiful. A man in his underclothes looks ridiculous.'

'I shan't think so,' she said. She sat on the bed, gazing at him.

He took off the jacket of his suit, and the waistcoat, loosened his cravat and undid the buttons of his collar and shirt. Unlacing and slipping off his boots, he then, reluctantly, removed his trousers. 'There. You see,' he said. 'Shirt-tails, underpants—they don't make a pretty picture.'

She smiled. 'Then take them off, my darling.'

He did so, slowly, turning aside. Nervousness and surprise had, for the moment, dampened his desire, but even so . . .

'Turn round,' she said. And then, 'Oh, you are beautiful, too, Edward—very beautiful and very handsome. Oh, what you must think of me! And yet, why should we be ashamed? We are as God made us, and perhaps we are as pleasing in His sight as in our own. Come, hold me, Edward.'

'Shall I turn out the light?'

'No.'

He went to her, and they lay on the bed, and he kissed and caressed her, and whispered his love. His mouth went to her breasts, and she drew in her breath in pleasure, and presently his fingers gently sought out her secret places, and he knew that she was ready for him. As he moved, she looked down at him, and for a moment there was shock and, he thought, fear in her eyes. He kissed her, so that she could no longer see that sight which had disturbed her, and manoeuvred himself into position, and thrust a little way, and met resistance, and waited, and thrust again, not

261

roughly, but with sufficient pressure. And she gave a little cry. Again he paused, waiting for her to indicate perhaps that the pain was too sharp.

'I hurt you.'

'Only a little, only a little. I really am a married woman now, Edward, am I not?'

'Hush!'

Slowly, slowly he began to move in her. He had expected that, in his excitement, it would soon be over, but, possibly because of his anxiety for her, his climax did not come quickly, and he was able to go on and on. And presently she began to pant, and to dig her fingers into his back, and her mouth on his became more demanding. And then she cried out, and her body convulsed, and, pounding now, Edward shuddered in his own little death, and moaned, too, in ecstasy.

Afterwards they lay together in contentment.

'Are you . . . sore?' Edward asked after a while.

'No. Well, only a little.' Suddenly she sat up. 'Edward!'

'What?'

'I never thought—the sheet, it must be . . .' Suddenly, she got out of bed. 'Yes, there's blood, and . . . Oh, Edward, what can we do?'

'Do?'

'We can't leave it like this. Whatever will they think?'

'It's no use worrying, my dear. I am sure they recognised us as a honeymoon couple—they say the people in hotels can always tell—so they will be expecting something like this. Perhaps they'd be disappointed if in the morning they failed to find evidence of our activities.'

'Please don't talk like that!' she snapped at him. 'You make it all sound so sordid. I'm surprised you don't suggest bringing them all in here to see!' She snatched up her nightdress, and fought her way into it, as though in a race against time. Then, she took a towel, and scrubbed at the marks on the sheet. 'It's no use!' she cried petulantly, and threw the towel down, and climbed back into bed, turning away from Edward.

He, taken aback by her attack, had the good sense to realise that silence was, for the moment, the best response. He put on his nightshirt and got into bed beside her. Then he realised that she was crying, and put out his hand and

262

gently touched her shoulder. 'What is it, my darling?' She did not answer, moving as though to evade his touch, but he persisted, lightly caressing her arm. 'Tell me, please.'

In little bursts, punctuated by sobs and shuddering breaths, the words came, some whispered so softly that he could barely make them out. 'Oh, Edward, I am so ashamed! I have behaved so immodestly. My mother brought me up to behave like a lady—she must be turning in her grave . . . Worst of all, what you must think of me . . . You must feel that you have married a harlot. Oh, God! And now these bedclothes! If I had not been so wanton, I would have kept my nightdress on, and it would have gone on that, and . . . Oh, God forgive me! I am so ashamed, so ashamed!'

He let her speak without interruption, knowing instinctively that it all had to come out before she would accept his comfort. He held her tight, and whispered, 'I love you, Alice. I love you very much. Nothing can change that, and nothing ever will.'

She turned away, crying softly into her pillow. He waited, and when she seemed calmer, again touched the satin skin of her shoulder. She did not reject the caress, and after a while, turned back to him. 'I'm sorry,' she whispered. He kissed away the tears, and then turned out the light, and presently they fell asleep in each other's arms.

In the morning, the breakfast Edward had ordered the previous night was brought to them promptly at eight o'clock. Once they had eaten it, he was ready for a little dalliance, but Alice immediately jumped out of bed, and washed and dressed quickly.

'Hurry up,' she said, 'or the water will be cold.'

As he was still shaving, she packed their cases.

'I'm all ready,' she said. 'You won't be long, will you?'

'What's the rush, my darling?'

'I want to leave, Edward.'

'Don't you like the room?'

'It's not that. It's . . . I want to be out of here before the chambermaid comes to make the bed.'

He was tempted for a moment to speak angrily, to tell her not to be such a little fool, but he caught the note of urgency in her voice and checked himself. 'All right, my sweet. Nearly ready.'

Later, as they sat alone in the first-class carriage of the train which was taking them to Cornwall, he decided the time had come for him to clarify a few matters. 'Now, my darling,' he said, 'I want you to listen carefully to your husband, and to obey his commands. You did promise to obey me, did you not?'

'Yes.'

'Very well, then. The first obedience concerns that hotel bedroom, that hotel bed and those hotel sheets. If those sheets are stained, firstly, I have paid for their laundry in the cost of the room, secondly, there is no shame in the way they were stained, and thirdly, the chambermaid will not know who you are and will not care to find out. So we will have no more of it, do you hear, Alice?'

'Yes,' she replied meekly.

Elated by his success, Edward continued, making his voice as stern and pompous as he could, 'But that is of minor concern. Of much greater importance is the matter of your wantonness.'

Alice looked at him in shock, her eyes wide.

'Yes. You behaved wantonly last night—you have already admitted it, and there is no other word for it. Now, listen to me, Alice, and make sure that you obey me to the last letter of what I am about to say. Will you do that?'

'Yes,' she whispered, apprehension in her eyes.

'I insist, I positively insist that . . .' He paused, dropped his severity of manner, and laughed. 'I insist that you continue to behave in exactly the same way for the rest of our married life.'

But his joke fell flat, for Alice wept again, and confessed herself mortified, and refused to be comforted. It took him until almost the end of their three days in Cornwall—he would not take more time away from Chetwynd's—to persuade her that he truly delighted in the behaviour which her upbringing told her was wicked and licentious. And together they learned how to give each other pleasure in many different ways.

*   *   *

When they arrived back at Rudleigh, they found that the entire staff of Chetwynd's was waiting to greet them.

They were cheered, and Alice was presented by Nancy Huggins with a bouquet of flowers, and then they were driven slowly to Fourways, their new home—slowly, so that those on foot could keep up with the trap.

Before the wedding they had received a large number of presents, and there were more now waiting to be undone. Prominent among them was a large, heavy parcel, addressed to them both in Frances' writing. The paper was covered in warnings in large letters: *'Fragile'*, *'Handle with Care'*, *'Breakable'*.

'How strange!' Edward said. 'The Bunns have already given us a present, have they not?'

'Yes, my love. The canteen of cutlery.'

'Then what can this be?'

When Edward opened it, he came first to a note from Frances. 'My dear ones, I suppose it is your doing really, Edward, but ever since you bullied me into preparing those designs for you, I have been thinking more and more in three-dimensional terms. I have taken to sculpting—at least that's what I call it, though my dear husband insists that it is merely messing about with mud. Anyway, here is my latest creation. Your uncle claims that it is a malicious caricature, but I rather like it, and I hope you both will, too. Lovingly, F.B.'

The statue, in unglazed terracotta, was an unmistakable portrait of Alfred Bunn. It was not altogether realistic, for Frances had slightly exaggerated the angularity of the limbs, and the position of the shoulders and the tilt of the head, but neither was it really a caricature. She had somehow captured the very essence of her husband, and had done so with obvious affection, but at the same time with humour.

Edward and Alice looked at it with delight.

'It's Uncle Alfred to the life!' Edward said.

'Yes. You know who it reminds me of?'

'Who?'

'Well, your uncle always makes me think of . . . And the slight exaggeration that your aunt has used makes him look even more like—like Mr Jingle.'

'Who?'

'Mr Jingle in *The Pickwick Papers*.'

'Oh.' Edward gazed at the statue. 'Yes,' he said absently. 'Yes. Now you mention it . . . Mr Jingle, eh? Dickens . . .

Now, if Aunt Frances could . . .' He looked at Alice. 'Are you thinking what I'm thinking?'

'Cast iron?'

'Yes. But not Mr Jingle. Mr Pickwick. And Oliver Twist.'

'And Sarah Gamp, and Mr Micawber, and Mr Squeers. Or you could have Pickwick with Tupman and Snodgrass. And all based on the Phiz drawings. Or are they copyright?'

'It's expired, I think. I believe it lasts for seven years after death, and Phiz—what was his name? Browne, wasn't it?—he died ten or twelve years ago, so there's no problem there. Alice, what a marvellous idea! They'll sell like hot cakes! Cast iron men! I'll write to Aunt Frances straight away.' He seized Alice and did a little dance with her round the room, laughing with excitement.

* * *

Everyone at Chetwynd's was enthusiastic about Frances' statuettes, which Walter Sales reproduced in wood so that moulds could be made from them. Most of the foundrymen could not read and had no knowledge of Dickens, but they could see the humour in the figures and recognised them as prototypes of Englishmen and women of their period. The designs were based on Phiz's drawings, but in making them three-dimensional, Frances had given them an extra vitality. The only dissenting voice was that of Beatrice Unwin. 'I can't abide, Dickens,' she said. 'I never could. So trivial, and often so vulgar. Now, Tolstoy—there's a novelist to admire. I've just read *Anna Karenina* for the second time. What a masterpiece!'

But even she saw the commercial potential of the statuettes, and was as pleased as everyone else when they proved to be a huge success. Edward and Alice were particularly gratified, feeling a proprietary pride in them, the whole idea having been sparked by one of their own wedding gifts. They were sold in two forms—plain and hand-painted—but the latter, although costing twice as much, were far more popular, and orders flooded in. The Mementoes of Love were also very successful, and Walter Sales was duly presented with the promised bonus—twenty golden sovereigns—which left him gasping, while Edward

266

thought how ironic it was that he had once wanted to pension the old man off.

These two lines gave them entrée to many new retail outlets, and although other firms eventually copied them, Chetwynd's led the field for many years. The immediate result was that Edward, with Jack Chetwynd's approval, built a new large shed, which became the paintshop, and then hired a number of young women who henceforth spent their days in painting Pickwicks and Micawbers and Sarah Gamps. As the months went by, it became clear that before long he would indeed need a larger foundry, too—provided, of course, that young Beeson continued to bring in the orders.

That young gentleman had prospered. He was earning considerable sums in commission, and now dressed very smartly, and smoked little cheroots, which he handed out with gracious liberality to friends and customers and workmen alike. And he had grown a luxuriant moustache. He had taken Edward's strictures to heart, and had become a voracious reader, but he still irritated Edward by the way he spoke.

'I'm going to take on more salesmen,' Edward told him one day.

'You dissatisfied with me, Mr 'Arcourt?'

'Not at all. But the time has come to expand. A couple of extra men would enable us to cover the outlets more fully and more often.'

'Would they be me equals, as it were?'

'That depends on you. I have been thinking—only thinking, mind—about whether to put you in charge of them. Now, *if* I decided to do so, we might think of calling you "Sales Manager", and adjusting your salary appropriately.'

'Thank you, sir,' Beeson said, and then added, 'Cor!'

'But there is one problem to be overcome before we can consider any such appointment. I've spoken to you about it before. I don't want a Sales Manager who speaks as though he's just come out of the gutter. You may think it sounds snobbish, Beeson, but people do take notice of such matters. And I know you can talk properly when you want to.'

Beeson's face broke into a smile. 'Lor' love a duck, Mr

'Arcourt! Is that all what's bothering you?' Suddenly the Cockney accent disappeared. 'You see, sir, I fit the way I talk to our customers. "Haigh-clarss" with those who expect me to be a bit of a swell, and in Newcastle I talk Geordie, bonny lad, and if I'm in Wales, I'm a reggerlar Taffy, isn't it?'

Edward laughed. It was always impossible to be angry with Beeson. 'Then why do you persist in being a Cockney when you're with me?'

'Two reasons. Firstly, you might think I was taking you off. And the second thing, Mr 'Arcourt, is that I feel I can sort o' relax with you, and be meself.'

Some weeks later, the two extra salesmen were taken on, and Beeson was appointed Sales Manager. He went straight from his interview with Edward in the latter's office at the foundry to Rudleigh House, marching into the room where Miss Unwin was at that moment berating Nancy Huggins for some minor error.

'Pardon me, Miss,' Beeson said, without waiting for Miss Unwin even to pause. To her astonishment, he then threw himself on one knee. 'Nancy 'Uggins,' he said, 'will you give me your 'and in marriage, and do me the honour of becoming Mrs Beeson? Say "yes", and you'll make me the 'appiest o' men. Say "no" and I'll throw meself under the four-fifteen from Shrewsbury to London.'

'Ooh, Freddie!' said Nancy.

'Get up at once, Beeson,' Miss Unwin said angrily.

Beeson scrambled to his feet.

'Ooh, Freddie!' repeated Nancy. She threw herself into his arms, and kissed him enthusiastically.

'Will you, then?' he asked her.

'Course I will.'

''Ooray!' He kissed her again, and then sobered. ''Ere, I got work to do. Sorry to disturb you, Miss Unwin. See you later, Nancy love.' And with a wave of his hat, he had gone.

Miss Unwin was not best pleased, and reprimanded Nancy in the strongest tones, threatening dismissal if she did not instantly calm herself, and get back to her work.

'Miserable old cat!' Nancy said later. 'I reckon she's jealous, not being able to get a man of her own, like.'

*   *   *

On Edward's twenty-sixth birthday in July of 1899, Alice presented him with a velvet smoking jacket and cap, which she had made herself, and then said, shyly, 'I have another present for you, my darling. But I'm afraid you'll have to wait for it for a while. Early February, the doctor says.'

'Early February.' Comprehension dawned. 'You don't mean . . .? Oh, Alice!'

'You are pleased, Edward?'

'Beyond all expression. Oh, Alice, I do love you. Come and sit down, my dear one—you have to take care.'

Alice laughed. 'Don't be absurd! The doctor says that I'm as fit as a fiddle, and I don't want to be treated as though I'm made of icing sugar. I am absolutely determined, Edward— I am not going to be like some women who have to be pampered and wrapped in cotton-wool the whole time. Unless the doctor tells me otherwise, I intend to lead as normal a life as I possibly can. I shall not change in any way—except in my figure. Oh, you won't care for me at all once I get to be like . . . like an elephant.'

'I shall love you even more.'

But however firmly she intended to control herself, at least in one respect she was unable to do so, as time went on, veering away from her normal level-headedness.

At first, she and Edward had kept the news to themselves, but before long everyone had to know. They told Mrs Chetwynd and Miss Unwin one evening when they were visiting them at Rudleigh House.

'I knew it,' Mrs Chetwynd said in her little voice. 'I can always tell.'

Miss Unwin shot an enigmatic look at Edward. 'I wonder that your husband did not allow you a longer period in which to become accustomed to your new status as a married woman, before forcing maternity upon you. But men are always thoughtless in such matters.'

'Beatrice! Beatrice!' her mother said.

'I'm sorry, but it is true.'

Mrs Chetwynd swiftly stepped in, with a spate of polite chatter, to cover up the awkwardness of the moment.

Soon after that incident, Doctor Bellamy strongly advised Alice that she and Edward should sleep apart.

269

Edward moved to a separate bedroom, and it was from that time that Alice began to behave strangely.

Within a week or so, she seemed convinced that she had lost all attraction for Edward, and that he was seeking his pleasures elsewhere. At first, he was totally baffled. Why on earth should she suspect him of infidelity with their maid, a girl whom he had hardly even looked at? Alice dismissed the girl, and for a few days there was peace between them.

Then one morning, to Edward's surprise, Alice came into the paintshop. He was standing by one of the girls who painted the Dickens statuettes—almost leaning over her, in fact, in order to study her work. As he straightened up Alice stared back at him, tightened her lips in an angry line, and stalked out. He hurried after her but she refused to speak to him, and it was not until that evening that she launched her attack, weeping and near to hysteria. He no longer loved her . . . he had seduced the girl from the paintshop . . . he was flaunting his mistress under his wife's very nose . . . The accusations seemed endless. Finally, she ran out of words, and leaned back against the cushions of her armchair, exhausted.

Then at last he was able to tell her that it was all nonsense; that he had no interest whatsoever in the girl; that he loved only his darling, darling wife, and always would. He had to repeat it over and over before she would believe it.

The same kind of thing happened again and again. And then, the worst time, when she had once more accused him of infidelity, she said bitterly, 'I suppose I could expect nothing else, with your family background!' Immediately, she regretted the words, and begged his forgiveness. 'I don't know what made me say that!' she exclaimed, wildly. 'Oh, I love you so much, Edward, and it wounds me to the depths of my soul that you no longer care for me.'

'But I do, I do!' he protested, trying to forget the hurt that her words had caused. His father was right, he thought— he should never have confided in Alice. Yet how could he not have done?

At his wits' end, he could think of nothing to solve the problem. He needed to be able to talk to an older woman, but his mother was miles away, even if she would have listened, and he could not have confided in Mrs Chetwynd. Suddenly he thought of someone, almost a stranger, which was what he needed most.

Mrs Woodham lived in a tiny cottage some two or three miles away from Fourways. Making the excuse of exercising Tando, the young Irish wolfhound he had given Alice, he went there one evening. She was surprised to see him, but bade him enter, and offered him a cup of hot buttermilk. Then she waited patiently, seeming to know that he would say whatever he had to say when he was ready and not before.

Eventually, stumbling over it, he told her the story, giving her every detail of the bizarre accusations that Alice levelled against him.

When he had finished, Mrs Woodham laughed. 'It's the baby,' she said in her thick accent. 'Takes 'em all ways. Some wants to eat coal, or live on blackcurrants. Others is sick all the time. It don't mean anything. She'll get over it, come her time. Don't you worry, sir.'

'You mean that's all it is?'

'Aye.'

'But where do these ideas come from?'

Mrs Woodham shrugged. 'Mebbe she's talking to someone, mebbe they just come out of her head. Don't make no odds. You let her say what she do like, and don't you take no notice.'

'That's easier said than done.'

'Ain't as difficult as what she's doing! Men got no cause to grumble. They gets the pleasure, women gets the pain. She'll be all right, when she's holding a babe in her arms. Mebbe before.'

It was easier after that. The accusations from Alice continued from time to time, but fortified by his belief in Mrs Woodham's diagnosis, Edward possessed himself in patience, simply reaffirming his love. He tried to discover the origin of the malicious stories, but she maintained that the knowledge simply came to her; that no other person was putting ideas into her head. And yet, something told him that she was lying. And that hurt, too, for she had never lied to him before, and it was unlike her.

Soon he had something else to worry about. Whenever Beeson made one of his sales trips to London, he acted as a courier between Jack Chetwynd and Edward, to whom he always reported immediately on his return. Edward enjoyed these meetings, even when Beeson remembered his manners and omitted his imitation of Jack's drawl.

But this time, instead of greeting Edward with his usual grin, Beeson looked solemn, almost apprehensive. 'You're not going to like this, Mr 'Arcourt.'

'Not going to like what? Surely Mr Chetwynd is not dissatisfied. Not with the profits we've been making these last few weeks.'

'I'm leaving.'

'What?'

'I'm leaving Chetwynd's.'

'Why on earth . . .? Where are you going? Not to Ironbridge?'

Beeson smiled at that. 'Not likely. I'm going on the 'alls.'

'I'm sorry, I don't understand.'

'The 'alls—the music 'alls. Mr Chetwynd's starting me off.'

'You're mad! You can't do that.'

'I'm doing it. Listen, Mr 'Arcourt, maybe I *am* mad, but I just got to try. When I was in London this time, I went to the Grenville, and they was 'aving what they call amachoor night. And I 'ad a go, and would you believe it, I won. They voted me the best o' the evening.'

'What did you do?'

'Imitations—what else? I did 'em all—'Arry Champion, Albert Chevalier, Little Tich, the lot. Told a few jokes and did a little dance. I thought of trying me 'and at a bit o' juggling, but you know me—I'd've dropped the lot! So I finished up with a couple of choruses of *The Old Bull and Bush*. Cor, it went down a treat, Mr 'Arcourt. And Mr Chetwynd 'eard it, which is what makes all the difference, 'cause 'e said 'e'd give me some introductions, and it wouldn't be easy without that.'

'But this is out of the question, Beeson. You've got a good job here, plenty of prospects, and—'

'Yes, I know that, Mr 'Arcourt.'

'Don't you think you owe me any loyalty? I brought you here, and gave you your chance.'

'Yes, I know all that, too, and I'm very grateful to you.

272

And I'm sorry, I am truly. But I got to do it. It's me destiny, you might say.'

'Listen,' Edward said. 'I'll pay you an extra one per cent commission.'

Beeson shook his head. 'It's not the money, Mr 'Arcourt, honest, it's not. You could offer me five per cent more, but I'd still want to do this. I think I've always wanted it, reelly.'

'And I've always wanted to fly to the moon! We can't always do just what we want—we have to think of other people. You've got security here, a job you're good at, employers who think highly of you—and you're going to give all that up for—for what? And what about Nancy? What's she going to say?'

'I got to talk to 'er,' Beeson said, without enthusiasm.

'Still going to get married?'

'Well, not immediately, but . . . Look, Mr 'Arcourt, I know all the arguments against what I'm doing, but I got to do it. I'm going to give it six months. If I don't make good, I'll come back with me tail between me legs, and you can say anything you like to me then.'

'There may not be a job for you.'

Beeson shrugged. 'I got to take that risk.'

'And when do you propose to leave us?'

'Beginning o' next month. Mr Chetwynd said 'e'd need a while to set up some contacts for me.'

'Right,' said Edward. 'I'll hear your report later, and in the meantime, you can get on with your paperwork as usual. Off you go.'

When Beeson had left the room, Edward sat and thought, deciding gloomily that this was just about the worst blow that he could wish for now that the business was really beginning to build up, and Beeson himself was gaining every day in experience and ability. There was only one way in which he might put a stop to it.

He sent a telegram, and hurried back to the house. Alice was sewing in the drawing-room. 'I'm going to London,' he said. 'I've got to see Jack as soon as possible.'

'Jack?' she queried, and he could hear the unspoken thought.

'Yes, Jack. I am not going to visit anyone else, not even Aunt Frances and Uncle Alfred, and I shall not so much as speak to another woman.'

'Why have you got to see Jack?'

He told her the story. 'I'm going to catch the next train,' he finished, 'and I'll be back early tomorrow.'

He went to Rudleigh House to tell Beatrice Unwin that he would be away for the rest of the day and the next morning.

She greeted him angrily. 'I wish you would tell Beeson not to come in here and upset my staff during working hours. Look at her!' She pointed to Nancy Huggins, who was huddled at her desk, weeping.

'I'm sorry,' Edward said. 'Come here, Miss Huggins.'

Nervously, the girl came and stood in front of him.

'Now, listen to me. I'm going to London to see whether I can persuade Mr Chetwynd to change his mind, or to change Beeson's for him. If I fail, you will simply have to come to terms with the situation, you understand?'

'Yes, sir.' She looked up at him, her face stained with tears, and suddenly she threw herself towards him, and her arms were around his neck, and she was sobbing, 'Oh, stop him, Mr Harcourt, stop him! If he goes on the halls, it's the end of any thought of marriage, I know that. He'll find some . . . some tart who's no better than she should be, and . . .' She dissolved into sobs.

'Such behaviour!' sniffed Miss Unwin, as Edward disentangled himself from the girl. 'It really is most provoking. Pull yourself together, Miss Huggins. You're better off without a man like Beeson—without any man, come to that.'

As he left, Edward could hear Beatrice Unwin continuing her diatribe against the male sex. He wondered why she should have suddenly developed so strong an antipathy, of which there had been no previous signs.

*   *   *

'He's got talent, Edward—he really has. That Friday night audience is the very devil to please, but your Fred Beeson not only pleased them—he had 'em in the palm of his hand.'

'But I need him. Chetwynd's needs him. For God's sake, Jack, how can you do this to me?'

'Is he irreplaceable?'

'Yes.'

'I mean, *really* irreplaceable.'

274

'No, I suppose not, but good Sales Managers don't grow on trees.'

'Neither do music hall stars, and that's what he's going to be.'

'And are music hall stars irreplaceable?'

Jack Chetwynd laughed. 'No. But I'll tell you this—Beeson's far more easily replaced as your Sales Manager than as a top-rate entertainer.'

'So I've had a wasted journey.'

'Oh, surely not, Edward. It's always a pleasure for me to see you, and I'm delighted to hear at first hand how well you're doing, and that the Dickens figures are so popular. I'm not surprised. Everyone admires my set tremendously.' He gestured towards an occasional table, on which stood a group of the cast iron statuettes. 'I tell 'em to go and buy 'em in the shops—and I think they do. I ought to get commission.'

Edward did not smile. 'Maybe you'd like to be my new Sales Manager.'

'Oh, stop being so sour, Edward. Be happy for Beeson—he's found his real niche in life, and that's rare enough. Go on—smile! That's better.'

'All right. I'll stop complaining, and wish him luck when he goes, and cope somehow or other with his fiancée—I just hope she doesn't go hysterical on me again—but what am I going to do about a Sales Manager?'

'Promote one of the representatives.'

'They've both been with us for so short a time.'

'Can you do without a Sales Manager for a few months, or do the job yourself?'

'I suppose so, if really necessary.'

'Right,' said Jack, 'then take on two more salesmen, and tell all four of 'em that the best one will be promoted at the end of six months. Then sit back and watch. It works. It's what I did at the theatre, with three sub-managers. They all worked like slaves, which was good for me and the business, and within a few weeks it was obvious that one of them was head and shoulders above the rest.'

'But suppose none of my men is suitable? I'm not sure that either of the two we've got has any desire to be a manager.'

'Don't you believe it, old boy. They're all looking for

promotion—everyone is. Anyway, when you take on the two new ones, make sure they're ambitious, and then you'll have at least two to choose from.' Jack yawned. 'Oh, I'm bored with this.' Then he sighed. 'As a matter of fact, Edward, old son, I'm bored with everything.'

Edward laughed.

'I'm not joking. It was fun setting up the theatre, but now it's nothing but problems. It's barely breaking even. And I'm bored with it. You ought to think yourself damned lucky, Edward—a thriving business, a job you enjoy, a beautiful wife, an infant on the way . . .'

'Perhaps you ought to get married.'

'Oh, there's not much chance of that—not with my reputation.'

The bitterness in Jack's tone surprised Edward. 'That sounds almost as though you've been turned down.'

Jack gave a short laugh. 'No. But I'm pretty sure I should be, if I asked her.'

'Who is she?'

'If you must know, it's Mary.'

'Which Mary? Do I know her?'

'Your cousin.'

'Mary!'

'We met at your wedding. We got on famously—at least I thought we did. And your old pal fell head over heels.'

'With Mary?'

'Yes. Why not? She may be your cousin, old chap, but she's a deuced attractive woman.'

'I know she is. It's just that—' Edward stopped short, anxious not to betray himself.

'Surprised, eh? Didn't think she was my type, is that it? But I can't get her out of my head, Edward. I think about her all the time.'

'Have you seen her since the wedding?'

'No.' Jack explained that he had written several times, inviting her to come to London, saying that if she wanted a chaperone he would happily pay for her mother to come, too. He had also angled for an invitation to Wensham. But all his efforts had failed. There was always some excuse to prevent a meeting—she was too busy at the hospital, or the weather was inclement, or her mother was having some old friends to stay.

276

'Perhaps she's trying to tell you she's not interested,' Edward said.

'I suppose that's possible, but her letters are very friendly, and she replies promptly to mine. I don't think she'd do that if she wanted to show that my attentions are unwelcome.'

'She told me once,' Edward said carefully, 'that she would never marry.'

That seemed to amuse Jack, and he suddenly regained his usual flippancy. 'Oh, piffle! All women say that sort of thing at some stage in their lives. Now, tell me honestly, old chap, have you any objection to me as a cousin-in-law? I assure you my intentions are honourable—in fact, they've never been honourabler.'

'I'd be delighted if it happened, Jack, I really would.' Edward meant it. If Mary could find happiness with Jack, the last vestiges of his guilt towards her would be wiped away, and she would undoubtedly be a good influence on him. 'Just don't hurt her, Jack, don't ever hurt her like—' He just stopped himself in time.

'Like what?'

'Oh, nothing. She was hurt very badly once.'

'Who by? How?'

'I . . . I don't know,' Edward lied. 'I just know that she went through a very bad time over some fellow, and I don't want it to happen to her again.'

'The swine!' Jack said. 'Anyway, you can depend on it—I'll never do anything to hurt her as long as I live. I swear it.' He grinned. 'Satisfied? Right, then this is what I want you to do.' And he explained his plan.

There was, however, little opportunity of putting the scheme into practice straightway.

On his return to Rudleigh, Edward went home first, anxious to know that Alice was still in good health, and had not been too miserable during his absence. She reassured him quickly, and then plied him with questions until he had accounted for every minute of the time he had been away.

Eventually, he said, 'I must go to the office, and find out what's going on. Besides, I've got to give Nancy Huggins the bad news.'

Alice tightened her lips at the girl's name, just as she had done earlier when he had mentioned Nancy while telling her of his conversation with Jack.

Nancy Huggins stood up as Edward entered the office, looking at him anxiously, but he motioned her to sit. 'I'll talk to you in a minute, Miss Huggins. I must have a word with Miss Unwin first.'

Beatrice Unwin looked flustered, two patches of colour burning on her cheeks, but nothing untoward had occurred during his absence. Orders had continued to come in, and payments had also been received as expected. No problems had arisen in the foundry. 'In fact,' she said, giving him one of her warmest smiles, 'everything has been entirely satisfactory. Except that Mama is confined to her bed.'

'I am sorry.'

'It is no more than a slight chill. She is almost recovered.'

Edward went and sat by Nancy Huggins' desk. 'I spoke to Mr Chetwynd,' he told her. 'He says that young Beeson has a brilliant future. In his view there is no question of the usual insecurity; Beeson will be a star, and will never be without work, or a proper reward for it.'

'So you're going to let him leave Chetwynd's, sir.' Her face crumpled, and tears formed in her eyes.

'I don't see how I can stop him. Mr Chetwynd is very firmly of the opinion that no one should stand in his way.'

She began to sob, and buried her head in her arms on the table.

'Come, come,' Edward said. 'Has he actually broken off your engagement?'

She shook her head.

'Then perhaps he is still planning your wedding soon.' He patted her shoulder sympathetically. 'Now try to stop crying.'

At that moment Alice entered the room. She took in the scene before her, glanced at Miss Unwin, and gave a kind of strangled cry. When she looked at Edward again, her eyes were pain-filled. She turned and left the room swiftly.

Edward hurried after her, running to catch her up. 'Alice, my darling, what is it?'

'That girl,' she said, 'that Huggins creature! You couldn't wait to get your hands on her, could you?'

'What do you mean?'

'Oh, don't pretend. I saw you with my own eyes. And I've heard. She was in your arms, wasn't she?'

278

Amazed at this accusation, Edward could only repeat, 'In my arms?'

'Oh, not now—before you went to London. With *her* arms around your neck. You were seen, of course. I heard all about it, so don't try to tell me it isn't true.'

One person only could have reported that scene to her, Edward thought. It took him the best part of an hour to calm Alice down, and persuade her that Nancy Huggins meant nothing at all to him, but by the time they had finished, he had established without doubt that it was Miss Unwin who had been pouring the poison into her ears. In the past few months, Alice had apparently taken to making frequent calls on her—always when she was certain that Edward would not interrupt them.

She begged his forgiveness for her stupidity. 'I'll try to control myself, Edward my dearest, but . . . well, sometimes these feelings get into me, and it seems that I can't do anything about them. I know I should, but I can't.'

Edward was tempted to tell her what Mrs Woodham had said, but decided against doing so. 'I understand, my sweetheart, and you're not to let it worry you. As long as you still love me, and I love you, nothing else matters. But what I don't understand is why Beatrice should have told you all these things which aren't true.'

Alice could not explain why, and Edward decided that he must have it out with Miss Unwin straight away.

It was a quarter past six when he got back to the office. He was surprised to find Miss Unwin alone. 'Where is Miss Huggins?' he asked.

'I had to send her home. She was no use to me in the state she was in.'

'I am glad, because I wanted to speak to you privately. I have just been talking to my wife. She tells me that you have been discussing me with her, and telling her stories about me. Is this true?'

'If she says so.'

'But why? Why, Beatrice—especially when you know that there is no truth in these tales?' When she did not reply, he went on, 'I just don't understand. Don't you see what damage you are doing? Alice is in a delicate condition, and her peace of mind is very readily disturbed.' To his amazement, she smiled. 'You smile,' he said, 'but it is no joke, I assure you. I forbid you to speak to her from now on. I shall also forbid her to come to this house except if I accompany her. I hope you understand this. I do not wish to have to speak of it again.' He went towards the door. 'One last thing. I should appreciate it if you would write a letter to my wife admitting the falsity of the stories you have told her about me. I think that you would agree that you owe me that.'

Suddenly she began to weep. 'Oh, God!' It was a terrible cry, wrung from the depths of her soul. Her whole body was shaking uncontrollably. 'Don't go! Don't go!' she cried. 'I'll tell you . . . everything . . . why I did it.' She slid from her chair and came towards him on her knees. Her words were broken by deep, shuddering sobs. 'Edward, oh, Edward! She's wrong for you. Can't you see that? She's no wife for *you*!' She was overcome again by her weeping, but then continued, her eyes wild, staring up at him. 'That's why I shall go on doing it. I'm going to drive her away, get rid of her.' She laughed hysterically. 'She doesn't trust you, Edward. She thinks she still loves you, but I'm killing her love, bit by bit. Soon she'll see it's hopeless, and she'll go away, and leave you to me.'

'Stop! Please stop!' Edward shouted.

She took no notice, but threw herself forward, clasping his ankles. Half sobbing, half laughing, all self control gone, she cried, 'Oh, Edward, Edward! I adore you! I worship you! Oh, tell me you love me, too!'

Horrified, he gazed down at her. He reached down and tried to pull her arms away. It was almost as ludicrous a situation as that earlier time when she had fallen on top of him. That had been on purpose, he thought angrily. Thank God she did not have her dog with her this time, and thank God, too, that Mrs Chetwynd was in bed and would not suddenly come in. He succeeded in releasing himself. She was still hysterical, kneeling before him. Perhaps again it was that time of the month . . . Her wild sobs were becoming even more uncontrolled. 'Slap her face,' he told himself, and suddenly his anger took control, and he hit her much harder than he had intended.

The hysterics stopped. Whimpering slightly, she looked up at him, with an expression almost of puzzlement, her hand rubbing at her cheek where he had struck her.

Somehow, a part of her hair had come unpinned, and straggled down over her face, giving her a sluttish look.

Edward stared at her with revulsion. 'You're mad,' he said, 'mad and evil. What you have done to Alice is wicked and cruel. I shall never forgive you, never. You should be put away.' For a moment he wanted to strike her again, but controlled his anger and left the room.

She would have to leave Rudleigh, he thought—she and her mother. It would mean going back to London to talk to Jack. As for Alice, in the meantime he would forbid her to speak to Miss Unwin again.

*   *   *

It was early the following morning that the incident took place, some miles away from Rudleigh. Some people wondered why she had gone so far away, but it was obvious: near to Ironbridge, the trains were slowing down to enter the station, or picking up speed as they left; where she had gone, they would be rattling along with lethal force, unable to brake in time.

It was also perfectly clear that it was no accident. In her room they found a note. It gave no reasons, made no accusations or excuses, but simply stated that she no longer wished to live. She had left the paper lying next to her copy of *Anna Karenina*, open at the pages describing Anna's suicide.

Edward was more distressed than anyone, realising that he bore a great responsibility for her death. Of course, there would be an inquest, and what should he say then? That he had been one of the last people to see her alive? That she had declared her love for him, and he had spurned her, and told her that she should be shut up in an asylum?

Naturally, he called upon Mrs Chetwynd. Wrapped in a shawl, she was sitting hunched up in the corner of a sofa in the sitting room. He was shocked at her appearance, for she seemed to have aged more than he would have believed possible. She looked like an old, old lady, fragile and vulnerable, her skin almost transparent. Her Prince snuffled on her lap, and beside her was her daughter's dog, Fido, which she caressed absently every now and then, as though conscious of a duty towards it.

281

'I just cannot believe it,' she said in her high little voice. 'If only she had given me some warning, some indication of how unhappy she was—for she must have been unhappy, must she not, Mr Harcourt? And yet, there was no sign of it when she came to say goodnight to me. I thought she had been crying, but she told me perfectly calmly that a log had fallen out of the fire, and the smoke had got in her eyes as she was putting it back. She did say that she was tired, but that it would be easier now that you were back again, Mr Harcourt.'

'She didn't say anything else about me?' Edward asked.

'No, I don't think so. I told her that I felt better and would probably get up in the morning, and then she kissed me goodnight, and went. I suppose I shall have to tell them that at the inquest, shan't I? And then they'll say that she took her life while the balance of her mind was disturbed. I always think that's such an unkind phrase, don't you?'

As he came away from the house, he thought of what she had said. If she repeated to the coroner what she had told him, then there would be no real reason why he need offer any evidence other than that, on his return from London, Miss Unwin had given him a routine report, in an entirely normal manner. That much was true. Was it a criminal act to conceal the extraordinary scene which had taken place later?

If only there were someone he could talk to about it. Normally, he would have gone straight to Alice, but it would not be fair, in her condition, to burden her with such a problem. She had been greatly distressed by the news, and indeed he had feared that she might even be on the verge of a miscarriage. Thank God, everything seemed all right, but obviously he would have to avoid upsetting her further. And then he realised that he *had* to discuss it with her—she already knew that he had had a difficult conversation with Beatrice . . .

He would also have to think about finding someone to look after Chetwynd's accounts. And extra salesmen, and re-allocating Beeson's responsibilities, and trying to engineer another meeting between Jack Chetwynd and Mary, as he had promised, and . . . 'Oh, Lord,' he thought, 'not single spies, but in battalions.'

He went into his house, and kissed Alice very tenderly,

feeling desperately in need of her love and support. Instinctively she knew that for once he had found himself wanting, and had come to her to ask her to lend him her wisdom and her strength and her courage, to bolster his own, and her heart was filled with joy, for it was the first time in their marriage that he had shown his dependence on her in this way. Usually, he refused all her offers of help. She had found it hurtful, until she realised that it was simply his nature to prefer to do everything he could on his own.

He told her everything that had happened between him and Miss Unwin the previous evening. 'If I repeat all that to the Coroner,' he said, 'I shall have to involve you.'

'I do not mind for myself,' she replied. 'I have been very foolish. I think I bear a responsibility, too. Perhaps, in a way, I encouraged her in her madness. And I have wronged you so very deeply. But if you were to reveal everything, you could not avoid pouring ridicule on poor Beatrice, and that is surely unnecessary. We should think of Mrs Chetwynd, too, and the additional distress it would cause her. There are not many occasions when the truth should be concealed, but I think this is one.'

He gave a sigh of relief, and nodded. 'Thank you, my dear.'

*   *   *

The next day when he returned from work, she was not in the house. The maid told him that she had gone out half an hour earlier, saying that she would not be long.

She returned almost immediately. He was in the sitting-room, and rose to greet her. 'No, sit down, please,' she said. She came to him and, clumsily because of her heavy body, knelt beside his chair. 'I have been to the church,' she told him. 'I went to confession, to cleanse my soul, to ask God's mercy on my wickedness. And now I want *your* forgiveness, my darling husband. I have been . . . out of my mind, I think. Those accusations! But never, in my heart, have I truly believed them. Never. Oh, forgive me, Edward.' There were tears in her eyes.

'I do, my darling—everything. Oh, do not distress yourself. I understand, and I love you very deeply.'

283

'But how can you ever forget what I said about your family, your background that day? I must have hurt you very deeply.'

'It is forgotten already. I knew you did not mean it.'

'No, I swear I did not. Oh, how I wish I could take back those words!' She was sobbing now. 'Do you remember saying that we must never let it come between us? And I did! I did!'

'It is forgiven and forgotten, Alice, and it will never happen again, I know. Now, dry your tears, my angel, and let us be happy in our love, and never think of this again.'

'You are the most generous of men, and I do not deserve your love. But I will make it up to you, I promise. I shall never again allow my mind to be poisoned in that way.'

'Let us talk of happier things.' He rose, and carefully helped her to her feet. 'Did you see Dr Bellamy this morning? And is he pleased with you?'

She tried to smile, and then went to his arms. 'Oh, Edward, Edward. I *do* love you.'

It seemed to him that their love grew from that day, becoming deeper and more lasting than before.

10

The inquest on Beatrice Unwin was brief. The train-driver gave evidence that she had deliberately thrown herself in the path of the engine, and that, together with the note that she had left, made the verdict inevitable. The Coroner, an old friend of the Chetwynds, kept the enquiries to a minimum in order to spare the family as much distress as possible, and Edward, to his great relief, was not even called.

Since she had committed suicide 'while of unsound mind', Beatrice could not be buried in hallowed ground, and a grave was dug, at her mother's wish, on a hillside overlooking the river.

The unhappy affair had caused a great stir in Rudleigh, but once the funeral was over, it was soon forgotten and the people of the village resumed their normal lives. Although he was still haunted by the thought of his partial responsibility for Beatrice's death, Edward in particular tried to put it all behind him. Many problems faced him, and he was grateful that Alice had regained her stability, for he was in much need of her support.

Mrs Chetwynd had appeared to accept her daughter's death calmly, but reaction soon set in, and she sank into a deep depression, mixed with periods of querulousness. After the funeral, Jack had dutifully, if somewhat half-heartedly, suggested that she could make her home with him, but she told Alice afterwards, 'I never cared for him, nor he for me. I'll be much happier here in my own home.' She was far from happy, however, and her fits of temper soon caused her servants to leave. Edward felt obliged to visit her from time to time, and became very worried when it was obvious that she was not eating or caring for herself properly.

Alice solved the problem by suggesting that the Widow Woodham might be willing to go and live with Mrs

Chetwynd, to be a companion, as well as to cook and clean, and Mrs Woodham, pleased to exchange her poverty for the luxury of Rudleigh House, accepted with alacrity. To Edward's astonishment, they took to each other, and became bosom friends.

His troubles with the business were more serious. Nancy Huggins, even when not in a state of near hysteria, was incapable of carrying the financial work of the company, and the double shocks of the suicide and Fred Beeson's departure made her virtually useless, so that the whole burden fell on Edward himself. All his evenings were taken up with writing up ledgers and preparing invoices and statements. He developed dark rings under his eyes, and Alice worried about him.

'You can't go on like this,' she said. 'Have there been no replies to your advertisements?'

'Two more today,' he replied. 'But no use. Far too inexperienced. I need someone like Uncle Richard's Mr Hill.'

'Why don't you write to him? Ask him if he knows anyone.'

'What, in Wensham? That wouldn't be much use.'

'I've got a sort of feeling about it. Something tells me that he'll be able to help.'

He laughed. 'Are you developing second sight, my angel?'

'Call it female intuition. It won't take a minute to write a letter.'

To humour her he wrote, and swiftly back came a letter from Mr Hill. 'Alas,' it said, 'I cannot be of any assistance. I would come myself, now that I am retired, were it not that I am now so ancient as to be in my second childhood, or so my dear wife tells me, and therefore incapable of adding more than single figures or counting beyond my twice times table.'

'You see,' said Edward, passing the letter across the breakfast table to Alice. 'It was a waste of time.'

'What's that other letter?' she asked. 'It looks hopeful.'

'Now, how can you say that? It's just an ordinary letter. And I thought we'd proved that your intuition wasn't in particularly good working order.'

'Open it, Edward, and don't try to catch me up so.'

The letter was from a Mr Robert Brown, an experienced accountant, who explained that he wished to change his present employment because his doctor had advised a move from low-lying Lincolnshire to an area of higher ground for the sake of his wife's health. 'I am, of course, willing to come for an interview,' he wrote, 'but if you wish first to take up my references, I respectfully ask you to apply to my present employer, Mr Albert Robinson of 19 Church Street, Spalding, Lincs., and to my previous employer, Mr J. Hill of Goodwin's Mill, Wensham, Norfolk.'

'There!' said Alice triumphantly, when Edward had read the letter to her. 'What did I tell you? I knew Mr Hill would help.'

'But he had nothing to do with it,' Edward protested, laughing at her.

'Of course he did. He must have written to this Mr Brown.'

'Then why didn't Brown say so? Anyway, I'll see what Mr Hill has to say about him.'

'How fortunate,' Mr Hill wrote. 'Robert Brown is a splendid fellow, and a most capable accountant, admirable in every way. I was most disappointed when he left Goodwin's to further his career.

'It is difficult to believe that his wife's illness, not of the most severe, will be cured by a move to Shropshire, but who am I to argue with the medical profession? And if you have a small mountain or two in the vicinity, perhaps she and he and you will all be suited.'

Robert Brown came for an interview, at which Edward took an instant liking to him, and three weeks later began work. His competence was of a high order, and since Nancy Huggins had by then regained something of her equilibrium, Edward was able to give up his daily toil on the accounts.

This left him free to concentrate on his other major problem, which was the sales staff. As Jack Chetwynd had recommended, he had engaged two more travelling salesmen, both of whom seemed to be satisfactory, though neither yet stood out as the sales manager he needed. He decided that it was essential to make a sales trip himself, and went to London.

On the day of his return the newsboys were shouting, 'War! All the latest! War in South Africa!' Edward bought a

287

paper. Volunteers to go and fight the Boers were being called for—young men in their twenties. Men like himself, he thought. But he had too many responsibilities.

''Allo, Mr 'Arcourt!'

Edward, sitting by the open carriage door of the train that was to take him to Shrewsbury, looked up. 'Beeson! What are you doing here?'

'Might ask you the same question, Mr 'Arcourt—'cept I know the answer. You're on your way 'ome, I'll be bound. Mind if I join you?'

'Of course not. You're the last person I expected to see. How have you been getting on, and where are you off to?'

'Same place as you, Mr 'Arcourt. Rudleigh. An' I been getting on famous.'

'Rudleigh?' Edward had a sudden flash of hope. 'Your job's still open, if you want it.'

'Sorry to disappoint you, Mr 'Arcourt, but that's not me intention.'

'No, I thought not. You're looking very prosperous.'

Beeson was dressed in smart, brand new clothes—a fawn jacket over a checked waistcoat, oatmeal-coloured trousers, and on his head, at a jaunty angle, a straw boater. 'You like the togs? Pretty smart, eh? You're looking well yourself, Mr 'Arcourt. 'Ow's the world treating you? And 'ow's business.'

'Not bad, Beeson, thank you, not bad at all. You'd earn a lot of money if you came back to us.'

'No, thanks. It was good, working for you, but this is the life for me. I'm in me element, Mr 'Arcourt, straight I am!'

'You still haven't told me why you're coming to Rudleigh.' A sudden thought struck him. 'It wouldn't be to tell Nancy that you're joining up, would it?'

'Joining up?'

'The war in South Africa.'

'Oh, that. No. I reckon they'll get plenty o' volunteers for that—'sides, it'll all be over in a week or two. And they won't expect married men to join up, now will they? And that's what I'm going to be.' He tapped his breast pocket. 'Got a special licence. I'm goin' to make an honest woman of Nancy, I am—always supposing she'll still 'ave me.' He laughed. 'She ain't got another feller since I been away, 'as she?'

'Not that I'm aware of,' Edward said.

'That's all right then. Mind you, I'm not marrying 'er to get out of going to South Africa—I don't want you to think that.'

'No, I didn't. But I understood there was no chance of marriage until you had established yourself on the halls. Surely you can't claim to have done that yet.'

'What would you say, Mr 'Arcourt—what would you say if I was to tell you that I got an engagement at the Al'ambra?' He leaned back, grinning.

'I'd say you'd done very well for yourself.'

'Starting next week. I'm opening the first 'alf, which ain't the best position in the world—but the Al'ambra! Can't do better than that, can you? This bloke sees me turn at Mr Chetwynd's theatre, and comes round the back after, and says—' Beeson adopted a deep, fruity voice. '"Not bad, laddie, not bad at all. How would you like to play the Alhambra for a couple of weeks, starting next Monday?" Well, o' course, 'e didn't 'ave to ask twice. So I tells Mr Chetwynd as I'm taking the last couple o' days o' this week off to go and get meself 'itched, and 'ere I am!'

'Are you really in a position to support a wife?'

'I know what you're thinking, Mr 'Arcourt. You're saying to yourself, "I bet 'e ain't got a penny to bless 'isself with—not after buying them togs *and* a special licence—so 'ow's 'e going to look after young Nancy, and what if a lot o' nippers come along, eh?" I bet that's what you was thinking.'

'Something like that,' Edward smiled.

'Well, you're right. I'm down to me last couple o' quid. But I've already paid for our digs for the next couple o' weeks, and I reckon Nancy won't care if we're a bit 'ard up to start with, and once the old ghost walks Friday o' next week, we'll be in clover. I'm on me way, Mr 'Arcourt. Give me a few months, an' I'll be topping the bill.'

'As soon as that?'

'Give or take a year or two! But I'll get there. I reckon you an' me's two of a kind, Mr 'Arcourt, if you'll pardon the liberty. There ain't nothing can stop us getting where we want to be—nothing!'

Edward laughed. 'I'm not sure that I've ever seen myself quite in that light.'

'Look at the top people in my profession—Marie Lloyd, Little Tich, 'Arry Champion—any of 'em you like to name. What 'ave they got in common? Two things: talent, and ambition. Single-minded, that's what they are. And if you ask me, it's the same in business, whether it's cast iron or . . . or making silk, like your ma.'

'M'm.' That comment seemed a little too close to home for comfort. Perhaps, Edward thought, he was more like his mother than he had realised, and that was why it was so difficult for them to get on together. He did not want to think about that.

'Now, take Mr Chetwynd,' Beeson went on, 'I'm not saying a word against 'im—'e give me me big chance—but 'e 'asn't got the same sort o' drive in 'im.' He paused for a moment, and then said reflectively, 'Mebbe it's because 'e's rich already. But it's nothing to do with money, reelly. 'E's not like you or me—'e don't care enough. Shame. 'E's a good chap, Mr Chetwynd is.' He shook his head sadly. Then his face brightened again. ''Ere, changing the subject, I was wondering, Mr 'Arcourt, I was wondering if you'd do me the honour of standing up for me, and being me best man.'

'I'd be pleased to, if you're sure.'

'I'm that right enough. Thanks, Mr 'Arcourt.' He laughed with pleasure. 'Ain't life wonderful?'

'You're really enjoying the theatre, aren't you?'

'Bless you, Mr 'Arcourt, it's . . . it's . . . I don't know 'ow to describe it. You waits your turn to go on—all butterflies in your stomach—shaking all over, I am—and then you 'ear 'em laugh, and they clap, and you feel like you're in 'eaven. And the people you meet! Laugh! There's this old girl— must be ninety if she's a day—she's on the same bill as me at Mr Chetwynd's theatre—singer, she is—well, the first time I sees 'er, she says to me, "Ay'm demeaning mayself," she says. "Hopera, that's may forte," she says. An' she goes on, and screeches away, and gets the bird, poor old duck, until the end of 'er turn, and then she picks up her skirts, an' she's got roller skates on, and she gives 'em the old two fingers, and skates off, and when she comes back for 'er bow, they cheers 'er to the rafters. Game old bird, she is.'

And for the rest of the journey, Fred regaled Edward

with tales of other performers, mimicking them and laughing all the while, and Edward could not remember a more enjoyable journey.

*   *   *

In Rudleigh, the wedding provoked far more interest and excitement than the war, which, after all, was half a world away. On the Saturday, Nancy Huggins became Mrs Fred Beeson, in a flurry of ecstatic elation, complaining happily that she had had no time to prepare, and that Fred had an awful cheek to spring it on her at such short notice, but that she would forgive him this time, if he promised never to let it happen again.

Edward performed his duties as best man, and provided the happy couple with a wedding breakfast, to which all his employees were invited. Alice had readily fallen in with the plan, and under her guidance, their servants, supplemented by several women from the village, had toiled ever since Edward's return to put on a spread which, even if far less grand than her own wedding reception, was generally agreed to have been the best party that Rudleigh had ever seen. After they had eaten and drunk to capacity, everyone went to the station to see Fred and Nancy off to London for two nights of honeymoon before Fred began his engagement at the Alhambra.

Nancy's departure meant yet another vacancy to be filled, but her younger sister approached Edward during the reception to ask whether she could take Nancy's job. He was doubtful—she was only sixteen—but she soon proved to have all her sister's flair for figures. Chetwynd's accounts had never been better kept than under Robert Brown, whose capabilities soon led Edward to treat him as his own right-hand man.

Soon after Beeson's wedding, the last of Edward's major problems was solved when a young man came to the house one evening and asked if Mr Harcourt would be kind enough to spare him a few minutes. He was smartly dressed, and something about him reminded Edward of Beeson, though he was rather more serious in his demeanour.

'My name is Farmiloe, sir, Henry Farmiloe.' He held out

his hand, and his handshake was firm. 'It's good of you to see me, sir, and I will try not to waste your time. The fact is, I am hoping that you may be able to offer me employment. I am at present the assistant sales manager at the Ironbridge Works, but I wish to leave.'

'Why?'

'I'm about to get married, sir. I could not agree with my superior concerning my future emoluments.'

'What are you paid at present?'

'One hundred and thirty pounds per annum, sir.'

'And how old are you?'

'Twenty-four, sir.'

'What experience have you had?'

'I joined the firm at fourteen, sir. Spent six years learning to be a foundryman, and then I was given my chance, and sent out on the road. Not by myself, at first, but later on I looked after the West Country. Then they brought me back into the office, and made me Assistant Sales Manager.'

'I see. A hundred and thirty pounds isn't a bad salary.'

'It's very good for a single man, sir.'

'But not to support a wife, too, eh?' Edward considered for a moment. 'Did you ask for an increase?'

'Yes, sir. They suggested an additional sum, but I do not consider it satisfactory.'

'How much?'

Farmiloe looked uncomfortable. 'I'd rather not say, sir.'

'Why not?'

'It makes them sound mean, sir, and they're not that—at least, not usually.'

Edward liked that. The young man obviously felt some loyalty to his employers. 'What was it—half a crown a week?'

Farmiloe hesitated for a moment, and then said, 'Less than that, sir. They said I would then be getting the top rate for anyone in the firm in an equivalent position.'

'And how much did you want?'

'I was hoping for ten bob, sir.'

'Do you think you're worth that?'

'That's not for me to say, sir. But there've never been any complaints about my work.'

'Have you told them that you're looking for other employment? Would they give you references?'

'Yes, sir, to both. I've got the reference here.' He brought out an envelope, and handed it to Edward.

It was an excellent testimonial, although it concluded by saying, 'The one fault that I can find, which is of no small importance, is that Farmiloe is over-ambitious for his age, and has perhaps too high an opinion of his own qualities.'

Edward smiled inwardly. The words sounded like those of an older man who saw in his assistant a young challenger, eager to step into his shoes. Ambition was not a bad trait. He remembered Beeson saying, 'You and me's two of a kind, Mr 'Arcourt. There ain't nothin' can stop us getting where we want to be.' Maybe Farmiloe was another of the same breed. In any case, he liked the young man, and his honest eyes. 'I'll give you a trial,' he said. 'A month's trial. During that month you will be paid two pounds fifteen a week, and if I'm satisfied, you can have the other five shillings from then on.'

Farmiloe did not smile. 'Thank you very much, sir,' he said gravely. 'I promise you you won't regret it.'

Edward did not. One of the salesmen he had taken on left the firm, disgruntled at having been passed over, but Farmiloe's energy and the control he exercised over the remaining three representatives made it unnecessary to replace the man.

Everything was going well. Edward felt that the whole business had been satisfactorily transformed from a one-man band into a kind of partnership, with himself at the head, and Brown and Farmiloe lending him wholehearted support.

The war in South Africa was never out of the news, and Mafeking, Kimberley, Ladysmith, and many others, became familiar names. Several of the younger men at Chetwynd's were fired at first with the idea of joining up, but in the end only two of the apprentices went. For the rest, South Africa seemed very remote. Why leave the security of a good job with a benevolent master, and the comfort of their homes, and the affections of their womenkind? There were plenty of volunteers in the big cities, for whom a call to the flag meant escape from squalor and degradation.

Many foundries were working exclusively on military contracts, and smaller firms, like Chetwynd's, gained considerable business as a result. Orders flowed in so fast, that Edward sent an urgent message to Jack, asking permission to build the larger foundry which he had had in mind for so long. Jack agreed, and since all the firm's previous debts had been paid off long ago, there was no difficulty in raising a bank loan.

Eager though he was to see this brainchild of his in operation, a fear lingered at the back of Edward's mind. The hoped-for speedy end to the South African conflict might mean that he would not have enough work to keep the new foundry busy, once it was built. He would have to keep a close watch for any opportunities to expand the business.

*　　*　　*

In February, 1900, Alice was safely delivered of a healthy child. The confinement took place in their home, and eventually Edward was allowed into the bedroom. Alice was lying in the bed, her head propped up by several pillows, while the baby had been placed in a bassinet by her side.

Edward smiled at her lovingly. 'My clever, clever darling,' he said, and kissed her. Her lips were cool, and though her eyes were happy, she was drawn and tired-looking. 'Was it very bad, dearest?'

She shook her head. 'If it was, I've forgotten it now. Are you pleased with your son, Edward?'

They had had long discussions about the name they would give the child. Edward's first impulse, if it were a boy, had been to call him Richard, but that might have caused embarrassment. On the other hand, he had no intention of naming his son Thomas after his own supposed father. In the end, they had agreed that he should be William, after nobody at all.

Edward looked at the little creature in the bassinet. The tiny bedclothes had been tightly drawn around the child, and he could not see very much—just a red, wrinkled face, and a tuft of dark hair escaping from under the bonnet. 'He doesn't look like a William somehow,' he said.

'Doesn't he?' Alice said, smiling. 'What should a William look like?'

'I don't know. Bigger.'

She laughed. 'He'll grow.'

Alice soon recovered from the birth, and the doctor expressed himself pleased with both mother and child. For his part, Edward was delighted, and liked nothing better than to nurse his son, who became more William-like every day as he put on weight.

*   *   *

The town council of Sullingford in the North Riding of Yorkshire had been debating from the beginning of 1899 exactly how to celebrate the beginning of a new century, eventually being persuaded that the relevant date was the first of January 1901, rather than 1900. Several schemes had been suggested, but the one which finally found favour was the installation of improved street lighting.

Alderman Albert Jones ('I'm Yorkshire born and bred, and so were me father and me mother, and their fathers and their mothers, so you can forget your comicalities about "Taffy Jones"!') made the speech of his political life, browbeating the council into agreeing that what they wanted was 'not any old lamp standards, such as our respected neighbours in 'Arkley might, in their ignorance, choose, but lamp standards which are things of beauty and will be a joy forever, as the poet says—summat to be proud of; summat to lead the world; summat to put Sullingford on the map, good and proper.'

Alderman Jones had thought it all out. How would they choose the design? A competition would be held for manufacturers of cast iron, and it would be judged, not by the Alderman and his cronies, as his political opponents had expected him to say, but by a sculptor and an artist, both to be nominated by the President of the Royal Academy of Art, no less, 'plus—because we all know, gentlemen, that artists sometimes 'ave their 'eads in the clouds—plus the Borough Engineer, to make sure that t' selected design is practical.' And the reward? Two suitably inscribed silver rose bowls—one for the firm, and one for the designer—a cheque for one hundred pounds for the designer, and the contract, at a fixed but generous figure, to provide two hundred and forty lamp standards.

The wrangling on the town council had taken months,

and the competition was not announced until March 1900. Entries were to be in by the end of October, and the judging committee would announce their verdict a few days before Christmas.

Edward saw the advertisement. Such a contract was exactly what he wanted. He made immediate contact with Aunt Frances and with Ralph Quennell. Both had become expert in their understanding of what could and could not be done in cast iron, and of the kind of design most suited to that material.

The drawings that they produced for the competition were typical. Quennell's lamp was elaborate and bulky, inspired, as he freely admitted, by the dolphin standards along London's Embankment, with two unicorns prancing around a central pole, which branched at the top to support a globe of glass housing the gas mantle. Frances, on the other hand, had used her favourite form, the slender, fluted column, depending on its carefully calculated proportions for its effect. The column split at the top, each half curving over gently so that there would be twin lights on each standard.

Alice had no doubt which she preferred. 'Mr Quennell's design is splendid, but not very practical, I fear. It is going to look overwhelming on ordinary pavements—the dolphins in London have space all around them, a wide road on one side, and the river on the other. What's more, I suspect that the unicorns' horns will break fairly easily.'

'It's going to be the very devil to cast, too,' Edward said. 'We can do it if we have to, but Aunt Frances' would be much easier.'

'And much more elegant,' Alice said. 'Are you going to enter them both?'

'Why not?'

*   *   *

William's christening was fixed for a Sunday in April, and this at last gave Edward the opportunity of carrying out the wishes which Jack had expressed when Edward had visited him to talk about Beeson. Alice's pregnancy had made it difficult to entertain visitors, but now there was every reason to invite Mary to Rudleigh, since she was to be

296

godmother to little William, and as Jack had agreed to be a godfather, they could meet without any appearance of contrivance.

Mary and Jack were not, of course, the only visitors. Sarah was to come, travelling up with Mr Prideau, while Richard and Louisa would accompany Mary, and the Bunns would complete the family. Edward had worried over the problem of accommodating them all—their house had only three spare bedrooms. They could take Sarah and Mr Prideau and the Bunns, but where were Jack and the Goodwins to go?

'Jack will stay with his stepmother, of course,' Alice said. 'And there's plenty of room in Rudleigh House, so I'll persuade Mrs Chetwynd to take Mary and her parents, too.'

It was a happy weekend for all of them. Sarah seemed a different person—almost as though in coming away from Brentfield she had been released from some wicked witch's spell. She scarcely mentioned the mill, and made none of her familiar complaints, and even managed to smile warmly at Louisa. To Edward's surprise, she seemed to like being a grandmother, and cooed and clucked over little William. 'I had all the trouble of bringing up Edward,' she said. 'I'm going to *enjoy* my grandson.'

Louisa tightened her lips in disapproval. She had greeted Edward and Alice with an attempt at warmth, but thereafter seemed much subdued for most of the time. When the ladies were alone together, she became rather more like her old self, and did not hesitate to give Alice firm instructions and advice on the right way to bring up the child. But when Richard was present, she barely opened her mouth, except to agree with anything he said.

The change was so marked that Edward, who had not seen her except when Richard was there, commented on it to Mary.

'Don't you believe it!' she said. 'She has changed, but it's only towards Papa. She still rules the household with a rod of iron, and she still knows what's best for everyone, especially me.' She laughed ruefully. 'She's a darling really, Edward, and I'm so happy that you and she get on better nowadays.'

Significant glances passed between Sarah and Richard

297

when he held his grandson, but the fiction that the child was no more than his great-nephew was carefully maintained. Even Mr Prideau, who had long guessed the truth, was careful when he said, 'You may be very proud to be a great-uncle, Goodwin, but I assure you it is as nothing to the pleasure of finding oneself a *great*-grandfather!'

And Jack at last had the opportunity of increasing his acquaintance with Mary. He made no effort to conceal his interest in her, managing frequently to sit or walk beside her, and they had many tête-a-têtes.

'I fancy Mr Chetwynd is greatly attracted to Mary,' Sarah said to Richard, 'and she is clearly not averse to his attentions.'

'Really?' Richard said, in surprised tones.

'Oh, you must have noticed it. And did you not see them at Edward's wedding? Very much taken with each other, they were. Mark my words, he'll be coming to you shortly to ask for her hand.'

'Oh, surely not. I think you are putting two and two together and making far more than four. They are the only two young people here who are unattached, so it is natural that they should talk to each other. I am sure it is no more than that. In any case, Mary told me a long time ago that she had no intention of marrying.'

'Oh, Richard!' Sarah laughed. 'You never did understand women, did you? All young girls go through a stage like that—I did myself—but when Mr Right comes along, those pious intentions go by the board. If I'm not mistaken, I hear wedding bells. Why, he may even propose to her this weekend.'

'They scarcely know each other.'

'You, above all people,' she said, with an edge to her voice, 'should know what a whirlwind romance is.' And then, to soften the implied criticism, she went on with a smile, 'I abominate that term, but I must admit that it is very expressive.'

'Yes, but surely he would not propose this weekend,' Richard said, still somewhat puzzled.

'Oh, Richard! Richard!'

She laughed again, that silvery sound which had so captivated him when they both were young—he the silk maker, and she the beautiful, capable wife of the owner of

Harcourt's Mill. If only, he thought . . . if only she had remained as she was then—vibrant and understanding, instead of totally obsessed, as so often nowadays, with the problems of her business. He stripped the years away, and remembered that afternoon of passion when Edward had been conceived, and thought how strange it was that the twists and turns of fate should have brought him now to Shropshire, and for such an occasion.

Jack did not propose to Mary during that weekend, but he did succeed in persuading her that he should invite her parents to come with her to London to visit him within the next few weeks. He would devote himself to them for as long as they cared to stay, and would be happy to guide them about the capital.

'But that would be putting you to great inconvenience, Mr Chetwynd,' she said.

'Will you not call me Jack? And may I call you Mary?'

She smiled. 'Very well.'

'It will not be the least inconvenience, Mary, and I insist upon it. I shall take the earliest opportunity of suggesting it to your father.'

That evening, after the whole family had dined at Edward's home, Jack and the Goodwins strolled back to Rudleigh House. Mary and her mother walked arm in arm, and Jack, as he and Richard followed, extended his invitation. Richard agreed to speak to his wife about it.

'Yes,' Louisa said when he told her of the conversation. 'Mary told me. I made it plain that I disapproved, but Mary insisted that I should discuss it with you. She takes no notice of anything I say. No one takes any notice of what I say. I am a mere cipher.'

'That is not true, my dear, and you know it is not.' She did not reply, simply looking at him challengingly, and he went on, 'I've been thinking about going to London. Perhaps it would be a good idea if we all went. You could do some Christmas shopping.'

'Very well, if that is your wish.'

'You'll enjoy it—you know you will.'

'We will stay with Frances and Alfred, I suppose.'

'No. That would be an imposition, and a hotel would be much better. There are several business calls I need to make, and it's much more convenient to be able to go in and out as one pleases.' He thought for a moment. 'If Mary is really set on this trip, then perhaps Sarah is right. She told me that she thought Mr Chetwynd would propose before long, and that Mary would accept him.'

'That is precisely what I am afraid of, and why we should not go.'

'If Mr Chetwynd is Mary's choice, then I certainly shouldn't stand in her way. I know he has a reputation as a bit of a tearaway, but he seems to me a very pleasant young man, much more serious than I had been led to believe. And Sarah says he is devoted to her. I'd like to see her married, and she would be very well provided for.'

'Since you never listen to me nowadays, but only apparently to Sarah, there is no point in my arguing. But I warn you that I shall do all in my power to persuade her against such a match.'

'She'll make up her own mind, my dear. I shall be content to leave it to her.'

*　　*　　*

Fred Beeson's success on the halls was such that he had risen from the lowliest place on the programme and now usually ended the first half. That was his position at the Grenville Theatre when Jack entertained Mary in his private box during her visit to London in early July. Richard and Louisa, who were dining that evening with the Leroys, had been reluctant to agree that Jack should take Mary unchaperoned to his theatre, but had finally allowed themselves to be persuaded, Mary having assured them that her experience in the hospital had taught her how to fend off unwelcome attentions from the roughest of men.

As Fred Beeson came on to the stage, he saw Jack. ' 'Allo, 'allo,' he said, 'the Guv'nor's 'ere.' He pointed up to the box. 'Ladies and gen'lemen, Mr Jack Chetwynd, the owner of this 'ere theaytre, and with a lovely lady, too. Give 'em a round of applause.'

The audience, in a good mood after the earlier turns, clapped and whistled.

'That's enough! That's enough!' Beeson cried. 'Go on like that, an' 'e'll make you pay double, just for the pleasure o' seeing 'im. Ever so mean, the Guv'nor is! 'E's so mean, if 'e gives an 'a'penny to a beggar, 'e charges 'im a farthing commission. 'E's so mean, 'e only buys one newspaper a week, and reads it all through seven times.' The jokes were feeble, but Beeson's personality and technique were so engaging, that the audience laughed uproariously. 'Only joking, Mr Chetwynd,' he called, and then, in an aside to the audience, ''Ave to say that, else 'e'll give me the sack. 'E sacked everyone on the bill the other night—comics, singers, dancers—the lot. Then 'e charged everyone in the audience to get out o' the theaytre. Said they ought to pay 'im for saving 'em from sittin' through such a load o' rubbish. Now, if 'e 'adn't 've sacked 'em, this is what they might 've 'eard.' And he launched into his repertoire of imitations, ending with a song and a comic dance.

The audience roared its delight.

'I wanted you to see him,' Jack said to Mary. 'He used to work for Edward—he was his Sales Manager. Did you notice, when he was imitating Harry Champion he sang, "Any old iron? Any old iron? Any, any, any old *cast* iron?" He always does that—a sort of reminder of his former employment. I was the one who persuaded him to go on the halls. He's got star quality, that boy. He's going right to the very top.'

'Yes. He was very good,' Mary said.

'And you laughed.'

'Yes. Yes, I did.'

But Jack knew that she did not really approve. 'Would you rather go?' he asked. 'We could have a spot of dinner, and still be back at your hotel in good time.'

She nodded gratefully.

'I'm sorry you haven't enjoyed it as much as I'd hoped.'

'I have. But . . . No, I won't pretend.' She hesitated. 'I'm afraid I just wasn't in the mood.'

'Never mind. We'll find a cab and go to the Silver Fountain.'

At the restaurant, Jack asked for a secluded table. On the way there in the cab, they had chatted easily enough of what Mary had been doing during her stay in London—shopping, visits to her relations, and the dinner which Jack had given for her and her parents in his flat the previous evening. But now, as they ate, she was quiet, almost

301

withdrawn. Jack gazed at her, sitting opposite him, admiring the clear skin, the fair hair, the blue eyes.

When their meal was over and they had been served with coffee, Jack leaned over towards her, and took her hand. She did not resist. 'May I talk to you, Mary?' he asked. It was almost a whisper.

'Of course.'

'You must know how much, how deeply I care for you. Mary, will you . . . will you please marry me?'

For several seconds she stared at him. Then she shook her head very slightly, and said, 'I'm sorry.'

'I love you very much. I would do anything for you. Please, Mary.'

'I'm sorry, but I can't.'

'I thought . . . perhaps you cared for me a little.'

'I do. I'm very fond of you, very fond indeed.'

'But you don't love me.'

'I think I do.'

'Then what is it? Is it because I own that theatre? I'll sell it.'

'No, it's not that.'

'It's not what Beeson said, is it? You don't think I'm mean?'

She smiled then. 'Of course not. No, I'm sorry, Jack. I'm deeply conscious of the honour you have done me, and I'm grateful, but I swore a vow—I swore it in the sight of God—that I would never marry.'

'But that's absurd! God would never hold you to that!'

'He might not, but I would. Oh, Jack, forgive me. Please may we go? I don't want to disgrace you by crying in public.'

'Of course.'

In the cab, they sat silent, in shared embarrassment. Arriving at Mary's hotel, Jack got out, paid the cabbie, and then helped Mary to descend. He held on to her arm. 'Mary, will you think about it? You can take as long as you like. I'll wait for you for ever.'

'It's no use, Jack. The answer would still be the same. I think it will be better if we do not see each other again. Thank you. Thank you for everything. And please forgive me.' She reached up and kissed him briefly on the cheek.

Jack could feel her tears on his face. 'Mary, please!' he called after her, but she had already disappeared into the hotel.

*   *   *

Soon after the Goodwins' visit to London, Mary wrote to Edward, telling him that she had decided that it would be better if she and Jack did not continue their acquaintance. 'It was painful for me, dear Edward, to reject his proposal when he did me the great honour of asking me to become his wife, but, as you well know, I became aware many years ago that God's plan for me did not include marriage. I believe Mr Chetwynd's feelings for me to be both deep-felt and genuine, but I hope he will soon forget me, and find some more deserving young woman on whom to lavish his affection. Please do not mention the subject to him—to do so would be, I fear, simply to re-open the wound.'

Edward naturally respected her wishes, but hoped that Jack would himself raise the matter. When Edward sent his progress reports, Jack had been in the habit of replying with a chatty letter, but he no longer did so, and when Edward sought his approval for the employment of four additional foundrymen, Jack's reply was brief. 'I really do not wish to be bothered with these trivialities,' he wrote. 'You should consider yourself to be in sole charge of the business, free to make any decisions you wish.'

Edward consulted Alice. 'It's so unlike him. He doesn't even call me "old boy"! Do you think it's because of Mary? Surely not. It's always been off with the old and on with the new, as far as Jack's concerned.'

'I think it's very sad,' Alice said. 'They would have been so good for each other. However, what's done is done. And, yes, I think it probably *is* Mary. You should go and see him, Edward. See if you can cheer him up. And while you're there, explain that it's not fair to expect you to take all the responsibility when you are not even a director of the company.'

'I'll write to him about that,' Edward said, 'so that he can think about it before we meet.'

But the reply came from Jack's solicitor:

303

Dear Mr Harcourt, Mr Jack Chetwynd has asked us to reply to yours of the fifteenth inst., and to inform you that it would be inconvenient for you to visit him at this time.

However, Mr Chetwynd desires to acknowledge your invaluable services to Chetwynd's Foundries, and he instructs us to put before you the following proposal:

As you are aware, Chetwynd's Foundries is a private company, all hundred shares in which are held by Mr Chetwynd. He wishes a contract to be drawn up whereby, every six months for the next two and a half years, five shares in the said company will be transferred to your name, at no cost and in addition to your salary, so that ownership of twenty-five per cent of the company will eventually be vested in you. The contract will also confirm your appointment as Managing Director, a title which Mr Chetwynd requests that you should assume with immediate effect. Your salary is also to be increased by five hundred pounds per annum.

Mr Chetwynd trusts that this arrangement will satisfy your justifiable desire for recognition of your position in the business.

The contract is currently in preparation, and will be sent to you for signature within the next seven days. However, we would ask that you immediately acknowledge receipt of this letter, and, without prejudice and subject to the terms of the said contract, signify your acceptance of the proposal as described above.

Yours faithfully, Carter & Sayers, Solicitors.

Edward was delighted, and wrote straightway both to the solicitors to signify his acceptance of the terms, and to Jack to thank him for his generosity.

It was extraordinary the difference that being a director made in his attitude towards his work. It was not a question of working longer hours or more diligently, but simply that for the first time he really felt free to make his own decisions, in a way that he had not done before, despite Jack's constant assertions that he wanted Edward to have full control.

Armed with this new-found freedom, he decided to put into practice an idea which had been in his mind for a long time—since before old Mr Chetwynd's death, in fact.

He sent for Thomas Yardman. 'I want to work in the foundry,' he said.

Yardman looked at him blankly.

'As an apprentice, I mean.'

That was greeted with another blank stare. Then Yardman shook his head. 'Wouldn't be right, sir. Not with you being the master.'

'On the contrary, Yardman, it would be very right. I intend to spend at least one day every week there, under your command.'

'But why, sir?'

'Because I can't run this business unless I am capable of doing the work of everyone in it—not as well as you, of course—but I want to improve on the few skills that I picked up when I first came here.'

'Won't be easy, sir,' Yardman said, stubbornly. ' 'Ave you thought how it'll be for the men? I reckon it'll put a bit of a blight on things, so to speak. It ain't easy to work natural-like when you know the master's watching every move you make. And supposing you tell me as you want to be treated just like one of the lads, and they all start calling you "Edward" or "Eddie" even; what's it going to be like when they have to come to see you as the master, and touch their foreheads, and call you "sir"? See my meaning, sir?'

Edward thought. 'I suppose so. Then how can I do what I want?'

Yardman did not reply at once. 'Late at night,' he said, as though thinking aloud. 'Late at night, when the others have gone 'ome. Begging your pardon, sir, but 'ow would Mrs Harcourt feel if you was to stay on a couple of nights a week?'

'What have you in mind?'

'I'd stay on meself, sir. Give you a little private tuition, as it might be, if I'm not taking a liberty in saying that.'

'And what would Mrs Yardman have to say to that idea?'

'Mrs Yardman does what I tell her, sir.'

Edward laughed. 'What makes you think that Mrs

305

Harcourt is any different? Are you sure you're willing to do that?'

'Always admire someone who's ready to learn, sir—always 'ave.'

'Of course, there'll be an extra bob or two, Yardman.'

It was Yardman's turn to smile. 'Thought there might be, sir. Not that that's why I said I'd do it, mind. But it'll be welcome, I don't deny it, and if the missus does create, it'll soon quieten her down. Thank you, sir. Is that all, sir?'

'Yes, thank you. We could start tomorrow evening, perhaps.'

'Yes, sir.' He went to the door. 'Course it'll be mostly what you might call theory, sir—you realise that. Can't really work the foundry with just the two of us.'

'I understand. But any additional knowledge will be useful to me.'

As Yardman had pointed out, the sessions were not as useful as Edward had hoped, but at least he learned more of such matters as the composition of the green sand, and when the molten iron was at the right temperature to be drawn off and poured into the flasks, and how two separate mouldings could be soldered together and any rough edges filed off. Additionally, when Edward was present in the foundry during the day, Yardman would often make a point of choosing that moment to show an apprentice the right way to perform this or that task, and only he and Edward were aware that he was instructing the master, too. Edward seized eagerly upon every piece of information that came his way, and gradually began to feel that he was better fitted to make judgements and decisions.

*　　*　　*

Edward and Alice were astonished in September to receive a telegram from Mary, asking if she could visit them for luncheon two days later.

'Luncheon!' said Edward. 'What on earth does she mean? She's surely not coming all this way just to have luncheon.'

'I expect she meant that she would be arriving in time for luncheon,' Alice said. 'I'll send a telegram to say that she *must* stay overnight, and preferably for at least a week.'

But the reply made it clear that Mary had meant exactly

what she said, though it still did not explain the reason for making such a ridiculously long journey for so short a time.

On the day of her visit, Edward left his office early and went to the station. When Mary alighted from the train, he embraced her, and kissed her formally on the cheek. 'You have no luggage?' he asked.

'No. It is all in London.'

'Then you really are going back this afternoon? But it's absurd, Mary! What is all this about?'

'I'll explain later, Edward. I want Alice to hear it, too.'

During the ride in the trap back to the house, the conversation was restricted to conventional enquiries about the health of the members of their two families, with most of the questions coming from Edward. Mary's thoughts seemed to be elsewhere. There was obviously something on her mind. Perhaps she had decided to marry Jack after all, and had come to announce her engagement . . . But if it had been that, surely she would have been bursting with happiness.

It was not until they were seated at the dining table that she revealed the reason for her visit. 'I'm going to South Africa,' she said.

Both Alice and Edward reacted with dismay.

'Oh, no, Mary, you don't mean it!' Alice said.

'They've been crying out for nurses,' Mary replied. 'The matron of my hospital asked for volunteers, especially those, like me, who had some years' experience. I'm twenty-one, so I didn't have to ask for Papa's permission, which I doubt he would have given. Several of us are going. I don't know how Matron will manage without us, but she said that the need was greater out there.'

'And when are you going?'

'We sail tomorrow.'

'Tomorrow!'

'Yes. That's why I could not accept your kind offer to stay.'

'And you've come all this way to . . .'

'To say goodbye. Yes. I wanted to see you, and my godson, before I went.' Again there seemed to be a sadness in the way she spoke, but she became more animated as she answered their questions. 'I'm not sure where I'm going— wherever the fighting's worst . . . Yes, I believe the conditions are very primitive—that's why we're so badly needed—we're taking a vast quantity of medical supplies . . . No, I don't know how long it will be for—as long as the war lasts, I suppose . . .'

When the meal was over, Mary played for a short while with William, who was now taking his first tottering steps under the proud eyes of his parents.

'Why, that's farther than he's ever walked before, Mary,' Alice exclaimed. 'Much farther. He must be doing it specially for you.'

Mary did not smile, but looked up at the ormolu clock on the mantlepiece. 'I think it's time we left, Edward,' she said.

'Oh, there's plenty of time. It only takes a quarter of an hour to the station.'

'I'd rather leave now, if you don't mind.' She made her farewells to Alice and William, hugging them both.

As the horse trotted gently along towards the station, Mary said, 'I wanted to leave early because I've something to say, Edward. Could we stop for a moment? Along here, where there's no one to hear us?'

He pulled up, and let the reins lie slack.

'I didn't want to say this in front of Alice,' Mary said. 'I'm not coming back, Edward.'

'What, back to Rudleigh?'

'No, no. Back from South Africa.'

'Not coming back? You mean you're emigrating?'

She smiled then. 'No, my dear. I mean that I shall die in South Africa.'

Edward, feeling an icy hand around his heart, tried desperately to joke. 'Die? Well, we shall all die some time, and why not in South Africa?'

'Oh, Edward, you are wilfully misunderstanding me, are you not?' There was no reproach in Mary's voice, just that same sadness he had noted earlier. 'I am going out to South Africa, and I shall die there before I am due to return.'

'When?'

'I don't know. Perhaps in a few weeks' time—perhaps longer. And how? I don't know that either. I simply know that death awaits me there.'

'But what nonsense! I don't believe in this sort of thing, Mary. God does not allow us to see our futures, and it's as well for us that He does not. It's just morbid to talk like that, morbid and superstitious.'

She smiled. 'Perhaps. But it doesn't change it. I just *know*, Edward. Don't ask me how, because I can't tell you.'

He gazed at her in frustrated silence for a moment. 'Then don't go!'

She smiled again. 'Oh, but I must. If I stayed here, I might live to be a hundred, but it would not be what was meant for me.'

'Just morbid superstition,' he repeated stubbornly.

'I don't think it is, really. It's not superstitious because it's true. And morbid? No, because death has no terror for me.' There was a long pause. Then she said, 'Now you know why I had to come and see you. To say goodbye. Drive on now, Edward, please.'

He sat for a moment or two, and then took up the reins, and the trap moved gently forward.

'Goodbye,' she repeated, in a reflective tone. 'God be with you. That's what it means, isn't it? One wonders how the pronunciation changed so that "God be with you" became "goodbye". I prefer "God be with you", I think.'

Edward realised that she was talking simply to fill the silence that would otherwise have hung between them. He could find nothing to say.

When they reached the station, he stood on the platform with her. 'Have you said anything like this to Jack?' he asked.

'No. And please don't tell him. I haven't told anyone else.'

'Are you going to see him?'

'No. It would be pointless, Edward. I'm going to stay with Aunt Frances and Uncle Alfred.'

'Give them my love,' Edward said, his mind full of so much else that it was simply an automatic reaction.

When Mary's train came in, she hugged him tightly, and kissed him on the cheek, and then laid her face against his. 'Goodbye, my very dear brother,' she whispered. 'Pray for me, Edward, as I shall pray for you. And try not to grieve when the news comes.' She stepped into the carriage, pulling the door to, and sat down facing straight ahead. She did not turn or wave as the train pulled out, and Edward knew that she did not want him to see the tears in her eyes.

'Why not, Mary?' he whispered. 'They could have joined with mine.' He watched until the train was out of sight, then brushed the wetness from his lashes, and drove back home.

11

By October of that year, Alice was expecting their second child, to be born the following May. Her health during her first pregnancy had been so good that she had no hesitation in making a journey to Essex to visit her grandfather and her mother-in-law. She returned with disturbing news. 'Your mother spends every day at the mill, urging the workers on to increase their output. She has the idea that if she can produce more, she'll be able to lower the price and bolster up the sales, though the warehouse is stacked to the roof with unsold crape, which she has already priced lower then ever before.'

'I suppose I should go and see what I can do,' Edward said.

'She's very bitter about you, my dear. She went on and on about how you had deserted her, and had no understanding of her problems or of the business, and when I said that I would ask you to come and see her, she said, "Oh, he'll never leave his stupid cast iron, and if he did come, he'd only argue with me. No, tell him to stay at home—I don't want him here." I'm sorry to say it, but—well, anyone would think, from the way she behaved, that she was losing her mind.'

He nodded. 'I know what you mean. I've seen it myself, more than once, though this sounds worse than before. Perhaps I'd better go, whether she wants me there or not.'

'No, Edward, no. It would only make you unhappy. I don't think I've ever spent such a miserable two days. She never asked about me or William once, and that was so unexpected, because she was very sweet when she was here for the christening. She really was very unkind.'

Despite her protests, Edward travelled the next day to Brentfield, and arriving in the afternoon, went to the mill.

Sarah was in her office. She looked at him coldly. 'What are you doing here?'

'I came to see you, Mama. Alice said—'

311

'Oh, no doubt she's told you all sorts of things about me. It was perfectly clear that she had come only to spy on me. I am quite all right, and I don't need your help. I'm also very busy, and I'd be grateful if you'd leave me in peace to get on with my work.'

'But, Mama, I've only come to see if I can help.'

She did not reply, returning to her writing. Then she stood up, and brushed past him. She turned at the door. 'Are you staying the night?'

'Yes, Mama, if that is all right.'

'Then I will see you at home. And now, as I said, I am very busy.' She left the room.

Edward went to the house, and waited. Sarah did not return in time for dinner, and he ate alone. It was half past ten when his mother came in, looking exhausted. She poured herself a large brandy. 'I shall take this up to bed,' she announced.

'Surely you're going to have something to eat. We could talk perhaps while—'

'I'm not hungry. In any case, there is nothing to talk about.'

'But, Mama, this is ridiculous! I want to help you.'

She laughed bitterly. 'The time for that was years ago, Edward. It's too late now, and I don't want your help. I didn't ask you to come, and I'd be glad if you would go. You can stay the night, but please leave tomorrow morning.'

'Mama, please! I know I upset you in the past, but can't we please put all that behind us? Believe me, I'll do anything I can. Alice and I will come back here if you like, and—'

'I can't say it any more plainly, Edward—I don't want you here! *I don't want you here!*' She went out of the room, slamming the door.

Feeling helpless, Edward waited for a while before going up to bed. On the way, he knocked at his mother's bedroom.

'Go away!'

He did not fall asleep until the early hours, and was awoken at about half past six by the sound of a horse and trap. He hurried to the window and looked out. Sarah was just driving off. He flung the window up and called after her, 'Mama!'.

312

She did not even look round. He washed and dressed and walked quickly down to the mill. At the entrance, his way was barred by a man whom he recognised as one of the oldest employees. 'Sorry, Master Edward,' he said. 'The Missus says you're not to come in.'

Disconsolately, Edward went back to the house, collected his bag and began the journey back to Shropshire.

Alice opened the door to him when he arrived home, and hugged him. 'I'm so glad you're back, my dear. Home isn't home without you.' He sketched a smile, but she could tell that he was deeply distressed. 'Have you eaten?' she asked.

'No, but I don't want anything just now.'

'Then come into the sitting-room.' She led the way, and poured him a drink. 'Do you want to talk about it?'

'It was . . . She wouldn't talk to me, she wouldn't let me help her. Oh, Alice, I've failed her. I've been thinking about it all the way home. I've been so selfish, following my own desires, and now that she needs me so desperately, I've . . . I might have been a total stranger—an enemy, even. She doesn't love me any more.'

'Oh, but she does, my dear. Of course she does. She's desperately worried, and perhaps she is unwell, and it has driven her affection for you out of her mind. But it's still there—deep down it's still there. Don't you see? She wants you to feel like this, she wants you to feel guilty.'

'Then she's succeeded.'

'Her mind is disturbed. And there is no disloyalty in believing that. It was she who drove you away from the mill, years ago, wasn't it? Wasn't it, Edward?'

'Perhaps. But I was pig-headed. I've been pig-headed about everything. I've thought about nothing but Chetwynd's and my own ambitions.'

'This is tiredness talking, my dear. You need to rest. Go to bed early this evening, and in the morning you'll feel better.'

'There's no need to treat me like a child, Alice. I've been going over it all in my mind. I know I've no real reason to feel guilty, but the fact remains that Mama is in trouble, and I can't help her, and it would never have happened if I'd had a bit more patience when I was younger. And look at my position here at Chetwynd's. I've got where I am by luck, by being in the right place at the right time—not by my own efforts. Mr Chetwynd spent his whole life in cast iron. I'm just an interloper, who has to pay the overseer to give him instruction. Oh, Alice, what am I doing with my life?'

Alice wondered what she could say which would drag him out of this slough of despond. What he needed, she realised, was to release all the emotions that were warring inside him, more fully than he'd done so far. 'Tell me about it, Edward. Tell me right from the beginning.'

'Oh, what's the use of going over it all again?'

'No, tell me. Did you have a good journey to Brentfield? When did you get there?'

Slowly, reluctantly at first, he told her everything that had happened. It took a long time. Alice hardly spoke, only occasionally encouraging him with a brief question or a nod of understanding. He told her not only of his conversations, if they could be so described, with his mother, but also of his thoughts, and the arguments that had been going on in his own mind, and gradually, to her relief, he began to relax and to take a more objective view. At last he was able to smile ruefully. 'It's all rather a storm in a teacup, isn't it? I've been a fool to let myself get so upset. But what can I do, Alice? I must do something.'

'Nothing yet,' she said. 'Perhaps the time will come later, but at the moment you would probably only aggravate matters. You have nothing to blame yourself for, so try to put it out of your mind.'

'I haven't even asked about you and William,' he said. 'How are you feeling, my darling? And has he been good?'

Alice thanked God silently that, in talking about the concerns which worried him so much, he had apparently been able to put them into perspective. It was strange, she thought, remembering her own absurd jealousies when she had been carrying her first child, how easily the most rational of beings could be thrown off balance.

*   *   *

At the end of November, Edward received a letter from the Clerk to Sullingford Borough Council, informing him that both his entries for the competition had been among the six short-listed, and requesting that he and Mrs Harcourt, and, if possible, the two artists, should attend a reception in Sullingford Town Hall during the second week of December, at which the result would be announced.

The letter had come at a most opportune moment. Even if they did not win, the short-listing would undoubtedly mean publicity for Chetwynd's and there would be a good chance of new business. And that would fully justify the decision to go ahead with a new foundry. It was nearing completion, and he waited impatiently for the day when it would be in working order. More than twice the size of either of the older workshops, Edward had designed it to allow of the most efficient possible workflow, working it all out with Thomas Yardman. He calculated that, though he would have to take on several more men, he would not need as many as were already working at Chetwynd's, and yet their output was likely to be more than doubled.

It was out of the question that, in her condition, Alice should go to Sullingford for what would amount to a public appearance, but she insisted that Edward should accept the invitation. Mr Quennell was eager to do so, but Frances replied to Edward's telegram that it seemed a long journey to make on the very remote chance that her design might be the favoured one.

'Send another telegram,' Alice said. 'Tell her she *must* come. I've got a feeling about it.'

'Like you had about my writing to Mr Hill?' Edward asked, indulgently.

'Exactly like it!'

And so Frances was persuaded to be present, accompanied of course by Alfred, and Edward began to think that Alice might be right when Alderman Jones was especially effusive in his greeting. 'Mrs Bunn! Pleased to meet you, Mrs Bunn, very pleased. And Mr Bunn, too. You must be very proud of your good lady, Mr Bunn. Our only lady designer, *and* on the short-list, too.' He wagged his finger roguishly. 'Not a long way from the top of it, either.' Nodding and winking, he moved on to greet another guest. Had that all been merely gallantry on his part, or was he hinting that Frances had actually won?

Presently, Alderman Jones announced that he was calling on Sir George Brooke, Associate of the Royal Academy, and the very distinguished chairman of the judges, to address the assembled gathering. Sir George was short and plump, and though undoubtedly an eminent sculptor, limited in oratorical skills. It was difficult at the back of the crowded room, where Edward and the Bunns and Mr Quennell were standing, to make out exactly what he was saying.

Alderman Jones got to his feet again. Used to public speaking, and perhaps determined to show up Sir George's failure in that respect, he thundered away as though addressing a turbulent council meeting. 'Mr Mayor, distinguished guests, it gives me great pleasure, as the instigator of this splendid scheme, which demonstrates Sullingford's readiness to advance into the twentieth century. And it is no coincidence, ladies and gentlemen, that I should 'ave decided upon—that is, that the council should 'ave decided upon—a plan to bring improved lighting to the streets of our well-loved town, symbolising both Sullingford's unceasing progress in this enlightened age, and its 'opes that the future may similarly be illumined by policies directed towards the improvement of conditions for our respected residents. I could cite many a case, ladies and gentlemen, of the far-sighted decisions of our Town Council, but I know that you are eagerly awaiting the announcement of the winners of this competition, and it gives me great pleasure to announce that . . .' He broke off and looked around with a self-satisfied smile. 'But before I give the names of the winning competitors, let me repeat that, as Sir George 'as said, our judges was faced with an insuperable dilemma, until I suggested that we could split the town's streets in two, as you might say—to wit, the main thoroughfares on the one 'and, and the side streets on the other—and give a runners-up award to the latter, provided that the judges could find a second design to 'armonise with the first. This they 'ave done, which explains the presence on this table not only of two magnificent silver rose bowls, but also of two silver epergnes.'

There was a murmur of approbation from the assembly, and some scattered applause. When it had died down, Alderman Jones continued, 'And now I will keep you waiting no longer. The company which 'as won the runners-up award and the contract to provide lamp standards for all side streets is Messrs William Bannister, Sons and Company of Bradford. They receive a silver epergne. And their designer is Mr Archibald Tonkin, 'oo takes away the second epergne and a cheque for seventy-five pounds. If they will kindly come forward . . .'

From the other side of the room, to the applause of all present, two men pushed their way to the front, shook hands with Alderman Jones and Sir George Brooke, and after a few words, retired, bearing their awards.

The Alderman stepped forward again. 'We now come to the major award. The judges was unanimous in selecting one design as the best in the competition, and the contract for lamp standards for the 'Igh Street, Kirkby Street, Victoria Avenue and Market Square, together with the rose bowls—silver rose bowls, I should say—and the cheque for one 'undred pounds, goes to . . .' He paused dramatically, and Edward took his Aunt Frances' hand, and squeezed it gently. '. . . the designs of Mr Ralph Quennell, to be cast by Chetwynd's Foundries of Rudleigh, Shropshire.'

Again applause filled the air. Frances looked at Edward with shining eyes. 'Congratulations, Edward!' She turned. 'And to you, too, Mr Quennell. I am so happy for you both!'

Alderman Jones raised his hand for silence. 'Before the presentation of these awards, why, you may ask, did not Mr Quennell's design receive the single award as originally arranged, and 'ave done with it? Well, ladies and gentlemen, that was where the afore-mentioned dilemma come in. The lamp standards in question was of such imposing appearance that they would be fitting only for the principal thorough-fares, where their full beauty could be appreciated. And also where they would not obstruct traffic. And now, if Mr Quennell and the representative of Chetwynd's would come forward . . .'

Later, as she and Alfred admired the rose bowls, Edward whispered to her, 'I was so sure it was going to be you, if we won at all. Alice was quite certain that you were going to take the prize. I wish you had.'

'I'm really rather glad I didn't, Edward. I wanted *you* to win, of course, but it's much better that it should be Mr Quennell, and not me. I'm not a designer really—I'm just a housewife, aren't I, Alfred?'

'If you say so, my dear, though I think you do yourself an injustice.'

'Perhaps this is a good opportunity, Edward, to tell you what's been in my mind for some time. I'm not going to do any more designing, if you don't mind. Not because I didn't win today—please don't think that—but because . . .' She linked her arm in Alfred's, and looked up at him lovingly. '. . . because there's only one real artist in our household.'

With a flash of insight, it was suddenly plain to Edward that she was sacrificing herself for the sake of Alfred's pride. He was tempted to fight her resolve, to tell her that Alfred was not the sort of man to feel aggrieved by his wife's success, but he realised that he stood no chance of changing her mind. This was something she had thought out a long time ago. 'Yes, I see,' he said. 'Thank you, Aunt Frances. Thank you for everything.' He kissed her.

'You'd better go and talk to Mr Quennell,' she said, smiling. 'He's going to burst if he doesn't get someone in a corner soon so that he can explain just how brilliant he is!'

As soon as he could, Edward excused himself and went out to send a triumphant telegram to Alice, asking her to pass the news immediately to everyone at Chetwynd's.

Later that evening, in their hotel, Edward, Mr Quennell and the Bunns drank champagne. Edward felt on top of the world. He looked again at the rose bowl the company had won. He would have a glass case made for it, he decided, and mount it on the wall of the new foundry. No. It was a rose bowl, designed to hold flowers, and it should be used for that purpose, even in the heart of the works. But would that not seem incongruous, and would the flowers not need to be renewed and the bowl itself polished every day? What did that matter? The prize belonged in the foundry, and should fulfil its proper function, just as everyone who worked there did.

*   *   *

As he stood with Alice, their glasses raised, listening for the chime of the mantelshelf clock, Edward could hear from the village the sound of voices and of pans being beaten. 'Some people are in a hurry to begin,' he said, smiling. 'I suppose it's impossible to get all clocks to tell

318

exactly the same time.' Their own clock struck . . . ten, eleven, twelve. 'Happy New Year, my darling! And Happy New Century!' He toasted her, and then kissed her with deep affection.

'1901,' she said. 'The twentieth century. I wonder what it will bring.'

'Just as well we don't know.'

'At least we can look forward to May, and our little daughter.'

'How can you be sure it'll be a daughter? I know—you've got a feeling about it!'

They both laughed happily.

*   *   *

But the New Year began sadly, with the death, towards the end of January, of the old Queen. It had long been expected, but nevertheless the whole country was sorrowful. She had been there so long, and during her reign Britain's power in the world had grown, with the expansion of the Empire, and the vast increase in trade that the new methods of industrial production had brought. Everything would be different now, and uncertain—who could tell what would happen with the throne occupied by Edward the Seventh, that libertine throw-back to the Prince Regent?

At Chetwynd's, however, prosperity reigned, and it was soon apparent that the firm was on the brink of a greater success than they had ever enjoyed before. Sales were increasing for every item in their catalogue, especially the new range which Ralph Quennell had designed to commemorate the accession of the new King.

The production of his lamp standards had provided many problems, but gradually they had all been solved. A deputation of councillors and other local bigwigs came from Sullingford to see the process of manufacture, and went away full of praise for all concerned. 'There'll be nowt to equal 'em in any town or city in the 'ole country,' Alderman Jones pronounced. 'Bar none!' he added. 'I tell you this—London'll look up to Sullingford, that it will!'

London might not in fact have been particularly impressed, but the competition and its results had been

319

closely watched in several towns which might more easily bear comparison with Sullingford, and over the next months, Edward began to receive a number of enquiries from official bodies eager to beautify their communities with decorative cast-iron—covered markets, lamp standards, fountains, statues, memorial plaques. Mr Quennell was kept constantly at his art-board, producing the designs.

*　　*　　*

At the end of March a letter came from Wensham.

> My dear Edward (Richard wrote), It is with great sorrow that I have to inform you that we have this day been notified of the death of our dear daughter, Mary, killed as she worked to save lives in a field hospital near Mafeking.
>
> You will understand, I am sure, that my heart is too heavy to allow me to write more.
>
> Your loving father, Richard Goodwin.

Even the fact that Richard acknowledged their true relationship lent no balm to Edward's distress. He put the letter down, staring blankly in front of him, living again the moments of Mary's farewell.

He had gone pale, and Alice looked at him in concern. 'What is it?'

He rose from the breakfast table, and handed her the letter. Then he walked slowly to the window, gazing out.

'Oh, Edward!' Alice said, when she had finished reading the brief note. 'Oh, Edward, how dreadful! Poor Mary! Come, sit down again. Let me get you some brandy.'

'No, I don't want that,' Edward said. 'I think . . . I think I will sit in the drawing-room for a moment.'

At the door, he turned and held out his hand to her. She hurried to him, and they went to the drawing-room, and sat together on a settee. For a long while neither spoke.

At last, he said, 'I wish I knew how she died. Do you think they have told my . . . father?' It was still difficult to say that word.

'Perhaps. It depends, I suppose, whether it was a telegram or a letter that was sent.'

320

'Yes.'

Another long silence followed. Then Alice said gently, 'Why not go and lie down, my dearest? It's been a terrible shock to you. A rest would be good for you.'

'No,' Edward replied. 'I ought to go into the office. I'm late enough as it is.' But he made no move, and after a while he said, 'I should like to go to Wensham. Do you think I should?'

'Why, yes. I am sure they would be happy to see you.'

'They might not want me there. It might remind them too forcibly of . . . of what happened between me and Mary. But I want to see the letter or the telegram—whatever it is they've had. I *must* find out how she died, Alice—I must.'

'Why is that so important to you?'

'I never told you what she said to me when I drove her to the station the last time she came here. It was her secret, and I couldn't tell anyone, not even you. Forgive me, my darling. Not even you.'

'Of course. I understand.' She did not, but she waited, knowing that he would need time if he were to tell her what was on his mind.

Eventually he began. 'She asked me to stop, just by Orton's meadow, and then she said, "I'm not coming back, Edward." And I said . . .' He repeated the conversation, and told how they had hugged at the station. 'Those were her very words, Alice. I shall never forget them. And that's why I want to know how she died.'

'But why, dearest? Does it really matter?'

'Don't you see? I want to know whether it was . . . well, an accident of war, or whether . . .'

'You mean she might deliberately have courted death? Oh, no—not Mary! She would not have done that.'

'No, but I must be sure.'

*   *   *

Edward arrived in Wensham that same evening. As the maid let him in, Richard came out into the hall. 'Edward!' he said. 'How good of you to come. I was glad to have your telegram.' He held out his hand, and then drew Edward to him, and embraced him. 'You will stay, of course.'

321

'Just for the night. I must get back tomorrow.'

'Come into the dining-room. I expect you're hungry. It's the cook's evening off, but I got the maid to prepare some cold meat for you. I hope that will be all right. I am sure your aunt . . . that is . . . I am sure she would have prepared a hot meal for you herself, but this news has prostrated her, I'm afraid. We had to call the doctor, and he has prescribed rest and total quiet.'

'I am sorry.'

'Yes. It has been a great blow, Edward, a great blow. Of course, in time of war, one must always be prepared to hear the worst, but somehow you don't ever let yourself believe that it will really happen.'

'Did she say anything to you before she went?'

'Say anything? What do you mean?'

Edward realised from Richard's tone that he must have been the only one to whom Mary had revealed her premonition of death. Hastily, he tried to cover up. 'I'm sorry, I don't know why I said that.' Hoping Richard would not pursue the matter, he went on, 'How did you hear?'

'A letter. I'll show it to you when you've eaten.'

At first, while Edward ate, there was an almost embarrassed silence between them. Then Richard said, 'I saw your mother last week.'

'Oh? How was she? I've been very worried about her since the last time I saw her. She really seemed to have become a little—what shall we say?—eccentric. I feel I ought to go back there, but you know what happens whenever I see her—before long we're quarrelling. God knows I try not to let it happen, but . . .'

'I know, Edward, I know. Your mother has become rather difficult to please. Life has never been easy for her, and now . . . Eccentric, you say? Yes, I suppose that is the word, but we had a long chat together, and discussed all her problems with the mill, and I think I got her to see sense about a great many of the things she's been doing. All this stock-piling, for instance. What she really needs is to lay off some of her workers, until the stocks have been reduced.'

'Or move into another form of silk manufacture.'

'Indeed, yes. I don't think anyone could persuade her to do that, but she did finally accept the idea of shutting the mill down for a fortnight, giving all the weavers and crape-makers a paid holiday, and then taking back only—well, I tried to get her to agree that she should cut the work force by half. Anyway, I think she's going to limit the numbers and reduce production, and . . . She's a stubborn woman, your mother, Edward, but I left Brentfield in a rather happier state of mind than when I first got there. I flatter myself that she has always been willing to listen to what I say, and I think we can expect some improvement in her situation.'

'I'm very glad to hear it, and very grateful to you.'

Later, when they were in the sitting-room, Richard produced the letter he had received from South Africa.

Dear Sir,

It is with great regret that I have to inform you that your daughter, Sister Mary Goodwin, was killed on active service in the recent battle at Lichtenburg, near Mafeking. I send you and Mrs Goodwin my sincerest condolences in your tragic loss, in which I share, for as Matron of the Field Hospital in which she worked, I looked upon her as one of my most capable and hard-working of nurses. Indeed, no other nurse upon my staff so much deserved the promotion to Sister which was hers a few short weeks ago. It is no exaggeration to say that Sister Goodwin was adored by those she tended, and many of our brave soldiers owe their recovery to her. I am very proud to have numbered her among my friends.

You will no doubt have read of the battle of Lichtenburg, when Boers under the command of De la Rey were, thank God, repulsed. Despite the clear indication that it was a hospital, the Boers directed much of their fire on the tents in which we were working, and one of their bullets struck your daughter as she was attempting to shield a wounded soldier from harm. In so doing, she undoubtedly saved his life. She died in my arms a few moments later.

It may be of some consolation to you to know that she did not appear to be in pain, and she died with the name of her Lord upon her lips. May God have mercy on her soul. I have no doubt that He will, for she was a true Christian, humble and devout, who sacrificed her

323

life, I believe, willingly, in the service of others. I am sure that she rests now in the bosom of her Lord, in the company of the saints, and that, too, must temper the sorrow which we all feel at her passing.

I am, Sir, with the repeated expression of my heartfelt sympathy, yours very truly, Dorothea Mansfield, Matron.

Edward handed back the letter, tears of mingled pride and sadness in his eyes, and relief in his heart. He would never have forgiven himself if . . . 'Thank you, Uncle,' he said.

'I wish,' Richard said, speaking with some difficulty, 'that you would call me "Father". I believe I have been most unjust towards you, Edward, not least in refusing to acknowledge the relationship between us. I beg your forgiveness, my boy.' He turned away, standing with his head cast down, as though fearing an unfavourable response.

Edward rose and went to him. He embraced his father and kissed him on the cheek. 'You must forgive me, too, Father. It was my fault that we became estranged.'

'No. If I had been honest and open with you from the first . . . our lives would have been very different. Mary might still be with us. I blame myself most bitterly.'

'But you must not. Perhaps you and I both changed her life, but once she had set her foot on her chosen path, I believe she knew it to be the right one for her.' He decided that he would, after all, tell Richard the secret. 'She knew that she was going to die, you see, and she accepted her fate willingly.'

'What do you mean?'

For the second time that day, Edward found himself relating that last conversation with Mary. 'But this lady is right,' he finished, 'this Matron. Mary has now met her Saviour—we must be happy for her.'

'Yes. I was very proud of my daughter,' Richard said, 'and I am also proud of my son. For the sake of your mother's good name, we shall have to pretend that you are no more than my nephew, but between ourselves there are no longer any barriers, are there, Edward?' He took out a handkerchief and blew his nose noisily. 'And now, my boy,

324

I have been very remiss again. I have not even asked after my daughter-in-law and my grandson. Tell me how they are. And is Chetwynd's flourishing? Your Aunt Frances told me about that competition that you won. I think she was rather pleased that her designs were not selected. She said that—what was her phrase?—that her Alfred's adoration had already given her enough of a swelled head. But why am I prattling on like this? Tell me about yourself and your family.'

They spent the next two hours in pleasant conversation, though Mary was never far from their minds, and every now and then one or other of them would mention her, and they would speak of her sadly, and yet somehow, because of what had passed between them earlier, with an acceptance of her death, and almost a sense of contentment for her.

In the morning, Richard and Edward ate their breakfast together, saying little, but occasionally smiling at each other, as though to acknowledge the new affection between them.

'I shall have to write to Jack Chetwynd,' Edward said, suddenly.

'I've already done so,' Richard replied. 'Before she left, Mary gave me a letter, to be opened if anything happened to her. Forgive me if I do not show it to you, but it is very personal—the letter of a daughter to her parents. She did not mention the belief that she would not return which she confessed to you, but she asked that two people should be informed if she should in fact die in South Africa. You were one, and Mr Chetwynd was the other.'

'Oh, it's such a waste!' Edward exclaimed. 'Such a wicked waste!' And I am sad for Jack, too.'

'You mean they might have married?'

'Oh, I don't know. I suppose not. I think Mary had decided firmly against marriage. But I wish they had—they would have been wonderful for each other.'

As Edward was about to leave, Richard said, 'I am going to have a plaque placed in our church to commemorate Mary.'

'I should like to share in it,' Edward said. 'May I do so, Father?'

'I had hoped you would. I will write to you about it. And

325

now, my boy, I think it is time for you to go. You must not miss your train.'

'Give my . . . my love to Aunt Louisa.' He paused. 'Perhaps it would be better if I continued to call her that. I hope she is soon recovered.'

'Thank you. And keep in touch, my boy. Remember, if you ever need me, I am here. And I hope to see you again before long, and your lovely Alice, and my little grand-boy.'

* * *

About a week after Edward's return to Rudleigh, he received a letter from Jack Chetwynd, summoning him to London. He went with a strange foreboding of what such an unprecedented message might mean.

Jack was in the most sombre of moods, scarcely able to raise a smile. He asked Edward to take a seat, and then, without preamble, announced, 'I'm going to America.'

'To America!'

'I've sold the theatre.'

'Sold the theatre?'

'Thank you for your letter about Mary, by the way.'

'My letter?'

'Oh, for heaven's sake, old chap, don't repeat everything I say.'

'I'm sorry. It's just that, though somehow I knew that you were going to tell me something like this, it took my breath away. What are you going to do in America?'

'I'm going there chiefly because it's a long way from England, and England has too many memories of the sort I want to forget. I'm sure I needn't go into details. I thought of joining up, but I'm too much of a coward. I should probably run a mile if one of those ghastly old Boers aimed a gun in my direction. On the other hand, I might be tempted into all sorts of foolhardiness, and that would be even worse.'

'What are you going to do in America?' Edward repeated.

'I'll make my mind up when something happens to make it up for me. The one thing that's certain is that I shall do something. No more Idle Jack.'

'And you've sold the theatre, you say?'

'Yes. It's not been the greatest of successes. Too difficult to get to for people outside the neighbourhood, I suppose, as you once said, and the locals couldn't fill it by themselves. I think it's going to be pulled down, so that they can build houses or something.'

'Did you lose a lot of money?'

'Enough, though I'm not exactly penniless. Anyway, I asked you to come down because I've decided to sell Chetwynd's.'

'Sell Chetwynd's!'

The corners of Jack's mouth twitched in the nearest he had come to a smile. 'There you go again, old chap.'

'Sorry,' Edward said. 'But you're mad. We're just starting to make really big profits.'

'Look, old boy, I'm going to America, and I'm going to stay there for the rest of my life. So I'm severing all my links with England.'

'Have you got a buyer?'

'I've someone in mind. Oh, don't look so worried, Edward. I was thinking of you.'

Edward looked at him in astonishment.

'The best person to work for is yourself, old boy.'

'Are you suggesting that I should buy Chetwynd's?'

'Yes. Are you interested?'

'Of course I am, but . . . well, it depends on the price, for one thing.'

'How many shares do you own now? Only five, isn't it? So that leaves ninety-five for you to buy. I was thinking of two hundred and fifty each. How about that?'

'That's a lot of money.'

'It's a fair price. I'm giving you first offer, Edward, because the old man thought very highly of you, and you've proved that you've got a real feeling for the work, but I'm not making you any concessions. If you don't want it, there are plenty of others who will, I believe. Two hundred and fifty a share comes to twenty-three thousand seven hundred and fifty pounds. Cheap at the price.'

'But I haven't got that sort of money!' Edward exclaimed.

'Of course you haven't, old boy,' Jack said irritably. 'You'll have to borrow it—your mother's got plenty, hasn't she? Certainly Mr Prideau has. And if you can't get it from them, then there are certain institutions known as banks.

327

They'll take a mortgage on the works, and cough up any extra you need; easy as falling off a log. No, don't say anything—you're clearly slow on the uptake today. Just sit and think about it, and when you're ready, we'll discuss the next move.'

There was sarcasm in Jack's tone, or bitterness perhaps. Edward thought he understood why his old friend was in such a strange mood. After a moment he said, 'I loved Mary, too, Jack.'

'Yes, I know.'

Edward looked at him sharply, trying to hide the shock in his own eyes. Had Mary told Jack the truth of their relationship?

But Jack went on, easily enough, 'Kissing cousins, weren't you? And yes, I'll answer the question you are asking—it *is* because of Mary that I'm leaving England. Everything here reminds me too painfully of . . . so many things. She sat in that chair, you know. She came to my theatre. We dined together.' He paused. 'How is Alice? And my godson?'

'They are well, thank you.' There was an awkward silence, and Edward began desperately to try to fill it. 'Alice is expecting again, you know. As for little William, he's a marvel. Walking everywhere nowadays, and chattering away, nineteen to the dozen. Can't always understand what he's saying, but "Mama" and "Papa" are clear enough. He's into everything, of course.' Jack said nothing, and after a moment he went on, 'Did you know that Mary had a premonition that she was going to die in South Africa?'

'No, I didn't.'

'When she came to Rudleigh to say goodbye, she told me—'

'Forgive me, old chap,' Jack suddenly interrupted, his voice taut, 'if I throw you out now. I . . . I'm not very good company these days, and I prefer to be by myself. I sometimes think I'd be better off in a monastery.'

It was meant to be a joke, Edward thought, but there was no humour in the voice.

'I suppose you'll have to go to Brentfield and Franton,' Jack went on, 'and you'll want to discuss it with Alice. You've got a clear week, Edward. After that I shall put Chetwynd's on the market.'

'That's not long. I'll certainly have to go to the bank, and you know how long they take.'

'Tell 'em you can't wait, and remind 'em that there are plenty of other banks who'd be delighted to help. You'll be surprised how quickly that'll sharpen their attitude.' He got up, helped Edward into his coat, and opened the door of the flat for him. 'Never be afraid of a bank, old boy,' he said, 'they're only money shops, and if one shop hasn't got the goods you want, you simply try next door.'

'I haven't even thanked you properly,' Edward said. 'I'm tremendously grateful, Jack. I'll be back before the week is out, so I'll see you before you leave for America.' About to go, he turned round. 'Give me your hand. I'm going to miss you. And I can't tell you how sorry I am about . . . everything.'

Jack nodded a little stiffly, and took Edward's hand. 'Yes. I know. Thanks, Edward.'

Well within the week, Edward was back at the Albany flat. It had all been much easier than he had expected. Mr Prideau had supplied the whole amount required without a murmur, and had not argued when Edward insisted that he would pay interest on the loan.

Jack presented Edward with a series of legal documents to sign.

'But these all have my name on,' Edward said in surprise.

'Of course,' Jack said. 'I was quite certain that you'd raise the wind, old boy, so I went ahead. It all saves time, you see.'

He was a little more like himself, as though he had begun to recover from the shock of the news of Mary's death. He spoke quite gaily of his forthcoming journey to America, and then said, 'I know I talked of severing all my connections here, but we shall keep in touch, old chap. I shall not neglect my duties as far as young William is concerned. And I have no doubt that I shall come back to England now and then for a holiday.'

As he travelled back to Rudleigh, Edward could scarcely believe what had happened. The owner of Chetwynd's! He was delighted beyond measure, but also faintly apprehensive. However little interest Jack had taken in the firm, while he owned it, Edward had always known that he was there in the background, ready to take action of some kind if things went wrong—though what exactly Jack would have been able to do, he was not sure. Now all the responsibility lay on his own shoulders, and that was alarming as well as exciting. For the first time, he began to understand something of his mother's feelings for Harcourt's Mill, and to sympathise a little more than he had done before with her insistence on having her own way.

He thought of the future. Some day, perhaps, young William would be working alongside him. He hoped that he, Edward, would never be as stubborn as his mother had been.

12

One evening in May, Edward and Alice were sitting in their drawing-room, when she suddenly broke off in mid-sentence, put her hand to her body and tensed. 'I believe it's begun,' she said. 'Go on, my dear—there's a little time yet.' But soon after, she interrupted him. 'I think I should go to our room, Edward, and you should send for Doctor Bellamy and Mrs Whitworth.'

Alice's first confinement had not been difficult, and this second birth was even easier. Some three hours after her labour pains began she was safely delivered of a daughter.

When he was allowed into the room, Alice was cradling the baby in her arms. Edward looked at them both with great joy, relieved to see that there were few signs of strain or tiredness on Alice's face. He kissed her. 'I'm so proud of you, my darling, and I love you so very much. I hoped we might be given a daughter.'

During her pregnancy, Alice had steadfastly refused to discuss what they should call this second child, but now she asked, 'What name shall we give her, Edward? Do you want to call her Mary?'

He did not answer immediately. 'No. There would always somehow be a shadow lying over her—a double shadow. You remember, my father—my real father—had another sister as well as Aunt Frances. Her name was Mary—she was the eldest—but she died, long before I was born. There was some mystery about it—she was only about seventeen, I believe. I could never quite find out what happened, but I was given to understand that she died in childbirth.'

'Was she married?'

'No. I've always imagined that some man got her into trouble, and then deserted her.' He paused. 'No, not Mary. But would you mind if we called her after my mother?'

331

Alice smiled and looked down at her daughter. 'Hello, little Sarah,' she said.

*   *   *

Some two months later, as the workers left Harcourt's Mill at the end of a long, hot July day, one of them looked up at the light still burning in Sarah's office. 'Our Missus!' he said, shaking his head. 'God help us all! God help us all!'

'What's up wi' you?' his companion asked.

'Mill's dying. Any fool can see that. 'Ow much longer afore we're all out o' work?'

'Our Missus'll pull it round. Always has. She'll do it again.'

'She'll need to work a bloody miracle, boy, I'm tellin' you.'

Sarah looked at the pile of papers on her desk—unpaid bills, letters from the bank demanding repayment of loans, and the pitifully small list of customers' invoices still unpaid. It reminded her of the chaos in the accounts which she had found when her father-in-law, John Harcourt, had taken his own life because he could not face the bankruptcy which seemed inevitable. She had saved the firm, bringing a new vigour to it in every department. And what she had done before, she thought, she could do again.

Suddenly, she stiffened in her chair, as though an electric shock had shot through her. She looked at her hands—they were not those of a woman in late middle age. She clenched her fists, feeling the power of the taut muscles, aware of the blood coursing through her veins. She stood up. She was no longer tired and worn, but the handsome Mrs Tom Harcourt, whose youth and sex had been no barrier to her dream of rescuing the family firm from disaster. 'I'll show them!' she said aloud. 'I'll show them. I'll start as I did before, with the workers.' She remembered the day so long ago when she had taken a broom herself and swept the mill floor, shaming the men out of their lazy, uncaring acceptance of inefficiency and squalor.

She hurried down to the weaving shed, and was amazed to find it in darkness. She knew the place like the back of her hand, and walked unerringly to where matches and tapers were kept, and then lit one of the gas lamps. Its light

332

was feeble, but it was sufficient to show her that the shed was deserted. 'Gone!' she said. 'Gone home early! I'll sack the lot of 'em!' She scurried around, lighting every lamp. 'I'll show you!' she screamed, the words echoing in the empty room. 'Swine! Traitors! If you won't do it, I'll do it myself. I can weave, you know! I can weave better than any of you! Bastards!' There were other obscenities, too, words that she had overheard but had never spoken before. She turned on the steam power of first one machine and then another, until all were clattering, pounding like her own heartbeat. She ran from one loom to another, trying to work them all, checking that there was still raw silk on the bobbins. And as she worked she laughed, until the laughter turned to tears, and suddenly she put her hands to her ears and sank down on the floor, sobbing.

It was there that the night watchman found her. He was an old man, deaf and with failing sight; a former weaver to whom Sarah had given this job out of charity, and because there was never any likelihood of trouble during the night which would be beyond his powers to cope with. A quarter of an hour had passed before he had become aware of the light in the shed, and had heard faintly the noise of the machines.

Sarah opened her eyes when he approached her. A stranger! A stranger in her mill! 'Who are you? What are you doing here?'

He leaned towards her. 'What's up, Missus? Are you all right?'

She scrambled to her feet, backing against the wall. There was a heavy brass measuring rod leaning there. She seized it gratefully, and threatened the old man with it. 'Get out!' she screamed. 'Get out!'

Fearfully, he backed away, relieved that she did not follow him, but simply stood there hurling abuse at him. He reached the door, and then hurried, as fast as his ancient, arthritic legs would carry him, to the cottage where the overseer of the weavers lived. 'It's our Missus!' he gasped. 'Gone off 'er 'ead, she 'as!' He explained what he had seen. 'I reckon it'll take more 'n one to grab 'old of 'er.'

Indeed, several men were needed to carry her, struggling and screaming, to Harcourt Place. She refused to swallow the sedative that old Dr Wood prepared, until he thought of slipping the drug into a glass of brandy. He shook his head gravely when he heard the men's story. 'Poor lady. It looks like a committal. I shall have to call in Dr Collins from Great Luckton. And I think you'd better send for young Master Edward.'

Not only young Master Edward, the men decided, and another telegram went to Mr Richard Goodwin.

Edward felt he had spent enough time that year away from Chetwynd's. There had been the visit to Wensham, and then the hectic week when he had become the owner of the firm, and the last thing he wanted was to be away again. Their order book was full, and everyone concerned with the business was working long hours and under great pressure. It was at times like this that any one of a hundred things could go wrong, and all those in a senior position needed to be more than usually vigilant. 'It couldn't have happened at a worse time,' he said to Alice. 'On top of everything else, there's a possibility that those people from Penswick may be coming to talk about us making lamp standards for them.'

'Mr Brown and Mr Farmiloe will be able to deal with them.'

'Yes. Thank goodness for them. I'll have a word with them, and with Yardman. I may own this business, but they're the three who really run it, you know. Sometimes I begin to think that I'm not needed there at all.'

'Don't talk nonsense,' Alice said fondly. 'Come, I'll pack a bag for you, and then you must be off.'

'Yes. The sooner I get to Brentfield, the sooner I'll be back.'

'You might have to stay there quite a time,' Alice said.

'Yes, I suppose so. My mother's more important than the firm, after all—much more important. But the thing that worries me is that if there is any kind of problem, Brown and Farmiloe will try to solve it by themselves, rather than bother me. They'll probably succeed, but that's not the point. Do you think you could keep an eye on things, Alice? Have a regular word with them—every day would be best—but try not to make it too obvious, because I don't want them to think I'm spying on them. Then, if I have to be away a long time, you could send me a wire if I'm badly needed.'

'Yes, of course,' said Alice, wondering how on earth she was going to find daily excuses for talking to the three men, whom she normally saw but rarely, without arousing their suspicions.

*　　*　　*

Edward was relieved to find Richard at Harcourt Place when he arrived. His support was very welcome, especially when it came to the decisions; the two terrible decisions.

Sarah had totally lost control of her mind, Dr Wood said, and he held out no hope whatsoever of a recovery. Dr Collins, much younger, and, he had to admit, more experienced than himself in such matters, concurred. Both were ready to sign the committal papers which would send Mrs Harcourt to an institution for the rest of her life.

'No!' said Edward. 'No!'

'But, my dear young friend,' Dr Wood protested, 'I cannot be responsible if your mother is left at large. She could become violent, she could cause considerable damage.'

'I don't believe it. She did not strike the night watchman —she only threatened him. And even that was simply because she was afraid of him.'

'Possibly. But the risk is still too great.'

'It's my *mother* we're talking about, not some stranger! Could she not stay in her own home, if we could find a suitable attendant for her? If the worst came to the worst, she could be locked in, the windows barred, but at least that would be better than an institution.'

'You have been reading *Jane Eyre*, I fear,' Dr Wood said drily. 'It is not nearly as simple as it sounds to look after someone in her condition. It is also very costly—there will be times when two attendants will be required, and the drugs . . . An institution is equipped to deal with all the problems of its patients. It really is advisable, Mr Harcourt.'

Edward turned to Richard. 'What do you think?'

'Is there no chance at all of her recovery?' Richard asked.

'She will probably have moments of lucidity. She may even appear to recover her wits entirely, but one would always have to be on one's guard. Constant attendance . . .'

'Surely a recovery would be more likely to take place if she were surrounded by her own possessions and the comfort of her home, rather than confined in an asylum.'

'Indeed, yes.'

'Then I support Mr Harcourt entirely, though of course the decision is his alone.'

'Very well,' Dr Wood said, controlling his irritation. After all, he was merely giving the best advice that he could, and pointing out the difficulties. Still, he reflected, he should be used to it by now—relatives and close friends often behaved somewhat irrationally in similar circumstances.

Shortly afterwards, he left, having agreed that he would find a capable nurse with all possible speed—indeed, the woman sitting at that time with Mrs Harcourt might be persuaded to accept a permanent position, which would be a blessing, since he could vouch for her character and her ability to deal firmly yet kindly with those whose minds were deranged.

Though caring for his mother was Edward's first concern, it was in some ways a more minor matter than the whole future of Harcourt's Mill. It would have made sense to close the mill completely, but that would mean depriving the entire work-force of their livelihood. There was no other employment available in Brentfield, and the majority of them were too old to pull up their roots and move from the village, even if another employer had been willing to take them on.

'The first thing you need,' Richard said, 'is Power of Attorney, so that you can sign on behalf of your mother.'

'I'm seeing her solicitor in Franton this afternoon.' He gave a short bitter laugh. 'It seems awful, when she's always been so independent.'

'Yes, but it's got to be done. As for the mill, if you're not willing to close it—and I think you're right in that—have you considered running it yourself?'

'I've been thinking about that almost ever since I heard Mother was ill. Do you think I should?'

Richard pondered. 'I don't think your heart is here, is it, Edward?'

'There was a time when I was prepared to give my life to Harcourt's,' Edward said. 'When I first came down from university. But Mother and I did not see eye to eye, and . . .'

'And why was that? Perhaps because you were committed

with your head, but not with your heart. Your mother is no fool. I expect she saw that you would never love the firm as she did.'

'Do you know,' Edward said, 'once I used to refer to you as "the cast iron man". That was a bad joke, and a pretty unfair one. But it's what I am now—a cast iron man. You're right, Father, my heart's in Rudleigh, not here.'

'Then you have only one option—you must sell. Prideau—'

'It would make my mother turn in her grave.' He drew a sharp breath. 'Oh, God! I'm talking of her as though she is already dead.'

'It would be the wise thing to do now. She won't know about it, and what the eye doesn't see . . . He'll give you a fair price, and he'll protect the workers.'

'I'm still reluctant. What about you, Father? If I'm the cast iron man, you're the silk maker. Why don't you run Harcourt's? After all, you helped to build its prosperity. It would be simple for you.'

Richard laughed. 'You flatter me, my boy. Now, if Harcourt's were a going concern, I might be tempted. But to take it on in its present state—no, that is out of the question. I have neither the desire nor the resources for such a task. After all, what is needed? Modernisation, which will take a great deal of capital investment; changes in working practices, in the product, in selling methods—a complete, radical shake-up of the whole business. Only a large, solid company, with a real depth of facilities, which would absorb Harcourt's without straining itself, could cope with all that. Prideau's is ideal, and the old man has already promised your mother that he'll retain the company name.'

It was exactly what Edward had hoped Richard would say. 'I'm glad you feel like that—it lessens my feelings of guilt.'

'You shouldn't feel guilty. Your mother should have sold out years ago.'

Edward went to see Mr Prideau, and told him about his mother.

Prideau raised his bushy eyebrows, and shook his head sadly. 'I am sorry to hear that, Edward, very sorry. Though I must confess I am not surprised. But if she is to be well looked after, that is good. And what about the mill?'

337

Edward smiled. 'I thought you might ask that, sir. Are you still interested in buying it?'

'It depends, of course, upon the price. But in principle, yes.' He opened a drawer in his large desk, and pulled out a document bound with lawyer's red tape. 'You might like to take this away with you and read it. I had it drawn up a long time ago, in the hope that your mother would eventually come to an agreement with me. It covers everything, I believe. It contains guarantees that the Harcourt work force will continue in full employment, and that the mill shall become a division of my company, to be known as the Prideau-Harcourt Mill, thus preserving the family name. Moreover, it covers the transfer of all deeds to property, all plant and stocks, and equally the assumption by Prideau's of all Harcourt's exterior obligations, whether in unfulfilled orders or debts or of any other nature.'

'That sounds very comprehensive.'

'It is. The amount of the cash consideration to be paid by my company remains to be added, of course, and if you agree, we will have an independent valuation of Harcourt's net worth. From all that I hear, the figure is likely to be quite small. You do understand that, Edward?'

'Yes, sir. I have no illusions on that score.'

'Good. There is one other clause which requires alteration. It was originally my intention to make your mother a director of my company, though in a non-executive capacity. That is obviously out of the question now.' He paused briefly. 'I want you to listen carefully to what I am going to say now. It is something which I have had in mind for a long time, and now is the time to put it to you with all the weight at my command. You should obviously take your mother's place on the board of directors, but I should like you to consider most seriously the possibility of making it an executive position.' He raised his hand. 'No, let me finish. I know that you are now your own master at Chetwynd's, and that is an enviable position to be in. But eventually you could occupy that position here, and in the meantime, you would be earning a very substantial salary—two thousand a year at least.'

'But I know nothing about your business,' Edward protested.

'Oh, administration is much the same, whether it is cast

338

iron or silk. You would soon learn all you need to know. Now, don't answer hastily—think about it.'

'I know my answer now, sir. I greatly appreciate the offer, but I cannot leave Chetwynd's.'

'Talk it over with Alice,' Prideau said, 'and then write to me. If your decision is still the same, then I suppose I shall have to accept it, in which case, I shall make you a non-executive director at an honorarium of a mere fifty pounds a year.'

His irritation was plain. Edward laughed. 'Agreed, sir.'

Prideau glared at him for a moment, and then suddenly smiled. 'You're as stubborn as your mother, do you know that?'

'Yes, sir.'

'Well, we shall see. There is one further matter. I have a strong suspicion that in recent years your mother has placed the larger part of her personal capital into the firm, without ever being able to replace it. Is that so?'

'I believe it is.'

'Then some provision will have to be made for her. This company should undoubtedly pay for the medical attendance that she will need, and a sum beyond that to allow her to live in the comfort which is her due.'

'I am quite willing and able to provide for her myself.'

'I am sure you are. And I know you too well to think that you would ever neglect your filial duties. But you have a growing family to provide for, and even without that factor, I regard this as an essential part of the deal between us.'

'That is most generous.'

'Not at all. It is no more than a small tribute to an erstwhile foe, who was always my most worthy adversary, even when later she became my friend.'

*   *   *

Edward stayed in Brentfield for some days, hoping that there might be a rapid change in his mother's condition, or that at least he could do something for her. But while her mind did not become any less confused, she seemed to have settled comparatively happily with her nurse in attendance.

339

She spent her days endlessly writing columns of figures in a ledger and adding them up. No one was sure what the sums represented, or how they came into her brain, but they kept her occupied, and only rarely would she look up from them to mutter unintelligible words, in an amiable way, at her companion. There was nothing that Edward could do.

He decided to return to Rudleigh, relieved that the major problems in Brentfield seemed to have been resolved, at least for the time being.

Although the final details of the transfer of the mill to Prideau's had yet to be settled, old Mr Prideau had already taken charge and moved his managers in. Before Edward left, he had insisted that the two of them should address all the workers to assure them that none need fear the sack, and to explain his intention that in future the mill should gradually be switched from the manufacture of mourning crape to a variety of other crapes, which were much more in demand.

'It is not certain at this stage,' he had said, 'exactly what position in the company Mr Edward Harcourt will hold, but he will undoubtedly be joining the board of directors in some capacity.' And he had again tried to persuade Edward to enter the firm.

Edward fulfilled his promise to discuss the matter with Alice. 'How would you like to go and live in Franton again?' he asked her, and saw her eyes light up. He explained Mr Prideau's offer as dispassionately as he could, wondering what he was going to do if she should be strongly in favour of his acceptance of it. It was obvious from her expression that she liked the thought of a return to the town where she had grown up, and the idea of his participation in her grandfather's business. 'Of course,' he said, 'if we were in Franton I'd be nearer my mother, too, in case anything happens.'

'Yes,' she said. 'Yes, that would be a good thing, wouldn't it?' Then a thought struck her. 'But you have said nothing about Chetwynd's. You could not run it from Essex, could you?'

'No. It would mean selling the company.'

The excitement faded from her eyes. 'Oh, Edward, you can't do that!' she said. 'I wouldn't want you to do that, not for anything.' She could see that he doubted her. 'I mean it, my darling, with all my heart.'

Edward hugged her. 'I knew you'd understand. But are you sure you don't want to go back to Franton?'

'I want to be where you are. And I want you to be happy. And if anything does happen to your mother, you can be there within a few hours.' She smiled. 'You needn't write to Grandpapa about it—I shall do so.'

Edward hugged her again. Then he sobered. 'I suppose one day . . . What will happen when he . . . ? He's not a young man.'

'When he dies, you mean? We'll face that when it comes, and not before. And now, my darling, I have good news for you. I didn't have to spy on Mr Brown and Mr Farmiloe. Mr Brown visited me each evening, and told me all that had happened during the day. The people from Penswick came, and they've placed an order—a huge order. I didn't send you a telegram, because their confirmation didn't come until this morning, but Mr Brown says we're really on the map now. Isn't that exciting?'

*   *   *

Other large orders soon followed, and Edward could see that, even with the recently-built foundry, they would soon be unable to cope with all the work if it continued to flow in at the same rate. He began to think about constructing a second new and even larger foundry. The two original ones, which had been there when he first came to Rudleigh, could be used as storage sheds, which they would undoubtedly need.

He discussed the idea with Farmiloe and Brown. The salesman supported the plan enthusiastically, but Brown was cautious. 'To make another large foundry economically viable, we shall have to maintain orders at a very high level,' he said, 'and no one can guarantee that—not even you, Farmiloe. If we stay as we are, we may have to extend the time between orders and delivery, but we shall still manage well enough.'

'I'm against that,' Farmiloe said.

They argued for a while, and then stopped, and Edward realised that both were looking to him for a final decision.

He no longer had Jack Chetwynd to fall back on—the responsibility was his alone. 'I shall sleep on it,' he told them. 'I'll give you my decision in the morning.'

In fact, he wanted to talk the matter over with Alice. There was no question of her making the decision for him—she would neither wish nor feel herself competent to do that—but he had discovered that, if he rehearsed all the arguments with her, she was almost always able to put her finger dispassionately on the strengths and weaknesses of the question.

'Of course they're both right,' she said, 'and they're both typical—salesmen always expect the best, and accountants are always cautious. What you need to do is to decide how much of Mr Farmiloe's optimism and how much of Mr Brown's pessimism to discount.'

Suddenly he realised that, however true it was that the firm was run by Brown, Farmiloe and Yardman, they could not do so without a leader.

In the morning, he sent for the architect.

*　　*　　*

Mr Prideau, slightly aggrieved that Alice had not visited him since the birth of her second child, journeyed to Rudleigh in September so that he could set eyes on his great-granddaughter for the first time. In the two months since Edward had seen him, he seemed to have aged. He walked with some difficulty, complaining of gout, and fell asleep frequently, dozing for short periods. Alice insisted that he should have early nights, and took him his breakfast in bed each morning and refused to let him get up for another hour or so. He grumbled that he was not an old man yet, but submitted to her cosseting.

However physically weary he might seem, his mind was as lively as ever, and he talked with great enthusiasm of what he was doing with Harcourt's. He had installed new machinery, cleaned and decorated the whole mill, and a new range of crapes was now being produced there. He explained everything in great detail, and indeed, it was only when he was playing gravely with young William or admiring baby Sarah that he seemed able to put Harcourt's out of his mind. Alice was pleased to see that he rarely repeated himself—at least there was no evidence of that sign of incipient senility.

He made no mention of his disappointment that Edward had decided to remain at Chetwynd's, and indeed complimented him on the way the business was run, and especially on the good relationship between Edward and the men. 'I learned long ago that concessions towards the contentment and prosperity of my workers brings major improvements in output and quality. The important thing is to be respected, rather than feared. I've put all the workers at Harcourt's on the same basis as in the mills at Franton and Macclesfield, and it's already paying dividends.'

As he left to return to Essex, looking rather more sprightly than on his arrival, he promised Edward that he would continue to keep an eye on Sarah, who, he said, was well, and, as far as one could tell, happy, though there was no improvement in the confusion of her mind, poor lady.

'He's really getting old,' Alice said, as they saw him off at the station. 'But taking over Harcourt's has given him a new interest in life. He's like a two-year-old with a new toy.'

'How old is he?' Edward asked.

'I'm not sure—about seventy-five or six, I think. I just hope Harcourt's is not going to be too much of a strain on him physically. The trouble is, he doesn't spare himself. I'm sure this little break has been good for him—given him a chance to rest.'

'I shouldn't worry, Alice. He's organised everything at Brentfield—he wouldn't have come here otherwise—and he'll be able to take things more easily from now on. He'll probably go on for ever.'

*　　　*　　　*

One month later the telegram announcing Prideau's death arrived. Taking two nurses with them to look after young Edward and Sarah, Alice and Edward travelled to Franton, shocked at the suddenness of the old man's going, and anxious at the thought of the responsibilities which might lie before them.

The funeral was very grand and impressive; Prideau's friends and business associates and all his workers flocking

343

to pay their last respects to him. Edward thought of the old man's words—'the important thing is to be respected.' He had certainly been that.

His will was very simple. After a few bequests to charities and some small sums left to his personal servants, everything was to go to Alice, including all the mills and other factories of which he had always retained full ownership. There was also a letter for her. It had been written immediately after his recent visit to Rudleigh.

My dear Alice, It has always seemed to me a futile practice to leave behind strict instructions as to the behaviour of one's legatees. They should be free to make their own decisions. However, I cannot restrain myself from at least making my wishes known.

I trust that you will never consider selling my businesses. They should remain under family control, and indeed the name of Prideau must be retained. Moreover, I wish to express most strongly my fervent desire that you and your husband, Mr Edward Harcourt, will personally assume the management of the companies. Your husband has his own interests, but despite his previous obduracy in the matter, I hope he can be persuaded that his business cannot compare with such an enterprise as Prideau's, with a turnover at least twenty times as big as that of Chetwynd's.

I have every confidence in Edward's abilities. I have been impressed by his business acumen since our first meetings, and all that I saw at Rudleigh reinforced my view. He should regard Prideau's as a challenge, and one which I believe he must accept.

If, despite these strongly expressed wishes, he declines to leave his own business, then you and he will have to look elsewhere for a manager. Let me warn you against any thought of handing control of the company to one or other of its present employees. Among them are many good men who have worked for me loyally, but none that I would trust with complete confidence. You will have to look outside, but be very, very careful in your choice, and ensure that at no point do you lose final control.

Enough. Like many old men I have a tendency to try

too hard to impose my will upon others. The final decision is yours.

I have been much gratified to observe the happiness of your marriage, and no doubt the affection between you and Edward will grow and develop even more strongly with the passing years. I have also been delighted and proud to see my great-grandchildren. It may surprise you that I have made no reference to them in my Will, but I do not wish to be unfair to any other great-grandchildren as yet unborn, and no doubt I can rely upon you to provide suitably for all your offspring yourself.

I send you my fondest love and admiration, my dear Alice.

Your affectionate grandfather, Jas. Prideau.

Alice handed the letter to Edward, and he read it with a sinking heart. The pressure to abandon cast iron in favour of silk was going to be even more intense this time.

Alice was watching his expression. 'You haven't got to do it,' she said. 'He says you haven't got to.'

'But you want me to. And the decision is yours. You are the owner of Prideau's now.'

'No. You are. A wife's property belongs to her husband.'

'Legally, yes. Morally, it is your company.'

'I couldn't run the business, and you could. And you wouldn't have to sell Chetwynd's.'

He shook his head. 'No. If I take on Prideau's, I should never be able to continue at Rudleigh, too. Even your grandfather could not have managed that.'

He thought of little else for the next few days, increasingly attracted to the prospect of becoming the head of so large and prosperous and influential a company. And yet every thought in such vein seemed to be accompanied by an even sharper tug back to Rudleigh and Chetwynd's.

He went to see his mother. She did not seem to know who he was, and at first refused to speak to him. Then his hopes rose as he saw recognition swim slowly into her eyes.

'Hello, Richard,' she said.

'It's not Richard, Mother—it's Edward.'

She ignored that. 'I just don't know what to do about

345

Edward, Richard. I wish you'd advise him. He's always taken notice of what you say, which I suppose is not surprising really.' The moment of comparative lucidity vanished. 'Who are you?' she said. 'I wish you'd go away. I want to get on with my figures. Go away! Go away!'

'There, there, lovey,' said her nurse. 'Don't get yourself upset now—the gentleman's going.' She whispered to Edward, 'Best if you go now, sir.'

Reluctantly, Edward left the room, sadly distressed. That his mother, his brilliant, beautiful mother should have come to this—her face lined, her once dark chestnut hair almost white, and her poor wandering wits . . .

The nurse had accompanied him. 'It's very upsetting for you, sir, I'm sure, but remember that most of the time she's perfectly happy, especially after she's had her little drop of brandy in the evening—well, quite a large drop, to tell the truth. She likes her brandy, Mrs Harcourt does.'

That seemed to make it even worse, and he drove away from Harcourt Place more downcast than ever. In his mind, he went back over his short conversation with Sarah, and suddenly realised what he should do. Why hadn't he thought of that before?

The next day he went to Wensham. Richard had been at Mr Prideau's funeral, of course, but there had been little opportunity for conversation.

'Come down to the church,' Richard said. 'I'd like you to see the plaque.'

It was a simple slab of white marble, lettered in gold. The inscription read, 'In fond memory of Mary Goodwin, killed in action at Lichtenburg, South Africa, March 3rd, 1901. Requiescat in pace.' Beneath, in much smaller letters, were the words, 'Erected by the loving members of her family, Richard and Louisa Goodwin and Edward Harcourt.'

They stood in front of it for a while.

'Very fine,' Edward said.

'Yes. Her mother wanted something more elaborate, and more details about the way she died, but Mary liked simple things.'

On the way back from the church, both were thinking of Mary, but once sitting in Richard's study, Edward began. 'I need your advice, Father,' he said. 'I went to see my mother yesterday. It was not very pleasant. She thought I was you.

346

But at least she helped me. She said, thinking I was you, "I wish you'd advise Edward. He's always taken notice of what you say." So I came.'

Richard listened carefully as Edward told him of his dilemma. 'And what does Alice say?'

'When Mr Prideau asked me to join him after my mother's breakdown, she understood that I had to stay at Chetwynd's. Now I think she wants me to give it up. But I know she'll accept whatever I finally decide.'

'Prideau's,' Richard said. 'There was a time when I'd have given my eye teeth to control that company. You'd be a fool to turn it down, Edward.'

'Yes, I know.'

'But sometimes the only wise thing is to be a fool. We decided some time ago, when we were discussing what was to happen to Harcourt's Mill, that your heart is with Chetwynd's. Nothing's happened to change that, has it?'

'No.'

'But your head is telling you that this is a very different proposition—Prideau's is a huge concern, and very profitable, and a challenge, not to mention the fact that it means a great deal to your wife. But you have to listen to your heart, Edward. If your head sends you to Prideau's, but your heart is still in Rudleigh, then that will do no one any good—neither you, nor Prideau's, nor Chetwynd's, nor Alice.'

Edward was silent for a long time. 'Then I must turn it down,' he said at last.

'You're sure?' Richard asked.

'Yes.' And he felt a kind of relief that the decision was taken. 'So what are we going to do? Where will we find someone to take it over? I suppose you wouldn't, Father.'

Richard laughed. 'Good heavens, no! I'm much too old.'

'Mr Prideau was still running it and he was even older than we thought—in his seventy-ninth year. And you just said that you'd have given your eye teeth.'

'Oh, that was a lot of nonsense!' But his eyes were bright with interest. 'How could I ask Louisa to uproot herself and move to Franton? How could I leave my own business? And don't you dare suggest that Prideau's would buy it! It's not for sale!'

Edward laughed. 'I wouldn't dream of it.' He felt like

347

singing and dancing. 'I tell you what,' he went on, 'how would it be if you were to run it for us on a temporary basis, with a brief of finding someone else really capable to take over from you whenever you felt ready to give it up? I know Mr Prideau said that there was no one in the company capable of taking over, but you might find someone there who could do so eventually.'

'The whole idea's quite absurd,' Richard said. 'But one thing's certain—somehow or other you've got to go back to Rudleigh, and get on with making cast iron.'

*   *   *

Christmas Day, 1901, was one of the most enjoyable that Edward could remember. William had played happily with his new toys, and little Sarah crawled all over the place, and cooed and gurgled and, amongst many unintelligible sounds, quite clearly said 'Mama' and 'Papa'. After the children were tucked up in bed, Mr Farmiloe and Mr and Mrs Brown, she now much recovered in health, arrived for Christmas dinner, which was eaten with great relish and considerable jollity. The guests did not leave until just after midnight.

Edward put his arms around Alice and kissed her. 'A very, very pleasant day, my darling. And you look quite ravishing.' He gave a little laugh. 'At least the year is ending well, but what a time we've had!'

'It wasn't all bad,' Alice said. 'There was little Sarah, and you becoming master of Chetwynd's, and all sorts of happy things.'

She was right, Edward thought. When you looked back on an old year, it was right to remember the sadness, but there were always blessings to be counted, too.

He looked at the Christmas cards on the mantelpiece. There was one from Franton, where his father, who had once been ignominiously dismissed from Prideau's, was having the time of his life as the undisputed master of that firm and its destinies, though he was still denying that he had any intention of staying in the company's employment.

And the Bunns had sent a card, too, giving the address of their new establishment which Frances' royalties on the Dickens statuettes had allowed them to purchase. And one of the largest was printed with the slogan 'A Score of Jokes in a Score of Voices', and inscribed, 'from Mr and Mrs Fred Beeson, and baby Frederick.' There were many others—from Ralph Quennell and Alderman Jones and the Leroys and dozens of other friends and acquaintances—and a letter had come from Jack Chetwynd, who sounded full of his old ebullience, saying that he had settled in New York and become involved in the theatre there.

No remembrance had come, of course, from his mother, but the nurse had written from Brentfield. 'Your mother suffered a brainstorm and lost consciousness,' she wrote, 'but on recovery seems to have regained at least a part of her senses, and Doctor Wood holds out some hope that she may eventually be restored to full sanity.'

And the greatest blessing of all, of course, was Alice and the children. Darling Alice, and William, and baby Sarah. He thought of that letter from old Mr Prideau—what was it he had said?—'I do not wish to be unfair to any other great-grandchildren as yet unborn.' Edward smiled to himself, and then at Alice.

'What are you smiling at?' she asked.

He could not tell her what had been in his mind at that moment. 'Oh, I was just thinking,' he said, 'of how lucky I am.' He sat in silence for a few moments, and then smiled at her again. 'I've been thinking of something else. You know, there'd be nothing to stop me, and I'm sure Jack wouldn't mind—I could change the name of Chetwynd's.'

'What to?'

'At one time I might have said "Goodwin's", but I'd better stick to the name by which everyone knows me. "Edward Harcourt and Company, Ironfounders"—how does that sound?'

'It sounds splendid,' Alice said.

'Yes,' said Edward. 'Yes, that's what I think, too.'